The
SCOUNDREL'S
Widow

The
SCOUNDREL'S
Widow

ANITA STANSFIELD

SWEETWATER BOOKS
An imprint of Cedar Fort, Inc.
Springville, Utah

ISBN 13: 978-1-4621-4245-3

Published by Sweetwater Books, an imprint of Cedar Fort, Inc.
2373 W. 700 S., Springville, UT 84663
Distributed by Cedar Fort, Inc., www.cedarfort.com

Library of Congress Control Number: 2022938961

Cover design by Courtney Proby
Cover design © 2022 Cedar Fort, Inc.
Edited and typeset by Valene Wood

Printed in the United States of America

10 9 8 7 6 5 4 3 2 1

Printed on acid-free paper

Titles by Anita Stansfield

Other Titles

A Promise of Forever*
A Star in Winter*
Someone to Hold*
Reflections, A Collection of Personal Essays*
Emma, Woman of Faith*

Where the Heart Leads*
When Hearts Meet*

The Gift, A Christmas Short Story*
The Empty Manger
(Included in the short story collection
A Merry Little Christmas)

Passage on the Titanic*

The Wishing Garden*
The Garden Path*

Legally and Lawfully Yours
Now and Always Yours

The Heir of Brownlie Manor

Color of Love

Lily of the Manor

Winter Angel
(A Christmas novella included in
the collection Christmas Grace)
Love and Loss at Whitmore Manor

The Stars Above Northumberland

The Heart of Thornewell

The Lady of Astoria Abbey

The House of Stone and Ivy

The Emerald Heart of Courtenay

The Angel of Grey Garden

The Heart of Christmas
(A Christmas novella included in the collection
All Hearts Come Home for Christmas)

Home to Somersby

The Heiress of all Things Beautiful

The Heart of Hampton House

The Dowry of Lady Eliza

---

* Latter-day Saint content

Chapter One

The Doppelganger

Kent, England — 1817

Sylvia Hewitt stood near the kitchen door and stared at her husband's boots, sitting there as if he'd worn them just last night to go out to the barn and see to the chores. It had practically become a ritual for her to stand in this spot every morning and allow her mind to drift back to the last time she'd seen him wearing these boots, the last time she'd felt his arms around her, their last kiss before he'd left her to never return. Something inside of her had believed he would become a victim of the war he'd been sent to fight in America. Still, she'd held onto the hope that he would come home to her alive and well—and changed for the better. She'd imagined a thousand times how it might have been if he'd returned to her a more humble and ethical man. Oh, how she'd longed to have the best of him back in her life. But the truth was that she didn't believe people could change— not to the extent Daniel Hewitt would have needed to change in order to relieve her of the continual anxiety of being married to a man who lived his life illicitly swindling and stealing from others. And yet it was all so complicated. Even with the years that had passed she still couldn't make any sense of her tangled web of emotions. All she knew for certain in that moment was the fact that each time she looked at his empty boots, she ached for him so deeply that it took every bit of strength she possessed to bring herself out of this daily trance, being immersed in a disarray of memories she wished to be free of forever.

Sylvia finally managed to bring herself back to the present as the distant rumbling of thunder reminded her of the storm she needed to face in order to accomplish the usual morning tasks. Rain was common and she was well accustomed to dealing with its effects, but the recent series of storms that were attempting to transform winter into spring had made her long to see the sun even a little bit more.

She stepped into Daniel's oversized boots, always liking the way she could slide her feet in and out of them so easily, and by using them every day she had a good excuse to always leave them next to the door; she didn't think she could ever bring herself to get rid of them.

Bracing herself for the trek to the barn, Sylvia flung the hood of her cloak up over her head in order to ward off the pounding rain as much as possible. She stepped outside and trudged through the mud toward the barn with clean buckets in each hand that were sheltered by her cloak and covered with clean towels that would protect the milk and eggs on their way back to the house. Her mood lightened once she entered the barn and left the storm behind. Very little sunlight emitted through the barn windows due to the storm, but it was sufficient for her to see how her cow and the four horses all looked toward her in greeting. She set the buckets down and went about her usual ritual of greeting the animals with some gentle stroking while she asked how they were faring and reassuring them that the noise of the rain beating on the roof—and the occasional rumble of thunder—was nothing to be concerned about. Sylvia knew that talking to the animals this way was definitely a symptom of her loneliness, but she didn't care. To her, they felt like friends, and she genuinely believed they enjoyed the attention she gave them.

Sylvia hummed a tune from her childhood while she fed the animals, milked the cow, and collected the chickens' eggs.

She knew that George would clean out the stalls, provide fresh straw, and take care of everything else that required more strength— chores he absolutely insisted a lady should not be doing. George Lyman and his wife Millie had been working for Sylvia for more than four years now, and she relied on them greatly for their companionship as well as their assistance. They worked together like a family, and indeed they were the only family she had left. She knew that Millie was at this moment beginning preparations for a fine breakfast, and George would arrive any minute to do his portion of the necessary chores related to the animals. Just the thought of their presence and the sincere care they put into their work warmed Sylvia's heart.

Assured that all was well for the moment, Sylvia again pulled the hood of her cloak over her head and was about to pick up the waiting buckets of milk and eggs when she heard a rustling of movement and a quiet groaning that no animal could have made; another human being was definitely somewhere in the barn. Pushing the hood back off her head so she could see clearly, her heart pounded and all of her senses became highly alert with the certainty that she was not alone. Having no idea if someone was in her barn merely trying to escape the rain or if she was dealing with an intruder who intended her harm, Sylvia slowly and carefully went to the corner of the barn where a loaded rifle was always kept hidden among the rakes and pitchforks leaning against the wall. The rifle needed a cap and powder to actually be fired and she had those nearby but she felt too unnerved to even attempt doing so.

Sylvia lifted the rifle to a threatening position and moved it slowly back and forth while she scanned the dimly lit barn for any sign of movement. With her back to the corner, she absolutely knew no one could possibly be hiding behind her, which gave her confidence as she called out sternly, "I know there's someone here. Come out and show yourself immediately or I will find you and—"

"Wait! Wait!" a man's voice called back, and Sylvia saw two hands come up from behind a mound of straw. "I was only looking for shelter. I'll not hurt you."

The man's accent let her know that he was from the north, possibly even from Scotland.

"May I come out?" he asked with a sincere humility that made her feel a little less afraid. "I confess that I'm injured, and I do need to sit down and—"

"Keep your hands where I can see them," Sylvia ordered, attempting to make it clear that she was in charge here and until she had more information regarding this intruder, she wasn't simply going to trust what he was telling her. Still, at the same time, his admittance to being injured caused her some concern, but not enough to lower her weapon until she could see for herself that he had no ability or intention of causing her harm. Most men would know that the rifle wasn't likely a real threat if they'd been watching her closely, but holding it still helped her feel more confident.

"I will," the man said. "I promise you."

Sylvia watched closely as he emerged from behind the mound of straw.

As he came into view, Sylvia felt anything but threatened. A quick scan from toe to head showed that his feet were bare—and filthy and possibly bleeding. His clothing looked as if he'd had nothing else to wear for weeks, perhaps months, and there was a makeshift bandage tied around his thigh that looked as if it had once been a shirt, now torn and wrapped tightly to help ease the bleeding of some kind of wound. There was a bloody stain on the fabric, and it was evident from the way he limped into the open that he was in a great deal of pain. His shaggy, dark blonde hair and overgrown beard made it difficult to see his face, especially when his head was bent as he focused on moving to a bale of hay where he could sit down. In fact, he didn't seem at all concerned with the fact that Sylvia had a rifle pointed at him. She had to believe he was truly in a great deal of pain, but still she kept the gun poised, uncertain of the situation. And for all she knew he hadn't come here alone.

Sylvia heard him sigh as he settled onto his makeshift seat and unwittingly rubbed his ailing leg, his head still down.

"Tell me everything," she said. "Why are you here, and how did you become injured? Are you alone or—"

"One question at a time," he said with a disarming chuckle.

He seemed somehow familiar, but given his present appearance and the fact that he'd not looked at her directly, it was impossible for her to recognize him.

"Yes, I'm alone," he said. "I've been traveling on foot at night in order to avoid being seen. I've completely lost track of the days I've been doing so. I confess there is someone out there who seems to want to kill me, but it's not because of anything I did. It's a terrible misunderstanding. It's complicated at best, but . . . I ask that you just . . . allow me to hide here in your barn until I heal up a bit . . . and then I'll leave you in peace. I mean you no harm; I swear to it. I'm just a desperate man in a desperate situation. I hope you can believe me. I'm begging for your help, miss."

"It's Missus," she snapped, wanting to defend her status even though she was long widowed.

"Forgive me," he said, and she realized that the way he kept his head down was unnatural. He was trying not to look at her, which left her suddenly suspicious just when she had been softening to his plea for help.

"Why won't you look at me?" she asked.

She heard him sigh deeply before he said, "I ask you to hear me out, ma'am, and not become alarmed. I confess that your farm has been my destination, and I've been trying to get here for many weeks, but the money I had for travel didn't last as long as I'd hoped it would, so I had no choice but to travel on foot. My shoes gave out some time ago."

"Why would my farm be your destination?" she demanded, sounding as alarmed as she felt.

"Because I knew your husband, Mrs. Hewitt," he said and she gasped, "and I know he died in the war because I was with him when it happened." His voiced quivered as if he were fighting the urge to cry. "He told me I should come here if ever I was in need, but I didn't want to impose upon you in any way. My intention was that I might be of some help to *you*. Although, I very much wanted to get way from the village where I'd grown up; there's nothing left for me there."

"And where is that?" Sylvia asked, her mind swirling with questions.

"So far north in England that I often walked to Scotland in my youth," he said, and his accent certainly verified the truth of that.

"And why would you not want to remain there?" she asked, wondering if he'd been telling her the truth. She wondered about his definition of a *misunderstanding* in regard to someone possibly trying to kill him.

"I was living alone with no loved ones with whom to share a home. And the farm I'd worked had been leased to another. The people I'd once felt comfortable with had come to feel like strangers. I couldn't stay there and be happy. So I sold all I had and headed this way." He once again sighed loudly. "The journey was far more challenging than

I had anticipated, but I swear to you that your husband and I became very good friends, together in the same regiment in America."

Sylvia recalled some comments littered throughout the very few letters she'd received from her husband about a man who had become his friend, but there had been no specific details. Although she doubted that most of his letters had ever found their way to her. Still uncomfortable with the way he wouldn't look at her—as if he had something to hide—Sylvia demanded, "Look at me. I need to see your eyes." She'd always prided herself on being able to discern sincerity from a person's eyes, and she'd never been wrong—even if there had been times when she'd chosen to ignore what she knew, much to her own detriment.

"I'm hesitant to show my face, Mrs. Hewitt," he said. The admittance was sincere, but it left her confused. "Allow me to tell you first that your husband and I *became* friends because of a strange happenstance that left us both baffled—as well as every man we served with."

Sylvia only felt more confused and insisted, "Just . . . look at me and then you can explain."

She held the rifle more tightly with sweating palms as this man slowly lifted his head, and then she had difficulty remaining on her feet as her limbs felt suddenly weak. She lowered the rifle and barely managed to hold onto it.

"That's impossible," she murmured, teetering slightly before she was able to steady herself. "Daniel?" she asked, knowing it couldn't be him. It just couldn't! But what she knew to be true and what her eyes were telling her were in direct contradiction.

"No," the man said, "I'm not your Daniel, but as you can see the two of us might as well have been born twins. Neither of us understood such a phenomenon, but we made good fun of it. Our superior officers always had to ask which one of us they were addressing, and our uniforms were even the same size. My name is Dougal Heywood, ma'am. So you see, even our initials were the same."

Sylvia became unable to speak or even move while she took in the face staring back at her. There was a scar on the left cheek that hadn't been there when Daniel had left her to fight in the war across the ocean, and the beard concealed a great deal. But if it weren't for the strange explanation this man had just given her, she would absolutely believe she was looking at Daniel Hewitt—the man she both loved and despised.

Dougal Heywood she repeated silently several times to try and convince herself of this man's identity. It was *not* Daniel! It was not! And she wouldn't want it to be. As much as she'd loved Daniel, and as much as she missed him, he'd brought so much trouble into her life with his lack of ethics and constant scheming that her relief over his death had far outweighed her sorrow.

Mr. Heywood remained quiet as if he sensed her need to take all of this in. After a reasonable amount of time had passed, he said kindly, "I apologize for the shock, Mrs. Hewitt. I knew it wouldn't be possible to meet you without it being a shock. I'm certain we have much to talk about, but . . . for now . . . I ask you to simply believe that my intention in coming here was to offer any help you might need, and my plans were foiled by . . . well . . . I already told you what I know about that, which is not much, and I do not understand, but . . ." He chuckled without humor. "For now I only ask that you help me until I'm strong enough to care for myself again, and then . . . if you want me to leave, I will. I'll not cause you any trouble," he added firmly, "and once I'm doing better, I'll work off whatever I might owe you for your efforts and—"

"There's no need for that," Sylvia said, hearing a tremor in her voice which she credited to the fact that she'd just seen the ghost of her dead husband. While returning the rifle to its place among the tools in the corner, she added, "George will be here at any moment. He and his wife Millie work for me. Thankfully they ask for little more than a roof over their heads and food to eat, because that's about all I can give them. And that's about all I can give you. But I *can* give you that, and I will. George can help you into the house and help get you cleaned up. I still have Daniel's clothes so that's convenient." She shook her head in disbelief, still trying to take all of this in while she thought about the fact that she was this very moment wearing a pair of Daniel's boots. But thankfully he'd owned a few pairs, and the others were collecting dust in the bottom of the wardrobe in the spare bedroom. She'd had his things moved long ago out of the room where she slept, not wanting to see them there. But she hadn't been able to bring herself to get rid of them. Now it seemed a strange kind of serendipity that she'd chosen to hold onto them, and they were already in the room where Mr. Heywood could sleep and recover from his ailments.

"Thank you," Mr. Heywood said with such deep relief she thought he might fall right off the bale where he was sitting. "I cannot thank you enough."

"Let's save the formalities for another time," she said, still reeling but trying very hard to pretend that she wasn't. "Let's just—"

The back door of the barn opened, and George entered, whistling as he often did. When he saw Sylvia standing there, he stopped abruptly. Normally she would have gone into the house with the milk and eggs long before now. Then his eyes turned to the man sitting there and widened.

"Are you all right, Missus?" he asked, and Sylvia could only think how grateful she was that she'd not taken George and Millie in until after Daniel had left for the war, so they had no idea what he looked like. The explanation of his strong resemblance to this man could wait until another time.

"I'm fine," Sylvia said with more confidence than she felt. "This is Dougal Heywood. He tells me that he was a friend of my husband's, and he has come far to find us and he's in need of assistance. Before you take care of the animals, could you help him to the spare room and get him all that he needs to clean himself up? He can use Daniel's things."

"As you wish, Missus," George said, looking mildly skeptical— but as always, George trusted and respected Sylvia's wishes completely.

"Come along," George said, looking Mr. Heywood over carefully as he put a strong arm around him and helped him to his feet. "My Millie's got some water on the stove for laundry, but that'll wait. We'll use it in the bathtub for you and then see what else you need."

"It might be best if we don't send for a doctor," Mr. Heywood said as George was helping him walk toward the door. "Not only because of the expense, but—"

"Don't you worry about that," George said. "We have all we need right here to take care of you."

Sylvia watched them walk out into the ongoing downpour of rain before she nearly collapsed onto a different bale of hay and hung her head. Now that Dougal Heywood was no longer present, her efforts to maintain her composure crumbled. She felt dizzy and had trouble breathing. She considered the fact that being confronted by a stranger in such a manner would have been enough to cause a terrible fright for any woman. But Sylvia had just looked upon the specter of her dead husband. She'd never seen Daniel with a beard, and he'd certainly not had any such scar on his face. And yet the resemblance was otherwise so remarkable that it took a few minutes to convince herself that her mind should not believe the trick her eyes had played upon her.

Mr. Heywood had clearly been prepared for how his appearance would affect her; she understood now why he'd kept his head down for so long while they'd been talking. He'd known Daniel well. The fact that these two men could have been identical twins had been a source of great humor to them and those they'd fought with. That certainly sounded like Daniel. He'd had a gift for finding humor in almost anything—to the point that it could be annoying. Well, Sylvia certainly found no humor in the present situation. But she needed to get hold of her wits and get on with her day. Dougal Heywood was in need of help, and he'd come *here* because Daniel had told him to. Sylvia had no trouble imagining how Daniel would have told Mr. Heywood—or any man he'd served with in the military—that they would always be welcome in his home. He'd likely not considered the possibility that he would be dead long before Mr. Heywood made his appearance. Nevertheless, Sylvia considered herself—above all else—a good Christian woman, and no Christian woman would turn away a stranger in need.

Sylvia finally managed to take in deep breaths and let them out slowly while she regained her equilibrium enough to stand up and take the eggs and milk into the kitchen where she knew Millie would be waiting for them. Just inside the door, she set the buckets down and removed her cloak, hanging it on a hook where it could dry. She slipped her feet out of Daniel's boots before she set the buckets in their usual place on the long worktable. Millie was busy stirring something on the stove at the other end of the long kitchen but looked up at Sylvia, her brow furrowed with concern.

"You all right, Missus?" Millie asked. When Sylvia didn't answer right away, Millie added, "Must've been quite a shock to find a stranger hiding in the barn."

"A shock indeed," Sylvia said, knowing that eventually she would have to tell Millie and George that the stranger they'd taken in was a near replica of Sylvia's deceased husband. *That* was a shock Sylvia felt dubious about ever being able to recover from.

"George helped him upstairs and then came back down for the hot water. He said he'd help the man get cleaned up and then take some breakfast up for him. I doubt he'll be going up and down the stairs with the condition he's in. The poor man could hardly walk with the way his feet are hurting him."

"I would think he'll be staying put for a while," Sylvia said, glad to think of him eating his meals in the bedroom he would be using rather than joining them at the dining table. She very much doubted her ability to keep looking at his face and not feel affected.

"I'll have breakfast put together in a few minutes for all of us," Millie added. "Why don't you clean up and we'll eat. Then we can help you tend to the man's wounds. I'm sure you'll know what to do."

"I'm sure," Sylvia repeated dully and hurried into the hall and toward the stairs and up to her own room to do as Millie had suggested. Even though she'd not gotten a close look at Mr. Heywood's sores and wounds, she had no doubt about her ability to help him— better than the only doctor that could be found around here, even if they could afford the foolish doctor's fees. But she dreaded even having to see her husband's twin again. She just kept reminding herself that while her eyes had shown her something that she desperately wanted to believe was true, she knew that it wasn't. Daniel Hewitt was dead, and the man George was helping in a room down the hall at the opposite end of the house had nothing to do with her beyond being a stranger she'd taken in. As long as she kept telling herself that over and over, she would surely become accustomed to the resemblance and stop feeling as if everything she knew about life and death had just been called into question.

Alone in her own room, Sylvia freshened up and put on her own shoes—which fit her feet perfectly—as she always did at the beginning of the day. Her skirt was slightly damp from the rain where her cloak had not covered it, but she had spared the hem from any mud by tucking the sides of the skirt into its waistband to hike it up. This was something she did *any* day that rain might threaten her ability to keep her clothes from getting muddy. But she felt embarrassed now to realize that Mr. Heywood surely would have had a perfect view of the oversized boots she'd been wearing, which were perfectly practical but looked ridiculous. She quickly asked herself why it mattered and immediately answered that it didn't.

Before going back downstairs, Sylvia looked in the mirror and smoothed the top of her dark blond hair where the hood of her cloak had ruffled it slightly. The rest of her hair had been spared the effect of the cloak since it hung down her back in a neat, practical braid—just as it always did. She didn't have time to be fussing with her hair when there was always work to be done. She took an extra moment to examine her own face in the reflection when she noted the shock and astonishment in her eyes. Her face was more narrow than round, and her features were more delicate than sturdy, all of which accentuated a gaunt appearance that hadn't been there before she'd gone out to the barn. Attempting to counteract an unusual paleness in her skin, she slapped her cheeks gently then pinched them, along with her lips, before she hurried back to the kitchen, grateful to know that George would make certain their guest had everything he needed so that she wouldn't have to.

In the kitchen, Millie was bustling about to see that all was ready for a hardy breakfast. The woman was tall and thin with a particularly long face, accentuated by a sharp chin and long nose. She was likely about ten years older than Sylvia's twenty-seven years, but Millie's dark brown hair had only recently shown just the slightest hint of gray here and there. Millie's husband was a little shorter than her with extremely broad shoulders and a burly chest that might have given him a menacing appearance if not for his almost constant smile. Even when he dozed in a chair in the parlor as he did on occasion, his face relaxed into a smile. If George scowled, Sylvia and Millie knew he was sorely displeased. His head was so bald that it was shiny, and Millie loved to give it a pat or a rub now and then in a teasing but affectionate gesture. Sylvia loved them both dearly and knew she never could have survived without their help as well as their companionship. They were the dearest of friends, but they were also loyal and hardworking, and between the three of them, they kept their simple life from falling apart.

"Oh, there you are," Millie said when she saw Sylvia, although she only took a quick glance since she was tending to the sausages that were frying on the stove. "You look a might better. It must have been quite a fright for you . . . having a strange man in the barn to greet you. I think I might have started throwing eggs at him." She chuckled in the deep rumbling way that was typical for her. "That would have taken him off his guard."

"And we'd not have had eggs for our breakfast today," Sylvia pointed out, getting the necessary dishes from a high cupboard. "And didn't I hear you say last night that you intended to bake a cake today? You'll certainly be needing eggs for that."

"You make a fair point, Missus," she said with another chuckle.

For all that Sylvia had tried to get Millie and George to call her by her given name, they both insisted that they worked for her and they would use a more respectful title, although there had been a compromise in her demanding that they not call her Mrs. Hewitt. Every time she heard her husband's name attached to herself, it bristled her with a barrage of confused memories and feelings. So 'Missus' suited her fine, although it wouldn't have been her first choice. Still, she'd become accustomed to it, and their addressing her in this way had not diminished the comfortable equality they'd come to share.

"Besides," Sylvia said, stepping into the dining room, which was just off the kitchen, "our visitor arrived filthy with mud. I suspect he did a great deal of traveling with no opportunity to bathe. Since George is helping him get cleaned up, I doubt he would have appreciated eggs being added to the problem."

Millie chuckled still again. "That too is a fair point," she added.

While Sylvia was setting the table for the three of them to share their breakfast as usual, going in and out of the kitchen to get what she needed, Millie added more seriously, "It's astounding that this man was a friend of your husband, but do we know anything more about him than that?"

Now that the table in the dining room was set, Sylvia had to sit down at a chair near the worktable in the kitchen, not far from where Millie was working at the stove. She nearly told Millie about Mr. Heywood's explanations but hesitated with the thought that she might just have to repeat everything after George arrived. She also wondered for a moment if she should tell them that this man who had stumbled into their lives bore an uncanny resemblance to her deceased husband—a man they had never met. But, of course, she needed to tell them. They were her dearest friends and the only family she had. She needed to tell them everything and be completely honest. Trying to keep secrets for any reason would never help any of them work together to nurse Mr. Heywood back to health and see him on his way.

"I'll be glad to tell you all he told me," Sylvia said, "but let's wait until George joins us so I don't have to repeat everything twice."

"Hmm," Millie murmured, which Sylvia knew was meant to express her agreement, then she added, "although he might be slow getting to breakfast with all he's doing upstairs. I'll take some breakfast up for our guest in a minute here and see how it's all going and if they need anything."

"Thank you," Sylvia said, never wanting to have to look upon Dougal Heywood's face again.

Sylvia watched as Millie arranged a tray with a pot of tea covered with a small, thick towel to keep it warm, and all that was needed to go along with it. She also put a plate there that was brimming with scrambled eggs, fried potatoes, and a couple of crisp sausages, and she quickly put a tarnished silver dome over the plate to keep the food warm. Millie added a glass of fresh milk and the proper utensils before she picked up the tray and headed toward the stairs.

"You keep an eye on the rest of those sausages," she ordered. "Some of them aren't quite done. Turn them over now and then so they don't burn."

"I will," Sylvia replied, glad that Millie and George weren't afraid to ask her to do something to help *them*, even if they worked for *her*. She stood and moved to the stove, shifting the sausages around with a long fork while her mind reviewed the encounter in the barn. All of her initial fear had vanished. Now she was more stuck on the issue of Mr. Heywood's friendship with Daniel—which in itself would have been strange to contend with—and even more so his striking resemblance, an oddity that still had her mind reeling. She kept having to remind herself that this was not her husband returned from the grave. It was nothing more than a strange coincidence, and she simply needed to give her mind time to adjust.

Millie returned to the kitchen just as Sylvia was moving the skillet containing the perfectly crispy sausages off the stove—just the way they all liked them.

"Our guest is much cleaner now," Millie reported, "although George intends to help him scrub that hair and beard later. One thing at a time." She began carrying food into the dining room and Sylvia followed her with the teapot and a pitcher of milk. "Our guest is tucked into bed wearing a clean nightshirt," Millie added as both women went back to the kitchen to collect more items for their breakfast. "And he was mighty pleased with his breakfast. I suspect he's not eaten for some time."

"Oh, that's dreadful!" Sylvia said, ashamed to realize that such a thought had not even occurred to her.

"I told him to take it slow and not make himself sick by eating too much too fast," Millie said in her motherly way, which came so naturally to her even though she'd never been able to have children. "But I do hope he enjoys it."

"I'm certain he will," Sylvia said. "You're one of the best cooks in the county."

Millie chuckled. "You just say that because you haven't tasted hardly a thing made by anyone else in the county."

"Perhaps not," Sylvia said. It was true that she'd not grown up here, and after she'd moved into this house with her new husband, there had never been much socializing with those who lived in the area, and certainly not with the villagers. "Nevertheless, everything you make is delicious and even the simplest meals are always a pleasure."

"You're too kind, Missus," Millie said before she declared they had all they needed to begin. She glanced toward the stairs and added, "I do think George will be down soon, but let's go on and say grace and start while the food is hot."

"We can wait if you prefer," Sylvia said. "It's not me who has to answer to George." She chuckled and Millie did the same.

"Ah, he don't scare me," Millie said with another chuckle. He didn't scare Sylvia either, but they liked to joke about his menacing appearance and his immense physical strength. Sylvia had seen him pick up things that she couldn't even push an inch with all of her efforts.

They were about to say grace when they heard George's familiar footfalls on the stairs, so they waited while he washed up in the kitchen and joined them at the dining table.

"How's our guest?" Sylvia asked, sounding much more nonchalant than she felt about the entire situation.

"He's gonna need a good washing and a trim on that hair and beard. He might as well have been living like a hermit in the woods for the way he looks. I'll help him with that after he's eaten and had some rest." George looked directly at Sylvia and added, "He's certainly in need of your concoctions to help what ails him. It's a wonder and a miracle that he made it here at all." George glanced over the breakfast on the table and smiled at his wife in a silent expression of appreciation. "But we can take that on later. I feel half-starved and this all looks good enough to feed royalty."

Millie offered one of her familiar chuckles before George spoke a simple blessing on their food and they proceeded to eat.

"Now that we're together," Millie said after her first bite of potatoes, "I'd love to be hearing what this man told you, Missus, about how he ended up here . . . so far away from everything as we are."

"Well," Sylvia said and swallowed the food she was chewing before she cleared her throat and attempted to gather the right words and an unaffected tone of voice, "our farm was his destination because he knew my husband in the war—that's where they became friends."

"Well, I'll be a donkey's dinner!" George exclaimed and wiped a hand over his shiny head. "If that isn't something!"

"Yes, it certainly is *something*," Sylvia said. "I was alarmed at first when I realized someone was in the barn, and I was quick to grab the rifle, but it didn't take long to see the evidence that he was in no condition to harm me even if that had been his intention—which obviously it hadn't been. He and my husband became very good friends and told each other a great deal about their lives. Mr. Heywood told me that—"

"Is that his name?" Millie asked, clearly pleased to learn more about the stranger they were now caring for in their home.

"Dougal Heywood," Sylvia said. "He told me he's from a village so far north in England that he could walk to Scotland."

"That would explain his way of talking," George said. "Seems a nice enough fellow."

"Yes," Sylvia said and forced herself to go on and get this over with. "Apparently my husband told Mr. Heywood he would be welcome here at any time, and Mr. Heywood found—for a number of reasons—that the place where he'd been raised had changed a great deal for him, and he no longer wished to remain there, so he headed this way to accept my husband's invitation but encountered many troubles along the way." Sylvia sighed and summarized, "I'm certain there are details he told me that I'm not remembering, but given the time that he will be in our home, I'm certain he can tell us those details himself."

Millie and George both nodded while they were eating, but Sylvia set her fork down, knowing there was one more thing that had to be said right now because she simply couldn't bear the tension of their not knowing. And since Mr. Heywood knew, Sylvia far preferred to be the one to disclose the strange situation, therefore she needed to do so now.

"There's something you both need to know," she said, and they gave her their full attention, their eyes wide with expectation. "I confess it gave me quite a fright at first, but I'm certain I'll become accustomed to the fact and—"

"What in the world are you talking about?" Millie insisted, clearly having picked up on Sylvia's sudden nervousness.

"Mr. Heywood and my husband are . . . well . . . could be . . . twins." Sylvia coughed, glad to have that much out.

"What?" George asked.

Sylvia took a deep breath and clarified. "Their appearance is identical," Sylvia said and heard Millie gasp. "When I first saw Mr. Heywood's face, it felt as if I were looking at a ghost."

"Oh, my!" Millie said.

"Then you *truly* had a fright!" George added.

"I confess that I did," Sylvia said and hurried on. "Apparently this was the reason they became friends because their entire regiment made quite a fuss over the bizarre coincidence, and my husband and Mr. Heywood likely had a great deal of fun with it." She drew in a long, sustaining breath. "So, that's that. Of course you needed to know. It feels . . . awkward and . . . strange to me, but I'll adjust with time. I know very well that my husband is long dead, but at the moment my mind is playing tricks on me, and I feel hesitant to even look at Mr. Heywood again." She sighed loudly. "Everything will be fine, and as always I appreciate the way you both help and support me. I just wanted you to understand why I might behave . . . strangely . . . around this man. The resemblance truly is . . . remarkable."

"Well, if that isn't just the cow wearing a hat!" Millie declared. It was an expression she used occasionally, but for some reason it made Sylvia laugh more than usual. Perhaps the humorous image of a cow wearing a hat seemed appropriate for a situation so bizarre, or maybe Sylvia was just relieved to have these two wonderful people to share this strange burden of caring for a man whose appearance made her miss her sweet Daniel more than she had in a very long time.

"I've heard it said," Millie interjected, "that each of us has someone who looks very much like ourselves somewhere in the world, but with as big as the world is, imagine the chances of these two men coming together like that."

"Well, you know what they say about coincidences," George added, puffing up his chest a little, which indicated he was about to say something he believed in firmly. "They say there's no such thing. That it's God showing His hand for some reason or the other, even if we mortals can't understand those reasons."

"Amen to that," Millie said and nodded firmly while Sylvia wondered for a moment if God's hand could have truly been present in bringing Dougal Heywood together with her Daniel.

"I dare say that I'm more prone to believe in simple coincidence," Sylvia declared, deciding she preferred that over the possibility that there was some deeper meaning to all of this.

"We're all entitled to our own beliefs, Missus," George said, "but it sure is a strange thing."

"Yes," Sylvia drawled absently while her mind wandered again to a sweet recollection of the love she'd shared with Daniel. But it only took a moment of indulging in happy memories with Daniel for Sylvia to recall the continual trouble he'd caused—for herself and a great many other people. And the presence of this man who looked so much like him had stirred up a great deal of anger and confusion as well. She would have preferred to leave her conflicted life with Daniel in the past, and she'd worked very hard since news of his death had come to her to do just that. And now all of her efforts to create a life without him and move on had come to a tumultuous halt, and she had to resist the ridiculous urge she felt to march up the stairs and slap Dougal Heywood good and hard for doing this to her. She knew he was innocent in all of this; he had nothing to do with the lack of ethics and integrity of the man Sylvia had loved so dearly. But he was a stark reminder of all she'd endured being married to Daniel Hewitt, and the precious moments they'd shared that had given her the illusion that love could compensate for all else that was wrong. She'd learned through much grief that such was not the case. But with Dougal Heywood in her home, she feared that she might very well have to learn it all over again.

Chapter Two

Patience with the Patient

After a satisfying breakfast, Sylvia helped Millie clear the table and clean the kitchen while George went out to the barn to care for the animals and see that everything was in order. George returned about the same time Millie declared the kitchen clean to her strict specifications. While removing his boots, he stated what should have been obvious to Sylvia if she hadn't been trying to ignore reality.

"I do believe we should tend to the ailments of our patient so he don't get no infection," George said. "And you're the one who would know what he needs."

He was looking directly at Sylvia, but it took her a moment to respond as she attempted to steel herself to face the patient. It was absolutely true that she had the knowledge and experience to be able to take on almost any physical ailment. Her grandmother and mother before her had been well versed in the use of herbs and plants to create tinctures, poultices, powders, and salves that had great healing qualities. There were many people in the area who came to her for assistance— even though they generally came under cover of darkness for fear of the gossip and possible ridicule that might come upon them if others in the community found out that they'd come to Sylvia for help.

The only doctor available in the village was an arrogant fool who was certainly well qualified in most medical matters, but in some regards he used methods that made no sense to Sylvia, and in her opinion were more likely to cause additional harm as opposed to promoting any healing. The incident that had sparked a terrible feud between herself and Dr. Belder was something she couldn't even think about without feeling upset, so she chose to push the matter to the back of her mind and focus on her personal dislike of the doctor instead. He was highly revered and respected by the vicar—in fact they were good friends—therefore many people believed if they were to be considered good Christians, they needed to go to the doctor for help with any medical needs. Sylvia had once been able to sell her homemade concoctions openly and people were generally pleased with their results. Now, out of sheer spite—or perhaps because he believed that his ways were the only right way—the doctor spread gossip throughout the area that Sylvia was something akin to a witch using potions and evil grogs, and that people should keep far away from her and her wicked ways of healing.

The entire matter made Sylvia angry if she thought about it too long, so she chose not to think about that either. Instead, she stayed away from the village and sent George and Millie to purchase goods when they were needed. And she found some satisfaction in knowing there were many people who trusted her above the doctor. It was simply ridiculous that they had to keep their purchases of her medicines secretive.

Right now Sylvia considered her knowledge a great blessing, along with the abundance of treatments labeled and stored neatly on shelves in a room that had once been a parlor. Thanks to George's carpentry skills, the parlor had been converted into a workroom where Sylvia could crush herbs and mix salves and tinctures and the like on a fine large table he'd built for her.

She didn't want that doctor anywhere near her home, but Mr. Heywood was certainly in need of medical assistance. She only wished that Millie or George could take care of the matter, instead of her having to face him again. She knew the notion was ridiculous; he would be living in her house for a few weeks at the very least until he recovered. She couldn't possibly avoid him, therefore it was best to just face him and get it over with—which would hopefully help her become accustomed to her reasons for wanting to avoid him.

"Yes," Sylvia finally said after several seconds of George and Millie both staring at her expectantly, "I will likely know what he needs. I hope it's nothing too serious."

"You're out of sorts because he looks like your Daniel," Millie stated with certainty.

"I confess that I am," Sylvia said, glad that they could discuss the matter openly rather than her having to try and make up an excuse to explain her strange behavior. "Nevertheless, it must be done." She sighed and pointed out what she considered an obvious problem. "I make and sell treatments for many things. I know how they should be used, but I don't actually treat patients myself. I believe it would be entirely inappropriate for me to care for the wound he has on his leg— and any other wounds that are normally out of sight when a man is fully dressed. Therefore, I'm going to call upon your help, George."

"How am I supposed to know what to do?" he asked in a panic.

"I have a plan and I'm certain we can make it work," Sylvia said. "I want you to scrub your hands so they're cleaner than they may have ever been while I gather what I believe we'll need, and we'll go and visit with the patient together."

George made a noise that sounded both disgruntled and skeptical, but he went to do what Sylvia had asked of him. Millie followed Sylvia to her workroom, as she'd come to call it, saying with more confidence than her husband, "I can help, as well. First of all, I can help you carry what you need because I suspect it will be more than you can hold. And I can assist George with whatever Mr. Heywood needs. I'm a married woman and my husband will be in the room. I'm not going to be embarrassed by seeing a man's leg, which I believe is where the biggest problem lies."

"Thank you," Sylvia said, attempting an even tone that wouldn't betray how deeply relieved she felt to know that she could give instructions and these good people who worked for her could carry them out, making it less necessary for Sylvia to spend much, if any, time with their patient. She considered what Millie had said and realized that she too had once been married, and she truly wouldn't be embarrassed to treat a man's leg, and with Millie or George in the room it wouldn't be inappropriate. She had to concede that it was the patient's resemblance to Daniel that was the biggest problem for her, but she decided to keep that thought to herself.

Sylvia opened the drapes so she could see the bottles clearly despite the ongoing rain, and she considered what she would most likely need. She knew that Mr. Heywood likely had sores on his feet from walking barefoot for quite some time, and she knew his leg was ailing him. She then recalled that he'd told her someone was trying to kill him.

"Good heavens!" Sylvia muttered and froze, wondering if he'd been stabbed or shot. And did that mean she was putting her household in danger by harboring him?

"What is it, Missus?" Millie asked, sounding mildly panicked in response to Sylvia having sounded the same.

"I just remembered," Sylvia explained, "that he said someone might be trying to kill him . . . that it wasn't because of anything he'd done, that it was some kind of misunderstanding." Sylvia looked directly at Millie. "It's possible that he's been shot . . . or stabbed." Millie gasped and Sylvia forged ahead with her suddenly overwhelming thoughts. "If he has a bullet wound, I'm not certain that any of us have the skill to remove a bullet."

"Oh, I do hope it's not that!" Millie said and added exactly what Sylvia was thinking. "Could we be in danger by keeping him here?"

"I don't know," Sylvia said, "but we certainly can't turn him out. We'll have to consider how we might deal with that . . . later—after we've taken care of Mr. Heywood." She sighed. "Oh, I do hope he doesn't have a bullet in his leg."

"I do hope for the same," Millie said, and Sylvia handed her a large roll of cotton bandaging, which was also something that Sylvia sold to her customers. But she stopped again and turned directly to Millie, adding in a whisper even though there was no one anywhere who might overhear them, "I can't deny the possibility that if Mr. Heywood believes someone is trying to kill him . . . it could very well be that he's been mistaken for my husband. I've told you and George everything I know about his escapades and schemes, although I'm certain there's a great deal I *don't* know. Mr. Heywood was clearly confused when he told me about it. I could be wrong, but I believe it needs to be considered as a possibility that he's the victim of a mistaken identity."

"Oh my!" Millie responded, also whispering. "We seem to have landed ourselves into rather a mess."

"Yes, it seems we have," Sylvia said. "But we must do the right thing and care for this man. We need to take on one problem at a time."

"I agree," Millie said, "but my George will help keep us safe. I'll talk to him about it later. We can be on the lookout and take extra care, and we mustn't worry 'cause worrying won't do us no good."

"I agree," Sylvia said, grateful for Millie's reassurance. She then turned her attention back to the labeled bottles. She picked up a jar of salve for the sores on Mr. Heywood's feet, a tincture that could be put into a drink that would help ease his pain, and two different kinds of disinfectant that had the ability to help prevent infection that could become very serious if ignored. She handed one of the bottles to Millie so she could hold the others securely before the two women headed out of the room and up the stairs. Sylvia's heart began to pound with the thought of seeing her husband's ghost, and she reminded herself with each step: *He is not Daniel. He is not Daniel. He is not Daniel.*

By the time they came to the door of Mr. Heywood's room, Sylvia almost believed she could maintain her composure and her dignity. She told herself that if she became emotional, she would hold it back until she was alone. Right now he was simply a man in need of medical attention, and she was inexplicably grateful for the assistance of George and Millie, if only so she didn't have to be alone in a room with a man who looked like the husband she knew to be long dead.

Sylvia followed Millie into the room where George was sitting in a chair beside the bed, chatting comfortably with Mr. Heywood who was leaning back against a stack of pillows, wearing one of Daniel's nightshirts, with the bedcovers up to his chest and his hands folded on top of them. Sylvia noticed then what looked like a dark brown mole on the small finger of his left hand. She was glad for the way it gave her one more piece of evidence that this was not Daniel. He was indeed sorely in need of having his beard shaved or at least trimmed and his hair cut, but he still looked much better than he had earlier in the barn. Now that Sylvia was actually looking at him again, she felt less uncomfortable than she'd expected. He didn't look as much like her Daniel as she'd initially believed, although she couldn't quite figure out why. The scar on his cheek wasn't too ghastly, but it was impossible to ignore. She wanted to ask him about it but knew that such questions could wait—or perhaps it would be impolite of her to ask at all. The diagonal line on his cheek was a few inches long but didn't look as if the wound had been very deep.

When Sylvia realized that Mr. Heywood was looking at her, she looked down and cleared her throat, feeling mildly embarrassed. Then she looked back up and asked matter-of-factly, "How are you feeling, Mr. Heywood?"

"Much better being clean and in such a fine bed," the patient said. "I can't thank you enough, Mrs. Hewitt. And George here has been ever so kind." He nodded toward Millie and added with a smile, "And breakfast was ever so delicious, Millie. Your good husband told me I must call you Millie, and that you were responsible for the excellent meal."

"Indeed you must call me Millie, and I'm glad you enjoyed your breakfast, although I dare say you must have been half-starved and anything would have tasted good." She smiled kindly at Mr. Heywood who smiled gratefully in return. "I'll be helping you get yourself right so you'll likely be seeing me often." Millie smiled again, almost seeming smitten with the man.

Sylvia appreciated his humility and gratitude, but she focused on more practical matters. "Can you tell us where you have been injured . . . or anywhere that you're experiencing pain?"

She saw Mr. Heywood eying the bottles and jars that Sylvia and Millie were holding, and his brow furrowed while his eyes showed curiosity.

George obviously noticed and, much to Sylvia's relief, explained, "Our missus here is rather gifted with growing herbs and such and gathering plants and making all kinds of concoctions that do wonders with healing. She learned from her mother and grandmother before her. There'll be no need to fetch the doctor; not that we'd want to. He's not the kind of man any of us would want looking after us when we're ailing."

"That's true, for certain," Millie added, and Sylvia felt mildly nauseous for a moment until she forced away the terrible memories related to George's statement.

Figuring that was sufficient explanation, Sylvia repeated her question. "Can you tell me where it hurts and why?"

"The bottom of my feet are in pretty bad shape," Mr. Heywood said. "And then there's where I got shot in the leg."

George and Millie both gasped but Sylvia simply asked, "Do you know if there's still a bullet in your leg or—"

"No, ma'am," he said. "It caused a nasty gash and it hurts something terrible, but there's no bullet. I got lucky there."

"You did, indeed," Sylvia said, counting herself lucky as well since she knew that dealing with such a complication was not something they were capable of handling without simply relying on common sense. "Is there anything else?"

"Only that I have some aching all over," Mr. Heywood continued, "but I think that's just from walking so much and sleeping in places that weren't meant for man to sleep. And I'm awfully tired."

"Probably for the same reasons that you're aching," Sylvia said. "And pain can make a person feel more fatigued. I'm guessing now that I think about it that your feet must have been awfully cold."

"I can't deny it," Mr. Heywood said. "I've been grateful that it's not the dead of winter, nevertheless it's still been very chilly. But once I gave up on my shoes, I've used my coat to cover my feet when I was sleeping or took a break from walking. Since that warm bath they feel much better, in that regard at least."

"I'm glad to hear it," Sylvia said. "Now let's see what we can do to help your wounds heal and hopefully prevent any infection, and then I've got something you can take to help with the pain so you can get some good rest. First, I'm going to have George look at the wound on your leg while I turn around, and he can follow my instructions."

"As you wish," Mr. Heywood said, and she wondered if it was her imagination that he was trying to subdue a smile. She had no sense that he was being unkind or considering her excessively prudish, but rather that he simply found the situation amusing. She resisted her impulse to say anything at all about his reaction, which was far too subtle for her to be certain that he'd shown any reaction at all. Perhaps it was her own strange feelings about the situation that were making it so terribly awkward. Whatever the reason, she forged ahead with her plan and turned her back to the patient, determined to rely on George to do what needed to be done.

"Now, George," she said, looking toward the open doorway that led into the hall while Millie moved close to her husband's side to provide him with what he needed. "Just move the bedcovers aside enough to look at the wound and tell me what you see."

Sylvia heard the rustle of bedding being moved then Millie said, "Oh my!" and George declared, "It don't look too good."

"Describe it for me," Sylvia said.

"Looks sure enough like a bullet took a path along the edge of his thigh—left a nasty gash. It looks bloody and . . . there's some pus there too, for sure."

Sylvia didn't like the sound of that but remained calm and in control. "Is there any foul odor?"

She could literally hear George sniffing before he said, "Not that I can tell."

"That's good," Sylvia said. "Mr. Heywood? How many days since this happened?"

"Two, I think," he said. "Maybe three. I confess I've lost track of my days."

"No matter," Sylvia said. "Now, George, I'm going to tell you how to disinfect the wound and then apply a poultice that will help draw out the infection before it's wrapped properly to keep it clean. Do you think you can do that?"

"I can help him," Millie said. "I had three brothers who were always getting themselves injured and it was me who dressed their wounds. Surely the two of us together can do this if you tell us what to do exactly."

Sylvia gave them instructions to first clean the wound thoroughly with a strong antiseptic that would hopefully begin the process of doing away with the infection. She knew when it had been applied by the way Mr. Heywood groaned and cursed under his breath.

"That's the most difficult part," Sylvia said to him with some compassion, her back still turned. "Unfortunately, we'll have to do that twice a day until there are no longer any signs of infection."

"How delightful," Mr. Heywood said with sarcasm, but he added more sincerely, "I'm very grateful . . . to all of you. Without your help I fear I'd be dead before long."

"It's highly possible," Sylvia said then proceeded with giving instructions on treating and dressing the wound. When that was done and she'd been assured that Mr. Heywood's leg was now once again beneath the bedcovers, she turned around and moved a chair to the foot of the bed where she had easy access to the patient's feet. "Now, let's see what we are dealing with here." She pushed back the sheet and blanket covering his feet and winced to see the open sores there that were a result of a great deal of walking on bare feet, likely having encountered a great many rocks and twigs and other things that should not be experienced without shoes.

"Is it as bad as it feels?" Mr. Heywood asked.

"I assume so," Sylvia said then proceeded to ask George and Millie to get her everything she needed, which meant each of them leaving the room more than once. Sylvia cleaned Mr. Heywood's feet more thoroughly before carefully disinfecting those wounds as well—which the patient hated very much, but he still expressed gratitude following his adverse reaction to the pain. A healing salve was also applied to each of the bleeding sores before Sylvia bandaged his feet to keep the salve from rubbing off, and to keep the wounds clean. She then put clean stockings which had once belonged to Daniel over the bandaging and declared, "There now. Those should keep your feet warm and keep everything in place. I would suggest that other than getting out of bed to see to your own personal matters, you stay off of your feet completely—at least for a few days—until those wounds show some evidence of healing. We will clean everything and change the bandaging twice a day until your wounds reach the point where exposing them to the air will be more beneficial to their healing. Between the three of us we'll check on you regularly and see that you have what you need."

"And I'll be seeing that you're well fed," Millie added proudly.

"You're all being so kind," Mr. Heywood said with a barely noticeable tremor in his voice. "There are no words to express my gratitude."

"We would never turn away *anyone* suffering or in need," Sylvia said, as if she needed to make it clear—for her own benefit—that they would have helped him even if he didn't bear a striking resemblance to Daniel Hewitt.

"Now," Sylvia went on, "I'm going to have Millie bring you a fresh cup of tea and I'm going to put a few drops of a tincture in it—you won't be able to taste the difference. It will help ease the pain so you can rest. I know you *are* in pain even though I suspect you'd rather not admit to it, and you certainly need to sleep. Sleeping helps the body heal."

Mr. Heywood nodded in response, and she sensed that he was presently incapable of speaking without getting emotional. What he'd been through to get here had obviously been traumatic, and a part of her wanted to talk to him about it—or rather give him the opportunity to tell his story since she knew well enough from what she'd been taught that the emotional aspects of enduring trauma needed to be addressed every bit as much as the physical wounds. But that could wait until another time—perhaps when she had become more accustomed to this man's appearance and she could stop continually having to tell herself that this was not her dead husband.

Forcing her mind back to the physical status of the patient, Sylvia felt certain the scar on his face had healed long ago, but in an effort to appease her curiosity, she asked him, "May I ask if the wound on your face is causing you any pain? How long has it been since—"

"Oh, it no longer hurts, but thank you for asking." He forced a smile and added, "It's not pretty, I know. But it could have been worse." Sylvia appreciated his attitude even though he'd told her nothing to ease her curiosity.

Sylvia resisted the urge to say that the scar didn't detract from the fact that he was a very handsome man—despite the bushy beard and scruffy hair that still needed to be dealt with. Instead, she told him, "Perhaps it will serve as a reminder of that very thing—that despite certain difficulties, things can most often be much worse."

"It does, in fact," Mr. Heywood said. "And I'm grateful to be alive and in such good hands. I thank you all again for your kindness and assistance."

The three caregivers all muttered something to express that they were glad to help and it was the right thing to do. Sylvia then sent Millie off to get some fresh tea, and George to take the used water to be thrown out and dirty wash rags to the laundry. Sylvia neatly arranged her remedies and bandages on top of the bureau before she asked Mr. Heywood, "Is there anything else you need at the moment?"

"No, thank you kindly. I'm doing very well."

"I will check on you later, then," she said. "I hope you can get some rest."

Mr. Heywood nodded again, and Sylvia hurried from the room, sighing with deep relief to come into the hallway, knowing she'd survived that necessary encounter with Dougal Heywood. She only hoped that she could quickly learn to not allow his appearance to affect her—or that she could completely rely on George and Millie to care for him. The latter suited her better, even though it didn't seem very hospitable.

Sylvia quickly got busy with some sweeping and dusting that needed to be done in order to keep the house tidy, which she had hoped would keep her mind off of the stranger now recuperating in her home, but she found it impossible to banish him from her head. The entire situation was just so bizarre.

Sylvia was glad to hear Millie's report that the tincture in Mr. Heywood's tea had been effective and he was sleeping soundly. They let him sleep through lunch, and Millie promised to check on him every little while, and once he was awake, she would see that he had plenty to eat. And George volunteered to be on hand to help their patient with any personal needs he might have that would be better seen to by another man. Sylvia was deeply grateful for their help and told them so, but she knew that seeing to Mr. Heywood's wounds was something she needed to assist with, which meant she couldn't avoid seeing him at least twice a day. With this in mind, she said, "We'll care for his wounds again before bedtime, and give him more of the tincture to help him sleep."

They were both happy to help Sylvia just as they had earlier, and Millie added, "I've got a little bell I'm going to give him so that he can ring if he needs something. Our bedroom is much closer to his so I believe we can hear it if he has a problem."

"We shall hope he doesn't have any problems that will interrupt your sleep," Sylvia said. "He *is* able to get around on his own. I'm certain it causes him pain to walk, and he shouldn't do so more than necessary, but that doesn't mean he isn't capable."

Sylvia was glad when their lunchtime conversation shifted to more ordinary topics, and they didn't talk about Mr. Heywood any further. Although, when they were clearing the table, George and Millie began to speculate over the details of this man's history and circumstances and his strange resemblance to the deceased Mr. Hewitt. They also briefly discussed the potential danger he might be in, but they agreed firmly that it didn't alter the fact that they had no problem with taking him in, and they would simply take some extra precautions in order to keep their household safe. It seemed logical that none of them had any reason to be concerned for their safety; they simply needed to keep Mr. Heywood hidden away, and hopefully no one had seen them bring him into the house. Sylvia was glad when she'd completed her usual work in the kitchen, and she announced that she was going for a walk to get some fresh air now that the rain had stopped.

Once she was properly dressed to go out, Sylvia exited through the front door, where there was a stone path that wound through the center of a blanket of grass that kept this side of the house from getting muddy when it rained. The path between the kitchen door and the barn was an entirely different matter, where rainfall always equated with mud.

The moment she closed the door behind her, Sylvia breathed in the scent of fresh rain and admired the beauty of the parting clouds and the way the sun peered through. She felt grateful to be out of the house where the very presence of Mr. Heywood had created a stifling effect. She knew that she needed to come to terms with this bizarre situation and not allow it to keep bothering her, but she also knew that it hadn't been so many hours since she'd been confronted with her husband's ghost, and she was certainly entitled to take some time to adjust. Still, the fresh air felt good, and she walked down the stone path across the lawn toward a meadow where wildflowers of various colors were peeking up out of the tall grass. Everything was wet from the morning's heavy rain, but Sylvia didn't care. She strolled lazily amidst the grass and flowers, allowing them to dampen her skirt and shoes, knowing she had a warm home and dry clothes to return to once she'd taken in the soothing effect of nature that was quickly calming her anxiousness.

Once Sylvia had gone a significant distance from the house, she indulged in a common habit of turning around to admire the home she'd grown to love. She'd never set eyes on this house until she'd come here as a new bride to Daniel Hewitt. As an only child, he had inherited the house and a vast amount of land surrounding it upon the death of his father, which had occurred in Daniel's twenty-fourth year. Since his mother had died before he'd been old enough to even remember her, he'd been left completely alone at an age when he was barely considered a man. He'd not even had any relatives on either side of his family. He'd told Sylvia many times how grateful he was for the way she'd filled his home with joy and laughter, and throughout the early months of their marriage, feeling joyful had been easy. Sylvia had loved caring for the beautiful home, which felt like a mansion to her in contrast to the little farmhouse where she'd grown up. The house that had become hers at the time of her husband's death had five bedrooms and a bathing room on the upper floor. On the ground floor—besides the much-used kitchen and dining room—were a parlor, her workroom, a pantry and larder, and a laundry room. These rooms all felt very luxurious to Sylvia since she'd grown up doing laundry in the kitchen with tubs that had to be moved about with great effort, and bathing had also been done in the kitchen with the same tubs and family members taking turns. In contrast to the house in which she'd grown up, the home Daniel Hewitt had given her was grand and fine, and a day never passed when she didn't feel an awareness of such a blessing. For all that Daniel had swindled and schemed in ways she couldn't begin to imagine, he had fought to protect the stability of the house and land he'd inherited from his father, and thus he'd left her with the security of always knowing she and those who worked for her would always have a home. There were also two homes with surrounding farmland some distance away but still a part of the land she'd inherited from Daniel. The rent she received each month from these farmers—who were good hardworking people with families—provided enough income for her needs to be met.

Admiring the house with beams of sunlight caressing the wet roof, Sylvia felt overcome with a calming sensation that helped counteract all that had happened—and her resulting tumultuous feelings—since she'd found a strange man hiding in her barn earlier this morning. For all of Daniel's faults and the trouble he'd caused, he'd loved her and she'd loved him. To her, this house and the surrounding land felt like tangible evidence of that love. And the appearance of this friend of his who looked so much like him changed nothing. As always, Sylvia forced her mind to focus on the good she'd shared with Daniel and let go of the rest. He was dead and buried; there was no changing the past. Peace could only be found in remembering the good.

Sorting through her own confusion, Sylvia realized she needed to be more clear with herself over the fact that Dougal Heywood and Daniel Hewitt were not the same man. Now that she'd had some time to adjust to that fact, she felt confident that she could interact with him and not be so strangely affected. She resigned herself to being more patient with him. She couldn't recall saying or doing anything that would have been considered impolite, but she knew her own thoughts and emotions had been overcome with a strong desire to leave his care to Millie and George, not wanting to interact with him at all. But he was not only in need of assistance, he was surely in need of compassion, and she needed to let go of her own selfish struggles and make an effort to not just care for his medical needs and see that he was fed, but also to express kindness toward him. She believed it was highly likely that the bullet wound on his leg—which could have been so much worse—was a direct result of his resemblance to Daniel. It was no fault of Mr. Heywood's that he had such a physical resemblance to a man who had earned many enemies through his unethical behavior and dubious acquaintances.

Sylvia purposefully took in deep breaths and blew them out slowly as she wandered aimlessly through the meadow, finding some measure of acceptance over the current situation, and a determination to let go of her own confusion and simply focus on Mr. Heywood. She reminded herself as she often did that she had always strived to be a good Christian woman, and that meant setting aside her own confounded emotions and simply be kind to this man. The story of the Good Samaritan came to her mind, making her realize that she had the means to care for this man without putting any strain on her household whatsoever. Neither Millie nor George had such a heavy workload that their time assisting Mr. Heywood would be a strain on them, and the same was true for Sylvia. Their household had been blessed with plenty of food and other supplies, and caring for someone in need was surely the only decent thing to do—no matter how much this man reminded her of Daniel and stirred up difficult feelings. But surely she would become accustomed to his appearance with time.

Sylvia finally made her way back to the house, arriving at the front door just as rain began to sprinkle again. Just inside the door, she sat down on a little, finely carved bench to remove her shoes, wet as they were, and carried them up the stairs with her. She paused on the landing and glanced briefly to her right, knowing that Mr. Heywood was resting in the room at the end of the hall. She uttered a silent prayer on behalf of his healing and turned the other direction to go to her own room at the opposite end of the hall. She stoked up the fire and set her shoes on the hearth to dry, then she exchanged her wet petticoat and skirt for dry ones, draping those that were wet over the back of a chair that she situated near the fire.

After putting an extra pair of thick stockings on her feet to help them warm up, she sat on the edge of her bed then plopped backwards into the softness of the quilt covering it while she wondered what her life might have been like if Daniel were still alive. She'd determined long ago—even before he'd left to fight in the war—that there were vast differences in the character of Daniel Hewitt; he was like the pendulum of a clock that swung back and forth with a tender and loving personality at one side, and a despicable tendency to scheme and cheat at the other, having no apparent sense of integrity. She had struggled greatly with the stark contrasts of her husband's character, but as time had passed, she had come to feel more and more that the trouble he was continually bringing upon himself—and subsequently her—was gradually smothering the love between them. To her, integrity and love were deeply intertwined and she had been unable to continue trying to ignore the lack of the former in order to keep the latter alive. With Daniel's absence, and then his death, she'd felt a deep relief in no longer needing to contend with the problems. But that hadn't kept her from grieving over her love for him. Perhaps in some ways it had been easier to allow her love for him to become more dominant in his absence.

33

Sylvia was surprised to awaken and realize that she had drifted to sleep. She knew she'd been immersed in strange dreams although she could recall very little except that she'd dreamt of Daniel as an apparition wandering the halls of this house, unhappy about the stranger being cared for here. The very idea left Sylvia wondering if she was being a fool to be so trusting of Mr. Heywood. She had taken for granted that everything he'd told her was true. But what if it wasn't? The very idea unsettled her so deeply that she abruptly pushed away any such thoughts. Right now he could hardly get out of bed, let alone cause any problems. Still, she resigned herself to the reality that she needed to remain guarded and careful. It would take time to know whether she could really trust this man, and with any luck he would be healed and long gone before the need to trust him ever became an issue.

Sylvia freshened up and resisted the urge to check on Mr. Heywood, choosing instead to go downstairs and ask Millie for a report.

"Oh, hello," Millie said from where she stood in front of the stove, stirring something in a large pot that Sylvia suspected was some kind of soup for tonight's supper. "I peeked in on you and found you sleeping, so I let you be."

"I hope I wasn't needed," Sylvia said and suppressed a yawn.

"You know I would have woke you up if you was," Millie said. "I've got some beef simmering till it gets tender then I'll add some vegetables later for a fine stew."

"Your stew is always divine," Sylvia said.

"George is in the barn repairing that broken stall before it gets any worse and causes problems."

"Excellent," Sylvia said, then added something she said often because it was true, "I don't know what I would ever do without the two of you."

"No need to ever wonder that," Millie said. "Finding work here in your home was a miracle for us when we needed one."

This was something that Millie said frequently, surely because to her and her husband it was true. The two of them had worked many years at a fine manor house where they met and had finally married after knowing each other for years. And then their employer had lost everything due to his ridiculously excessive gambling habits, and he'd taken his own life. His wife and children had gone to live with family elsewhere, and the purchaser of the manor had brought his own staff with him, and thus all of the servants had been left without employment. This had all occurred about the same time that Daniel had gone off to war and Sylvia had realized she needed help to care for the house and the farm, and she'd also needed company. With the income she received, she couldn't afford to pay them very much, but she could offer them security, and they had sufficient funds to all live comfortably as long as they all worked together to see to the needed chores. She'd interviewed multiple people who had responded to her advertisements, but it was Millie and George who met her every qualification. And now she couldn't imagine how life had been without them. Given some terrible challenges she'd unexpectedly faced not many months after she'd hired them, their being here had come to feel like a miracle, and Sylvia had never let go of that feeling.

As if Millie had read Sylvia's mind, she answered the very question Sylvia had been thinking only moments earlier. "I peeked in on Mr. Heywood not so many minutes ago and he was still asleep. We didn't give him enough of that tincture to put him out for too long. I suspect it just helped him relax and now his poor tired body has taken over in giving him the rest he needs."

"I would have to agree," Sylvia said and didn't realize that her mind had wandered very far away until Millie startled her.

"Are you all right, Missus?" she asked and set down the spoon she'd been using to stir before putting a lid on the pot.

Sylvia had no reason to try and hide her true feelings from Millie; they'd become very good friends, and Sylvia knew she could trust her completely. "Mr. Heywood's resemblance to my dead husband just has me unsettled somewhat."

"I should say," Millie declared and both women sat down at the worktable.

"Even if he didn't look so much like my Daniel—which is disarming to say the least—the fact that they had become friends, that they knew each other so well, it's . . . well, it's as if all of my efforts to come to terms with Daniel's death are now becoming . . . unraveled, somehow."

"I doubt there's any person on God's green earth who wouldn't feel the same," Millie said. "And from the way you were behaving earlier, I'm guessing you'd prefer to avoid him as much as possible. If that's what you want to do, me and George can take care of him. We have a comfortable life here, thanks to you, and we'll do whatever you ask of us—you know that."

"I *do* know that," Sylvia said.

"Still, I got to say that . . . maybe avoiding him isn't the best way to make your feelings right, Missus. Sooner or later he's going to be up and about more, although I don't think we'll be kicking him out the door the minute he's barely able to walk without hurting."

Sylvia actually preferred that option but had to say, "No, that wouldn't be very kind."

"It's my thinking that you *should* spend time with him. He was a friend to your Daniel. Now, I know your feelings toward your husband—may he rest in peace—are more than a bit messy with love all mixed up into the bad stuff he was doing. But still, Missus, you loved your Daniel, and this man came to know him well. Maybe—just maybe—talking about Daniel with someone who spent time with him before he died might help you with your healing. That's just my tuppence of a thought. What you do is up to you, and me and George will take care of whatever needs taking care of."

"Thank you," Sylvia said and reached across the table to squeeze Millie's hand. "Your advice is much appreciated. I will give it some thought."

"You do that," Millie said and came to her feet. "Right now, I need to be making some bread to go with that stew. I assume you'll be helping me."

"I would love to," Sylvia said, well aware that Millie knew how much Sylvia loved the feel of bread dough in her hands as she kneaded it to the perfect consistency Millie had taught her.

"Then we'd best get to it so it'll have time to rise and bake before supper," Millie added, gathering the necessary ingredients and setting them out on the table. Sylvia set to work helping her in a way that had become a comfortable routine for the two women. But she found herself wishing that Dougal Heywood had never found his way here, and then there would be no need for her to determine the best way to deal with his presence in her home and the complicated thoughts and feelings it evoked. She would rather just knead bread dough without any concerns whatsoever.

Chapter Three

The Lie

When supper was ready, George took a tray upstairs for the patient and returned to report that Mr. Heywood had everything he needed and was very appreciative of the meal.

"Told me he got some good rest with that concoction you gave him," George added, nodding toward Sylvia as they all sat down to eat their own supper, "and he's already feeling a little less pain."

"I'm glad to hear it," Sylvia said with sincerity, and she was also glad that George had been the one to check on him and see that his needs were met.

Throughout supper Sylvia mostly listened to George and Millie speculating over Mr. Heywood's past, his reasons for coming here, and his friendship with the late Mr. Hewitt. She found it interesting that despite their all being aware that Mr. Heywood had been brutally attacked and had declared that his life was in danger, the subject was not addressed and no one seemed concerned. Sylvia preferred not to bring it up herself and assumed that the consensus would be that there was simply nothing more they could do to protect their patient or themselves beyond what they were already doing. It was easier to focus on the simpler facets of interest regarding their guest. While Sylvia distinctly felt curious over these things as well, she had no desire to fruitlessly try and guess the answers to questions that only Mr. Heywood could answer. She felt certain that with time they would all have their curiosity satisfied.

While Sylvia settled in to help Millie put the kitchen in order and clean the dirty dishes, George announced he was going upstairs to help Mr. Hewitt trim his beard and hair. "I'm no expert," he said with a jolly chuckle and rubbed his bald head, "but there was a time when I had a full head of hair and wore a beard myself, and I managed to keep them trimmed and not look like a heathen. It's not like he's gonna be going to any grand socials or nothing." He chuckled again. "But I do believe he'll feel better without all that extra hair getting in the way."

"I'm glad for your willingness and your expertise," Sylvia said, watching George retrieve a small basin and a good pair of scissors. "I wouldn't know where to begin."

"Glad to help, Missus," he said with a smile. He also picked up a tin pitcher of warm water before he headed up the stairs, saying over his shoulder, "After I get him more presentable, I'm guessing you'll want to be changing his bandages and such."

"Yes," Sylvia called. "Let us know when you're finished."

When the work in the kitchen was done, Sylvia sank into a chair and leaned her elbows on the table. Millie sat across from her and proved her keen perception when she stated, "This Mr. Heywood being in the house has got you a good deal more upset than you're trying to let on."

"I cannot deny that's true," Sylvia said. "I find myself thinking about him far too much—which is ridiculous because I know very well he's not my Daniel."

"But I dare say seeing someone who looks so much like your Daniel has stirred up a great many memories." Millie's voice was as compassionate as her vague smile as she reached her hand across the table and put it over Sylvia's.

"I think that's exactly what's happening," Sylvia said, "although I'm not certain what to do about it."

"And Mr. Heywood having known your husband in the war is . . . well . . ." Millie hesitated, struggling for the right words, "he spent time with your Mr. Hewitt long after you last saw him. That surely must feel strange too."

"Yes, you're right about that, as well," Sylvia said. "I know I need to just get all of this straight in my head and not be hesitant to even look at the man, but . . . it's proving more difficult than I had anticipated, and for all that everything you've said makes sense, it feels to me as if a great deal of my being upset *doesn't* make sense. I think I'm making far more of this than it is, and I just need to set aside my own confusion over the matter."

"Perhaps," Millie suggested, "you should have some conversations with the man. Maybe hearing Mr. Heywood's account of his friendship with your husband could help you."

"That makes sense," Sylvia said. She could see the wisdom in such an endeavor, but she still didn't want to do it.

"For now let's go and see how the men are getting on," Millie said as she stood, "and we'll care for the wounds while we're at it."

"Yes, of course," Sylvia said and reluctantly followed Millie up the stairs, down the hall, and into the open doorway of Mr. Heywood's room. She was surprised to see the patient sitting in a chair rather than in the bed. Thankfully the nightshirt he wore was long and showed nothing of his legs. He was still wearing the stockings she had put on his feet earlier. Initially Sylvia didn't get a good look at his face because George was blocking her view, but when George moved aside, Sylvia took in a sharp breath and had to consciously will herself to appear unaffected. Mr. Hewitt's hair was now shorter, and its curliness easily disguised any flaws there might have been in the lack of George's skills—so much like Daniel's hair, although Mr. Hewitt's hair was a darker blond than Daniel's had been, and she found herself wondering if the comparison was just her mind playing tricks on her. But more striking was the way the neatly trimmed beard made his features more visible, and Sylvia was struck afresh with this man's disturbing resemblance to Daniel.

Sylvia was glad for the way that Millie was fussing over how fine the patient looked. It gave her a few moments to steady her composure and remind herself of the facts versus the mental deception of what her eyes were telling her.

"You do look much better," Sylvia said. "More comfortable, dare I guess?"

"Very much so," Mr. Hewitt said, "thank you. And supper was delicious, Millie," he added, smiling at her. "Thank you for that."

"A pleasure," Millie said. "But Mrs. Hewitt helped make that bread."

"It was excellent," he said with a disarming smile that Sylvia tried to ignore. "Thank you."

"Of course," Sylvia said nonchalantly. "We wouldn't let you go hungry." Before any further niceties could be exchanged, she hurried to add, "Now let's see how your wounds are faring and make certain we're doing all we can to help them heal as quickly as possible." She couldn't help thinking as she said the last part that the sooner he healed the sooner he could be on his way and this continual reminder of Daniel would no longer be living beneath her own roof.

Mr. Heywood walked carefully on his ailing feet to the bed with George's help. Once he was comfortable, leaning back against pillows that softened the hardness of the headboard, Sylvia took over removing the bandages from his feet and inspecting the sores there, glad to see that there was no excessive redness or any other sign of infections. Still, she disinfected them carefully, which was a painful process, but Mr. Heywood exhibited patience even though it obviously hurt. Sylvia applied salve and bandaged his feet again, putting stockings on him to keep the bandaging in place and to keep his feet warm.

Sylvia once again allowed George to oversee what needed to be done for the wound on Mr. Heywood's leg while she kept her back turned. George reported that it looked better since he saw no sign of pus. When the wound was disinfected and a poultice was applied once again, the patient was tucked beneath the bedcovers and Sylvia took a chair beside the bed, putting a great deal of effort into maintaining a nonchalant countenance. "Tell me how you're feeling, Mr. Heywood. How is the pain?"

"It was good to get some sleep," he said, "although I still feel very tired."

"That's to be expected, I think," Sylvia replied. "And the pain?" she asked again.

"It's still there," he said, "but with the help you're giving me, I'm confident that it will improve and for that I'm more grateful than I can say."

"I'm glad that we're able to help," Sylvia said and stood up, suddenly needing to get out of the room when the visage of Daniel in front of her brought on a sudden urge to just lean over and wrap her arms around this man. "I'll have Millie bring you some tea with the tincture in it that will help you sleep, and I'll check back with you in the morning."

"Thank you, Mrs. Hewitt," he said, and she nodded.

"And you can ring if you need anything," Millie added.

"Might take us a minute or two to get here," George said in an apologetic tone, "but we can hear the bell from our room and we'll come quick enough."

"I don't think there's any need for me to wake anyone," Mr. Heywood said, "nevertheless I appreciate your thoughtfulness on that count. I assure you if I need something I can't manage on my own that I will ring."

Sylvia hurried from the room, saying to Millie as she left, "I'm going to bed myself; I will see you in the morning as usual."

"Sleep well, Missus," Millie said and Sylvia felt as if she couldn't get to the safety of her room fast enough. The long hallway that went down the center of the upper floor felt eternal as she went from Mr. Heywood's room at one end all the way to her own room at the other. A lamp left burning on a table at the top of the stairs gave off enough of a glow to guide her through the darkness until she entered her room, closed the door, and leaned back against it as if some kind of monster might be after her. She took in a few deep breaths and blew them out slowly before she felt her way to find the lamp on the little table to her right, and a match to be able to light the wick so she could see. The room was chilly but she felt no incentive to build a fire, knowing she would be warm enough in her bed.

Sylvia had just begun to unbutton her dress to change into a nightgown when she heard a light knocking on her door.

"Who is it?" she called, even though she knew from the sound of the knocking that it was likely Millie; still, she didn't want to open the door with her dress unbuttoned if it were George.

"Tis me, Missus," she heard Millie say and Sylvia held the front of her dress together with one hand while she opened the door with the other.

"Is something wrong?" Sylvia asked.

"No, Missus," Millie said, "but Mrs. Ripple is here saying her son got himself a bad cut on his leg and she needs to purchase some remedies.

"Of course," Sylvia said, sorry to hear about Mrs. Ripple's son, but glad this had nothing to do with Mr. Heywood. It wasn't at all unusual for people to come late in the evening to get supplies from her, and fortunately it was rare that anyone came so late that she'd already gone to bed. But they definitely waited until after dark; no one wanted to be seen coming to her house, or even heading this direction—since this house was the only one this far out from the village, and beyond a distant crossroads, the road led nowhere but here. "Tell her I'll be right down."

Millie just nodded and left, holding a lamp to guide her way. Sylvia hurried to button her dress and smooth her hair before she picked up her own lamp and went downstairs to find the plump, middle-aged Mrs. Ripple pacing in the parlor, clearly concerned for one of her seven children, and exuberant to see Sylvia when she entered.

"Oh, Mrs. Hewitt," the woman said with adoration, "I cannot tell you how glad I am that we are blessed enough to have you here with your wonderful remedies. Not one of us at my house likes that doctor one bit, and I could treat a great many mishaps with your remedies for the price of one of his visits."

"You're very kind," Sylvia said and led the way to her workroom, asking some questions about the specific nature of the injury. Sylvia often had to just stare for a minute or so at the bottles on her shelves in order to logically assess the correct remedy and examine her feelings on the matter. She'd learned to trust her instincts when it came to these things, and over the past few years she'd rarely been wrong. When she *had* been wrong, she generally discovered there was missing information and then she was able to offer the proper remedy. So, she'd learned to ask a great many questions before offering what she believed would be the correct solutions.

Sylvia finally settled on three different products, which she moved from the shelf to the table while she offered careful instructions that could not be misunderstood.

"Wonderful!" Mrs. Ripple said. "And may I buy some bandages from you, as well? Yours are cleaner and softer than what I can come up with, and I'm certain we'll need to keep that nasty cut of his covered for a while yet."

"Of course," Sylvia said and picked up one of the clean cotton bags she made for customers. She put everything in the bag while Mrs. Ripple asked what she owed and Sylvia told her.

"A bargain, to be sure," Mrs. Ripple said and counted out the money, setting it on the table.

"I'm glad that I can help," Sylvia said and meant it. The money helped but it wasn't her biggest reason for doing what she did.

After walking Mrs. Ripple out the front door where Sylvia now realized *Mr.* Ripple was waiting with a trap to drive her home, Sylvia locked the door and headed back up the stairs with her lamp, gratified by her ability to help good people like the Ripple family.

Once in her room again with the door closed, Sylvia hurried to get ready for bed and climbed beneath the plentiful bedcovers where she knew she would soon be warm enough to sleep. With the lamp now on her bedside table, Sylvia debated about reading from the book she'd left open there but decided she wouldn't be able to concentrate, so she extinguished the lamp and focused on breathing deeply with the hope that her thoughts would remain on the steady rhythm of her breaths and not be capable of wandering elsewhere.

But that only lasted a few minutes. She simply couldn't push away all of the reminders of Daniel that had burst back into her life since she'd gone to the barn this morning as part of her usual routine. She realized that today felt as if it had been three or four days; perhaps that's why she felt so physically exhausted even if she couldn't get her mind to stop circling through a barrage of memories—some sweet and tender, but most of them distressing and troublesome. That's how her marriage had been: the love and tenderness between them had always been overshadowed by the trouble that had continually followed Daniel Hewitt.

Sylvia forced her mind to focus on only the good, and she was finally able to relax.

Her next awareness was the distant crowing of their resident rooster, and the hint of sunlight peering between her partially closed curtains. Her initial response to being greeted by the signs of a typical morning was a pleasant sigh while she stretched the sleep out of her limbs. For all that her life was simple and isolated, she felt safe and content here in her home with George and Millie to help her and offer good company. She had everything she needed and felt very blessed. Her normal morning thoughts suddenly rushed away in lieu of recalling the events of the previous day, and Sylvia gasped then sighed then groaned as she considered how Dougal Heywood's arrival had made her realize that she had not dealt with Daniel's death nearly as well as she had believed, but she doubted there were many widows who were forced to contend with facing what seemed an identical twin to their deceased husbands. Sylvia actually considered the possibility that Daniel had been born a twin, and his brother had been given to another family to be adopted and raised elsewhere, and the two brothers had been unknowingly reunited by the hand of fate. The idea made a good story—and it was a more plausible explanation in her mind than the fact that two men simply looked so much alike—but she instinctively knew such an idea simply couldn't be true, and she had to accept that it was nothing more than a strange coincidence. Daniel had told Sylvia many times of how his parents had wanted a large family but his mother had been unable to have more children after his birth. If they'd been blessed with twins, they would have been thrilled.

Sylvia groaned again before she forced herself to get out of bed and prepare for the day. Again, she chose not to build a fire since she wouldn't be in this room long enough for it to do her any good. Right now, she just needed to get the milk and eggs and deliver them to Millie in the kitchen, and then she could warm up near the stove in the kitchen where she knew Millie would be busy cooking a sustaining breakfast. It gave Sylvia comfort just to think of being able to eat delicious food with her dear friends.

As Sylvia slipped her feet into Daniel's boots—the same way she did every morning—her mind went back to the previous morning when she'd been on the brink of confronting Daniel's ghost, completely oblivious to how this man's appearance in her life would be so upsetting. But thankfully it wasn't raining as it had been yesterday, and she was able to enjoy the sunlight peering over the east horizon as she made her way to the barn to do her usual early morning chores. She tried not to think about what had occurred here the previous morning while she greeted the animals and talked to them the way she usually did. It occurred to her that Mr. Heywood had surely over-heard her doing so while he'd been hiding in her barn, and she felt mildly embarrassed. But there was nothing to be done about that.

Sylvia hurried through her usual routine and returned to the house with the buckets of milk and eggs which she left in the usual place for Millie to use. She went to her room to clean up then returned to the kitchen to help Millie put breakfast on.

"You know you don't have to cook such an elaborate breakfast every morning," Sylvia said. "We'd do fine with bread and butter, I'm sure."

"So you've said a great many times," Millie said while she expertly turned over a griddle cake to cook the other side, "and as I've said a great many times: there's nothing like a good, hardy breakfast to start the day, and unless I'm down in bed, that's what we'll be having."

"Well," Sylvia chuckled, "I can't deny that it is a delight—espe-cially with your fine cooking."

Millie chuckled deeply and flipped the cooked griddle cake out of the skillet before she poured more batter into the pan to make another. Sylvia watched over another skillet where slices of bacon were sizzling. She'd learned from Millie how to tell when they were cooked to perfec-tion, and she was determined to tend to them carefully so they turned out as well as if Millie had cooked them herself. Sylvia had been able to do a fair amount of basic cooking and baking before Millie had come to live in her home, but Millie had excellent skills in the kitchen, and Sylvia had learned a great deal from her about how to make meals delicious as well as satisfying. It was Millie's belief that the food God provided was meant to be enjoyed as well as necessary for survival. Sylvia was glad that she had the money to purchase such fine food for Millie to then spin into her culinary masterpieces. The extra income she received from her medical remedies helped make that possible, and George and Millie had both agreed that they would far prefer having Sylvia spend extra money on fine food as opposed to giving them a raise in their salaries since they had everything they needed and more.

When breakfast was ready and the table had been set, George took a tray up for Mr. Heywood. George reported that he'd already been in to check on their patient who had enjoyed a fairly good night's sleep and by all accounts was doing well.

"Tell him we'll change the bandages after we finish breakfast and clean up the kitchen," Sylvia said, glad that she didn't feel as much dread over that prospect as she had the day before.

When Sylvia and Millie arrived at Mr. Heywood's room and stepped through the open door, they found George sitting in the chair near the bed while the two men laughed boisterously.

"Something must be terribly funny," Sylvia said, drawing the men's attention to the fact that the women were standing there.

"I doubt we could repeat it with the same humorous effect," Mr. Heywood said, still chuckling.

"No need to try," Sylvia said, although she felt glad that George and their patient were developing a comfortable rapport. In fact, she noticed the same easy interaction between Millie and Mr. Heywood. He was polite and humble and always appreciative. And he was easy to like. Of course, Daniel had possessed those same qualities—the very same traits that had allowed him to be such a swindler. But it was because of Daniel that Sylvia had developed what she considered a keen ability to discern sincerity in a person. And thus far she had no reason to believe that Mr. Heywood wasn't completely sincere. As they went through the usual routine of cleaning, treating, and bandaging the wounds, she found herself surprised by how comfortable she felt in his presence when she had believed not so long ago that she only wanted to avoid him as much as possible until he was healed enough to leave. But she'd become more accustomed—although not entirely—to the absolute fact that this man was not Daniel, and she was able to see him more as a completely separate individual from her deceased husband.

When they were finished, George asked Mr. Heywood if he needed anything else.

"Not at the moment, thank you," the patient said. It was evident that George had already helped him get washed up and into a clean nightshirt.

George and Millie left the room ahead of Sylvia, and she was nearly to the door when the patient said, "Mrs. Hewitt?"

"Yes?" she replied and turned toward him, her heart quickening a little as her confidence over having adjusted to his resemblance to Daniel wavered. It *was* easier than yesterday, but she felt certain there would always be unexpected moments when the resemblance would take her off guard—just as it did in that particular moment. "Do you need something?"

"I know you must be very busy," he said, seeming mildly nervous, "but . . . I wonder if we could talk . . . just for a few minutes. I won't keep you long, but . . . there are some things I've been wondering, and . . ." His stammering ended as he motioned subtly toward the chair beside the bed where George had been sitting.

Sylvia hesitated for a long moment while she settled her mind firmly on the fact that this was simply a few minutes of conversation, and it was surely nothing to be concerned about. She moved to the chair and sat down, unconsciously smoothing her hands over her apron as if that might somehow protect her from the strangeness of this situation.

"I have a few minutes," she stated, hoping that would prevent their conversation from going on too long.

"Thank you," he said. His humble gratitude always reminded her of the best of Daniel, but it also reminded her that as time had passed, Daniel had been less and less humble *or* grateful about anything in life, and their marriage had mostly disintegrated. She'd never stopped loving him, but she'd lost every bit of trust and respect, and the combination had been brutal.

Sylvia snapped her thoughts away from Daniel with a firm reminder that he had nothing to do with the man sitting in front of her. "What can I do for you, Mr. Heywood?" she asked.

"First of all," he sounded astonished, "you can never call me Mr. Heywood again. I only think of my father, and I wasn't necessarily fond of the man. I'd be grateful to have you call me Dougal—it is my name. It's a Scottish name. My mother was Scottish and named me after her father, and I was very close to both my mother and my grandfather, so I prefer the name for many reasons."

"Very well, Dougal," she said and returned to the point. "What can I do for you?"

"It's just that . . . well . . . I don't want to be at all intrusive or inappropriate, but . . ."

Sylvia felt nervous already after such a preamble, but she just listened.

"The thing is . . ." he stammered, something Daniel had never done. "Well . . . Daniel often told me he was concerned for you . . . that he hoped you were well. He was worried about you being alone, and . . . worried about your needs being met. I know he's gone and . . . it's surely none of my business, but . . . I suppose he spoke of it enough to put it in my head, and . . . now you've taken me in and you're feeding me well and taking very good care of me, and . . . I just . . . well . . . perhaps I only want to know . . . on Daniel's behalf, maybe . . ." He shook his head as if he regretted his words. "I've no right to ask anything on Daniel's behalf, ma'am. Let me just say that I would like to know you're doing well . . . and that your needs are being met. I feel as if I came to know you through Daniel, and now you're being so kind and—"

Sylvia stopped his stammering—which was beginning to wear on her nerves—and just told him what he wanted to know; she certainly had nothing to hide. "The house and a great deal of land are mine, which gives me security. There are two farms with families living on my land. The leases for these farms provide a sufficient income. I hired Millie and George not long after Daniel left. We'd talked about my taking on someone to help me and keep me company. I don't have much salary to pay them, but I can give them a place to live and meet their needs and our arrangement is excellent, especially since we've all come to feel like family."

"I'm very glad to hear it," he said. "And thank you for telling me—you didn't have to."

"I don't mind," she replied, finding their conversation not entirely unpleasant now that he'd stopped stammering. "I have no secrets, Dougal." She'd almost called him Mr. Heywood but managed to stop herself. "You should know that I also supplement my income a little by selling the remedies I make from the herbs I grow."

"That's wonderful," he said with a kind smile. "How clever you are! I recall now that George said you had learned such things from your mother and grandmother. Your skills are obviously excellent since I can already feel much improvement."

"I'm very glad to hear it," she said, "but be careful about your admiration of my skills. I only sell my remedies under cover of darkness with the promise of never telling anyone the identity of my customers. And I never personally leave the farm. George and Millie take the wagon into town whenever we need supplies."

"Why?" Dougal asked, his brow furrowing, his eyes narrow with confusion.

"Because I'm a witch," she said, and his eyes widened before she laughed. "Forgive me. Allow me to rephrase that. There are a great many of the villagers who have decided that I am a witch; that my 'potions and concoctions,' as they call them, are something evil and therefore forbidden. The reality is that our local doctor is a charlatan and an arrogant fool who won't tolerate any competition to seeing to the medical needs of the community. He charges exorbitant prices for his services to people who cannot afford them and so they are always in debt to him if they have medical needs. And the vicar is his friend and in my opinion doesn't have the strength of character to think for himself so he is easily swayed by those who have the ability to benefit his life in any possible way. The doctor makes generous donations to the vicarage, and therefore the vicar has become incapable of seeing anything but the best in the doctor, and therefore believes everything this man has told him. The result has been wave after wave of ridiculous gossip about me, and the result has been my being labeled a witch." Sylvia thought briefly about one very large part of this story that had contributed to the feud between her and the doctor, but she couldn't imagine ever speaking of such things aloud to a stranger. Instead, she pressed on with the same topic. "Children actually run away from me if I show myself in the village, so . . ." Sylvia managed to swallow any indication of the sorrow she felt over the situation, ". . . I just enjoy my simple life here and I'm very grateful for the help that Millie and George give me."

"I admire your positive attitude, Mrs. Hewitt, but may I say . . . that is truly terrible!"

"I agree, it is. And there is nothing to be done about it beyond accepting the reality as it is, so I make the best of all I've been blessed with."

"And you have so generously shared your blessings with me," he said. "I want to apologize for the fright I gave you yesterday. Finding a stranger in your barn must have been terrifying enough, but I'm absolutely certain that my resemblance to your husband was surely shocking."

"I can't deny that," she said and coughed slightly, again pressing her hands over her skirt. "Although I've recovered from the shock and I'm glad that we can help you heal."

"I will make it up to you when I'm on my feet again, Mrs. Hewitt. I'm more than happy to do any work you would have me do and—"

Sylvia's mind got stuck on the possibility of him staying on longer and she stood up in order to conclude the conversation. "Let's not worry about that right now," she said. "But please call me Sylvia. Like you, I find my surname attached to some uncomfortable memories." He nodded and she said, "Is there anything you need right now? Did Millie give you something to help you rest or—"

"She asked but I declined. Perhaps later. Right now I'd like to stay awake, and the pain is tolerable."

"Something to read, perhaps?" Sylvia offered, certain that sitting in bed like this had to be terribly boring.

"Oh, that would be grand!" he said with enthusiasm.

"I'll see what I can find," Sylvia said and left the room.

After locating a handful of books she thought Dougal might like, she sent Millie upstairs to deliver them. She was glad for the little bit of conversation she'd had with him, and felt like such little snippets of time in his presence would help convince her more and more that he was not Daniel. Still, she'd had enough of being in the same room with him for now and was only too glad to have Millie deliver the books.

The remainder of the day progressed as most days did. Dougal informed Millie that the pain had worsened, so after lunch he accepted some tea with a few drops of Sylvia's tincture added so that he could take a nap. Sylvia and Millie worked together to make a cake since Millie's intention to do so the previous day had been lost in their adjustment to having Dougal Hewitt to care for. While the women worked in the kitchen, George sat in the parlor to read from the newspaper he'd picked up in the village the day before Dougal had appeared in their lives. Millie and George went into town once a week to purchase whatever they needed, and he always bought a newspaper from London. The news was always a week or two old, but reading it was one of George's favorite pastimes. He always read for a while after lunch before he went back to work doing whatever needed to be done.

A loud knock at the front door startled Sylvia, and she heard Millie gasp. "Who on earth at this time of day?" Millie asked in a voice that made it difficult to tell if she was afraid for some reason, or simply taken off guard by such an unusual occurrence.

Sylvia's customers always came after dark, and beyond them they'd not had a single visitor in months. Their last visitor had been the wife of one of their tenant farmers asking if George could come and help her husband with a needed repair on the farmhouse. George always went to the farms to collect the rent, and he also checked in on them every couple of weeks to make certain all was well, therefore it was rare for their renters to have a need to come visit—especially since it was likely they too believed the rumors about Sylvia being a witch.

Sylvia didn't want to answer the door, but she was mostly watching Millie work on the cake, and she knew George was relaxing with his newspaper, so she went to the door, pulled it open, and immediately found herself in the position of exerting every bit of strength she possessed to not appear astonished or alarmed, and to maintain a countenance of courage and confidence. The two men standing in front of her looked more fierce and menacing than any human being she'd ever encountered. She guessed them to be not much older than herself, and their ruddy features looked nothing alike, yet the way they were dressed like laborers, and their obvious lack of hygiene, made it difficult to distinguish one from the other.

"May I help you?" she asked as nonchalantly as she could manage, proud of herself for sounding so unaffected by their frightening appearance.

"Good mornin', ma'am," one of them said, tipping his hat as if he were a gentleman, and his smile widened, giving Sylvia a better view of his terribly crooked teeth. "We're lookin' for a man we have some business with—a friend of ours—and we last saw him not many miles from here, and since there isn't much out this way, we're just checkin' all the houses t' see if he might o' been found. He was hurt, ye see, and we got separated, and we was worried about his state o' bein'."

"I see," Sylvia said, remaining expressionless. She absolutely knew that the man they were looking for was Dougal Heywood, and he was certainly not their *friend*. In fact, she was almost certain these were the men that Dougal had said might be trying to kill him. She didn't know *why* they had shot him, or what their disagreement with him might be. She'd wondered if the circumstances might have something to do with Daniel, but in truth he'd been gone for years, and in that moment, she had to consider the possibility that Dougal had brought this trouble upon himself, somehow. Sylvia knew absolutely nothing about the situation—except that she truly believed Dougal was a kind and decent man, and these two heathens standing at her door appeared to be anything but.

Sylvia was vaguely aware of Millie and George now standing at her sides and just a little behind her; whether they'd come out of curiosity or to offer support and protection, she was glad to have them there. It only took Sylvia a moment or two for words to form in her head that then flowed unheeded out of her mouth without any thought of the repercussions. "I'm afraid I can't help you. There's no one here except the three of us and my husband, and he's not feeling well, so he's bound to his bed at the moment." Sylvia could almost feel the silent astonishment of Millie and George; she only hoped they weren't allowing it to show on their faces.

"This husband o' yer's . . ." the other man said, sounding suspicious, ". . . I think we'd very much like t' meet him."

"As I told you, he's ill and in bed," Sylvia declared more firmly. "I don't know what he could tell you that I haven't already told you. We haven't seen anyone around here at all."

"No, we haven't," Sylvia heard Millie say.

"Not a soul," George added.

"Word around town," this despicable man continued, "is that this husband died in the war, so that makes me wonder if ye're tellin' the truth."

"I'm wonderin' the same," the other man said. "No offense, ma'am."

"Well, I *am* offended!" Sylvia insisted as if she didn't feel the slightest intimidation from these men. "If you're going to pay heed to gossip in the village, you should make certain you get all of the correct information. I am socially ostracized from this community and there's not a soul who will even speak to me because of what they believe."

"And what's that?" one of them asked.

"That I'm a witch," Sylvia said, leaning forward slightly and almost hissing that last word, finding delight in the way it made these men each take a step back as if they feared she might immediately cast an evil spell on them. "My servants here," she casually motioned to Millie and George, "go into town as minimally as possible to purchase supplies, but due to their association with me, they do not engage in conversation with anyone they encounter there. No one in the community has cared a wit about us for years, so why would anyone know that my husband's reported death was a mistake and he returned home—much to our surprise—months ago. But the war was hard on him, not to mention the journey to get here, and he's never been the same. My husband's health has nothing to do with your missing friend, and I will not have you disturbing his rest for any reason."

Much to Sylvia's pleasure, these two men looked disarmed and put in their place as they took another step back. "Sorry t' have bothered ye, ma'am," one of them said.

Sylvia softened her tone and stated with some kindness that she hoped would win their favor and help keep them away, "I do hope you find your friend, and I hope he's all right."

"Thank you, ma'am," the other one said. They exchanged polite nods and Sylvia closed the door, leaning back against it as her fear of these men suddenly burst past her efforts to hold it back. In the same moment everything she'd said came rushing back to her and she muttered quietly—as if the villains who had just visited them might be able to overhear, "What have I done?"

"You have saved the life of that poor, dear man upstairs," Millie said with complete confidence, as if she would defend Sylvia's lies in a court of law.

"I was real proud of the way you stood up to them," George added.

Sylvia appreciated their support, but had to point out the obvious problems. "But . . . I just told them my husband is here . . . and alive . . . and . . ." she put a hand over her suddenly pounding heart, ". . . if they go back to the village and utter even a word of that to anyone, people will believe it to be true, and . . . and . . . then what?"

"I don't think those two blackguards are gonna be gossiping in town," Millie said. "I can't see how this changes anything . . . except that it got those despicable creatures to leave."

"I wonder why they would be so keen on finding our Dougal," George said.

Sylvia was a little taken aback by the reference to *our* Dougal. It was as if they'd not only taken him in, they had accepted him as a part of the family.

"And I'd wager," George added, "that it was them who shot our friend."

"I wonder why on earth they'd be wanting to harm Dougal," Millie said. "He did say it was a misunderstanding and I believe him. I can't think of any reason why someone like Dougal would have anything at all to do with men like that."

"And yet we don't really know anything at all," Sylvia pointed out. "We've taken what Dougal has told us as the truth, but how do we know for certain? If he—"

"Begging your pardon, Missus," Millie interrupted, "but that sounds a little bit like you're judging Dougal according to the things your Daniel did. Dougal won't be going anywhere for a long while yet, and we will have plenty of opportunity to talk to him about all of this, but I say he deserves to be trusted until he proves otherwise."

"Does he?" Sylvia asked cynically even though she knew that doing so only helped prove Millie's point.

"I agree with Millie," George said and then none of them said anything for a minute or more as they all mentally sorted out all that had just happened and their opinions on the matter.

"Well," Sylvia said with a heavy sigh, "whatever it is that actually happened . . . and whatever the truth may be . . . I need to tell Dougal what just occurred . . . and perhaps it's time he told *me* about this misunderstanding that put his life in jeopardy. It will hardly do him any good to heal from his current state only to go back out there and be in danger again. I'd prefer that my efforts to get him healthy didn't result in having him end up dead."

"Reasonable enough," Millie said with a little smile that Sylvia found mostly annoying in her present mood.

Sylvia headed toward the stairs and George said, "I don't think you should try to talk to him now."

"Why not?" Sylvia demanded.

"Because," Millie explained, "as you should recall we gave him some of that tincture after lunch and he's sound asleep."

"Ah," Sylvia said, "so we did." She sighed. "Then I'll speak to him later." Turning her mind back to what had been happening before their menacing visitors had arrived, she added, "I suppose we should finish that cake."

"Yes, we should," Millie said and led the way to the kitchen while George returned to his newspaper.

Chapter Four

Acting Lessons

Through the remainder of the day, while everything going on around Sylvia felt normal, nothing inside of her mind was normal at all. She enjoyed a delicious supper with Millie and George after George had taken a tray up to Dougal and returned to report that he was doing fine. After supper was over, Millie suggested that they all enjoy a piece of cake together in Dougal's room, with the explanation that, "He must be terribly bored and lonely up there."

"Yes, he must be," Sylvia replied, trying very hard to sound like she meant it. She *did* agree with the statement, but she was more preoccupied with her need to tell Dougal that she had declared to strangers that he was her husband, and it was impossible to predict if her lie might turn into a rumor which might very well create some difficulties that she didn't even want to think about.

Dougal's obvious pleasure over the cake and especially the company made Sylvia feel a little guilty for being so preoccupied with her own concerns. She didn't at all begrudge having taken this man in and helping him, despite the strange circumstances of why he'd ended up *here*. But there was something going on that she didn't understand, and she had unwittingly put herself into the middle of Dougal's problems by impulsively lying in order to try and explain Dougal's presence in the house and to draw attention away from him having been the man who had been shot—presumably by one of the men she'd lied to.

Sylvia mostly listened to the conversation taking place while they enjoyed their cake, and nothing at all was said about their visitors. Setting her empty cake plate aside, Sylvia's anxiety in her need began to rise. She needed to just tell him and get it over with. And she certainly wanted to know exactly *why* these men were apparently trying to kill him. She'd told a terrible lie in order to protect him; she thought it was only fair that she know exactly what kind of mess she had stepped into.

"Dougal," she said when there was a lull in the conversation, "there's something I need to tell you, and . . . I need some information from you in return."

"Very well," he said, setting aside his own plate even though he'd not finished eating his piece of cake. "What is it?"

"We had some very strange visitors this afternoon," Sylvia went on, then told him what they'd looked like and their claim to be searching for *a friend*. The way Dougal's expression filled with terror let Sylvia know that these were indeed the men who had shot him.

"What did you tell them?" Dougal asked fearfully. "You've all been so kind, and the last thing I would ever want is to bring trouble upon your house for any reason and—"

"But I'm guessing," George said, "that you also don't want to be found by these blackguards."

"No, I do not," Dougal said, "but I'm doing better, and if you think I should leave now, I will. I can leave tonight . . . and travel in the darkness as I was doing before, and . . ."

"You can't leave," Sylvia insisted. "For one thing, I would never let you leave in such a condition. You are far from adequately healed. Without more days of careful attention to your wounds, they would surely become infected, and . . . I just won't have it. Besides, I . . . well . . ."

George stopped her from stammering when he said, "She lied to them . . . to protect you." Dougal turned from George to look at Sylvia with astonished eyes until George continued his explanation and Dougal looked his way. "She told them there was no one else here except her husband who had returned from the war months ago. That he'd been believed dead but it had been a mistake and he'd come home, and no one in town knew about it because they never talk to any of us." George shrugged. "That part's true."

Dougal stared at George a long moment as if taking in what he'd been told, then he turned to Sylvia. "And what does that mean for you? I don't wish to cause you trouble. I—"

"I don't know what it means," Sylvia said. "If these men go on their way and don't go back into the village, then it will mean nothing. If they go back to the village and tell someone what I said, then the entire village will believe it before supper tomorrow."

"And then I suppose you'll be needing a husband to keep up appearances," Millie said with a little laugh, but Sylvia didn't think it was funny, and Dougal obviously didn't either.

"Or your husband could just . . . leave again," Dougal said. "After a few people who knew him see him from a distance . . . enough to believe that what you said was true . . . he could just, well . . . leave you and mysteriously never return."

Sylvia felt unexpectedly angry over the comment and snapped back, "Because Daniel Hewitt was simply known to be the kind of man who would impulsively go chasing after some wild, dangerous scheme and leave his wife behind."

The room became eerily quiet as the truth of what Sylvia had just impulsively declared in anger seemed to fall from the ceiling like snow, dusting each of them with the chilling reminder that for all the love she'd felt for Daniel Hewitt, she'd never been able to trust him.

Dougal didn't look as astonished as she might have expected, and he verified the reasons for this when he said somberly, "Yes, because that's the kind of man he was known to be."

"You guessed that from your conversations with him?" Sylvia asked, trying to sound less agitated.

"I didn't have to guess, Sylvia," he said. It was the first time he'd spoken her given name, but he spoke it with a compassion that helped her feel calmer. "He talked to me freely about his schemes to cheat people out of their money, about his careful thievery, about his tendency to leave his wife on her own for extended periods of time while he traveled about to do what he did best. He told me often that he purposely went far from home to engage in his wicked deeds, which kept trouble and danger away from home. He always made certain no one he stole from would ever know where to find him." Dougal sighed. "But now *I* have brought trouble and danger to your home, and I cannot begin to express my regret. You've been so kind and . . . I would never want to bring any difficulty your way, and yet it seems I have."

Sylvia recognized that his regret was sincere, but she had to say, "Tell me what you know of these men, Dougal. Tell me what happened. We cannot solve this problem if we don't understand what it is they want."

"I know nothing!" Dougal said.

"You told me someone might be trying to kill you," Sylvia said. "You have the bullet wound to prove it. You said you were traveling on foot at night in order to not be found. Do I understand all of that correctly?"

"Yes," Dougal said. "All I can tell you otherwise is that I was sitting in a pub and . . . well, this was only a few days into my journey from home . . . when I still had money enough to pay for passage on a coach and at least one good meal a day. It was late in the evening, so the pub was dim. I was eating a quick meal while the drivers of the coach were changing the horses, and I saw two men eying me suspiciously, so much so that I lost my appetite and felt quite afraid. I attempted to ignore them and finish my meal anyway, knowing I'd paid good money for the food, and it would be a great many hours before I would have the opportunity to eat again, and then I slipped out carefully and into the waiting coach. I'd believed to have escaped them, but days later I believe I saw them again. And it was some days after that I used the last of my money to purchase as much bread and cheese as it would buy, and I set out to finish my journey on foot. A few nights later when I was sitting next to a fire I built for warmth before getting some rest, a bullet came from out of nowhere and hit my leg.

"I dropped to the ground and threw some water on the fire before I grabbed my knapsack which held my food and crawled deeper into the woods where I stayed hidden . . . and that was when I started traveling only at night. My shoes were not so good to begin with and quickly gave out on me. I rationed my food as best as I could, but I wandered about a great deal instead of coming here directly since I could only use the sun and the stars to calculate my direction until I came to certain landmarks Daniel had told me about. My food ran out a couple of days before I got here, and . . . well . . . you know the condition my feet were in . . . and the bullet wound was . . ."

He stopped and hung his head, and once again a chilled silence descended over the room. Hearing Dougal's story in detail left Sylvia filled with heartache on his behalf. But she now didn't feel as certain that this had anything to do with Daniel, or Dougal's resemblance to him.

She was surprised when he lifted his head and cleared his throat and added, "From your description of the men who came to your door earlier, it could be the same men. But they don't necessarily believe I'm here, do they?" he asked, sounding mildly afraid. "Didn't they say they were asking at many homes? I can't believe they could have followed me here. I was really trying to be careful and remain unseen. You would think if they'd found me during my travels, they would have finished off the job and killed me."

"I was thinking the same thing," George said. "And even *if* these men are suspicious about not being able to actually see the man of the house here and be assured it wasn't their *friend,* our missus led them to believe her husband had been home for months—a story that's not hard to defend given the isolated way we live, and how no one in these parts cares a lick about what goes on out here."

"That's all true," Millie added, "however, if they are the least bit suspicious . . . if they want to get a look at Mrs. Hewitt's husband before they move on . . . they'll not be moving on until they do. And if they get a good look at him, they'll see that he's the man they were following, and indeed the man they tried to kill. Assuming it's the same men, and if you ask me, I'd say it's highly likely. There's far too much coincidence for any other option to be very possible, I'd say."

"I agree," Sylvia said. "So, we have two problems: one is to convince these men that you are not the man they are looking for, and the other is to potentially convince anyone else around here that you are my husband."

"It's just come to me," Millie said, "that if you first saw these men earlier in your travels, is it not more likely that their interest would be in *you* as opposed to Mr. Hewitt?"

Dougal looked astonished and then deeply thoughtful and troubled. He only said, "That may very well be."

Sylvia said nothing about how this had already occurred to her. Strangely enough she found the idea intriguing, but it also seemed like a question that could not be answered with the limited information they had. She felt more concerned with the problem directly before them.

"What of the scar on his face?" George asked. "The resemblance between Dougal here and your husband—may he rest in peace—is a bizarre coincidence at best, but no two men could have such a distinctive scar exactly the same."

"That's an excellent point," Sylvia said, "but it's impossible to know what these men believe about the scar because we have no knowledge of their motives. I believe we should be more concerned about the possibility that someone from the village will likely come face-to-face with Dougal, believing he is Daniel Hewitt, and we need to be prepared for that possibility. If it doesn't happen, we may have wasted our time, but I don't think we can take that risk and remain unprepared—especially when Dougal's life is in danger."

"I don't understand, Missus," Millie said.

"Well," Sylvia motioned toward Dougal, "he certainly looks like Daniel Hewitt—the man everyone in the village knew before he left to fight in the war—but he doesn't sound at all like him. The accent would give him away in an instant. And . . ." She looked at Dougal and spoke to him as opposed to just talking about him in his presence. "Your . . . mannerisms and such, it's all wrong."

"So . . ." Dougal drawled thoughtfully, "you're saying I need to . . . learn how to speak like Daniel . . . and . . ."

"*Be* Daniel," she said.

"Like an actor," Dougal said with enlightenment. "Like an actor in a play. I saw one of Shakespeare's plays many years ago. It was something I'll never forget. And those people surely learned to speak and behave in a way that would allow them to play their parts." He looked firmly at Sylvia, and she forced back the sensation of being unnerved by his resemblance to Daniel, especially given the fact that they were discussing a plan to make him behave and sound like Daniel. "I just need you to teach me how to talk like Daniel . . . to sound more like people around here, who live in the south, as opposed to where I come from in the north."

"Yes," Sylvia said, "and . . . a few other things, as well."

Sylvia stood, unable to bear any more of this conversation right now—and the implications of it. "We will do the best we can. Perhaps with time we'll come up with more ideas." She glanced at Dougal. "No one can see you until you're healed . . . which means we must continue with the ruse that you're ill. And before you're up and about, you'll be needing to sound exactly like Daniel."

With that point summarized, Sylvia hurried to her own room, feeling her way along the wall through the darkness. Once behind the safety of her own door, she leaned back against it then slid down to sit on the floor, suddenly overcome with a strange weakness. What had she gotten herself into? Not only had she told the biggest lie in her life, but she had also committed herself to spending a great deal of time with Dougal so that she could teach him to speak and act like Daniel. Sylvia wasn't even certain she knew how to do either. She could listen to Dougal and watch him, clearly hearing and seeing the differences between him and Daniel, but that didn't mean she had the ability to guide him through this transformation. She was already struggling to contend with his appearance, and now their goal was to turn him into Daniel as much as it was possible. And this surely meant that he might be staying here longer than she had hoped.

"Oh," she muttered and pressed her hands over her face, "what have I done?"

Sylvia slept little and fretted and stewed a great deal over the situation with Dougal. It was so utterly bizarre she could hardly believe it was real. Even though she managed to drift in and out of sleep enough to get *some* rest, she was wide awake before the sun came up, and already in the kitchen making scones before Millie appeared to begin her day's work.

"What on earth are you doing, Missus?" Millie asked. "I thought you'd be out gathering the eggs and—"

"Already done," Sylvia said while she mixed the scone dough with her hands to the perfect consistency.

"Then what are you—"

"I'm making scones," Sylvia stated. "It's always nice to have fresh scones." Before Millie could point out that this was not the question she'd wanted answered, Sylvia added, "I couldn't sleep. It wasn't doing me or anyone else any good to just remain in my bed and worry."

"Worried about . . ." Millie left the sentence unfinished while she put on her apron.

Sylvia had no reason to not be completely honest with Millie. "It's been difficult for me to interact with a man who looks so much like Daniel, so the very idea of spending a great deal of time with him in order to help him sound and act like Daniel is not appealing to me in the slightest. And perhaps it won't even matter; perhaps no one will ever even speak to him before he leaves. Perhaps we're worried over nothing."

"I'm inclined to believe that it's more likely something will come of it," Millie said. "I think the decision to do this is wise. It's better to be prepared than end up in trouble."

"And yet I fear we could already be in a great deal of trouble that can't be fixed no matter *what* we do. I'm not saying it's Dougal's fault, but we don't have much information about the situation to help us, now do we." She slammed down the large wad of scone dough with a hefty thud before she began rolling it out with excessive vigor.

Sylvia stopped taking out her frustrations on the dough when she felt Millie's gentle hand on her shoulder. "Everything will be all right," Millie said. "We'll take this on one day at a time, and if you ask me, the more time you spend with Dougal, the more you will be able to separate him in your mind from Daniel. They're not the same man, and we all know it. Just . . . be patient with yourself, and with him. It's not his fault that he was born to look so much like Daniel, nor that they both fell into the same regiment. It's a strange story, mind you, but we're all in this together."

"Thank you, Millie," Sylvia said and took a moment to turn around and hug her, being careful not to touch her back with flour-covered hands. "I don't know what I would ever do without you."

"You never need to wonder about that," Millie said, squeezing Sylvia tightly before they both focused on preparing breakfast, and nothing more was said about the despicable strangers that had shown up at the door the previous day, or the way Sylvia dreaded the time she would need to spend with Dougal. For all she knew, he wouldn't even be able to change his voice enough to sound like Daniel. It could all be a waste of time and effort, and it might do nothing more than increase her stress and frustration.

As usual George took a breakfast tray up to Dougal and returned to report that all was well before he sat with Sylvia and Millie to enjoy their own breakfast. After their meal was finished and the kitchen put in order, the three of them went upstairs to work together to treat and bandage Dougal's wounds. Sylvia found his feet looking much better and declared, "I think it's time we kept the bandaging off during the day. Being exposed to the air will aid their healing best at this point. We'll use the salve and bandage them at night, but we'll keep your feet bare during the day. If your feet get cold, we'll stoke up the fire."

"I trust your judgment," Dougal said to her.

"Very wise," George added.

"From what George is telling me about the wound on your thigh," Sylvia continued, "I'd say it's improved a great deal, but I still think we should keep it covered for now since we're still trying to get rid of the infection." Dougal nodded and Sylvia added, "Has the pain improved? That can be a great indicator of your progress."

"Oh, it *has* improved!" Dougal said with enthusiasm. "In fact, I'd very much like to get out of this bed and walk around a little more."

"Your ambition is admirable," Sylvia said, "but I think it's wise to stay off of your feet as much as possible for at least a few more days so those sores don't start to bleed again, and I dare say if you start walking too much too soon you will *definitely* begin to feel more pain."

"Very well," he said with a smile that made her heart quicken while her mind scolded her for it. "You have convinced me, Missus." She scowled at him, and he added. "George and Millie call you that. I just thought that . . ."

Sylvia replied firmly, "George and Millie work for me, even though I'm deeply grateful that we've developed comfortable friendships. I'm not necessarily happy that they choose not to call me by my given name, and I truly prefer that you simply call me Sylvia. Let's not have to repeat such a trivial conversation ever again."

Dougal nodded and smiled again, as if he found the whole of this conversation amusing. Sylvia did her best to ignore him—and the effect he had on her—to finish up the routine of making certain his wounds were cared for, glad to know that George would help him with anything else he needed.

After George and Millie left the room and Sylvia was following them out, Dougal stopped her by asking, "When will we begin my lessons to become Daniel Hewitt?"

In that moment as their eyes met, Sylvia both wanted to spend every possible minute with him and also to avoid him completely. She knew that these lessons he referred to would not be taking place all day every day, which would allow for a balance in accommodating her confusion and a general desire to avoid him. While she couldn't think of any practical reason not to begin today, she also felt that she needed just a little more time to prepare.

"Tomorrow morning after I've helped Millie put the kitchen in order after breakfast. I need to take care of a few other things—including seeing to your ailments—and then we'll begin."

"I'm looking forward to it," he said with a smile that not only quickened her heart but also left her with a warm sensation. She had to acknowledge that his smiles were always genuine. In fact, everything about him seemed genuine—which was a far cry different from what she'd experienced with Daniel. When it came to her husband, she'd never doubted his sincerity when he'd professed his love for her, but in retrospect she wondered if she'd ever truly been able to trust him regarding anything else he'd said. Over the years, the evidence had mounted against him, and eventually she'd been left alone with the cold, hard reality that her husband had been a liar and a cheat, probably in ways she couldn't even imagine.

The day unfolded without event while Sylvia mentally attempted to prepare herself to spend a great deal more time with Dougal tomorrow. Again, she had difficulty sleeping as her mind engaged in a battle between the dead Daniel Hewitt and the very-much-alive Dougal Heywood. After a good, long while of analyzing the situation and the present state of her feelings, Sylvia could acknowledge that she'd adjusted a great deal in not seeing Dougal as her late husband, but seeing him more for himself. His dramatically different accent and mannerisms had helped with that a great deal. The conundrum for her was the way her heart often quickened when she was conversing with him, and her stomach frequently fluttered even at the sight of him. At first, she knew such sensations were due to her mind not being able to discern a distinction between Dougal and the man she had loved for many years, and had very much missed since his death—even if she didn't miss the manner in which he'd lived his life. But she had come to see Dougal more clearly now as himself.

And now she had to wonder if her reactions toward Dougal were simply about him, and had nothing to do with Daniel. Sylvia had been lonely for a very long time. Daniel had been dead for a couple of years, and away at war for a long time before that. But even before the war, he had frequently left her on her own for weeks—sometimes months—at a time while he traveled to engage in his deplorable escapades. And now there was a very kind and engaging man staying in her house, and she was beginning to enjoy his company.

Sylvia finally managed to force all thoughts of Dougal—*and* Daniel—out of her head and fell asleep, glad to wake up to a sunny day and realize she had gotten some good hours of rest. The morning routine went forth as usual, with Sylvia helping Millie in the kitchen after breakfast while George helped Dougal get cleaned up and into a fresh nightshirt. Afterward they cared for his wounds as usual, then George and Millie went off to see to their work while Sylvia sat down in a chair that gave her a perfect view out the window to the seemingly endless meadows stretching away from the house, and she had an equally good view of Dougal where he was sitting up in his bed. She took a long moment to just look at him and assess the feelings that had been swirling around inside of her, and she was glad to note that she saw Dougal before her, and it was indeed becoming steadily easier to not think of Daniel when she looked at him.

Sylvia noticed his scar and realized that she'd already come to overlook it and be able to see beyond it. But now that they were here and ready to delve into their lessons of voice and mannerisms, she impulsively decided to try and ease her curiosity before they began.

"May I ask," she spoke in a tentative voice, "about the scar on your face? If you don't want to tell me about it, that's fine. I've just . . . wondered." She recalled that he had been vague in discussing it before. "Did you have it before the war or is it a result of—"

"There is no problem with your asking," he said comfortably. "You may ask me anything you like. I've no secrets to keep from you, Sylvia. And no, I did not have the scar before the war, however it was not a result of anything that happened on a battlefield. It happened on a night we were off duty. A group of us went to a tavern just to have a few drinks and relax, some enemy soldiers came to the same tavern. If we'd wanted some liquor, we should have purchased it discreetly and enjoyed it in our own tents rather than putting ourselves in such a public place. We weren't wearing our uniforms, of course, but I guess it was the way we talked and such that made it evident who we were. We were trying to just leave but a few of those men seemed determined to fight it out—as if we could resolve the war then and there by who survived a brawl in a tavern. One of them went after a friend of mine, and I got in the middle of it. Then, he took out a knife, and I would say that using a knife in a fistfight just isn't any form of fairness."

"I'd think not!" Sylvia agreed, not liking this story at all—except that she was very glad Dougal was willing to tell her.

"I don't remember exactly what happened except that I felt the pain on my face, and I didn't have any more fight left in me. I know it might have been much worse, and I'm grateful it wasn't."

Sylvia nodded and said, "I think that when people get to know you, they will stop seeing the scar. I hardly notice it anymore. It is surely no indication of your character."

"Thank you for saying that. I do hope that's the case. I suppose time will tell whether that's true."

They exchanged a smile and a strange silence stretched between them before Sylvia cleared her throat and looked out the window in order to break their gaze. Looking back at him she said, "Shall we begin our lessons?" She laughed softly. "Although I don't know exactly *how* to begin. The only idea that's occurred to me is for you to try and imitate the way that *I* talk, simply because I speak with an accent that's typical, and then perhaps I will be able to hear in your voice whether or not it sounds like Daniel, and help correct you."

"That makes sense," he said.

"And rather than trying to just think of things to say," she added, "I was thinking that you could read aloud to me." She nodded toward the books on his bedside table.

"Oh, that is a very good idea!" he said. "I confess I've been a little nervous wondering what I might come up with to say when I'm not known for being chatty."

"So . . ." Sylvia motioned with her hand toward the books, "pick one and let's get started. We won't know how well this will work until we try it."

Dougal nodded and picked up a book which he opened to the first page, then cleared his throat and began to read with great hesitancy. It only took one sentence for both of them to recognize that he only sounded like himself.

"Do this," Sylvia said. "Read a sentence, then I will say the sentence and you can try and repeat the way I say it. Then we will move on to another sentence so we don't get too bored. And you mustn't be hard on yourself. I suspect it will be difficult at first, but once you've had some practice, I think it will settle in and you'll be able to do it without hardly thinking about it."

"I appreciate your confidence," he chuckled, "but I'm not certain I share it."

"Just . . . read that sentence again," she said, and he did, then Sylvia repeated it, and he repeated it again with an attempt to say it as she had. They both laughed at his effort, but she just told him to read the next sentence and they continued. After a few pages, Sylvia could already hear Dougal sounding more like Daniel, which brought up that strange sensation she'd had before that forced her to keep the division between the two men very clear in her mind.

Dougal let out a surprised laugh when he heard the improvement in his own voice, and Sylvia laughed with him. "You see," she said, "with some time and practice you will be able to do this."

"I think I now actually believe it might be possible, but . . ."

"Is something wrong?" she asked when he hesitated.

"It's just . . . strange . . . trying to . . . make myself into Daniel, so to speak. And it must be strange for *you*. All of this must be strange for you."

"I confess that it is," Sylvia admitted honestly. "Although I'm becoming more accustomed to your resemblance to Daniel, and I'm certain I'll become accustomed to your speaking like him." Not wanting to focus too much on the emotional facets of the situation, she motioned with her hand, saying, "Now, let's continue."

They went on with their lesson for more than an hour when they both agreed that an hour at a time was likely sufficient, and they would do another hour in the afternoon, and perhaps another in the evening.

"I'll keep practicing," Dougal said. "I can read aloud even when I'm alone and continue working at it."

"Excellent," she said. "With any luck this won't even be necessary, but better to be prepared."

"I agree in every way," he said, and Sylvia made certain he had everything he needed before she left the room.

Over the next few days, Sylvia's routine was adjusted to include spending some time with Dougal each morning, afternoon, and evening. There were times when she doubted he would ever be able to truly sound like Daniel. He was trying very hard, and his efforts were bringing him closer to the correct accent, but it wasn't quite right, and she found it difficult to explain to him exactly what the problem might be. Despite their lessons being challenging, Sylvia found herself looking forward to the time she spent with Dougal each day. Intermixed with reading sentences back and forth, they chatted comfortably, and she came to learn a little more each day about the village where he'd grown up and his experiences there. She shared with him the situation of her own upbringing, with her father being a farmer, and how her family of seven had shared a rather small house. And yet their needs had always been met and her parents had been kind, good people.

"Because I was the youngest of my siblings," she continued her story on a drizzly afternoon, "I was the only one left living at home when my parents passed."

"Oh, I'm so sorry," he said with sincerity.

"Thank you, but . . . it's been years now. I miss them now and then, but I've adjusted. Because I moved here when I married Daniel, I most often think of them and just feel as if they are still in the home where I grew up, happy together and doing well. Even though I know that's not true, I do believe they're in a better place—still happy together and doing well."

"I'd like to think that's the case," Dougal said, talking more like Daniel than himself. He'd decided the previous day that he was going to begin speaking that way all the time in order to keep practicing, and also on the chance that he might actually need to convince someone he was Daniel, as they all feared he might.

"I hope so," Sylvia said.

"How did they die, if you don't mind my asking?"

"My father went very suddenly," Sylvia said. "He just . . . collapsed in the kitchen, and he was gone. The doctor said it was probably his heart, that it just gave out. My mother passed less than a month later. She simply went to sleep one night as usual, and in the morning I found her dead. She'd grieved so deeply for the loss of my father that I convinced myself she'd died of a broken heart."

"Maybe she did," Dougal said. "It's nice to think that two people would love each other so much that after sharing decades of life together, they would simply not be able to live without the other by their side."

There had been a time when Sylvia had wanted to believe the same was true for her and Daniel. The love they shared in and of itself had never been a problem between them, but other challenges had only left her confused over such things. She forced her thoughts away from Daniel and focused on the present.

"That's my thought exactly," Sylvia said and found herself sharing a rather intense gaze with Dougal. The quickening of her heart startled her, and she looked away. "That's all there is to know about me, really," Sylvia said. "I'd met Daniel not long before my parents' passing. He had been staying with a friend in the village and we met when I went to purchase some things we needed at home. Daniel and I walked right into each other on the street. We were both distracted while we were walking and literally bumped into each other." She laughed softly at the memory. "If he'd not taken hold of my arms, I would have fallen right over. We started talking and before I knew it, I had invited him to our home for Sunday dinner. My parents fell in love with him almost as quickly as I did, and we had already discussed the possibility of marriage before my father passed. Daniel was so kind and supportive during that time, coming by every day to make certain my mother and I had all we needed. He stayed with his friend longer than he'd intended so that he could be there for us." Sylvia sighed. "That was the best of him. He could be so tender and caring. And I don't know what I would have done without him. He officially proposed soon after my father's funeral, since he'd asked my father for my hand only a day or two before his passing. Our plan was that he would move into our home after we were married and help take care of me and my mother, although he did talk about the house he owned and the possibility of our moving there. 'But we have plenty of time to make such decisions,' he would often say. And then my mother passed, and . . . well, with her gone I felt so out of place there. The house I'd grown up in no longer felt like home, and since Daniel's home was elsewhere, we were married just a few days after my mother's funeral and then we came here. That's all there is to tell, really."

"I'm glad to know your history," Dougal said with keen interest, "however I know that's not all there is to tell."

"What do you mean?" she asked, genuinely confused.

"You haven't told me how you came to be a witch," he said with a little smile that reminded her of Daniel—which made her stomach flutter. But she looked away long enough to break their gaze and laughed softly.

"I did not become a witch, Dougal," she clarified. "I came to be *known* as a witch due to a great deal of nasty gossip and ill intentions by certain people in the community."

"Yes, I know," he said with a little chuckle that indicated he'd been teasing her—which also reminded her of Daniel. "But I am curious about how all of that came to be."

"It's not complicated," she said. "My mother taught me how to grow herbs and gather certain plants with healing qualities, and then how to make them into healing remedies and use them properly. She'd learned all of this from my grandmother, who had learned it from *her* mother. I believe the knowledge goes back many generations. The general belief is that God gave us all of the plants and herbs we have here on the earth, and He created them with the purpose of helping His children. I was blessed to be able to learn such skills from my mother and grandmother. But I never expected to be ostracized in such a way because of what I do. Such a thing never happened to any of the women who came before me." As always when the topic came up, Sylvia couldn't help but think about the traumatic experience that had truly been the initial source of the harsh disagreement between her and the doctor, but she doubted she would ever be able to speak of it again for as long as she lived, and she hurried to push thoughts of it away.

Dougal went on to say, "From what I've heard, it's mostly due to the jealousy and arrogance of the local doctor who is obviously influencing other people who look up to him and can't recognize his true nature."

"Jealousy?" she echoed. "Truly?"

"Well, of course," Dougal said. "I'd guess he's actually concerned that you might steal away his business, and since he doesn't understand what you do, he's probably intimidated by it. But of course a man like that could never admit such a thing. In fact, we men are often prone to choose arrogance over admitting we might be intimidated."

Sylvia let out a small laugh. "Are you putting yourself into the category of such men who would deem me a witch rather than just accept that what I do is a good thing?"

"I do not agree with such men in the slightest," he said. "I'm only saying that I've been able to see in myself—and in most men I know—varying degrees of a tendency to react badly when feeling vulnerable. I think the horrible reality of war helped bring this home to me, and I've tried to do better since then. I could look back and see that my father had very much been that way, and I made a decision to try and do better."

"That's very admirable," Sylvia said and meant it.

"Oh," Dougal chuckled, "I didn't say I was good at it; just trying."

"Simply being aware of such a thing is good, I believe," she said. "Perhaps if my Daniel had been more aware of such things, we might not have . . ."

"Have what?" he asked when she stopped.

"It's not important," she insisted. "He's gone and there's no need for me to be wishing things had been different, or . . . to be making comparisons that simply don't matter anymore."

"Very well," he said. "Just know that if you ever need to talk about Daniel, I don't mind at all listening to your thoughts. In fact, I feel rather honored to have you share your thoughts with me."

"Honored?" she repeated and almost laughed over what felt so absurd until she realized his expression was entirely serious, perhaps even severe. She simply added, "Thank you. That's very kind. And the same is true for you. I'm happy to talk about anything you might feel the need to talk about." Dougal nodded, and she shifted the subject by saying, "You're doing remarkably well with your speech. I think we might be able to get away with this . . . if the need arises. With any luck, it won't. Perhaps tomorrow we can work on your mannerisms . . . even though I'm not quite certain how to go about that."

"I did know Daniel, if you'll recall. I think I might be able to mimic some of his mannerisms. I've been working on trying to remember. I believe we'll be able to figure it out," Dougal said, sounding so much like Daniel that it felt eerie.

"I believe we will," she said, encouraged by the fact that they'd been able to transform his speech, and also the fact that he'd known Daniel well. Surely they could work together to smooth over any other issues. She considered the fact that no one in the area had seen Daniel for years, therefore any tiny differences might not be noticed at all. Still, they had to do the best they could in order to keep them all safe.

Sylvia reluctantly left the room, wondering why she'd come to thoroughly enjoy every minute she spent with Dougal. And she could sincerely say that it had nothing to do with his resemblance to Daniel. She liked him very much and enjoyed his company. It was as simple as that. But his being here was only temporary, and she had to remember that becoming too attached to this man would only bring her heartache, and she'd had far too much of that already in her life. She didn't need to put herself into a situation that would only cause her more grief.

Chapter Five

Sharing Secrets

The following morning in the middle of breakfast, a loud knock at the front door startled Sylvia so much that she actually gasped. But George and Millie both gasped as well, which made her feel less foolish.

"Who on earth could that be?" Millie asked, sliding her chair back.

"What a question to ask," George said. "We won't know until we open the door."

"Fine," Millie said, "I'll open the door, but if it's those frightening men again, I'll be expecting the both of you to be right there with me."

"Of course," Sylvia said.

"I won't let no one hurt either of you ladies," George said with sincere gallantry.

Sylvia listened carefully as Millie went to the door and opened it. Their curiosity was immediately satisfied when they heard her say with astonishment, "Vicar?"

Sylvia understood the astonishment. The man had not once come here since only days after she had arrived at this house with Daniel as his new bride.

"What might I do for you?" Millie asked while Sylvia and George remained where they were, keeping very still in order to eavesdrop discreetly.

"I heard a rumor in town . . ." he began and Sylvia cringed. Not only did the man's voice grate on her nerves—most likely due to his past cruelties—but those six words let her know that her fears had come to pass. ". . . That Mr. Hewitt had returned home after having been believed to be dead. Such a miraculous occurrence naturally has the entire town talking and I thought that I should come visit myself and verify the good news so that we don't have false gossip spreading."

Sylvia rolled her eyes at this. Thinking of how this man had perpetuated the rumor that she was some kind of witch, the very idea that he would claim to be concerned about the spreading of false gossip made her angry. George made a disgusted expression that tempted Sylvia to laugh, but she kept quiet.

"Mr. Hewitt did indeed come back alive," Millie said in such a convincing tone that Sylvia never would have suspected her of lying. She hoped the vicar was equally convinced. "There was some misunderstanding over in America after a battle when he was wounded and got sick after, and a letter was sent to the missus telling her that he'd died. Him having been declared dead and all, he had a hard time of it trying to get back to England, but he finally made it, although he was awfully worn out and done in and he's been mostly stuck in his bed since he come back."

"And when was that, exactly?" the vicar asked with barely disguised suspicion. Sylvia *knew* he'd spoken to the devils who had come to her door in search of Dougal. She just *knew* it. She wanted to think that a vicar would have no reason to become involved in the business of such men, but this particular vicar had always clearly been a hypocrite in Sylvia's eyes. In fact, Daniel had felt the same about him, and he'd known the man many more years than Sylvia.

"Oh, it was before Christmas," Millie said quickly and with firm confidence. "It's a wonder he survived the cold. But it was a Christmas miracle for all of us, it was. The missus especially." Millie added in a voice that carried its own brand of suspicion, "Why are you asking about Mr. Hewitt? You've not set foot here in a good many years. I never saw you here in all the years I lived in this house with the missus. I only know you because I've seen you in town."

"Perhaps if you attended church," the vicar said, his voice mildly scolding, "along with your husband, we would be better acquainted."

"Me and my husband won't be going to any church where my missus is not welcome," Millie said with a tinge of anger. "And if you've no further business here, I'd say it's best you be on your way."

The vicar spoke in a false niceness that made Sylvia shudder visibly. "I'd very much like to speak with Mr. Hewitt, if I may."

"That sounds a bit like you might think we're lying about his being here," Millie accused.

"Not at all," the vicar laughed with the same kind of falseness. "As his clergyman I would simply like to offer my best wishes in person for his recovery."

"I'm not certain his seeing you would do any good for him, especially when he knows well enough what you think of the missus . . . and all the nasty gossip you've spread around about her."

"I assure you I had nothing to do with that," the vicar defended himself hotly. "And perhaps you would be wise to consider the possibility that it's not necessarily gossip if it's true, and—"

He stopped at the sound of Sylvia noisily pushing back her chair to stand up. She'd had enough of this. As she appeared in the doorway next to Millie, the vicar actually took a few steps back as if he feared she might turn him into a snake. The thought amused her given that she believed he was already a snake, even if he didn't look like one. Although his excessively pale complexion combined with his long, sallow face and thin body did give him a degree of resemblance.

"What is all this about?" Sylvia demanded, making no effort to conceal her anger over his reasons for coming here. She would prefer to never see the man again and she doubted there was *any* reason he could come here that wouldn't make her angry. George followed her and stood just behind the two women. Sylvia was glad to know they had his support, and he could look very menacing when he wanted to.

The vicar said somewhat sheepishly, as if he were truly afraid of Sylvia, "I was just explaining that—"

"I heard what you said," Sylvia declared. "But I see no reason that I'm bound to offer you proof my husband is here. He's resting and—"

"I'm right here," Sylvia heard Dougal say in Daniel's voice, and she gasped before she turned around to see him moving tentatively down the stairs on his feet that still had to be extremely tender to walk on. He was wearing a dressing gown and slippers that had belonged to Daniel. For a long moment Sylvia was lured into that place in her mind where it truly felt as if Daniel had come back from the dead and he was standing before her. With the exception of the scar on his face, the man appeared to be Daniel in every respect—and he'd done well in learning the accent as he convincingly added to the vicar, "What is it that you want? Given the way you've treated my wife, I see no reason for you to believe that you are welcome here." Dougal exuded a commanding presence that was *not* like Daniel, who had generally left Sylvia to deal with her own difficulties. But it had been years since the vicar had seen Daniel, and Sylvia doubted he would notice anything except the fact that the man standing before him looked and sounded like Daniel Hewitt.

"I've no wish to offend anyone," the vicar said, and Sylvia knew *that* wasn't true; he simply went about his offensive ways with such subtle undercurrents that people often couldn't even discern that they were being offended—or even deceived. "I only wanted to check in on you after I'd heard that you'd returned." After a moment's pause, he added, "I've been told that you returned before Christmas. Is this really true?"

"Why would you think this good woman," he motioned toward Millie, "would lie to you?"

"It's just that . . . no one in the village heard a word of your return, and—"

"No one in the village cares to show any kindness toward anyone from this household," Dougal continued in his portrayal of Daniel. "Why would you think that either Millie or George would care to converse with those who have made it clear they have no desire to share conversation for any reason? Now that you've gotten what you came for, I will thank you kindly to leave my home and stay off of my property. As long as you disparage my wife and spread your contemptuous lies, you are not welcome here for any reason."

The vicar nodded, unable to hide the fact that Dougal had just instilled a good amount of fear in him. Sylvia found it interesting that the vicar made no attempt to defend himself against the accusations of disparaging Sylvia and spreading lies. But she felt better after Millie slammed the door, which declared a loud finality to the unpleasant exchange with the vicar.

Sylvia turned and hurried toward Dougal as he sat down on one of the stairs with clear evidence that his feet hurt terribly.

"Are you all right?" Sylvia asked, sitting on the next step down, leaning her back against the wall while Dougal leaned against one of the poles supporting the banister.

"I'm fine," Dougal said, and before Sylvia could ask any more questions, he added, "I could hear enough to know that we had a visitor, and Millie was speaking loudly enough that I knew she wasn't pleased—even though I couldn't hear exactly what she was saying. So, I found the dressing gown and slippers and moved to the top of the stairs . . . both curious and concerned, given what I know about the last visitors who came here. Once I heard enough to get the gist of the problem, I . . . well, you know what I did."

"Yes," Sylvia said, marveling at how well he'd taken on Daniel's accent and was continuing to speak that way. They had agreed this was best—both in order to continue his practice but also to never be caught off guard if anyone might come around with any kind of suspicion. "And you did beautifully. It's evident the men who came here *did* go into the village and repeated what I told them, and I'm very grateful we were prepared."

"As am I," Dougal said. "I will do anything I can to help keep trouble away from your home—especially since it followed me here."

"And with any luck," George said, "we can figure out why that happened so we can fix the problem—whatever it might be."

"You're all so very good to me," Dougal said.

"That's not hard," Millie said with a smile, and Sylvia smiled as well, silently adding her agreement. "But I think you should get yourself back to bed and—"

"I confess that the bottom of my feet are still giving me a great deal of pain," Dougal said, "but if I'm being truthful, I also have to admit that sitting in bed in that room has become awfully boring. Since I've made it this far, would it be all right if I come downstairs and—"

"Oh, of course!" Sylvia said and immediately stood up, offering her arm to help him stand up and continue walking down the stairs. "You can make yourself comfortable in the parlor for as long as you like. George spends some time with his newspaper there to relax between chores. And perhaps you can make it to the dining room to sit and have lunch with us there."

"I'd like that very much," Dougal said, and Sylvia could hear a hint of his own accent sneaking through now that he wasn't putting so much effort into acting like Daniel.

With Dougal settled in the parlor, showing an interest in the pile of newspapers that George had read but didn't want to burn just yet, the others finished their now-cold breakfast—assured that Dougal had finished his own before the ruckus had occurred. When it was time for lunch, Dougal joined them at the table and they speculated over the reasons for their recent visitors—and what their motives might be—while they shared a simple but satisfying meal. After lunch, Dougal expressed dismay that he couldn't be on his feet long enough to help them clear the table and clean the dishes, but he was reassured that his only responsibility for now was to get better.

"A little later," Millie said to him, "I'd be glad for your help peeling and cutting some vegetables for the soup we'll be having for dinner. You can do that sitting at the table. I assume you know *how* to do that."

Dougal chuckled. "Yes, Millie, I know *how* to do that—my mother made certain of it. And I'd be very glad to help."

"There's that settled," Millie declared and carried dishes into the kitchen.

Dougal made his way slowly on his tender feet back to the parlor where he continued reading newspapers, mentioning to Sylvia when she passed through the room that it was interesting catching up on news that had occurred while he'd been taking his long journey from the border of Scotland to the meadows of Kent.

"How long *were* you traveling?" Sylvia asked him.

Dougal shook his head. "I honestly cannot tell you. I lost track of time rather quickly, and the days and nights blurred together. I can only say that it was a great many days—perhaps weeks. It felt like a great many weeks, but I'm not certain."

"Well, I'm glad you're here now where you can heal and get your strength back," she said, keeping to herself that she had every hope of him quickly moving on once he was physically able to do so. Despite having become a great deal more comfortable around him—and even enjoying his company—his presence was still often unnerving to her for reasons that were difficult to define.

"I'm very glad of that myself," he said. "I can't bring myself to even think of what would have become of me if you'd not taken me in."

Sylvia just nodded and smiled, then moved on through the parlor into her workroom where she set to work crushing some dried herbs that could be used for a variety of teas that had beneficial purposes. Using the knowledge she'd gained from her mother and grandmother, she'd been able to grow a large quantity of herbs in pots during the cold months of winter as long as she kept them near the south-facing windows in the house where the winter sun gave them plenty of light. In the summer she always moved the pots outside to take advantage of the warm sun and rain. But wherever her precious herbs might be, she always tended to them carefully. She'd recently picked a great many mature stems and had hung them up to dry, and now they were ready for the leaves to be crushed with her mortar and pestle.

Sylvia hummed while she worked, and her mind went to Dougal and how strange—if not unsettling—it was to see him in different rooms of the house, settling comfortably into their home and their lives, almost as if he'd always been here. Given how they'd purposely been working to make him a convincing replica of Daniel in order to reassure the locals, she shouldn't have felt surprised that she was finding it difficult to keep her mind straight on the facts regarding this man living under her roof. But how could she not look at Dougal sitting at the dining table, or in the parlor—and hear him speaking so much like her Daniel—and not be reminded of the man she'd loved and lost?

Her mind was so preoccupied with the ever-increasing strangeness of the situation when Dougal's voice startled her, and she gasped. "And what are you doing in here?" he asked, then chuckled when he realized she'd not heard him approaching the open doorway. "Forgive me. I didn't mean to frighten you."

"It's all right," she said.

"May I come in?" he asked. "Or is this room off limits?"

"You're welcome to come in," she said, motioning toward a chair he could use. "Although I doubt there's much of any interest here."

"On the contrary," he said, his eyes examining the rows of jars and bottles on the shelves behind her, "I find what you do very fascinating."

Sylvia focused on her work and ground the herbs currently in the mortar especially fine with extra vigor, attempting to be unaffected by Dougal's presence.

"So," he drawled as a preamble for whatever he was about to say. "This is what qualifies a woman to be labeled a witch." She heard a tinge of anger in his voice that validated her own feelings on the matter, but it was mixed with a smidgen of humor, which was also validating since what had been defined as witchcraft by some of the locals was just utterly ridiculous.

"I suppose this is it," she said. With mild sarcasm she added, "How dare I grind up herbs for healing purposes? Oh, and sometimes I boil things to make them into tinctures or salves. Perhaps I should get myself a cauldron for that purpose and make the situation more convincing."

"You do know that it's all just very silly, don't you?" He posed his question with evidence of concern on her behalf.

"Yes, I do know," she answered solemnly, "and for the most part I've learned not to be bothered by their assumptions and gossip, but there are times when I can't help but long to fit in. To be able to go to church . . . to socialize with other women . . . and . . ." She cleared her throat to stop herself from musing over things that were simply not possible. "And yet the situation simply is what it is. I do my best to focus on all that is good in my life . . . all that I *do* have, rather than what I *don't* have. I have a fine and comfortable home, my needs are more than met, and I have wonderful friends here who help me as much as they keep me company. I'm very blessed, in truth. And I am able to help a great many people—even if they only come to buy my remedies under cover of darkness." She laughed softly. "I dare say the doctor, the vicar, and their closest friends would be astonished by how many people in the village are secretly using what I make as opposed to calling on the doctor. And these people are very committed to keeping it a secret because they want to be able to continue having access to my products."

"You find it fulfilling then . . . what you do to help others this way?"

"I do," she said firmly.

"That's good, then," Dougal said. "I only wish it didn't come at the cost of your being ostracized from the community. That just isn't right."

"Right or wrong there is nothing to be done, but I do appreciate your kindness."

Sylvia dumped the crushed herbs into a bottle that was already labeled with a little rectangle of paper she'd glued onto the glass. She put the bottle on the shelf, wiped the mortar and pestle clean and moved on to crush some dried lavender.

"Oh, that smells very nice," Dougal said as soon as she'd started. "What is it?"

"Lavender," she told him. "It grows wild in abundance, but I grow it in pots during the cold months. This process releases the fragrance of the plants. Some have a stronger aroma than others, and some are pleasant while others are the opposite. But lavender has a lovely fragrance."

"And what is it used for?" he asked, seeming genuinely interested.

"Oh, lavender is a miracle!" she said, unable to hide her enthusiasm. "It does good in a great many ways. It can help clear up infection, and also reduce swelling. It's also helpful for insect bites, and even burns. But my favorite benefits of lavender are its soothing effects. It can reduce anxiousness and even lift one's spirits. For some people it can be very relaxing and help them rest. Just the right amount also tastes delicious in a cake or even scones."

"Truly?" he asked, intrigued rather than skeptical.

"You've eaten it more than once while you've been here," she said and kept working, filling a jar of crushed lavender little by little.

"Isn't that remarkable!" he said. "I can only say that everything I've eaten here has been especially delicious. Millie is an excellent cook, and you are as well."

Sylvia laughed softly. "Millie is in charge in the kitchen. She is the one with all of the knowledge and skills that produce all the good things we are blessed enough to eat. I simply assist her and do what she tells me. I'm learning, but before Millie came along, I confess that my cooking skills left much to be desired." She laughed again. "It was a good thing that when Daniel brought me to live here that he already had a woman employed as a housekeeper and cook—although she left not long before Daniel did because she had family who needed her. I do well enough at cleaning and other chores, but it's far better for everyone if the cooking is left to someone who knows what they're doing. My mother did fair enough in the kitchen, although I can see now that compared to Millie's skills, hers were very simple and basic, which is a polite way of saying that the food she prepared was generally bland and meant for survival rather than enjoyment. My mother focused on teaching me *these* skills." Sylvia motioned nonchalantly toward the shelves of jars and bottles behind her.

"We all have something we're good at, I believe," Dougal said, "and it's a good thing this world is filled with a great variety of talents, or we'd not be able to provide needs for each other."

Sylvia thought about that for a moment. "That's true, and an interesting insight. If people were all good at the same thing, the world would surely be in trouble."

"Indeed," he chuckled, and silence followed but Sylvia kept working and tried to ignore the fact that she was enjoying this conversation far too much. Just having Dougal in the room soothed the loneliness she'd never become accustomed to feeling.

When the silence grew mildly strained, Sylvia was glad to think of something to ask him. "And what are *you* good at, Dougal Heywood?"

"Oh," he drawled with a tone of hesitancy, as if he were weighing whether he should tell her. Sylvia stopped crushing lavender long enough to look at him and definitely saw dilemma in his expression before he said, "I'm not certain I can answer that honestly without leaving you sorely disappointed in me. In fact, you might even evict me promptly, and I wouldn't blame you." Sylvia stopped working and put the pestle down. Already such a confession reminded her more of Daniel than anything about him had before. He looked directly at her, and she was relieved to see genuine humility in his eyes. She had always been able to tell when Daniel had been lying to her—or at least she'd learned to after it had happened so many times.

Without even thinking about it, Sylvia sat down, preparing herself to hear something that—as he had said—might very well disappoint her or even prompt her to evict him. She steeled herself for such feelings and said, "I think we've come to know each other well enough that we should be able to speak with complete honesty—and be willing to face the consequences. Since you brought it up, I think it's only fair that you tell me what you're referring to." He hesitated and she added, "Should I be worried that you'll steal from me? Cause us harm? Are you—"

"No, Sylvia, there's no need for you to worry about anything, because I'm a changed man." He sighed loudly and looked at the floor as if he were ashamed. "I've wanted to tell you this ever since you took me in; you've been so kind despite the fact that I know my resemblance to Daniel has been difficult for you."

Sylvia wanted to insist that it *hadn't* been difficult, but she had just stated that they should be completely honest with each other, so she said nothing.

"The truth is that . . . before I went to war, I was very much like Daniel in the way I lived my life. And I'm speaking from what Daniel told me about his own life. But Daniel had the good sense to travel some distance from his home when he engaged in his schemes. The people I swindled were in my own community. Since the war, I've been working to repay my debts to those people; offering apologies and working for them to do whatever they needed help with until I came to a place where I had sincerely done everything I could to make restitution, and I ended up on good terms with most of these people."

"That's excellent," Sylvia said and meant it. Such an endeavor would have taken a great deal of courage and humility, and she couldn't help but be impressed with his efforts, especially when her instincts were insisting that he was being truthful.

Dougal went on to say, "I'm well aware that you and Daniel loved each other very much, but you were often angry with him once you'd become aware of his reasons for traveling so much, and the large amounts of money that he would have in his possession for which he could give you no explanation. He admitted freely to me that he had swindled and cheated a great many people and he knew it—and he was contending with deep regret. It was so odd the way we were drawn together because of our looking like twins, but as we shared many conversations, it became evident that we also had a great deal in common in the way we'd lived our lives. As I said, I too was a swindler and a cheat, Sylvia." She took in a sharp breath and had trouble letting it out. Despite his admitting to the restitutions he'd made, she hoped and prayed he would say something that would make her believe she should *not* evict him from her home. She wanted to believe he *had* truly changed, and she paid close attention to her instincts as the conversation unfolded, telling herself that he wouldn't likely make such confessions if he were attempting to swindle her in any way. If he had any hidden motives, he would surely want to keep them hidden.

"Daniel and I understood each other very well," Dougal went on. "But we were also in complete agreement that facing death on the battlefield had given us both good cause to reconsider the kind of men we should choose to be. We talked about it a great deal, and you should know that your Daniel was deeply thrilled over the intention of coming home to you a changed man, a man you could be proud of, a man you could trust, a man who would work hard to make an honest living in order to care for you properly."

Sylvia felt tears sliding down her cheeks before she'd even realized she felt the urge to cry. How could she not feel grief over the thought of such a possibility and knowing it would never come to pass? She'd grieved deeply over Daniel's death—she'd missed him so much! But she'd actually soothed her own grief with frequent reminders that all the good she'd shared with Daniel had always been tainted by his unethical nature and stark lack of integrity. Now she was hearing evidence that he'd changed, that he'd been determined to set those ways aside. If that had truly been the case, Sylvia could easily imagine sharing a life with Daniel that might have been practically idyllic. But he was dead, and such a possibility would never come to pass.

"I've upset you," Dougal said, startling her.

She hurried to wipe a hand over her cheeks and coughed before she said, "It's just that . . . I loved Daniel dearly, and . . . it was my deepest wish for him to change his ways. If he'd not died, and . . . if he'd come home to me with such a change of heart . . . it would have been . . ."

"Then I'm guessing that such knowledge is likely to enhance your grief," he said with compassion.

"Yes, I suppose in a way it does, except that . . . it also warms my heart. Just to know that he'd changed his thinking gives me a strange kind of comfort." She looked directly at Dougal, whose brow was furrowed with concern. "I'm glad you told me."

"Then I'm glad I told you," he said. "And I hope that my confessions won't change your opinion of me too much. I'm well aware that you don't know me well enough to know whether you can trust me, but I swear to you, Sylvia, that I am not the same man I was before the war. You asked me what I was good at, and I gave you an honest answer. Since I returned to England with the determination to live a life of integrity and make an honest living, I've been quite out of sorts. I was raised on a farm, so I know something of that kind of work, but I don't own any land and therefore my life is quite upended. Nevertheless, rest assured that I did not set out to come here looking for any kind of assistance. I didn't anticipate getting shot or needing to travel on foot for so long which left me in the position of being quite desperate for your help—and I'm grateful. But my biggest purpose for coming here was to convey to you the message that Daniel had changed, and his motivation for changing was *you*. He loved you very much, Sylvia. You were the most important thing to him, and I saw and heard much evidence of his anguish when he had faced the possibility of death and it brought him to his senses . . . made him realize how much his bad behavior had affected your life. He wanted nothing but to come home to you so he could make things right. Neither of us believed that he would not live long enough to make that happen, but I was with him when he died and . . ."

The same moment Sylvia realized she was crying again, she heard a tremor in Dougal's voice and saw his chin quiver before he bowed his head abruptly. She took advantage of his not looking at her to wipe her hands over her face to dry her tears, but more tears came and after three attempts she just had to let them fall, lifting her apron to cover her face and absorb the unending stream flowing down her face.

"Now I have *really* upset you," she heard Dougal say and hurried to wipe her face with her apron before she let it drop and forced herself to look at him, even though she was still crying.

"I can't deny that what you're telling me has brought my grief to the surface. Nevertheless, I'm so very glad to know . . . that he'd changed . . . that he loved me that much. I do believe my tears are a mixture of joy and sorrow. I deeply wish I could have lived the rest of my life with Daniel at his best, but he's been gone long enough that I've accepted his death and I've made peace with it—for the most part. I have times when I miss him and my sorrow overtakes me, and perhaps it will take some time and effort to come to terms with what you've told me, but that doesn't mean I'm not glad to know it." She took a deep breath and wiped away more tears. "And I *do* believe you're telling me the truth. I *do* trust you, Dougal. I hope and pray you don't give me any reason to regret trusting you. Please don't prove me wrong. A part of me was convinced that a person couldn't change so drastically, while at the same time something deep inside of me desperately wanted to believe Daniel had the ability to change . . . to become a better man. You've admitted that the two of you were very much the same. I'm going to give you the same consideration. I'm going to believe that you've changed, and you are a good man. I believe you've been honest with me."

"I would not lie to you about something so difficult and tender as a man's determination to change his ways. I swear to it."

Sylvia nodded and silence descended while Sylvia attempted to take in everything she'd just learned about Daniel. She knew it would take time to fully accept this news and its impact on her, but she *was* glad to know. Recalling that Dougal was still in the room, she attempted to focus on the present situation and said, "May I ask you a question?"

"Anything," he said.

"And please be honest with me, even if it requires admitting to your having done something unsavory in regard to these men. I promise that you can stay here until you heal regardless of anything you tell me."

"That's very kind," he said and motioned toward her with his hand. "Please . . . ask your question."

"The men following you . . . the reason you were shot . . ." She coughed and took a deep breath, not certain she wanted to know, but knowing she needed to. "Do they have anything to do with something from your past misdeeds? Is there a legitimate reason they might be wanting to do you harm . . . or to kill you? You told me before that you didn't know the reasons, but I realize you were in a desperate situation, and I can understand why you might have felt the need to deny any knowledge of their motives. But now . . . I need to know the truth."

Dougal took a deep breath and looked nervous—perhaps even ashamed—which made Sylvia's heart begin to pound. Dougal had just committed to being completely honest with her, but she wondered if prior to this conversation he might have been less than forthcoming, as she'd just suggested. She had promised to harbor him until he was able to manage on his own, but the possible answer to her question was suddenly very unnerving.

"Well?" she asked when he hesitated too long.

"I had never seen them before I saw them staring at me in the pub that night I told you about. But I have a suspicion over why they might be after me and want me dead. And I sincerely apologize if I misled you in any way. You're right, I was desperate. I was so cold and tired and hungry that I don't even remember what exactly I said to you. I hope you can forgive me."

Sylvia nodded, hoping that was a sufficient response to what he'd just admitted to. She *did* understand. But she still needed the answer to her question. He hesitated again as if he were trying to find the right words, and Sylvia said with some impatience, "Are you going to tell me? I can understand your wanting to keep it to yourself, and I would respect your right to do that . . . except that I am obviously in the middle of all this, and I would prefer to know what's going on."

"I believe you have every right to know the truth," he said, leaning his forearms on his thighs and looking at the floor. "Despite all of my efforts to prove myself a changed man to the people in the area where I lived and grew up, there was one family that would not be convinced. They always hated me, and I think they very much would have preferred that I'd died on the battlefield." He sighed loudly while Sylvia tried to imagine anyone being so cruel, but she had certainly dealt with a great deal of cruelty herself that was often difficult to comprehend. "I can't know for certain," Dougal went on, "if these men were sent by the people I'm referring to, but . . . in my mind it's the only possibility I can think of. I never would have thought they would lower themselves to such depraved methods to rid me from their lives, but I can't deny that it's a possibility."

"All right," Sylvia said after giving him some long moments to go on but he didn't. "What is this possibility? Who are you talking about specifically?"

Dougal sat up straight and looked at her directly, which she always found a little unnerving, but she returned his gaze, believing she could sense whether he was telling her the truth if she could see his eyes. "Before the war, I was married," he said and she held her breath, wondering why such a possibility had never occurred to her—or perhaps she was more prone to feel upset over the reality that he was no longer married, and in fact was stranded so far from his home, alone and trying to heal from a very traumatic experience. Sylvia listened with a quickened heartbeat as he went on. "Mary and I fell in love with each other when we were very young. We grew up not living far from each other. We were playmates and then sweethearts, and we wanted to get married as soon as it was possible. Once I had a place for us to live, I proposed marriage, but of course I had a bad reputation, and in that respect I can't blame her parents for their concerns in not wanting her to marry me. Although even then I was *trying* to change my ways and earn a living as a farmer, they still despised me. Mary knew the truth about me, she believed in me, she made me want to be a better man, and I'd been trying very hard to put my bad ways behind me. And then . . . she died . . . giving birth to our daughter."

"Oh goodness!" Sylvia murmured. "I'm so very sorry!"

"Thank you," he said somberly. "I miss her still sometimes, but it's been years. Time may not take away the sorrow, but it does allow you to become accustomed."

"Yes, I know what you mean," Sylvia said.

"I'm certain you do," he replied, let out a harsh breath, and continued. "My father had passed before then, and my mother moved in with me to help care for the baby. Rachel's a beautiful little girl, so much like her mother. She was four when I had to leave for the war, and by then I was caring for her on my own while I worked the farm the best I could because my mother had passed."

"Good heavens," Sylvia said, "you have endured a great deal of loss."

"As have you," he countered, and she couldn't deny it. He sighed as if a blanket of shame fell over him. "I confess that in my desperation of caring for a child on my own and having no help, I fell back into indulging in some illegal activities in order to keep us fed and cared for; the farm simply wasn't enough. But as I've already told you, I've done my best to make all of that right." He sighed again and went on. "Since I had to leave, I had no choice but to leave Rachel in the care of Mary's parents. I never felt comfortable with it given the fact that Mary never liked her parents much and had been glad to get out from under their roof. But they were well off and could afford to care for Rachel and at least keep her safe and see that her needs were met. In fact, they could give a little girl everything she could ever want." He coughed and looked at the floor. "I always found it ironic that they refused to give any assistance to Rachel when it was needed, but they were more than willing to take over her care when I was leaving."

Dougal sighed again as he looked up, and Sylvia had a thought that made her wonder if she'd figured out what he was leading to. "Are they well enough off to send someone to kill you so that they don't have to give your daughter back to you?"

Sylvia immediately saw moisture gather in Dougal's eyes, then tears trickled down his face. "Yes," he said, "they are—and I believe they would. I tried and tried to see my Rachel and they wouldn't allow it. With some sneaking around I managed to speak to her for a few minutes a couple of times, and I was glad to know that she remembered me and she even asked to come with me. She told me she didn't like living there. But Mary's parents told me I would never get her back, that I could never be a good father to her given the kind of man I was, and there was no convincing them that I'd changed and I *would* be a good father to her. She's my daughter. She is rightfully mine."

"Yes, she is," Sylvia said emphatically.

"But they spread some nasty and utterly false rumors about me which made it all the more impossible to try and get Rachel from them, and then it became impossible to even remain there."

"So you came here," Sylvia said.

"I just needed some time to consider what I might be able to do to get my daughter back, but they found a way to block my every effort. And since I'd done all I could to make right all of my wrongs, my next priority was to come here on behalf of my friend and let you know how Daniel had changed, and there was nothing more important to him than you."

Hearing Dougal's story, his efforts on her behalf meant even more. His delay in coming here now made perfect sense, and his sacrifices in doing so meant more than she could even grasp. But she attempted to focus on Dougal's tragic situation as opposed to her own sensitive emotions.

"What will you do about your daughter?" Sylvia asked, feeling some degree of panic on Dougal's behalf, "You must be heartbroken!"

"I admit that I am," he said with distinct sadness in his voice. "But what *can* I do? I have nothing, Sylvia. No way to provide for a child—and certainly no means to contend with the power of her grandparents." He blew out a long, slow breath and Sylvia could see the heaviness of his heart. "For now, I simply have to find a way to make a new life for myself with the hope that eventually I will be able to have her in my life."

Sylvia felt helpless and frustrated on his behalf, but she couldn't come up with any helpful ideas. She could only say, "I truly hope you'll be able to get your Rachel back."

"Thank you," Dougal said. "You're ever so kind." He looked firmly at her and added, "I want to just say once again . . . because it is the reason I came here . . . Daniel had truly changed . . . for you. You were his motivation to become a better man. It's my hope that your knowing this will help you find peace . . . even if doing so takes time."

Sylvia wiped her cheeks again, murmuring softly, "I do believe it *will* help me find peace. I also believe that it *will* take time. Hearing this makes me miss him more than I have in a long while." She laughed softly. "The problem between us was never a lack of love. I loved him dearly; I still do, I believe. The problems that created all the tension and arguing had to do with his . . . well . . ." She coughed then cleared her throat. "We've already talked about that. I only wish that he'd lived long enough to make good on the changes occurring in his heart. We could have been so happy together."

"And for that, above all else, I am truly sorry, Sylvia," Dougal said with such sincere compassion that she was drawn to look directly into his eyes. She found it strange that even his eyes reminded her of Daniel—although they were different, even if she wasn't certain exactly how to describe it. Still the similarities between them often took her off guard, and given the very personal and tender nature of this conversation, she had to firmly remind herself once again that it was Dougal to whom she was speaking, and Daniel was long dead—along with his desire to become a better man.

"I should leave you to your work," Dougal said. "I think I've shared more than enough for you to think about. If you have any questions for me, well . . ." he chuckled wryly, "you know where I live."

"I do indeed," Sylvia said as Dougal stood slowly and tentatively upon his tender feet. "Please . . . do not be on your feet any more than necessary. They will heal more quickly without the weight of your body pressing down upon them."

"I'll do my best," he said, "although it is very nice to be out of that room. Not that I'm complaining because you've all taken very good care of me. But I think that I'd prefer spending my days here on the ground floor—unless that's a problem."

"No," Sylvia said, feeling as if she were lying, "it's not a problem." In truth, she liked it better when he was confined to one room and she could prepare herself mentally for the time she spent with him. If he was going to be in other rooms of the house, she had to accept that she might come upon him unexpectedly at any given time. But it was a fact she simply had to come to terms with.

"And perhaps," Dougal added, "if nothing else, I can help Millie in the kitchen with tasks that can be done sitting down. It's nice to feel like I can contribute even a little."

"I'm certain she'll appreciate that," Sylvia said. "Millie works too hard and would do well to put her feet up a little more. I've told her as much many times but she's a stubborn woman."

"I'll see what I can do to help encourage her in that regard," Dougal said with a smile that quickened Sylvia's heartbeat. Before he left the room, she felt compelled to ask him a question that kept hovering in her mind, and she wasn't certain when they might have another opportunity to speak privately—or perhaps it was more accurate that she wanted to have the question answered now so she could stop wondering.

"I *do* have a question," she said, and he sat back down.

"Anything," he encouraged.

"You said you were with him when he died. *How* did he die?"

Dougal's eyes widened while his brow furrowed. He didn't want to talk about it, that was obvious enough. But Sylvia added, "I know it's difficult. My intention is not to bring up ugly memories for you— even though that's surely what I'm doing. It's just that . . . even though

I know it sounds strange, I've wondered a thousand times exactly how he died, and I think—even though the answer is surely disturbing—I will still be more likely to find peace if I know how it happened. Did he suffer? Was he alive a long time after he'd been wounded? Did he . . . Well, I don't need to go on. You can get the idea. Those are questions that have haunted me, and even if he *did* suffer, I feel like I need to know."

Dougal nodded then remained silent for more than a minute with a tight, stern expression—as if he were measuring his words carefully while at the same time contending with difficult memories. She sincerely felt regret for urging him to recall an experience that was surely horrifying for him. But she needed to know, and she waited patiently to hear what he might tell her, trying to ignore the sweat rising on her palms and the mild nausea smoldering in her stomach.

"He . . . uh . . ." Dougal began. "We . . . were on the ground . . . on our bellies . . . our rifles aimed toward the enemy line. He was right beside me. We had to keep our eyes straight ahead so we couldn't look at each other. We were whispering . . . talking about trivial things . . . I suppose to distract ourselves from knowing that the shooting would start at any moment and . . . . . . it was . . . well, quite frankly it was . . . terrifying. Then the bullets started flying, and . . . I didn't even realize . . . what had happened until . . . it occurred to me that he wasn't talking to me . . . anymore. When I turned to look at him, I sincerely expected to see that he was just intent on reloading his rifle, but . . . he was dead. A bullet had hit him in the forehead." Dougal put a finger on his own forehead, just above his left eye. He gazed distantly at nothing and remained silent for several moments before he seemed snapped out of a trance and looked again at Sylvia. "No, he didn't suffer. He was gone instantly; alive one moment and dead the next. I hope that tells you what you need to know."

"Yes, thank you," Sylvia said with more tears trickling down her cheeks, but she figured they were warranted. "It's difficult to hear, but . . . knowing how it happened will keep my mind from trying to conjure up the endless possibilities." She sighed and asked, "Are you all right? I mean . . . telling me can't have been easy, but . . . how do you cope with such memories? And I'm certain that Daniel's death was far from the only one that you observed."

Dougal chuckled with no hint of humor. "It's kind of you to ask," he said, "and the truthful answer is that I don't think I cope at all. I have nightmares, and . . . even sometimes when I'm wide awake I'll find my mind drifting to those terrible memories as if I have no control over it. Sometimes certain noises that remind me of gunfire will actually frighten me . . . and I feel like a little boy that wants to hide in a cupboard."

"It's nothing to be ashamed of," Sylvia said.

"Isn't it?" Dougal countered very quickly as if he'd contended a great deal with feeling shame over his reaction to his memories.

"Not at all," Sylvia said. "What you've been through is indescribably horrifying. Surely no man could endure such things and not contend with such reactions."

"I don't know about that." He shook his head. "I just know that for me, I . . . well, I hate it. I wish I could just forget all about it, but I fear it will haunt me for the rest of my life."

Sylvia searched her mind for some kind of insight or wisdom that might help soothe his fears, that might help him more easily contend with this struggle—but she could think of nothing. After a grueling stretch of silence, Dougal stood up and said in an unnaturally cheerful voice, "I think I will make my way back upstairs and see if I can manage a nap. I still tire easily."

"Of course," Sylvia said. "Do you need anything or—"

"No, no," Dougal insisted. "I'm fine, but thank you." He paused on his way to the door and nodded toward her, smiling as he did. "It's been lovely talking with you, Sylvia. I hope that we will be able to have more conversations."

"That would be nice," she said, omitting the thought she knew he shared that conversation would be nice as long as they avoided his terrible memories of the war.

Long after he left the room, Sylvia pondered what she'd just learned about Daniel's death. She was so glad to know he hadn't suffered, but she did have difficulty with the mental image of how he'd died. She felt certain with time she would come to terms with it, and she felt certain that whatever difficult images she might have in her mind were only a drop in the ocean compared to what was swirling around in Dougal's mind.

Thinking of Dougal and the lengthy conversation they'd just shared, Sylvia's mind went to his daughter. It was dreadfully unsettling to think that he had a daughter that was being kept from him. Surely the rights of a father outweighed those of grandparents, especially when he'd worked so hard to make restitution for his misdeeds. She wondered for a long moment if he had told her the truth about all of that, and instinctively she knew that he had.

Suddenly overwhelmed by too many things to think about, Sylvia returned to her work and hummed a familiar tune as she did so. Dougal's arrival had certainly created a great many complications for her household, and yet for the first time, she felt distinctly glad that he was here. Just thinking of him made her feel less lonely for reasons that were difficult to define. He was not her Daniel, but he was kind and compassionate and easy to talk to, and he made her miss Daniel much less. How could she not be grateful for that?

Chapter Six

Healer Woman

It took a few days for Sylvia to become accustomed to seeing Dougal around the house. He also started sitting at the dining table to share meals and joining them for tea in the parlor in the afternoons. The wound on his leg was healing nicely, and although he reported that he still felt some pain, it was minimal in contrast to what it had been. According to George's reports, the wound on Dougal's leg looked better every day. Sylvia could attest for herself that the bottom of Dougal's feet were also much improved. Most of the sores had scabbed over, and some of them had scabs coming off. Dougal reported that his feet were still tender to walk on, but they were so much better than when he'd first arrived that he considered it a miracle. He kept stockings on his feet in order to keep the scabs from causing him problems when he walked, although given the fact that they were barely beyond winter, the floors in the house were too cold to *not* wear stockings.

Each day Dougal helped Millie in the kitchen with tasks he could do sitting down, and Sylvia enjoyed hearing them talking and laughing, which had become quite common. Dougal had also helped Sylvia in her workroom a few times, following her instructions in order to help fill the contents of jars and bottles that were stored on the shelves for when they were needed. Herbs and other dried plants were crushed and some of them were stored dry to be used for teas. Others were boiled and then cooled to be mixed with other ingredients to create salves and tinctures. Dougal showed a great interest in the process, and fresh astonishment that for this reason she had been labeled a witch by many in the community.

The conversations they shared became more and more comfortable, although it was mostly light and trivial—unlike the first time he'd sat in here with her, sharing deep secrets about himself and his life. It occurred to Sylvia that there were secrets regarding her own life—things she didn't want to talk about—that Dougal was oblivious to. But she wasn't ready to talk about certain things just yet—and maybe she never would be.

She knew that Daniel had shared a great deal with Dougal about her, since every once in a while something would come up that he already knew and he would readily admit that Daniel had told him. Initially Sylvia felt disconcerted over such a fact, but she quickly adjusted; Daniel was dead, and the fact that he'd talked about her to a friend he'd cared for and trusted was more of a comfort than anything. But there were things that had happened in her life after Daniel had left, things he never would have known about. Millie and George knew all of her secrets, but she knew they would never repeat such personal matters without her permission. It occurred to her that perhaps she would eventually feel comfortable enough with Dougal to tell him, and then she would recall that he was not staying here permanently. Once he was sufficiently healed, he would be on his way and the friendship growing between them would be over and irrelevant. But Sylvia refused to think about that now. For now she enjoyed the time she spent with him and was glad to have him there.

A day came when Sylvia and George agreed that it was time to prepare the garden for planting. The topic came up at supper one evening and Dougal was full of questions. George answered most of them, telling him how they grew a great variety of vegetables—enjoying them when they were each in season, drying some to be used in the winter months, and storing the root vegetables in the cellar where they would remain edible for many months. He also told Dougal how he and Sylvia did the plowing and planting, the weeding and watering, while Millie kept the household functioning and provided good meals—as she always did.

"I would like to help," Dougal said sincerely.

"That's very kind," Sylvia said, "but I believe your feet need some time yet before you do something like that. I know you're bored and frustrated, but please give the healing a little more time; those sores were dreadful when you arrived. Let's not do anything to aggravate them."

Dougal nodded sullenly, like a child who had just been reminded that he had been denied privileges due to bad behavior. Sylvia was glad when Millie changed the subject and nothing more on the topic was said.

The following day, Sylvia went out to the barn with George right after breakfast. He fastened the plow to the horse and insisted that he should be the one to use it. "I know you could do it if you had to," he told her. "But I'm here and a man's strength is better suited to maneuvering the plow."

She knew he was right, but she felt mostly useless while this stage of preparing the soil was completed. If nothing else, it gave her some empathy for what Dougal had to be feeling. While George plowed, Sylvia took care of *everything* else that needed doing for the animals and in the barn and the household that George usually took care of. She even chopped wood and mucked out the animals' stalls.

After three days, the large rectangle of land that was likely bigger than the house was finally ready for planting. George's skill with the plow had left nearly straight rows where the vegetables could be planted, and Sylvia had a map she'd created years earlier in order to keep track of what was planted where, and to take advantage of the ways the bees would pollinate the plants. This subject fascinated Dougal, and Sylvia enjoyed telling him all that her father had taught her about this. Dougal's own farming experience had been with simply planting and caring for one kind of crop; he'd never done anything like this before.

On the second morning of planting seeds with George's help, Sylvia caught movement from the corner of her eye and stood up straight so she could fully take in the effect of Dougal walking toward her dressed in Daniel's clothes, looking so much like him that her heart began to pound and her stomach seemed to flip over inside of her. The black boots looked so familiar, but even more so were the dark trousers he wore—although they looked a little large on him, but they were held up nicely by the braces he wore over a dingy white shirt that was clean but had been worn to work in so much that it had lost its vibrancy a long time ago. The shirt also looked a little large, but the breeze pressed it against the muscles of his arms and chest, taking Sylvia's breath away. Something more rational in her mind snapped her back to reality. This was not Daniel. What she saw before her was an illusion. *He's the wrong man,* Sylvia told herself. *The wrong man.*

"What are you doing?" she asked as he came closer.

"I'm going to help you," he said. "My feet are fine," he insisted. "I'm not feeling any pain at all, and I'm going to help you."

"Very well," she said, not willing to argue with him. She could admit to herself that she'd likely exaggerated his need to stay off his feet in order to keep him from being around her too much, but she would never admit that aloud. A part of her never wanted him to leave. She had begun to rely on his company, and she felt increasingly drawn to him. But the entire situation was confusing to say the least, and she really didn't want to think about it too much.

"Are you all right?" he asked and she realized she'd been staring at him.

"Yes," she insisted. "I . . . I just . . ." She cleared her throat. "Just . . . seeing you in his clothes . . . brought back memories, and . . ."

"I hope it's all right," he said, mildly panicked as he brushed his hands down the front of his shirt.

"Of course," she said as if it were nothing when in truth it was far more difficult than she'd expected. "I told you when you first came here that you could use his clothes. No sense in them gathering dust." She nodded toward his feet. "The boots fit you?" she asked.

He lifted one foot to look at it a moment before he set it back down. "A tad large but not so much that it's a problem. After walking so far on bare, bleeding feet I'm very grateful to be wearing such fine boots."

"Then you must take them with you when you go," she said, hoping that might remind him that he *would* leave and free her from this strange torment he caused in her. She both loved his presence and his companionship and also hated the acute resemblance he bore to Daniel.

"How about we get the garden planted before we talk about when I should leave?" he said with a smile, motioning toward where George was hard at work, not caring about the conversation taking place between Sylvia and Dougal.

"Very well," she said.

"Tell me what you'd like me to do," he said, and she gave him instructions on how to plant the corn in short rows to create a square, since the stalks grew much heartier that way. He quickly got to work and Sylvia returned to what she'd been doing before he'd come out of the house and caused such a ruckus inside her.

The three of them all worked in different areas of the garden until Millie's voice could be heard calling them into the house for lunch. Inside the kitchen door they all removed their dirty boots before they each went to get cleaned up. They were all a few minutes into eating their meal when Millie chuckled and said, "It's always true that when you're working hard you eat more; good thing I cook more food to keep you going. Glad to see you've all got a good appetite."

"And everything tastes delicious, as always," Dougal said.

"Indeed it does," Sylvia added, and George made a noise of agreement with his mouth full.

After lunch they went back to work outside. Occasionally Dougal would ask Sylvia a question to make certain he was doing the work correctly according to her specifications.

"I thought you had experience as a farmer," she said.

"Oh, I do," he replied. "But we only ever grew wheat and barley. We bought our vegetables or traded for them. This kind of garden is a new experience for me."

"Oh, that's right," she said. "You told me that before and I forgot. Well, you're doing splendidly." She went on to answer his questions and give him further instructions before he went back to work and she did the same. She preferred working at opposite ends of the garden from him, and tried to keep her back turned, still finding it difficult to see him looking far more like Daniel than he had since he'd shown up here so unexpectedly.

The planting was accomplished quicker than usual with three pairs of hands instead of two, and within a few days the garden was ready to be left to soak in the rain that fell for days after they were finished. While the four occupants of the house remained inside as much as possible when the weather was wet, they all commented a number of times on how fortunate it was that they had been blessed with warmth and sunshine while they'd been planting.

Sylvia realized she was becoming more accustomed to having Dougal around, and since he was determined to remain engaged in helping out in any way that he could, she found it difficult if not impossible to even think of telling him that he needed to make plans to leave now that he was healed. He'd told her more than once that he believed it was only right for him to do repairs and help wherever he could in order to earn off all that she had given him. Her assurances that this was absolutely unnecessary fell on deaf ears, and she had to accept that he wouldn't be leaving anytime soon. But his presence was bothering her less than it had in the past, and she felt some degree of confidence that she could abide having him nearby—even though his appearance still often caught her off guard.

As days passed, Sylvia realized a new problem presented itself when she found it difficult to be unaffected by Dougal. Dougal—not his resemblance to Daniel which she was becoming accustomed to—Dougal himself. She was finding that she enjoyed his company very much.

He was kind and good and they could always manage to find the means for stimulating conversation, no matter what they might be doing. In fact, Sylvia had to acknowledge that she was attracted to Dougal and she had to acknowledge it had nothing to do with his physical appearance. There were moments when her mind was assaulted with some measure of confusion over the matter, but it would only take a quick reminder of the situation to set her thinking straight. She couldn't deny that she liked Dougal very much, which made her begin to hope that he would *not* leave. But the future was full of uncertainty, and she had no intention—at least not yet—of admitting to her feelings aloud. Therefore, the only solution for the time being was to press forward, taking on each day as it came, while she continued to observe Dougal closely, as if she had to make certain he had no hidden flaws in his character that might one day arise and cause her the kind of grief that Daniel had brought into her life. As of yet, she'd found nothing at all in Dougal that even hinted at anything distasteful. He'd confessed the misdeeds of his past and she sincerely believed he'd been telling her the truth, and that he had fully put behind him any kind of unseemly behavior.

A couple of days after the planting of the garden had been completed, Sylvia went up to her room at bedtime and sat to read before changing into her nightclothes. On the chance that someone might come to the house late in the evening to purchase medical remedies from her, she sometimes felt inclined to put off changing—just in case. It wasn't that she hadn't many times met her customers and helped them while wearing a dressing gown over her nightgown, but on the evenings when she didn't feel terribly tired, she waited to change until she was ready to fall asleep—even though her efforts were most often wasted since customers rarely came.

Sylvia was actually startled to hear a pounding at the front door and she hurriedly set her book aside, took up the nearby lamp, and headed down the stairs. She was startled to come upon Dougal at the top of the stairs and he seemed alarmed. "Who could that be?"

"Likely just a customer," she said. "No need for concern."

"Oh, of course," he replied, immediately appearing reassured.

Still, he followed her down the stairs and she said, "This happens all the time, Dougal. There's no need for you to—"

"I feel restless and I'm bored," he said. "Is there a reason you don't want me to accompany you or—"

The very moment he asked the question, Sylvia felt a strange shuddering sensation rush over her, as if to warn her that something wasn't right. "Actually," she said, stopping on the stairs which forced him to do the same, "I think I'd very much like to have you accompany me."

"Is something wrong?" he asked.

"I don't know," she said. "I just felt . . . something strange. I can't explain it. Perhaps it's nothing, but . . ."

A repeated pounding on the door startled her, and she hurried into the parlor and opened a drawer on one side of a small desk, where she kept a loaded pistol.

"Oh, my," Dougal said as she picked up the gun and put the hand holding it behind her so it couldn't be seen, and she handed Dougal the lamp so that her other hand was free.

"Stay with me," she said, still unable to discern if what she felt was valid.

"I promise," he said, and she couldn't deny being much less afraid with him beside her.

They went to the door which she unlocked then opened only to have her fears begin to pound painfully in her chest, and she could almost feel Dougal going tense beside her. The two grisly men who had come to her home weeks ago in search of Dougal were standing before her—although one of them was barely upright, held up mostly by the other, who had an arm around him.

"Ye must help us!" the man said who was supporting his cohort. "I wouldn't blame ye if ye didn't. We got a way o' bein' frightenin' and all; we knows that. But . . . Biff here got a stab in a fight and . . . that doctor won't have nothin' t' do with us, and . . . I swear to ye ma'am we mean ye no harm." His eyes went to Dougal, and he added firmly while his eyes retained a plea for help combined with a spark of astonishment. "I don't know if ye're the man we harmed or if ye do indeed just look very much like him. I don't know how it's possible but . . . if ye help my man Biff here I swear t' ye I'll tell ye everything about what we done and why, and we never would o' killed ye—or the man who likes like ye, I swear it—even though that's what we'd been hired t' do." His eyes went back to Sylvia and the pleading in them deepened. "I'm beggin' ye, miss. Ye gots a reputation for bein' able t' help with such things. I can't lose my man Biff, I just can't."

Sylvia pulled together all of her courage and strength, instinctively believing what this man was telling her. She declared firmly, "I'll not have any weapons. Turn them over now."

The man was eager to comply, but what followed was an awkward and almost comical effort to pass over three pistols and four knives from the man who told them his name was Rodney, and he also knew where weapons were hidden on the barely conscious Biff. Dougal set all of the weapons aside before he patted both men down from top to bottom to make certain everything menacing had been relinquished. Dougal then followed Sylvia's instructions to help Rodney get Biff to the big table in the workroom. It wasn't comfortable but she could assess the problem there more easily and then have him moved to a more appropriate place to rest. Sylvia sent Dougal to get more lamps so she could see the situation more clearly, and she told him to hide the weapons he'd just confiscated. Since Rodney was in the room with her, attempting to reassure his friend, he wouldn't know where Dougal had put them. Sylvia discreetly put her own pistol in a nearby drawer for easy access while Rodney was distracted. But she very much doubted she would need it.

Surprisingly enough, her fear had left her regarding these men. Biff was in a very bad way, and Rodney's humility over that fact was very clearly genuine. She found it strange to observe how Rodney's fears on behalf of his friend—and Biff's fear for his own mortality— had completely changed the motives and behaviors of these men. And with Dougal close by, she felt confident they were safe enough. She noted that George and Millie had made no appearance, and she suspected they had already gone to bed and had likely been asleep before the pounding on the door had occurred. If it had stirred them, they would have assumed it was a customer for Sylvia and would have known she'd take care of it before they'd gone quickly back to sleep.

After Dougal had gone in and out of the room a few times, bringing lamps and turning up the wicks as high as they would go, Sylvia discreetly nodded toward the drawer where the pistol was now hidden. Dougal made it clear that he understood her meaning, and discreetly showed her how he had one of the confiscated pistols tucked into the back of his trousers, which made her feel even less afraid.

Sylvia quickly set to work assessing the knife wound on the side of Biff's abdomen. It was bleeding so much that she found it difficult to see the exact nature of the problem. But Dougal kept handing her clean rags according to her instructions so that she could press them against the open wound firmly enough to hopefully stop the bleeding. If she couldn't do that, there was no other remedy she had that could help Biff, and she told Rodney so, wanting to be completely honest with him. "The wound *should* be stitched closed, but right now there's so much bleeding that I can't even see *where* to stitch. We must get the bleeding to stop or at least slow down."

"Oh, I do hope it stops!" Rodney said with a whimper that led Sylvia to believe he was trying not to cry. "We been friends for so many years, I just don't think I can . . ." His voice faded and he slumped to his knees beside the table where he was holding to one of Biff's hands.

Sylvia thought frantically about the best course to take in order to hopefully save Biff, and she knew that pressure on the wound was the only hope of slowing the bleeding enough to stitch the wound. With the strength of Dougal and Rodney, they followed her instructions to help wrap bandaging firmly around Biff's abdomen to hold clean rags tightly in place over the wound. When that was done, Sylvia instructed the men to take turns pressing tightly over the folded rags covering the wound. They did so while the three of them said nothing unless Sylvia had instructions to give them. Biff drifted in and out of consciousness, mumbling mostly indiscernible phrases to which Rodney replied with reassurances that he'd found the *'healer woman'* and if anyone could help him, it would be her.

Sylvia exchanged a surprised glance with Dougal upon hearing this, and they continued their vigil while the two strong men took turns putting pressure on the wound. With Biff unconscious again, it became eerily silent in the room, then he jolted into consciousness again and reached for Rodney, who was at his side while Dougal was taking his turn tending to the wound.

"We never woulda killed him," Biff muttered to his friend, barely audible. "No matter how much those snobbish folks was willin' t' pay us, we never woulda done it. Th' man ought t' 'ave 'is daughter; nothin' wrong with that."

"I know it, Biff," Rodney said and sniffled. "I know it."

Again, Sylvia exchanged an astonished gaze with Dougal. It was impossible for a man in Biff's condition to be lying; only truth could escape the lips of a person in such a terrible state. In fact, Sylvia doubted that Biff could hardly even be aware of what he was saying.

Biff fell unconscious again, and Rodney wiped his dirty sleeve across his face to dry tears before he came around the table and traded places with Dougal. The two men exchanged a nod but no words.

After nearly two hours of this routine, Sylvia was pleased to note that the bleeding had indeed mostly stopped, although she was keenly aware of the pile of blood-soaked rags on the floor, and the puddle of blood surrounding them. She was careful not to draw attention to the gruesome image that was evidence of how much blood Biff had lost. She didn't want to upset Rodney, but she sincerely doubted that Biff would survive. Still, she felt compelled to try and offer some hope, praying they might be blessed with a miracle. Rodney was thrilled to hear that Biff was bleeding very little now, and that Sylvia was going to do her best to stitch the wound now with the hope that it would help. But she realized that she had to be honest with him, and added in a cautious voice, "Nevertheless, he lost a great deal of blood, and such a thing can be difficult if not impossible to recover from. I have no way of knowing what kind of damage might have been inflicted by the knife inside of his belly, and I don't have the knowledge to do anything about such things. If he survives the loss of blood and the internal damage, I will do everything in my power to use my remedies to fight off infection and to help the wound heal, but I cannot make you any promises, Rodney. It's truly a terrible wound."

Rodney nodded and bowed his head. "I understand, miss," he said humbly. "I thank ye greatly for doin' all ye can."

"Of course," Sylvia said and set to work stitching the wound while Dougal held a lamp right above it and handed her everything she needed. "May I ask what happened?" she asked, mostly trying to distract Rodney, and grateful that Biff was unconscious so he couldn't feel any pain. You don't have to tell me, but—"

"Ol' Biff was at the pub drinkin' too much as he does. Ever since he lost his wife and little one from a fever, he's always prone t' drink too much. After we'd left the pub and I was walkin' him back t' a place in the woods where we'd been hidin' out and sleepin', a man as drunk as Biff bumped into us and then started shoutin' at us like it was our fault and I just tried to move along but this man pulled a knife on us and b'fore I knowed what was happenin', he just stabbed my man Biff and run off. That's all I know. But it don't seem right. It's just not right."

"That is for certain!" Dougal said with enthusiastic compassion and Rodney looked directly at him for the first time since this ordeal had begun.

Rodney was overcome with tears again as he said with sincerity to Dougal, "We never woulda killed ye. When Biff shot ye, he made sure it wouldn't do ye much harm. It was just enough t' be able t' tell those who'd hired us that we'd tried, but . . ." He hung his head with regret.

Dougal shared a concerned glance with Sylvia, which she took to mean that Rodney believed he was speaking to Dougal Heywood and not Daniel Hewitt, despite all he might have been told about the strange resemblance. Sylvia didn't know what to do about that, but this was not the moment for such concerns.

"We can talk about that later," Dougal said. "Why don't you try to get some rest and I'll sit with Biff for a while."

"Oh, that's most kind," Rodney said, "but I couldn't sleep a bit if I tried. I'll sit with my man Biff . . . and God willin' he'll make it through the night."

"God willing," Sylvia repeated, not feeling a great deal of confidence in that respect. While she worked carefully to stitch the wound, regularly dabbing away some intermittent bleeding, she strongly suspected that irreparable damage had taken place inside. And she wondered what on earth they would do with Rodney should he lose his friend to this untimely death. Or what they would do with him if Biff hung on and needed weeks of medical care. Or what they would do with Biff's body if he were to die in their care. Questions and confusion and complications swirled around in her mind while her body felt as if it might collapse from sheer exhaustion. She was glad to have her task completed but wished that she felt more hope that it might have made a difference.

"Why don't you wash up and try to rest," Dougal said quietly to her.

Sylvia was simply too tired to argue. "Thank you. I'll be on the sofa in the parlor if I'm needed. Will you tell Rodney?"

"Yes," Dougal said, and Sylvia left the room, wishing she had insisted that Dougal also get some rest, but she figured he could do so if he wished. She wasn't at all worried now that Rodney might do harm to any of them, nor did she worry he might steal from them or any such thing. He was sincerely overcome with grief and fear, and she believed his humility and gratitude were genuine.

Sylvia fell asleep the moment her head relaxed on one of the sofa cushions. Her next awareness was Dougal's voice telling her she was needed while he nudged her shoulder gently. She sat up abruptly then took a moment to make certain she wasn't dizzy, aware that the room was filled with the light of dawn.

"What is it?" Sylvia asked as she stood and went with Dougal toward the workroom.

Dougal spoke quickly and walked slowly, as if he wanted her to have all of the pertinent information before they arrived at their destination. "The patient has mostly been unconscious beyond some brief bouts of muttering that we couldn't understand. Rodney hasn't left his side and I felt the need to stay awake and be there if I was needed—for any reason."

From the way he said it, Sylvia wondered if Dougal was implying that Rodney might very well be sincere and there was no reason to feel threatened by him, and he simply might have needed help with his ailing friend, but they also couldn't be completely sure they could trust him.

Sylvia simply said, "Thank you. I don't know how you managed to remain awake."

"I might have learned that ability during the war," he said, and Sylvia didn't have time to comment as they entered the workroom. She was glad to know that she and Dougal would have the opportunity to talk later about this situation when they had the time and privacy to do so.

Sylvia paused after coming through the open doorway when she realized that Biff was coherent—in a weak and dazed kind of way—and he was speaking with strain to Rodney in a voice that could barely be heard. Rodney was holding tightly to Biff's hand and mostly nodding as Biff spoke, while tears left streaks down Rodney's dirty face.

"I promise ye," Rodney said to his friend. "I promise ye I'll make it right. Don't ye fear none, now. Ye can meet yer maker free of guilt, my friend. We both know yer heart is good, and we knew why ye felt ye had t' do what ye did—and I'll make it right for both o' us. I promise ye."

Sylvia felt concerned to hear what were clearly dying promises. Her instinct was to rush forward and do something—anything—to try and save this man's life. But her eye was drawn to the evidence of lost blood on the floor. She wondered for a moment if she should have remained awake, but she immediately knew there was nothing more she could have done. If Biff survived the loss of blood, then she could treat the wound—but only from the outside. As she'd told Rodney last night, there was no way of knowing what damage there might be inside of Biff's belly.

Sylvia took a step forward but felt Dougal's hand on her arm, holding her back as he whispered, "Let them have their time. He's barely been breathing for more than an hour, and mostly unconscious. It's been evident for quite some time he wouldn't last long. We both know you did everything you could."

"How do you know he wouldn't last long?" she whispered back, glad to note that Rodney had no apparent awareness that they were even in the room.

"War gave me far too much exposure to dying men," he replied with a severe glance before he turned compassionate eyes toward Rodney and Biff. As if he'd read her mind, Dougal assured her once again, "There's nothing more you could have done, Sylvia, with the amount of blood he lost. Now I think we just need to help our new friend Rodney deal with this."

"Our new friend?" Sylvia echoed. "They tried to—"

Dougal put his fingers over Sylvia's lips to stop her. "Given what we've heard, we obviously need a more extensive conversation with the man, but I have a feeling that he can help us a great deal—given the situation."

Sylvia wasn't sure what he meant, but before she could question him, Rodney began sobbing Biff's name over and over in a way that made it clear his friend was gone. Sylvia rushed to Rodney's side and quickly pressed her fingers to Biff's throat to see if she could feel a pulse. She could feel nothing.

"Is he truly gone?" Rodney asked like a frightened child and Sylvia couldn't help but feel compassion for him.

"I'm afraid he is," Sylvia said gently. "I'm truly sorry, Rodney. I wish I could have done more."

Rodney pressed his face to Biff's shoulder and wept uncontrollably. Sylvia and Dougal exchanged a concerned glance but at the moment there was nothing either of them could say or do but allow Rodney to be able to express his grief and shock. They both sat down in respectful silence, with no idea how long they would have to wait, but it was only a matter of minutes before Rodney seemed to lose his strength and he reluctantly let go of Biff, stumbling backward onto a chair that was behind him. Sylvia was grateful for the way that Dougal rushed to move another chair right next to Rodney's where he sat and put an arm around the man's shoulders.

"I'm so sorry, Rodney," he said. "We both wish we could have done more, but—"

"I know ye did all ye could," Rodney said, looking at the floor. "Th' healer woman is a kind one. Ye was both kind t' let us into yer home after what we did. I'm glad my man Biff died here and not out in th' woods somewhere. I'm surely grateful t' know we did all we could instead o' wonderin' if he coulda been saved, but . . ." He seemed to run out of the strength to finish his words.

"But he *couldn't* have been saved," Dougal said with compassion, "still, he left this world knowing he had the best of friends in you." Rodney nodded and sniffled loudly. Dougal glanced toward Sylvia, silently declaring that he had no idea what to do now. Sylvia shrugged to indicate she had no idea either. She was grateful when Dougal said to Rodney, "We have some decisions to make and much to talk about, but right now I think you should get cleaned up and get some rest. Everything else can wait until you're rested enough to think more clearly."

Rodney thought about Dougal's suggestion for several moments before he finally nodded and said, "That's awful kind of ye, sir. I confess I feel so tired I don't think I can even . . ."

"Come along, my good fellow," Dougal said, urging the man to his feet. "I'll help you get settled."

Sylvia gave Dougal a nod of appreciation before he left the room with Rodney, leaving Sylvia alone with Biff's body. She wondered for a moment where he'd gotten a name like Biff, and what they were supposed to do with his body. Her mind wandered for a few minutes through matters of life and death before she was startled by the thought that George and Millie would be up and about soon, and she had much to tell them, but she didn't want either of them coming upon the dead body and the gruesome amount of blood in the workroom.

She hurried to find the key to the door, a key she hadn't used in a very long time. With the key in one hand, she put the other on Biff's shoulder with a reverent farewell to this stranger who had died in her home before she left the room and locked the door, not wanting to think about all they had to contend with this day.

Sylvia was glad to get up to her room before George and Millie came out of *their* room. The water there was very cool, but she was still glad to have it to freshen up while she thought of Rodney needing to use water the same temperature to clean up. There certainly hadn't been time to heat any water, but they could prepare the man a nice hot bath later.

Sylvia changed her clothes and smoothed her hair before she went downstairs to go out to the barn to milk the cow and gather the eggs before Millie even got to the kitchen. She was glad for the fresh air and early morning light that somehow helped cleanse away the awfulness of the night's events. Once alone in the barn, the reality of watching a man die overcame her in waves and she sank onto a bale of hay as she sobbed helplessly, glad to be alone and far from the house.

After many minutes of crying, Sylvia managed to pull herself together and focus on her tasks while her mind swirled an endless string of questions about this bizarre situation. She finally banished all pointless thoughts from her head, knowing such questions could not be answered until later when they were able to speak more with Rodney, and she would very much need Dougal and George and Millie to help her know how to solve certain problems—and to help deal with the presence of Rodney in her home. She wondered what kind of strange alignment of the stars and planets might have occurred that was bringing strange men in need into her home. But she was certainly grateful to have Dougal here to help her deal with Rodney and the dead body of his friend.

Sylvia finished her chores and took several deep breaths before she headed back to the house with the buckets of eggs and milk, covered with clean towels. She entered the house and set the buckets down in the usual place before she slipped her feet out of Daniel's boots. She turned around to see both George and Millie in the kitchen, unaware that anything unusual had happened during the night. Millie was just beginning to prepare breakfast and George was about to go outside to see to a few chores before eating.

"There's something I need to tell you and it can't wait. Let's sit down." She motioned toward the chairs around the table and they both looked astonished and concerned as they hesitantly took their seats and she sat down across from them.

"We had late-night visitors," Sylvia began.

"We heard the knock at the door," George said, "but we was already in bed and thought it would just be someone wanting to buy your remedies, so we went to sleep. Should we not have done—"

"No, it's fine," Sylvia said. "I'm glad you both went to sleep. If I'd needed you, I would have come to get you; you know that."

"What's happened?" Millie asked, sounding deeply concerned. They had both surely picked up on Sylvia's especially somber mood.

"Well," she drawled, giving herself a few more seconds to think of the right words to begin, but she realized she just needed to tell them the story from the beginning. There was no careful wording that would change the fact that there was a dead body in the workroom. And adding to the drama, a man they'd formerly believed to be a villain was upstairs in one of their extra bedrooms.

Sylvia had barely told them *who* had come to the door and why before Millie bellowed, "Well, if that isn't just the cow wearing a hat!"

"I'm sure it is," Sylvia said too severely for such an outlandish expression. "Likely more than it has ever been before." She continued with her story, telling them everything, and they both gasped when she told them that Biff had died. She went on to tell them how upset Rodney was, taking extra care to explain the man's humility and multiple apologies before she told them that he was currently upstairs with Dougal. This seemed to surprise George and Millie, but they had no protests. It seemed they understood that this was the only possible thing they could do for the man. Rodney's regret seemed sincere, and he'd also been divested of his weapons. Sylvia also mentioned that Rodney didn't seem to know if the man helping him was Dougal Heywood or Daniel Hewitt, and they would have to consider what exactly to tell him in that regard. But that could certainly wait.

When there was no more to say, Sylvia waited through a grueling silence for their reactions, and George finally said, "Well, I'll be a donkey's dinner!" He sighed loudly and there was more silence before he added, "I doubt any one of us could have imagined such events."

"No, we certainly couldn't," Sylvia said.

"And now we've got some problems to deal with," George added, and she was grateful for his insight, since she couldn't deal with the present challenges without their help.

"Yes, we certainly do," she said but couldn't think of anything else to say so she added, "but let's just have breakfast and do our morning chores while Rodney rests—and Dougal surely needs some rest as well, and then we'll talk about what to do exactly. I think we need more answers from Rodney, but we can't talk to him until he's gotten some sleep."

"Of course that's what we should do," Millie said and stood up to return to preparing breakfast. George followed her example and headed outside to work on his chores until it was time to eat. Sylvia just sat there, her mind swirling once again with questions she couldn't answer and problems that wouldn't be easy to solve.

Chapter Seven

The Stranger in the House

Sylvia was grateful to be startled out of her troubled thoughts when Dougal came down the stairs to report that Rodney was settled into bed in a spare room and he was hopefully exhausted enough that he would be able to sleep despite his overwhelming grief.

Dougal sat at the table near Sylvia and said, "He was glad for some water to wash up even though it wasn't at all warm. Apparently these men have been sleeping on the ground in the woods, or sneaking into people's barns at night. I don't know the entire story yet, but it's evident they have very little money and they've been using what they have to purchase bread to keep themselves fed—and liquor, which I suspect they put a high priority on because they are both ridden with a great deal of guilt and confusion." Dougal sighed. "Rodney is deeply broken by Biff's death." He shook his head. "I sincerely believe we don't have anything to fear from him."

"I agree," Sylvia said, "but we'll keep all of the weapons in the house hidden anyway."

"Very wise," Dougal agreed and went on. "I let him use one of my clean nightshirts, which was a little snug on him, but it worked. I think the clothes he was wearing ought to be burned, and once he's rested and had something to eat, he needs a good scrubbing from head to toe and the bedsheets ought to be well cleaned too before they're used again." He shook his head once more. "As you know, I've had my own experience of having to sleep rough, with nothing to my name. I don't know what drove these men to do the same. We have some clues from the things they said, but there's still a great deal we don't know. Still, I do hope you're all right with giving the man a place to rest and food to eat for at least a day or two."

"Of course," Sylvia said.

"And I suppose we'll be digging a grave for poor Biff. I don't suspect we can call on the undertaker without causing problems for Rodney—and perhaps ourselves."

Sylvia hadn't even thought about that—which made her glad that Dougal *had* thought about it. She was more grateful to have him here than she ever could have said—especially when she felt too numb and overcome to say much of anything.

"Thank you for your help," she managed to murmur.

"I'd do anything to help you," he said with a glimmer of devotion in his voice that surprised Sylvia, but she was too distracted to think about it for more than a moment. "I'm glad I was here to help."

"Even though these are the men who tried to kill you?" Sylvia asked.

"If we believe they were telling the truth—and I think we do—I can't speak for you, but I don't think either of them were in any condition to be lying. It all sounded honest to me—which means they didn't actually try to kill me. They are guilty of *shooting* me, but it seems there's a lot we don't know about that, and we won't know until we can speak to Rodney. I believe we'll be far more likely to get that information from him by giving him shelter and food and assistance burying his friend than we would if we turned him out."

"I would do my best to offer him those things anyway," Sylvia said, "but you make a fair point." After a brief pause, she said, "There's something else." Dougal's attention became even more intent. "I think Rodney is confused as to whether you are the man they shot or Daniel Hewitt who was supposedly here for months before then. And I'm not certain what to tell him."

Dougal looked as dumbfounded and confused as Sylvia felt. He finally said, "That's something I think we need to think about and discuss further before we say anything to him on the matter."

"I agree," she said, glad to know she didn't have to deal with *that* alone. In fact, she didn't feel alone at all in facing these new challenges.

Of course, George and Millie were always here and willing to do whatever was needed. But Dougal's kindness and assistance buoyed Sylvia up and she felt deeply grateful to have him here. "Thank you," she said, wanting to say more but fearing her words would only come out sounding foolish.

Nothing more was said before they set to work helping Millie put breakfast on. After Dougal had eaten, he gladly followed Sylvia's firm instructions to go to his room and get some sleep. George declared that once his mandatory chores were done, he would sit in the room where Rodney was sleeping to keep an eye on him and be there when he woke up to make certain he had what he needed.

"I bet he'll be mighty hungry," Millie said. "I'll put a plate in the oven for him to keep it warm."

"Thank you both," Sylvia said. "I think I'm going to try and get a little more rest myself. I have a feeling it's going to be a long day."

"Would seem that way," Millie said, and Sylvia dragged herself up the stairs, grateful beyond words for those who were here to help her, otherwise she would be utterly defeated.

Sylvia was glad that her rumbling thoughts hadn't kept her from sleeping. When she awoke, the clock let her know that she'd missed lunch, but she wondered what else she had missed. She hurried to freshen up and went down to the kitchen where she found no one, but voices conversing led her to the dining room where she was surprised to find everyone—including Rodney—sitting around the teapot, with a cup and saucer on the table in front of each of them. Before anyone noticed her, she saw a cup and saucer in front of an empty chair next to where Dougal was sitting and she knew it was intended for her. As she stepped farther into the room all eyes turned toward her.

"Oh, there you are, Missus," Millie said. "Did you get yourself some sleep?"

"I did, thank you," she said and stopped when Rodney came to his feet. She was quick to notice that he was wearing a set of George's shirt and trousers. The clothes were a tad too short and a little large around the waist but were being held up by braces. She assumed the boots he wore were his own. He was dramatically cleaner, and his face had been shaved. In fact, she hardly recognized him, given such a drastic change in appearance.

"Mrs. Hewitt," he said, his voice humble while he looked more at the floor than at her. "I must thank ye once again for all ye did t' try and save my dear friend Biff. It's hard t' let him go, but I'll rest easier knowin' that someone so kind tried so hard t' save him."

"You're very welcome, Rodney," she said. "I wish I *could* have saved him, but . . ." Her words became lost as she struggled to think of a way to finish the sentence that wouldn't sound insensitive.

"I understand, Missus," he said, apparently following the example of Millie. "There's no need t' explain. Ye was awful kind t' take us in at all after what we done. I just . . . needed t' thank ye again."

Sylvia nodded and moved past him to be seated and Rodney sat back down, his countenance heavy with grief. She was glad to hear Millie break a growing tension in the silence when she stood and said, "You must be starving, Missus. I've got your lunch keeping warm in the oven."

"Thank you," Sylvia said and poured herself a cup of tea. Before she was finished stirring in a little milk and sugar, Millie was setting a plate in front of her. "Thank you," Sylvia said again and took a bite of her food while Millie sat back down. Silence ensued as she began her lunch, but after Sylvia had chewed and swallowed without anyone saying a word, unable to bear the silence, Sylvia said, "I had no idea I would sleep that long. Now that I'm awake, there are things we need to take care of, and—"

"Everything is taken care of," Dougal said quietly. "Our deceased friend has been properly buried in the woods, and the workroom is clean."

"Truly?" Sylvia asked, unable to eat until she heard more of an explanation. "How did you manage?"

George explained, "We didn't figure anyone would come out this way and happen upon us doing such a deed that could appear suspicious without knowing what had taken place, but just to make certain we avoided any trouble, we moved the wagon close to the back door and carried him out—respectfully covered with one of the blankets you keep in the workroom, those that you sometimes give to others in need when they come for remedies." Sylvia nodded and he continued. "We men went deep into the woods where the trees are thick and we'd not be seen. Together we dug a proper grave and laid poor old Biff to rest."

Rodney sniffled and Dougal added, "We sang a hymn and spoke a prayer and Rodney had some lovely words to say."

"We did it right proper," Rodney said and sniffled again, wiping his face with a clean handkerchief that had apparently been given to him for this purpose; she suspected that it too belonged to George.

"I'm glad to hear it," Sylvia said. "Every person who leaves this world deserves a peaceful resting place and a proper farewell."

With that said Sylvia continued to eat since she was very hungry, but she wished that someone else at the table would engage in some conversation as opposed to the only sounds in the room being her fork occasionally meeting with her plate, cups being set into saucers, and Rodney's occasional sniffling. She finally brought up a topic that she considered obvious. "Rodney, you told us some things last night that answered some questions for us, but what you said also left me with many other questions about the situation. I don't know if you've all had this conversation while I was sleeping, but I—"

"Actually," Dougal said, "we've been rather busy cleaning up the workroom, and . . . taking care of the burial and . . . then we all needed to clean ourselves up. Once we'd had lunch, I think we all just needed to . . ."

"Just sit and have a nice cuppa," Millie said when he hesitated. "And in you came, Missus."

"I'll tell ye everything I know," Rodney declared firmly. "I owe ye that and much more. I wonder though if ye could answer me a question first."

"We'll surely try," Sylvia said, almost certain she knew what the question was.

"How is it," Rodney asked, his expression looking almost child-like with overt confusion, "that the Dougal Heywood we was paid t' deal with looks so much like ye, Mr. Hewitt? Or are ye Mr. Hewitt? Bein' so upset about Biff, I think I didn't know who I was talkin' to when I talked t' ye, and I'm still mighty confused over which man ye are. Assumin' ye're Mr. Hewitt, where did Mr. Heywood disappear to once he got t' these parts?"

"That is a *very* good question, Rodney," Dougal said, and Sylvia held her breath, wondering how he might answer, "and I can only say that the uncanny resemblance between Dougal Heywood and myself is something that was a mystery to both of us." Rodney's eyes widened to hear even that much but he said nothing, listening expectantly to Dougal's explanation—as he continued to pretend he was Daniel. "You see, Dougal and I were in the same regiment in the war. We had great fun at times with the tricks we could play on our comrades due to our resemblance, but we also became very good friends and told each other a great deal about our lives."

Dougal cleared his throat and looked down for a long moment as he said, "Of course in the middle of war a man knows he could die, and yet in some ways it still seems impossible and difficult to prepare for." He looked back up at Rodney. "When Dougal was killed, I knew I needed to take care of some things on his behalf—given how good a friend he'd been to me. So I went to the village where he'd grown up and I worked off his debts to the people he'd swindled and cheated— actions which he had come to deeply regret. And then I did every- thing I could to get his daughter away from her grandparents, people he despised and did not want raising his daughter; a man certainly has the right to care for his own child, and I believed from what he'd told me about his deceased wife's parents that I could care for her far better than they could. They have money to spoil her, certainly, but it's love a child needs."

Dougal coughed slightly and glanced at Sylvia for a moment before he went on. A part of her felt relieved over the way his explana- tion made sense, but she also felt the deepening of a lie that affected them all. But what could they do? "When I made the decision to do this on my friend's behalf," Dougal went on, "I knew it meant allow- ing my wife to believe that I was dead, but my intention was to get little Rachel and bring her here and beg my wife's forgiveness. As I'm sure you've come to see she is a remarkable woman. She even went so far as to lie on my behalf and allow people to believe that I had been here at home longer than I actually had been, which I'm certain must have been very confusing for you. But then, we didn't know your side of the story; we had no idea what we were actually up against."

Dougal sighed deeply and gave Sylvia a convincingly poignant glance, as if they were truly husband and wife.

"I was not able to get Rachel away from her grandparents, and I'd wasted so much of what money I'd earned in trying that I ran out long before I got here. Thankfully my good wife was willing to take me in despite all I'd done to hurt her." He offered her a warm smile before he looked at Rodney again. "I am guessing that it's Dougal's father-in-law who hired you and Biff . . . to kill me . . . so that I wouldn't ever come back and try to retrieve Rachel again."

Rodney became shrouded with shame as he admitted, "That would be the truth of it, but . . . I hope ye can all believe me when I say that me and Biff ain't never killed anyone for any reason. We done things we weren't proud of, and we certainly broke th' law on some occasions. We was livin' in the next village over, hidin' there cuz we was in trouble with th' law where we'd come from in the west, and I s'pose we had a reputation cuz one night we got knocked out after leavin' a pub and dragged into a carriage and we woke up in some stables fancier than we'd ever seen. We was told we would get paid more money than we'd ever imagined if we did a job for the man we met there, though he had lots o' other men there protectin' him, lookin' all fierce and frightenin'. Thing is, it wasn't like he was offerin' us a job; it was more like he was tellin' us we had to do this or he'd do us both harm. We told 'em no and got out o' there, but then . . . some things changed, and . . ."

The shame in his countenance deepened and Sylvia wanted to ask what exactly had changed but she didn't want to halt his momentum so she remained silent while he finished his explanation.

"The next night we met up with a couple o' his men who went to a pub with us t' show us who we was s'posed t' get rid of, and it was you—but it weren't you, cuz . . ." Rodney shook his head. "How is it possible for two men t' be like twins when that's not so?"

Dougal shook his head. "Me and Dougal and all who knew us both often speculated over that very question. Our only conclusion was that it happens; sometimes a person just looks like another person. But it seemed even more incredulous that we ended up in the same regiment. We often talked about the possibility that perhaps there was a reason; that perhaps God had brought us together to accomplish some kind of good. After Dougal was killed, I believed that reason was my ability to *become* him and make right all of the things that he'd desperately wanted to make right." Dougal shrugged. "But only God knows for sure. And since I was not able to get Rachel, I feel as if I let him down."

Sylvia listened to Dougal's explanation—speaking as if he were Daniel—and it was evident he'd given the story a great deal of thought. Of course, Dougal was speaking from personal experience regarding nearly everything he was saying; he simply had to say it as if he were in truth a different man. And his acting skills had become very convincing.

"Then we gots t' go and get her!" Rodney declared, sounding both angry and determined. "The child belongs here with good people . . . not with th' likes o' them who would pay t' have a man killed."

A chorus of gasps followed Rodney's declaration, and then silence fell hard as those seated at the table all exchanged astonished glances as if they might be able to discern each other's opinions and know what to say by some kind of supernatural phenomenon. What Rodney didn't know was the fact that Dougal was pretending to be Daniel Hewitt. Dougal did indeed deserve to have his daughter with him, but they'd given Rodney the impression that the intention had been for Daniel and Sylvia Hewitt to take in the child of Daniel's deceased friend. Dougal had come here with nothing; he was in no position to take on the care of a child, which meant that Sylvia was now in the position of deciding whether or not she was in a position to do so— and if she was willing.

With her thoughts scrambling around in her mind like a dozen frightened mice scurrying away from a cat, Sylvia was glad to be able to find some sound words she could say, "That is . . . something I think we need to think about and discuss. It's a complicated situation, to be sure. There's no question about what is right, but we need to consider what we are actually capable of doing."

"Yes," Dougal said, and she appreciated his support. "It's a long ways to travel with a great deal of uncertainty—and even danger— regarding the possibility of whether we would even be able to get the child—short of kidnapping, and it wouldn't do any of us any good to create more trouble; I think we all have enough trouble from the situation already. There's also the matter of money; traveling costs money."

Sylvia looked at Dougal and almost said, *But it's your daughter!* She caught herself and instead murmured with the compassion she felt, "But it's Dougal's daughter, and Rodney has made a fair point that I think perhaps we need to consider more seriously than we have done previously. I have some money put away; I don't know if it's enough, but I do have some saved and I would gladly contribute what I have to this cause. How can we just abandon the child to—"

Dougal stood up abruptly which startled the others. "As you said, we need to give the matter some thought. We'll talk later. I've got some chores to see to."

Sylvia didn't know what chores those might be since he regularly helped in many different ways, but no one was counting on him to do any specific chores. She suspected that the issue regarding his daughter was tender for him and he was likely very upset to have been reminded so keenly of how he was being denied the right to have his daughter in his life. Hearing Rodney's side of the story had surely pressed old wounds to the surface, although there were still aspects to Rodney's story that were missing and Sylvia longed to ask him more questions, but not without Dougal present.

"Perhaps we all just need to—"

"Get some rest, I'd say," Millie interrupted Sylvia. "I'll find Mister Hewitt and tell him the same. It's been a long day already and there's nothing that needs attention that me and George can't take care of. Those of you who was up in the night should attempt a nap."

Sylvia wanted to remind her that she'd not been awake from her last nap all that long, but she didn't want to discourage Rodney from getting some rest. He looked as if he might slide off of his chair into a puddle.

"Come along," George said to Rodney, urging him to his feet with a gentle hand on his arm. "I do believe my missus is right. I'll make sure you don't miss supper. My Millie has already got some lamb in the oven, and you're going to love what my Millie can do with lamb."

Rodney nodded and Sylvia saw his lip quivering slightly. She was glad when George and Rodney left the room, and she waited until she'd heard their footsteps reach the top of the stairs before she said quietly to Millie, "This is a fine mess we're in now. How did all of this happen? Not so many weeks ago, life was simple and uncomplicated and . . . peaceful. And that's the way I prefer it."

"Perhaps," Millie said with the hint of a mischievous smile, "you shouldn't be taking in strangers right and left."

"And what was I to do? Leave them to suffer and—"

"No!" Millie reached across the table and put her hand over Sylvia's. "Of course not. That's what you need to remember. It's not in you or any of us to turn away a person suffering or in need. You did right. And we will work the rest out. We *do* need to all think on it and talk about the situation, but not while we're all so tired and overcome as we are now. All that grave digging and mopping up blood along with everything else is enough to handle for now, I think."

"It all sounds very macabre when you put it that way," Sylvia said, then couldn't help smiling when she added, "if the people in the village knew about *that,* my fate as a witch would surely be sealed."

Millie chuckled as she stood and picked up the teapot. "Then it's a good thing they don't know about *that.* And they never will."

Millie went into the kitchen and Sylvia took a bite of her now-cold lunch while her thoughts went to the little girl living with devious grandparents somewhere near the border of Scotland, and to her father who was living here—likely with a broken heart. How could she not help him? How could they not at least try to do everything in their power to get her back? She wished she had been more firm on this stance before. She wanted Dougal to know that she would do whatever she could to help him get his daughter back. But he'd seemed resigned to having given up for now. However, Rodney's declaration had now put the problem in a new light which made it impossible to ignore.

Sylvia needed to find Dougal and make certain he was all right. Given his reference to doing chores, she assumed the most likely place to find him was the barn. She entered to see him there hard at work, flinging straw with a pitchfork in a way that made it clearly evident he was upset—and she couldn't blame him.

"Dougal," she said. He gasped as he turned to look at her for only a second before he stuck the prongs of the pitchfork into the ground and leaned on it, looking away, which gave her a perfect view of the tight muscles in his face. "We need to talk, I think."

"You're kind, as always, Sylvia, but this is not your responsibility. I did not come here to bring trouble to your doorstep and yet I have. And I certainly did not come here to burden you regarding any aspect of this situation with Rachel."

"But she's your daughter," Sylvia said with a plea of urgency. She couldn't even imagine how all of this must feel for him. "And even if she were not, how can we stand by knowing an innocent child is in the care of such people when we could do something about it?"

"And *what* exactly could we do?" he asked, looking at her sharply.

"I have four good horses and a carriage," Sylvia declared, gesturing around. "We can simply . . . go and get her."

"No, we cannot!" he countered, sounding angry. "Do you think I didn't exhaust every possibility of getting her away from those people? I had a great deal of time to think while I made my way here, Sylvia, and I've accepted the fact that I have to let her go—at least until she gets older. I have to just . . . do my best to think of the positive facets of her situation. Her grandparents will leave her in the care of nannies and governesses, and perhaps they will be kind and help her find her way with some goodness. And at least she will never go hungry . . . she will never go without." He turned a hot gaze toward her and added, "I have nothing to give her, Sylvia; nothing. How can I possibly care for a child when I can't even care for myself? I am completely at your mercy for now. I should find work and move on, and I will, but . . ." He looked down as if he were drawing courage. "My business on your husband's behalf is not finished, and I can't leave here until it is." He looked at her again while Sylvia's heart took to pounding.

She was wondering how to ask what on earth he could be talking about when Dougal said more calmly,

"We should sit down." He motioned toward the bales of hay that had become more like furniture than something to feed the animals.

Sylvia was glad to get off of her feet when she realized her legs were trembling slightly and she didn't want them to give way. *What could he be talking about? What business could he possibly need to see to on Daniel's behalf?*

After Dougal was seated, he leaned his forearms on his thighs and looked at the ground. His countenance was carved into shame and regret, and he was clearly trying to avoid looking at her. Following a long moment of silence while Sylvia feared he might hear the thudding of her heart, Dougal cleared his throat and said, "I meant to tell you the first day I was here. It was, after all, one of the biggest reasons he wanted me to come here. He told me many times that if he didn't survive, you had to know about this. I should have said something long ago, but the time just never seemed right, and . . . now . . . it feels more wrong than ever, because . . . you're talking about the money you have . . . and offering it to help me go and get Rachel—which I still believe is an impossible venture, so don't be thinking that what I'm about to tell you is meant to influence you in that regard. But it can't wait any longer, and—"

"Will you just tell me what it is you're trying to say?" Sylvia snapped impatiently. "Tell me and then we can determine whether or not I should be angry with you . . . or if it has anything at all to do with my desire to help you get your daughter back. Just tell me!"

Dougal took in a loud breath and looked firmly at Sylvia, as if he'd drawn all of his courage to do so. "Daniel left a great deal of money hidden here, and he desperately wanted you to know about it and to have it." Sylvia found it difficult to even draw breath while her mind swirled with a barrage of questions, and thankfully Dougal continued. "He told me where it's hidden, and—"

"And you've not been tempted to seek it out on your own?" she asked, sounding far too accusatory.

"No, Sylvia. It's *your* money. I thought I had proven myself trustworthy by now. You told me that you trust me, and yet you question my motives and—"

"Forgive me but this is . . . not something I ever expected to hear and I'm having trouble taking it in. And . . . I'm not sure I want to know about this money, or to ever have it in my hands. He swindled and cheated people out of money. It's not really *mine*, now, is it? But I don't have the means to return any of it to its rightful owners, therefore it feels . . . tainted. If he meant to offer me some kind of security with this knowledge, I'm not sure that I—"

"Please let me finish, Sylvia," he said, putting a hand over hers where it was gripping the bale of hay in her attempt to remain steady. She nodded and he went on. "He told me there is a ledger with the money that clearly states where the money came from and who it belongs to . . . which would give you the means to return it to the rightful owners."

"Oh," Sylvia said, feeling herself sit up straighter. The very idea of having *that* burden lifted was deeply heartening. She felt certain there was a great deal of money Daniel had spent through the years—money that she had certainly benefitted from—and it would be impossible to return everything he'd acquired illegally. But to know that she could at least return some of it helped her feel better about Daniel's illicit dealings than she had in years.

Sylvia's mind was so caught up in imagining herself being able to send money back to people from whom it had been taken illegally that she was startled to hear Dougal say, "And not all of the money was obtained through illegal methods, Sylvia. Daniel was a gambler; I'm certain you know that."

"I suspected more than actually knew for certain," she admitted, embarrassed to realize how little she'd really known her husband in some respects.

"He played a great deal of poker, and he was very good at it. He won an enormous amount of money legitimately. When a man gambles in this way, if he puts money down on the table to make a bet, he's declaring his willingness to lose it if another player wins. I don't know how much money is there, Sylvia, but I know where it is, and I can help you return what's owed to others according to the ledger he kept. And whatever else is left belongs to you. He wanted you to have it so your needs would be met."

"My needs *are* met," Sylvia declared, feeling angry without entirely understanding why—although it wasn't difficult to assess that discussing Daniel's methods of acquiring money had always irked her. Suddenly overwhelmed by all of this, she stood abruptly and declared, "I cannot deal with this right now, Dougal. I'm glad you told me, and . . . I ask you to leave the matter alone until . . . I'm ready . . . and then we'll find it together. I would indeed appreciate your help in making things right with it as much as possible, but . . . there is too much on my mind . . . too much drama has occurred already today. I just . . . need to be alone."

Dougal sighed and said, "Then you should be alone. When you need to talk . . ." His sentence faded as Sylvia hurried out of the barn as quickly as she could walk without actually running. And with every step she became more and more angry. If money and a ledger had been left behind by Daniel, would he not have been wise to inform his wife before going off to war? Sylvia's needs were met well enough, and she felt very blessed in that regard. She had her home, the animals, the land, and the income from the farms she leased. The issue that angered her was not so much the money itself but the principle of the matter. No man could go to war and be certain he would return home. Why would Daniel not have told her? It was just one more facet of his behavior that infuriated her. He'd always been prone to keeping secrets from her, and she hated him for it!

Sylvia decided to go for a walk before going back into the house since she was still bursting with anger, and she didn't want to encounter anyone else until she'd had the chance to calm down. Despite her anger, she couldn't deny her gratitude for Dougal telling her, and she *would* have him help her as he'd offered. The thought of being able to return money to at least some of Daniel's victims gave her the hope of feeling some degree of peace and perhaps redemption on Daniel's behalf. Sylvia herself was not guilty of any crime, but Daniel was her husband, and if she could make right on his behalf even a little, she believed it might help her feel better about letting go of her difficult feelings toward him. Nevertheless, for the moment she just needed to be angry.

Sylvia walked with excessive speed in an attempt to eliminate her anger and confusion. Her pace slowed as her body proved that it simply wasn't capable of maintaining such speed. She finally felt ready to return to the house even though she knew she still had a great deal to think about. As she opened the back door and stepped inside, all of the other recent drama rushed back over her. A man had died in her home despite all of her best efforts to save him. He'd been buried in the woods and the blood had been cleaned away, but Sylvia's memories of the experiences made her shudder. And Rodney—a man who had once left her terrified—was staying in one of her spare bedrooms and she felt no threat from him whatsoever. Oh, how quickly life could change! She thought of the changes in her life—and in her home—since she'd found Dougal hiding in her barn and found she could hardly recall what life had been like before his arrival.

All of Sylvia's deep thoughts fled as Millie approached her in the hall, speaking with quiet urgency, "Oh, you're back! Praise heaven!"

"What's happened?" Sylvia demanded, also speaking quietly as she wondered if Millie's tone indicated that she didn't want them to be overheard.

"It's taken care of now . . . at least for the moment, but . . . our new friend Rodney was in such a state!" Millie put her hands on both sides of her face. "I don't know that I've ever seen a man so upset. We all tried to talk to him and say the things a person needs to hear when they've lost someone dear, but it made no difference. Eventually we realized that he's upset over more than his friend's death, although he said he couldn't talk about it. Dougal kindly assured him that we could not offer assistance if we didn't know the problem, and Rodney got more upset, mumbling about how he didn't deserve assistance from us and on and on like that."

"Oh, my," was all Sylvia could think to say, increasingly grateful that she'd taken a very long walk so that she'd been spared the drama being described to her. "You said it's taken care of for the moment. How do you mean?"

"I insisted he drink a cup of tea to help him calm down, but I didn't tell him I'd added some of your sleeping tincture to it. He's now resting deeply, bless him. Whatever the problem might be, I'm certain that such a lack of sleep and the grief of losing his friend was making it all the worse. It's my hope that he'll be able to speak with us more rationally after he's had some rest."

"That's very good thinking," Sylvia said, "and we can only hope that's the case." She sighed and admitted, still speaking softly, "I'm glad that we were able to help him. There's nothing we could have done to save Biff, but at least Rodney can have the peace of knowing we tried . . . and we did give the man a proper burial. But now I'm not certain what exactly to do with Rodney. He seems sincere enough and I don't feel threatened by him anymore. In fact, I think he's got a rather soft heart beneath all of that gruff exterior."

"I would agree with that, Missus," Millie declared firmly.

"Still, I wonder how long he might intend to stay or—"

"It's your home and you can politely inform him that he needs to go whenever you feel it's the right time. You owe him nothing. You're a good and charitable woman, Missus, but that don't mean you gotta care for everyone in need."

Sylvia just nodded and said, "Thank you. I'll give that some thought. And perhaps when we're able to speak with him when he's in a more rational mood, we can assess exactly what his needs might be and make a plan to help him be on his way."

"Let's hope," Millie said and hurried away as if she had work to do.

Once alone, Sylvia went quietly up the stairs to her room where she freshened up and removed her shoes before crawling into her bed. She didn't feel as tired as she thought she might, but she did feel the need to just try and relax with the hope that doing so might help her think more clearly. She thought of little Rachel living with cold and devious grandparents and her heart ached even though she had no connection whatsoever to the child. She thought of Dougal being without his daughter, and all he'd gone through to try and get her back, and then all he'd gone through to come *here* in order to honor Daniel's last wishes. The thought of father and daughter being separated made her feel mildly nauseous. The situation was just horrible! And then she needed to add into that situation the fact that Rachel's grandparents had actually hired Rodney and Biff to follow Dougal and kill him. Although, from the way Rodney had told the story, it sounded less like they were hired and more like they'd been threatened. But it occurred to Sylvia that there was an aspect of this story that didn't make sense. Once Rodney and Biff had come to believe that Dougal was actually Daniel Hewitt, why had they continued to remain in the area? Had they believed—for some reason—that Dougal Heywood was still hiding somewhere around here? Well, he was! But they weren't to know that. Therefore, why had they remained so close, especially when they'd had no place to stay? She intended to ask Rodney and hoped he could give her an answer that made sense.

All things together, Sylvia was stunned over the complicated drama that had taken place within her own home—a drama that was far from resolved. And then there was the matter of Daniel's hidden money and accompanying ledger. She knew she had to find it and deal with it, and she would need Dougal's help since *she* certainly didn't know where it was. But that was a fact that made her angry all over again when she thought about it. Daniel had gone off to war and left a great amount of money hidden without telling his wife about it. If he was still alive, she'd slap him good and hard. But the moment that image went through her mind, she started to cry, knowing she would have immediately regretted it if she'd done any such thing. She more wanted to kiss him and hold him in her arms.

And then she found her thoughts wandering to a place where Dougal was holding her and kissing her as if he were the husband she'd lost. Their physical resemblance did not change the fact that Daniel was long dead, but neither did it alter the reality that Sylvia's feelings for Dougal were becoming something she had to acknowledge, even if she didn't want to. In her heart she knew that what she felt for Dougal had nothing to do with his looking so much like Daniel, but she doubted she could ever convince anyone else that such was the case—as if she would ever admit to her feelings aloud. She still believed the best thing for all of them would be for both Rodney *and* Dougal to leave her home and resume their lives elsewhere. Dougal was healed enough to manage on his own. He could surely find work and make a fresh start. And Rodney was fit and capable of working. He didn't need their charity beyond what they had already done for him.

Sylvia was surprised to feel herself jolt awake when she never would have expected to fall asleep, given the tumultuous and overwhelming nature of her thoughts. She could hear sounds from the kitchen that made it evident supper was being prepared. Sylvia hurried to freshen up and went downstairs, knowing she should help, and also wondering about Rodney's current condition. It occurred to her that he might still be sleeping but she entered the kitchen to find him sitting at the worktable, looking glum and somewhat dazed while Millie was busy at the stove.

"Oh, there you are," Millie said when she saw Sylvia, and Rodney glanced toward her as well. "I'm glad you got yourself another nap. The men have gone out to see to the evening chores with the animals while I finish up supper. I'm afraid I'm a little behind tonight."

"No need to apologize, Millie," Sylvia said. "I'm certain you'll see that we're all fed very well no matter what time supper is ready."

Sylvia habitually felt the need to help Millie but instinctively she knew that she needed to show some compassion toward Rodney first. While she was wondering what to say to him, he glanced up at her again quickly before he looked toward the window and said, "I done offered to help with the chores but I was told t' rest for t'day. I feel useless just sittin' here after all ye good people have done for me."

"Don't you worry about that," Sylvia said and resisted the temptation to ask him questions she wanted the answers to. She would be foolish to start talking about such things without having everyone present. "Did you get a good nap? You must have been exhausted."

"Yes, Missus. I didn't think I could sleep but I did."

"I'm glad to hear it," Sylvia said, exchanging a discreet mischievous glance with Millie. Sylvia added with compassion, "You've had a very trying time, Rodney. I'd say you well deserve to just relax while we get supper on. For tonight you are our guest. Tomorrow we will discuss how we can help you get along with your life." She hoped he would understand the implication that she wanted him to cease being her house guest, but again she determined that whatever conversation they needed to have should take place when everyone was present.

Sylvia got to work helping Millie, and they were just beginning to set dishes on the dining table when George and Dougal returned from the stable, leaving their boots by the door before they went to wash up.

Through the majority of their meal, little bits of conversation were exchanged that had absolutely no substance whatsoever. In between were long stretches of silence in which it was starkly evident that Rodney was barely managing to eat, and the cloud of grief hanging over him was so palpable that Sylvia almost expected it to start raining directly over Rodney's head. As Sylvia's mind wandered, she felt startled to consider all that had happened since bedtime the previous evening. A part of her wished that it had never happened, but there was no good in trying to wish away the past when it couldn't be changed, so she chose instead to be grateful that the worst was over. She hoped to never have to live through such an experience again. The only problem now was how to contend with Rodney and his grim visage that seemed to radiate melancholy throughout the room.

When Sylvia had eaten her fill, she felt the need to contend with the problem in a straightforward manner and stop trying to ignore the facts. They all knew Rodney was terribly upset about more than his friend's death, but according to Millie he'd said that he couldn't talk about it. With the help of the tincture in his tea, he'd been able to get some rest and calm down, but there was obviously something very wrong. Rodney and Biff had been sent to kill Dougal, and while Rodney obviously had regret over that, and apparently had never had the intention of actually killing him, there was clearly a great deal more to the story than what he'd told them thus far. Rodney now believed that Dougal was Daniel Hewitt, and he was clearly confused over that fact. Beyond that there were so many unanswered questions that needed to be answered before they determined the next logical steps. Sylvia didn't want Rodney staying in her home any longer than necessary, but she also didn't want him to leave until they were able to get as much information as possible from him so that Dougal could be safe. Since this was her home, she realized it was up to her to address the problems they were facing and, with any luck, the five of them seated at the table could communicate enough for them to all under-stand what had happened and why, and if there was still a threat to be faced.

Chapter Eight

Buried Treasure

"Rodney," Sylvia said, purposely maintaining kindness in her voice so that he wouldn't be put off by her questions. She felt frustrated and overwhelmed, but that wasn't Rodney's fault, and she didn't want any indication of her own present struggles coming through in the way she spoke.

"Yes, Missus?" he said politely, lifting his head to look at her, although she distinctly saw shame in his eyes.

"I know that losing your friend is very difficult for you, and we all have a great deal of compassion for what you must be going through. I feel the need to ask you some questions about the strange situation we're all in. I believe it's important for all of us to understand all that we can about what's happening so that we can solve the problems. I want you to know that my desire to talk about this and gain some understanding in no way contradicts the compassion I feel for your grief. Do you understand what I'm saying?"

"Yes, Missus," he said, looking down again as he set his fork on his plate and put his hands in his lap. At the moment he looked very much like an overgrown little boy who was expecting a good scolding.

Sylvia noticed that everyone else had also stopped eating, but unlike Rodney, they had mostly cleared their plates. George, Millie, and Dougal all wore very serious expressions, knowing this conversation was necessary and important, and they all looked at Sylvia with something akin to relief since she was the one taking charge.

Knowing she just needed to forge ahead and get this over with, Sylvia ignored everyone but Rodney and said gently, "You were very upset earlier . . . about something beyond your friend's death. We've opened our home to you, Rodney, and we did everything we could to help Biff."

"I thank ye for that," Rodney said, still looking down. "And I thank ye for helping see that he got a proper burial." He sniffled. "I can't thank ye enough for such kindness, and I want ye t' know that I'll be on my way as soon as ye want me t' go. I could go now. Ye have no duty t' let me stay and—"

"It might be best if you *are* on your way soon," Sylvia said, "but you can't set out this late. You need to at least stay tonight, and we need to talk about your situation. Do you have any kind of work to support yourself or—"

"I got money enough for now," Rodney said. "Me and Biff was sleeping in the woods so we could save the money we had. I have enough to manage, and I'll be fine. Thank ye, Missus. I'll set out t' leave first thing t'morrow."

"Before you go," Sylvia pressed on, "you told us when you first arrived that you would explain everything to us. You promised Biff when he was dying that you would make things right . . . or something to that effect. And yet earlier you said that you couldn't talk about it. Not one of us begrudges helping you, Rodney, nevertheless I think it's only fair that in return you tell us everything you know." Sylvia motioned toward Dougal with a dramatic flair that got Rodney's attention and he looked up. "Whether this man is Daniel Hewitt or Dougal Heywood, there are clearly people who would merely glance at him and assume him to be one or the other without any proof. If he is in danger, we need to know. What exactly is your role in all of this, Rodney? We will not be angry with you for telling us the truth, even if the truth you tell us might be . . . upsetting. Please, Rodney. Tell us what you know."

Sylvia felt confident that her plea had been well-spoken, and it had driven home the seriousness and necessity of this conversation. She believed that Rodney would be convinced to tell them what he knew, but she was wholly unprepared to have him hang his head and start crying with as much intensity as when Biff had died. The others at the table all exchanged glances of alarm while Rodney cried for several minutes, and everyone simply allowed him to vent his sorrow.

Sylvia was relieved when Millie stood and said, "I'm going to clear the table. George, why don't you men help Rodney to the parlor and we can all visit there after the supper's cleaned up."

Sylvia hurried to stand and help Millie, deeply grateful for an opportunity to be free of just watching Rodney cry and feeling utterly helpless. As she cleared the table, she saw George and Dougal kindly urging Rodney toward the parlor, and it seemed that Rodney was calming down a bit. Sylvia was grateful for Millie's insight, and it also occurred to her that the leftover food from supper needed to be stored properly so it wouldn't spoil. Even if they didn't have time this evening to clean all of the dishes, a certain amount of work had to be done in the kitchen so that breakfast could be prepared in the morning. Assuming they could get Rodney to start talking and tell them all he knew, they had no idea how long that might take, and it was better to have the work in the kitchen completed first.

Sylvia and Millie finally went to the parlor to join the men, who were all sitting in silence, and Rodney had that dazed expression on his face again.

"We're here now, Rodney," Sylvia said to alert him to their presence. At first she thought it was a silly thing to say since their entering the room would have been obvious, but the sound of her voice seemed to startle Rodney from some kind of trance and he looked up and nodded in response. He *hadn't* noticed the women coming into the room, but now that they were all gathered again, Sylvia prayed they could have this conversation and get it over with.

When nothing was said by anyone, Sylvia realized that she would likely need to take the lead once again. While she was considering the words she might use to help convince Rodney to talk openly with them, she was relieved beyond measure when Dougal leaned toward Rodney, looked him in the eye, and said gently but with a firmness that demanded attention, "Rodney, my good man. Will you not tell us what happened to bring you here? And why you're still here? I promise that not one of us will repeat what you share with us, and perhaps we are in a position to help each other." This made Rodney's eyes widen, as if it had never occurred to him that they could help each other.

Before Rodney could speak, Dougal asked a question that surprised Sylvia. "Rodney, despite what we told you before, I dare say you must be very confused over wondering for certain whether I am Dougal Heywood or Daniel Hewitt."

"I do feel confused," Rodney said. "I can't deny it, even though your story makes sense t' me. But me and Biff agreed that ye're th' man he shot; we just could never figure for certain how that was possible. How could ye be that man and also the man who had been here months before that time? Or was that just what ye told that dreadful man who claims t' serve the Lord our God? He's a hypocrite if ever I saw one, and I can understand why ye'd lie t' him t' stay safe, and ye didn't know nothin' about me and Biff except that we might be after ye, and we didn't blame ye none for doin' what ye had t' do t' protect yerselfs." He shook his head in disbelief. "I still don't understand how two men could look so much alike . . . or maybe it just feels . . . hard t' understand because we thought we was after one man and it turns out that we coulda made a terrible mistake because o' something we never thought could happen."

"I can assure you, Rodney, that you are not alone in your confusion and disbelief. Although I've heard many times since it came to light in my life that it is something that happens; it's rare but it does happen. I believe what's important right now is . . . well . . . you told us that Rachel's grandparents . . . forced you to follow me and kill me; that the two of you lived in a village a short distance from them and they'd heard of your reputation."

Rodney nodded. "We did things that weren't right, but we never killed no one and we never woulda done that. But . . ." Rodney hung his head in shame again and Sylvia sensed that he was once again on the verge of breaking down into helpless sobbing.

Not wanting this conversation to be delayed any further due to Rodney's excessive emotion, Sylvia hurried to say, "It's all right, Rodney. All of us have made mistakes. We are not going to judge you for your past crimes. We only need to know everything that *you* know regarding what you were sent here to do. I keep wondering why you remained in this area after you realized that the man you could have killed but only wounded might very likely have been the wrong man."

Rodney shook his head and muttered, "I *do* need t' tell ye all the truth. It's just that . . . they told me if I told anyone—anyone at all—that they'd kill my boy."

"What?" The word burst out of Sylvia's mouth. It was the last thing she'd expected to hear him say, although she couldn't deny that it already made a great many things make more sense—even though they still knew almost nothing.

"Me and Biff told them no, we wasn't gonna do it. Biff got no family. His wife and little one died. It's just him on his own. My wife died too, bringin' my little Bob int' the world. Biff lived with me and my Bob. We helped each other out and we was doin' better in the ways we made our livin' and such. That's why we told 'em no, that and we ain't never killed nobody. Next day . . ." Rodney's chin quivered, "little Bob went outside t' play and when I went out t' check on him he . . . was gone." Rodney was fighting to not get upset again but his struggle was visible. "A note was nailed to a tree not far from the door. I could have my boy back when I brought proof that you were dead." He nodded toward Dougal. "But I don't even know for sure if ye're the man they want." He threw his hands in the air and coughed to choke back a sob. "But how would I convince them o' that? So ye see, me and Biff has been in a quandry . . . not wantin' t' hurt anyone but . . . wonderin' how t' get my boy back and . . ." He finally gave into his emotional battle and hung his head to cry. "Oh, my poor boy. It's been so long. What if somethin's happened t' him already? What if . . ." Rodney completely broke down.

Sylvia gave him a minute or so to vent his emotion before she asked, "Rodney? What kind of proof? How can you prove that someone is dead when they live so many miles from here?" He sniffled and wiped his nose with his handkerchief, clearly trying to prepare himself to answer, but Sylvia felt impatient and asked, "Do you need to take back some possession of his or—"

"No, Missus," he said then surprised them all by speaking directly to Dougal, "How is it possible for you to be Daniel Hewitt if Dougal Heywood has that very mole on his finger?"

Sylvia gasped softly the same moment she saw Dougal look startled—and guilty. Rodney had just figured out the truth, despite everything he'd been told, and how hard Dougal had worked to be able to impersonate Daniel.

While Sylvia was wondering what they could possibly do next, Dougal did the only thing possible when caught in a lie: he told the truth. "You're right, Rodney. I'm not Daniel Hewitt, but that doesn't mean the story I told you isn't otherwise true. And it's vitally important for people around here to believe that I *am* Daniel and I think I speak for my friends here when I ask you to please not tell anyone the truth."

"I promise ye that," Rodney said. "Ye've been good t' me and I'd not do nothin' t' cause ye any more trouble than I already have." He sighed loudly. "I thank ye for tellin' me; it makes things less confusin' for certain, because . . . well . . . gettin' back t' the proof these people wanted from me . . ." He hesitated and grimaced, making Sylvia wince in some kind of preparation for the answer; she had a strange feeling it was going to be something quite macabre. "His finger, Missus. The one with the mole." Rodney nodded toward Dougal's hand which was planted on his thigh before he looked at the floor with that ashamed countenance that was common for him.

"Oh, good heavens!" Sylvia said as the idea fully sunk in. "They truly wanted you to bring back the finger of a dead man?" Rodney nodded without looking up. "What kind of people are they?"

George finally entered the conversation, sounding angry. "They're the kind of people that have little Rachel in their care—and Rodney's boy too. Now, I know I'm not in charge around here, Missus, and I'll do whatever you would have me do, but . . . I don't know how we can just sit around here in our comfort and leave these little ones with such people. Don't we need to at least try to get them back? To see that they're safe and cared for by people who'll love them? I know traveling costs money . . . but we can take as much food as possible from home that won't spoil; we can take turns sleeping in the carriage. I know that it's possible to leave our horses in a reliable livery and we can borrow other horses along the way to keep them fresh so we don't have to stop for long. I can drive the carriage, Missus, and I will. We need to go and get them! Me and Millie got some money put away. It's not much but we would give it to help."

"We certainly shall!" Millie declared as if she might challenge these despicable grandparents to a duel. "I'd give every penny we have to help those poor little ones."

"But you're saving that money to—"

Sylvia was interrupted by Millie saying, "Doesn't matter. Me and my dear George don't even have to talk about this. I think it's evident we are in agreement." The two exchanged a nod, a smile, and a wink almost in perfect unison.

"But you can't drive all day every day, George," Sylvia said.

"I can drive a carriage and four," Rodney said, looking up with something new showing in his countenance—hope.

"As can I," Dougal said.

"I'll stay here and take care of the house and the animals," Millie said firmly, "and if you travel as fast as George has said, you'll be back in no time at all—hopefully having gotten those children away from such . . . devils."

"I think Sylvia needs to stay here with Millie," Dougal said. Sylvia was briefly distracted by the fact that were it not for the money that he'd told her was hidden somewhere, they likely wouldn't have enough to embark on this venture—even if they put together all of what they had. But everyone seemed determined to make this happen—perhaps on faith. And if Daniel had truly left money behind, perhaps that faith was warranted. "There's nothing she can do. The trip will be exhausting, and it's best if you're not left alone here, Millie."

"I'll think for myself, thank you very much," Sylvia said to him.

"I beg your pardon," Dougal said with mild sarcasm. He then nodded at Rodney, showing a hint of a smile, "We have all learned not to argue with the missus when she makes up her mind to something." Dougal turned to Sylvia and said, "I can understand why you would want to go, and you need to make up your own mind, but this could be a dangerous endeavor, and I think we would all feel better if you remained safely at home."

"I . . . don't know. I need to think about it." She let out an exasperated sigh. "I don't doubt that we need to do this. I agree that we cannot in good conscience leave these children in such a situation. I just think we need to . . . sleep on it, think through the details. Might we talk at breakfast and decide a feasible plan? I think we're all exhausted."

"The missus is right," Millie said.

"As always," Dougal said and winked at her in a way that made her stomach flutter and she looked away quickly. But there was something in her that felt grateful Rodney knew the truth. While she'd not had time to think about it much, the idea of Rodney figuring out that Daniel was actually Dougal had been adding to her stress. At least that was one less thing to worry about.

"Is there anything else you need to tell us, Rodney?" Sylvia asked.

"Not that I can think of at the moment," he said, "but I feel as if my mind's gone t' porridge."

"It's been a very difficult time since you arrived here last night," Sylvia said. "George will make certain you have all you need for the night, and Millie will fix you a cup of my special tea to help you relax." She gave Millie a discreet nod that Millie returned.

"I'd like that very much," Rodney said. "Thank ye. Ye're the kindest people I think I've ever come t' know."

Sylvia was relieved to have Rodney in the care of George and Millie, and especially relieved to simply know that this day was over. She could go to bed and wake up with a rested mind and body before she had to determine exactly what should happen next. She could only see two impediments to her getting a good night's sleep, the first being her sudden inability to even get out of her chair, let alone all the way up the stairs. Her second concern was the myriad of thoughts and dilemmas consuming her mind. She could only pray that God would help her sleep by making the exhaustion of her body overcome the busyness taking place in her mind.

"Are you all right?" Sylvia heard and looked up to see Dougal still sitting across from her even though the others had left the room.

"Just . . . very tired, and . . . overwhelmed," she admitted.

"Understandably so," he said with sincere compassion. "Talk to me. Tell me what's troubling you most."

"I don't have any doubt that we need to go and get these children, but exactly how to go about it is . . . well . . . overwhelming." She focused more directly on Dougal and added in a whisper, "We need to find that money. I'd give all that I have to see that these children are safe." She lowered her voice even further. "Rachel is your daughter, Dougal. She should be with you. This is simply not right."

"I cannot argue with that," he said. "Nevertheless, you've already done so much for me. I cannot tell you how much I loathe to impose on you further—especially in such an enormous way. That money—the money Daniel came by legally—is *yours*, Sylvia. You should not be spending it on strangers to—"

"I shall spend it how I choose. Rodney is practically a stranger, although I feel that he's been far too consumed with grief and fear to have been putting on any kind of false front with us. I believe we've come to know him well in the short time he's been here, and I believe he's telling us the truth."

"I would agree."

"But you are not a stranger, Dougal," she said and heard far too much devotion coming forth in her voice. She'd wanted him to know her words were sincere, but instead she'd sounded downright adoring. The last thing she wanted him to know was how thoroughly attracted she'd come to feel toward him, but she knew she needed to stop analyzing the situation and just say what needed to be said. "You have become a friend, and you are in trouble. You were Daniel's friend, you were with him when he died, you came here at his request, a journey that caused you great suffering. I must do everything I can to help you get your daughter back. I consider myself a good Christian woman. How can I not consider the story of the Good Samaritan? He helped a stranger in need and spent his own money to see that the injured man was cared for. I am going to help you whether you like it or not, and helping you will help Rodney get his own child back. In the morning we can plan the details of the journey—and what to do when we've arrived. But we need that money. I need you to tell me where it is, and now that the others have gone to bed, it might be our only opportunity without having one of them become suspicious."

Dougal nodded. "I intended to get the money into your hands regardless. Now is as good a time as any—even though I have to say once more that you are not obligated to spend a bit of it for the sake of my—"

"I've already explained that," she stated. "Enough said." She stood up and put her hands on her hips, making him stand to face her. Her determination to have that money in her hands—and all that it represented—had given her a sudden burst of energy that staved off her exhaustion. "Now, where is it?"

"In the barn," he said, and Sylvia headed toward the back door where she lit a lantern with a handle. She then slipped her feet into Daniel's boots and put on a lightweight coat suitable for summer evenings and the gloves she wore to work. Dougal put on a work shirt of George's over his own and donned a pair of gloves and followed her out, closing the door very quietly so as not to alert George or Millie.

Once they were in the barn with the door closed, Sylvia immediately asked, "Where?"

Dougal was quick to give a memorized answer, and for a moment Sylvia imagined Daniel giving him careful instructions and having Dougal repeat them back to make certain he had all of the information memorized correctly. "In the corner beneath the rakes and shovels." Sylvia thought about how there was a loaded rifle discreetly leaning there among the tools, the very rifle she had pointed at Dougal when she'd first found him here. Dougal chuckled softly and added, as if he'd read her mind, "And I remember well that there's a rifle there too."

"I imagine you would," she said, and they both began moving the tools and the rifle and setting them aside except for a shovel that Dougal kept in his hands with the clear intention of digging a hole in the dirt.

As Dougal pushed the shovel into the hardened earth, Sylvia noticed that it hadn't been disturbed in a very long time. In fact, if not for what Dougal had told her, she would have believed that it had never been disturbed at all.

"He said the box wasn't very far down," Dougal said after removing four or five shovelfuls of dirt. And then the shovel hit something that made a clanking sound—metal against metal.

"Oh, my," Sylvia said, feeling a little breathless. She wasn't at all surprised that Daniel had kept a secret like this from her, but she had to swallow her temptation to feel angry again and just be grateful that she'd been given the means to find it.

Sylvia watched with anticipation as Dougal used the shovel to loosen the earth around the edges of the box before he went to his knees and lifted it out of the ground, brushing the dirt off the top of what appeared to be a plain rectangular metal box with a latch. He set it on the ground and knelt in front of it, and Sylvia knelt down as well.

"You should open it," Dougal said, sliding the box toward her. "It belongs to you."

Sylvia nodded, finding it difficult to speak as it occurred to her what this meant to her—if the box indeed held what Dougal had been told it held. The opportunity to make right at least some of Daniel's misdeeds would surely be healing for Sylvia, and the possibility of having some extra money to help aid a worthy cause now warmed her heart. She found it easier to think of truly letting go of her difficult feelings for Daniel if he had indeed left behind the means for her to do these things.

Sylvia took a deep breath before she removed her gloves and attempted to lift the latch, but it wouldn't budge. Dougal observed the problem and left for a moment and returned with a claw hammer. She watched as he wedged the claw end of the hammer beneath the latch and pulled it loose. He then slid the box back toward her and set the hammer and his own gloves beside where he was kneeling. Sylvia took another deep breath and lifted the lid with some difficulty, since it too was reluctant due to having been in the ground for so many years. A small book with an aged leather cover sat on top of a bulky fabric bag.

"The ledger," Dougal said as Sylvia picked it up and opened it, hearing the leather binding crack as she did so. She was quickly able to surmise that there was only writing on the first few pages of the book and the remainder of the pages were blank. But it was certainly Daniel's handwriting, and it was indeed a list of people's names along with information of where they lived and an amount of money.

Giving the pages a closer look, she noticed something written at the top of the first page, which she began to read aloud before she'd even bothered to realize what it said. *"While the people listed below would surely disagree with me, I always considered the money taken from them to be a loan, and when it is all returned to them, my debts to them will be cleared and my conscience lightened. I have worked hard to legitimately earn the money to repay these debts and to care for my sweet Sylvia, even if my methods are unconventional. Now I can only pray that she and God will forgive me for the error of my ways. D. Hewitt.'"*

Sylvia didn't realize she was crying until she felt Dougal's fingers on her cheeks, wiping away her tears. She felt more comforted than alarmed by his touch as she attempted to explain the reason for her tears. "He truly had a good heart, and I loved him with all my soul. I only wish he'd lived to be able to . . ." She found it difficult to finish speaking her thought as her emotion grew and gathered in her throat.

"But you and I will make it right on his behalf, Sylvia. Don't you see? Two men with an inexplicable resemblance brought together in a way that could only be considered a miracle. And both of these men carrying the burden of guilt resulting from many bad choices in their lives, and facing death in the midst of war, wanting to make right all of their wrongs. While both men knew there was a possibility of dying, they agreed that on the chance at least one of them made it out alive, the survivor would do all he could to make everything right for *both* of them. That's why I came here, Sylvia. I did everything I could to right my own wrongs and to get Rachel away from her grandparents. Once I realized I'd done all that I could, I came here to make things right on Daniel's behalf. He begged me to tell you how dear you were to him, how he loved you so deeply. And he made me promise to get this box into your hands and to help you make certain the money was all properly repaid. I considered more than once just writing you a letter, but I really wanted to be able to tell you in person—even though it took some time."

Sylvia could only nod, unable to speak. She was so overcome with everything Dougal had just said, combined with her memory of him telling her how Daniel had been killed. Against her strongest self-discipline, she began to sob and was grateful to feel Dougal's arms come around her. She set the ledger aside and they both sat on the ground. She held to him while she mourned once again for the death of her sweet Daniel, and she wept tears of joy and relief over the evidence that even before the war he'd been working hard to change his ways and he had a plan in place to make some degree of restitution for his crimes.

When Sylvia had finally calmed down, she felt reluctant to let go of Dougal and the sweet comfort she felt in his embrace. She'd been brutally aware of her loneliness for years now, but it was as if having Dougal's arms around her had deepened that awareness even further, to a point that the cumulative effect of all her years alone were suddenly overwhelming and unbearable. Instinctively she lifted her face from his shoulder and looked up at him, as if doing so might somehow ease the barrage of emotions assaulting her.

She wasn't surprised to see compassion and kindness in his expression, but she was completely taken off guard to see something else as well, something she'd wanted to see but at the same time it frightened her. Before she had even a moment to consider the enormity of its implications and complications, he bent his head toward hers and kissed her.

She'd imagined him kissing her and couldn't deny that something in her had been longing for such a moment. Perhaps that was the reason that one kiss quickly turned to two and then three while she pushed her hand into his hair and he drew her closer, making her feel as if he'd been lost in the desert and she could quench his thirst. And then he eased back slightly, looking at her with his brow furrowed.

Before Sylvia could ask him what was wrong, he said in a husky whisper, "When you look at me like that, I always wonder if you see *me,* or if you're seeing the husband you loved and lost. I want you to see a man who would never betray you, never lie to you, never leave you. I want it so badly, Sylvia, but . . ."

Dougal seemed unable to explain any further, and Sylvia could find no words to adequately explain the complexity of her feelings. Instead, she just kissed him again, glad that he seemed to silently agree to talk about such things another time and simply enjoy this moment for whatever it might mean.

"Oh, Sylvia," he murmured and pressed a hand over her face while he seemed to be forcing himself to stop kissing her. "I've wanted to do that for so long."

"And I have wanted you to," she admitted, then felt the need to offer him at least a partial answer to the question he'd posed a moment ago. "When you first came it was difficult to look at you and not see Daniel, but now that I've gotten to know you, I feel as if . . . well, you're very much like all of the best parts of Daniel, and yet I see you as a completely different man. I know that this situation is complicated at best, and we need . . . time . . . and we need to talk more about what we feel . . . and what's best, but . . . for now . . . I don't want you to leave here. I want you to go and get your daughter and bring her back here and . . . maybe . . . just maybe . . . we can find a way to be a family . . . taking things in their proper and appropriate order, of course, but . . . oh my goodness, I think I'm rambling and . . . we just . . . need to talk . . . and we need time. That's all for now."

"I understand," he said and smiled before he kissed her quickly once more. "I'm just glad to know that you might at least consider sharing a life with me. I have nothing to give you, Sylvia. And you have everything you need without me. You could easily believe that all I'm looking for is a home and security by attaching myself so conveniently to a woman with a home and land and a reliable income. I assure you that's not the case, and yet I realize you have no good reason to believe I'm telling you the truth. If not for the way I feel about you, I could walk away from here tomorrow and find my way back to Rachel and just keep trying to get her away from them. But I can't walk away, Sylvia. To even consider leaving you feels as if my heart might shatter within my chest and I would spend the rest of my life just struggling to breathe. Nevertheless, you're right, we need time. I hope you can believe me when I tell you that I didn't come here expecting to fall in love with the woman Daniel left behind . . . but I have, and I'm glad that you finally know how I feel."

Sylvia took in a sharp breath when she heard the word *love* emerge in the midst of his declarations. But she could only nod in response, not certain if she could say for certain that she loved him too. It was possible, but she'd not considered it enough to be able to tell him, and she wouldn't tell him something unless she knew it to be true beyond any doubt. She was glad when he kissed her again, and both relieved and disappointed when he said, "I think we should do what we came out here to do and focus on the challenges before us. Perhaps when everything is properly taken care of we will be able to talk again and consider the situation—and our feelings—more practically."

"Yes, of course," Sylvia said, grateful his words had given them both a bridge to stand on until all of the complications in their lives were settled.

They both went to their knees again and turned their attention to the box where something covered in fabric —presumably money— still remained untouched.

"Go on, then," Dougal said to her, nodding toward the box.

Sylvia tentatively reached into the box with both hands, able to get her fingers around the fabric bag. As she lifted the contents out of the box, she was able to say with certainty, "It's a pillowcase . . . used as a bag."

Sylvia set the pillowcase on the ground and reached inside before she realized it would be easier to just turn it upside down and dump out the contents—so she did. And the amount of money that fell onto the ground—banknotes tied in bundles—was incomprehensible. Sylvia heard herself breathing in short gasps as she touched the money and picked up the bundles to look at the numbers printed on them while her mind attempted to tally how much was there, but she simply couldn't do it.

"I'm not very good with numbers," she admitted breathlessly. "Are you? Can you estimate how much is here? I can't believe he had this much money in his possession."

"He was very good at cards, Sylvia. I saw evidence for myself in the card games we played with our comrades when there was nothing to do. And he assured me that he had legally acquired enough money to pay back all of his debts and more."

Sylvia nodded, glad to hear this—more than she could ever say. She wanted to be able to make restitution on Daniel's behalf to those he'd stolen from, and she also wanted enough money to be able to help Dougal and Rodney get their children back. Dougal began counting the money by thumbing through each bundle while Sylvia just watched, still unable to fully catch her breath. Once he'd figured out how many notes were in each bundle, he began stacking the bundles while she kept quiet, aware that he was making figures in his mind. She sat down when her knees began to hurt from kneeling. When Dougal had apparently come up with an estimate of the amount of money that had fallen almost magically out of the pillowcase, he looked at what was written in the ledger, line by line, and she could see his lips moving subtly while he counted the amount of money that was owed to each person listed there. He finally set the ledger beside him and sat down as if his own knees had begun to hurt, and he looked rather astonished himself.

"Sylvia," he said, "I can only estimate in my head without being able to actually write anything down, but . . . I think I can safely say that once all of these debts are paid, you will still have . . ." he took a deep breath as if it took a great effort to finish the statement, ". . . more than twenty thousand pounds."

"What?" Sylvia squeaked and then she started to cough, as if speaking the word had been equivalent to choking on a drink of water that had gone down wrong. She coughed so hard for more than a minute that Dougal took hold of her shoulders, looking at her in concern. "I'm fine," she managed to say between her loud, unfeminine squawks. "I'm fine."

Dougal began to chuckle as if he found her response amusing now that he knew she truly *was* fine.

"It's not funny," she finally managed to say and coughed again a few times. "Twenty thousand pounds?"

"Yes, Sylvia," he said and chuckled again. "Now you'll be all the more prone to believe that I only love you for your money." He laughed as if he were finding the entire situation terribly amusing. His laughter finally calmed down along with Sylvia's coughing, and he said more seriously, "But you can kick me out if you choose and I'll leave as penniless as I arrived, grateful for all you've done for me."

"I could never," she said then suddenly felt startled by all that had just happened between her and Dougal. She sat up straight, putting distance between them and added very practically, "Returning money to its rightful owners will take some time and it will have to wait. Getting Rachel and Rodney's son to safety must be our main priority for now."

While she spoke, she stuffed the bundles of banknotes back into the pillowcase except for one bundle that she tucked into her apron pocket and patted it as if that might help keep it safer there. She didn't know how much money she'd kept aside, but she felt certain it was more than enough to fund the journey the men needed to make in order to retrieve these children. She had no idea how they were going to go about making that happen but this treasure that Daniel had left behind boosted her confidence. While it was difficult for her to define, she believed somewhere deep inside that this strange and stark resemblance between Daniel and Dougal was a miracle that had been orchestrated by God's hand to bring about good things. Already having Dougal here—pretending to be her husband—had blessed her life in many ways, not the least of which was his knowledge of the money they had just found. And even Rodney and Biff coming to her home in the midst of crisis seemed somehow meant to be. They were in a position to help Rodney, and the information he'd given them offered a great advantage to the situation.

Sylvia returned the pillowcase full of money and the ledger to the box and hooked the latch while Dougal got to his feet. She handed him the box and he offered his free hand to assist her in getting her to her feet. Once she was standing, he handed the box back to her and said, "Do you have a safe place to hide this? Or should we put it back for now?"

Sylvia thought about that for a moment. "I have a place to keep it. We should fill in the hole and put the tools back so that no one will be able to see that the area has been disturbed."

"I can take care of that quickly enough," he said, and Sylvia watched as he put his gloves back on and quickly filled in the small hole with the dirt that had come out of it. Sylvia put on her own gloves to help him return the tools—and the gun—arranging them carefully to try and make them look the way they had before they'd been disturbed.

They walked together back toward the house while Dougal carried the lantern and Sylvia held the box of money tightly against her. Neither of them had anything to say, but Sylvia wondered if he was thinking about the tender and thrilling affection they'd shared in the barn, just as she was. She suspected he had been when he stopped her at the door and kissed her as if in parting, since they certainly couldn't be kissing in front of the people with whom they shared their home. She was inexplicably glad when he kissed her still again. In fact, she felt almost giddy with delight, and from the little chuckle she heard from him, she suspected he felt the same.

"I dare say," he murmured with a little smile and pressed his forehead to hers, "this is a night we will never forget."

"I dare say you're right," she said, and he kissed her once more before he opened the door.

Before they had even stepped inside, Sylvia became aware that Millie was in the kitchen, making herself a cup of tea. She was grateful for the way that Dougal moved to stand between her and Millie, which gave her time to tuck the box beneath a little pile of gloves and mufflers that was always on the little bench there. She then stood beside Dougal to slip her feet out of the oversized boots she was wearing.

"Oh, hello," Millie said to them as Dougal locked the door and set down the lantern to remove his coat. "I assumed the two of you had gone to bed. I couldn't sleep and hoped some chamomile might help."

"It should," Sylvia said in a toneless voice that gave no indication she had just found an enormous amount of money, and she'd shared an unexpected exchange of affection with Dougal. Their little outing had certainly been an adventure!

"Where have the two of you been off to so late?" Millie asked, adding some honey to her tea while Sylvia removed her coat and gloves.

"We just decided to take a little walk and talk about what might be best to do from here forward," Dougal said. "Since we both felt restless, it seemed a good option."

"And have you come up with any new ideas?" Millie asked, seeming wholly convinced he was telling her the truth, but then she had no reason to believe otherwise.

"Possibly," Sylvia said, "but I think we all need to get some sleep and we'll talk about it in the morning." She *did* have some ideas, and she suspected Dougal did too, but they hadn't discussed them, and she felt certain trying to talk about them right now would only prove that they hadn't been talking about that at all.

"Well, good night, then," Millie said and went up the stairs with her tea.

"Good night," Sylvia and Dougal both said before Sylvia retrieved the box of treasure and held it closely against her as she turned toward Dougal. "I suppose we should say good night, as well. A great deal has happened since we went up to bed last night."

"It has indeed," he said and kissed her brow before he murmured softly. "Sleep well. I will look forward to seeing you in the morning."

"And you," she said, smiling up at him before she headed toward the stairs herself, so overcome with all that had happened—and a deep exhaustion that was likely as emotional as it was physical. Her legs felt heavy as she forced them to carry her to her room, where she locked the door long enough to figure out where to hide the money—both the box containing the majority of it, and the bundle she had in her apron pocket. She only had to think for a moment before she recalled a time when she'd been vigorously deep cleaning in this room and discovered that if the bottom drawer of the bureau was pulled out, there was space between the drawer and the floor. She quickly went to her knees and pulled the drawer out, which was filled with a variety of worn stockings and underclothing—the kind of things that she knew she should mend but wanted to just throw out, so she'd simply stuffed them into this particular drawer where they could be ignored. She pulled the drawer out and set it aside, thrilled to realize the box would fit in the space there, and then pushed it as far back as it would go before returning the drawer, which took some effort to maneuver so that it slid in and out normally.

Sylvia tucked the little bundle of money intended for the use of rescuing the children in the drawer that housed her nightclothes. She put it at the back and beneath the folded nightgowns, certain she'd be getting it back out very soon, once a plan was put in place and they could estimate how much money might be needed. Given the fact that both Dougal and Rodney had traveled from this area of the country not so long ago—and Dougal had ran out of money—she felt certain that between them they could estimate how much they might need, and with the amount of money she now knew she had in her possession, she would of course send them with extra just to be certain they weren't left stranded should they encounter any unexpected challenges.

With that taken care of, Sylvia's exhaustion suddenly washed over her, and no purpose or task could keep her from getting the rest she needed. She was grateful she'd been able to nap earlier, but given the enormity of all that had happened since Rodney and Biff had come to her door late the previous evening, she sincerely wondered how she had gotten through the day. She hurried to get ready for bed, only with the motivation that once she *was* ready, she had a comfortable bed waiting for her. She slid beneath the bedcovers thinking of how it had felt to be kissed by Dougal Heywood, and with such pleasant memories foremost in her mind she quickly fell asleep.

Chapter Nine

The Mission

Sylvia woke to a room filled with daylight. The angle of the sun shining through her bedroom windows made it evident she'd slept much later than usual. She could hear sounds coming from the kitchen below—sounds that normally would have awakened her, but she'd slept right through any indication that the rest of the household was awake and busy. For a moment she felt tempted to panic, thinking of the chores she was expected to do early each morning, then it occurred to her that Millie would have awakened her if she'd truly been needed, and her friends had likely wanted her to sleep for as long as she could.

Sylvia got ready for the day quickly but without rushing. Then she went downstairs to find George, Millie, Dougal, and Rodney all seated at the dining table eating a breakfast of griddle cakes and sausages. It was a common breakfast in this house, but one they all enjoyed.

"Good morning," Millie said. "Food is still hot, so you're right on time."

"I slept so long," Sylvia said apologetically.

"I'm certain you needed it," Dougal said and stood to help her with her chair.

While Sylvia was taking her seat with Dougal's assistance—which seemed rather silly for breakfast in the kitchen of her home—she said, "But what about the milk and eggs and the—"

"All taken care of," George said. "Dougal and Rodney did your chores for you, and they even helped me with mine."

"Least I could do," Rodney said, looking very shy but also more rested and calm.

"Just enjoy your breakfast," Millie said, passing food toward Sylvia. "We all wanted you to get as much rest as you could, and as you can see, the house is still standing."

"So it is," Sylvia said and began piling food on her plate, suddenly feeling very hungry as she realized her appetite had not been very good the previous day, which she suspected was true of everyone else. She noticed that Rodney was eating well, and he'd just picked at his food the previous day, so he was likely experiencing the same kind of delayed hunger. Or perhaps there was a determination among the people gathered around the table to build up their strength, knowing they were about to set out on a long journey with many uncertainties involved.

"Now," Millie said in an authoritative voice, "once we've all got our stomachs full, we need to make a plan to get those little ones back in the care of their fathers. I think we all have some ideas, but we need to talk the matter through thoroughly so that we have a solid plan."

Sylvia looked around and realized she was the only one still eating, while the others were sipping coffee or tea to wash down their breakfast. "No need to wait for me," Sylvia said after she'd swallowed what she'd been chewing. "Although I'd like to say this much: first of all, I think we need to spend today doing as much baking as we can, while someone goes into town to purchase a good amount of cheese and fruit. We have a fair supply of dried meat in the cellar. I do believe that will provide much of the food we'll need for the journey, although I do have enough money put away that we can certainly stop here and there and eat a decent meal to keep up our strength. I was also thinking that when we arrive in the area, we would actually be wise to locate the constable and enlist his assistance. What's happening with both children is surely against the law in many respects. Rachel is being kept from her father when fathers surely have more legal rights regarding a child than grandparents. And Rodney's son was kidnapped—plain and simple—for the purpose of manipulating him into committing a crime. I really do believe that getting legal assistance would be to our benefit, unless you men know something about the constable in the area that might go against—"

"As far as I know the constable is a fair man," Dougal interrupted, "but Sylvia, I truly don't think you should go."

Sylvia had just put another forkful of food into her mouth and had trouble not choking.

"It's going to be a long and difficult journey, what with traveling continually to get there and back as quickly as possible. There is absolutely nothing you can do that we men can't do. And I know you're capable of doing *anything*—we all know that."

Sylvia appreciated his words of good faith, but she had to acknowledge in that moment she'd already been leaning toward the practicality of it being better for her to remain at home. She knew she'd never learned to drive a carriage, and the men would be taking turns at it in order to each get some rest. It also occurred to her that the interior of the carriage was not very large and having one more person *would* make sleeping in it more difficult. The men would also always have to be concerned about being appropriate due to a woman being in their presence. These were all points that she felt certain the others had discussed but didn't likely want to bring up with her. Nevertheless, she was intelligent enough to see the obvious and knew she had to concede, even though she wanted to go with them so badly that remaining behind would be more difficult than she wanted to admit.

Dougal continued in a kind voice. "It will not require four of us to carry out this endeavor, and I for one would feel more at ease to know that Millie is not here all alone. I know George agrees with me."

Sylvia looked at George as if he might have betrayed her, but he only gazed back at her with a silent indication that he felt very strongly about this and he would not be swayed. "He's right, Missus," George said. "Your being willing to go and all is admirable. We all know you want to help these children. But I would ask that you not leave Millie here alone."

While Sylvia could feel George, Millie, and Dougal all expecting her to argue the point, she took a deep breath and said, "I understand. Everything will be more complicated with an extra passenger and a woman among men. As much as I *do* want to go, and I *do* want to help all I can, I see your reasoning, and . . . I'll remain here with Millie. I only ask that you all be very careful."

"So you was wanting to come with us to watch over us like a mother hen?" George asked lightly. "Making certain we mind our manners?"

"Maybe," Sylvia said, forcing a light tone herself that did not at all express how she was really feeling.

She was glad when George and Dougal began talking of their plans for the journey and she was able to just eat her breakfast while she attempted to become fully accustomed to the fact that she would be remaining behind. She noticed that Rodney said very little, but he was keenly aware of everything being said. Mostly he just interjected comments about how he only wanted to get his boy back, and how grateful he was for their help.

Sylvia was glad to be done eating her breakfast so she didn't have to sit at the table with the men while they discussed this grand endeavor of which she would not be a part. After offering some helpful suggestions, she stood and began clearing the table, and Millie did the same.

As soon as breakfast was all cleaned up, Millie and Sylvia got to work with their baking projects. Dougal went out to the barn to carefully check the carriage and make certain it wasn't in need of any repairs in order to carry them a long distance very quickly. He also did a careful check of each of the horses to make certain their shoes were in good condition and they had no signs of ailment, since they would need to be at their finest.

George hitched the wagon to a horse and went into town for supplies the women would need while the men were gone, and to get the "good amount of cheese and fruit" Sylvia had suggested for the journey, along with a few other things. Rodney had wanted to go along and help but they had all agreed he should stay out of sight, given how strangely suspicious some of the villagers could get over the silliest things, and it was likely best that Rodney and George weren't seen together. Instead Rodney worked hard in the barn to put everything in pristine order to make it easier for the women to care for the animals.

The day remained busy, only stopping briefly for lunch and tea— both of which were especially simple given that the women were focused on preparing food for the journey. Although Millie did have beef simmering on the stove for a hearty stew she would be preparing for supper, knowing they all needed a good meal before the men headed out the following morning before the sun came up.

When the men had done all the preparations they could do, they joined the women in the kitchen, taking orders from Millie to knead bread, cut vegetables for the stew, and help get scones in and out of the oven. The warm bread and savory stew they had for supper was satisfying for all of them. Sylvia expected them to discuss their plans further while they were gathered and all sitting down, but it seemed they'd already said all that needed to be said. The only comment that came up was George asking, "Are we certain we have enough money to get us there and back? I'll bring all that me and my Millie have saved but—"

"There's no need for that, George," Sylvia said. "You and Millie need to keep that money. You might need it in the future. I know I've not mentioned it before, but we have a fair amount of money put away for emergencies, and I assure you we have ample. I'm only too glad to see some of that money used for such a purpose."

Nothing more was said about the money until late that evening when everything was packed and ready to go, and George, Millie, and Rodney had already gone to bed. Sylvia retrieved the bundle of money from her drawer and found Dougal in the parlor with a cup of tea. She wondered if this was a regular evening habit of his that she simply hadn't noticed, or if he'd known they needed to talk. He certainly needed money in his possession in order to carry out this mission.

"Hello," he said when she entered the room where a single lamp was burning dimly.

"Hello," Sylvia said and set down the candle she'd brought with her to illuminate her way.

Sylvia sat across from Dougal while he lifted his cup toward her and said, "I confess I've become rather fond of enjoying one of your relaxing teas at bedtime." He took a quiet sip. "And it's rather tasty, too."

"I'm glad you enjoy it," she said then hurried to take care of the necessary business. Holding the money out toward him, she said, "You'll be needing this. I trust you'll keep it safely hidden and see that it's properly cared for."

She was surprised when he didn't take the money but instead took another sip of his tea. "I will do whatever is necessary to keep it safe, but . . ."

"But?" she echoed.

"First of all, we will not be needing that much, I'm certain."

"I have no idea how much it costs to take such a journey, but I'd far prefer you have extra than for there to be any possibility of running out. You've already experienced *that* challenge. I don't want anything like that to happen again."

"I appreciate that more than I can say," he said and nodded toward the money. "Still, with the way we are traveling, we won't be needing that much."

"Fine," she said and set the bundle of notes down on the table between them, "you take what you think you'll need . . . and some extra, and . . ." She thought about it a moment and changed her mind. "No, take all of it. Maybe you'll need some money for . . . bribery or something. I don't know. I only know I'll feel better knowing you have extra money with you. So take it." A new thought occurred to her and she added, "Besides, we're planning for two children to be coming home with you, and they will likely be needing things. You should get anything they need or want to make the journey easier."

Dougal took another sip of his tea and chuckled softly. "That is a kind thought regarding the children. Thank you. I do hope we don't have to resort to any kind of bribery, but . . . if you want me to take it all, I will. I'll take very good care of it, and I'll return everything we don't spend into your hands when we return."

"Very good," she said and relaxed more into her chair.

"Although I have something to ask you, and I need you to be completely honest with me."

"I have never been anything but completely honest with you," she said firmly.

"I didn't mean to imply otherwise. I just . . . needed to clarify that this is important for me to understand . . . and perhaps for you to reconsider." Sylvia motioned impatiently with her hand for him to continue and he got to the point. "Why are you not giving the money to George? You've known him far longer than me, and I know you trust him completely. I've admitted to you that I've swindled people out of their money a great many times in the past. Why would you put that much money into my hands, Sylvia?"

"You told me you'd changed, that you didn't do that kind of thing anymore," Sylvia said. "I *do* trust you, but if there's some reason I shouldn't . . . if you're playing me for a fool, Dougal, I would appreciate it if you would be completely honest with *me* and just tell me. *Is* there some reason I can't trust you with this money?"

"You can trust me, Sylvia," he said severely. "I will keep it well guarded and I will spend it wisely. I'm just wondering . . . why you would—"

"I don't know," she said and looked down. "Perhaps I just want very badly to know that I *can* trust you."

"So, this is a test?" he chuckled mirthlessly. "A very expensive and risky test. Although, I must say, any man who would take advantage of you after all you've done for me . . . and all you're willing to do to help get Rachel back, would be the worst kind of blackguard. Even at my worst I can't imagine ever being capable of such betrayal."

"There you have it," she said, feeling a little unsettled over the conversation, but not for the reasons he believed. She just wasn't certain if she was ready to fully examine those reasons, and she certainly wasn't ready to talk about them.

"And you're also willing to give of what you have to help our new friend Rodney," Dougal said with mild astonishment. "He told you his story and you were willing to help—even willing to make the journey, which I can assure you would be terribly miserable. You truly are the best of women."

"I dare say there are a great many people in the world who would be willing to give what they have to help others. I don't think I'm as rare as you're implying. Is that not what any Christian should do?"

"It might be what they *should* do, but I've not encountered very many people who truly live what they claim to believe—until I came here. I'm just trying to say that I'm grateful, Sylvia, and also that I think you're a remarkable woman. I'm not trying to embarrass you, but I had to say it. I swear to you that I will not repay your kindness and generosity by betraying you in any way."

"Then my trust in you is valid," she declared and came to her feet. "I think we'd do well to get some rest. You will be leaving very early, and I will be up to see you off."

"Wait," he said, setting down his cup and saucer very quickly before he stood and stepped toward her. "Tomorrow . . . before I go . . . the others will be with us, and . . . I just . . ." He stopped stammering and took her face into his hands before he gave her a lengthy kiss. "I wanted to kiss you goodbye," he murmured close to her lips and kissed her again.

Sylvia took hold of his upper arms and whispered, "I'm so glad you did. Be safe. Please come back safely to me."

"I will," he said. "I promise."

Sylvia wanted to point out that he couldn't possibly keep such a promise when life was so unpredictable. Even barring the potential danger of the situation, they could be confronted with terrible weather or an accident or any number of things that could go wrong. But she forced herself not to think about that, and she forced herself not to think of how attached she'd become to Dougal. It truly was as if he'd brought the very best of Daniel back to her, even though she had sincerely stopped seeing Daniel in him. She was only glad for the way he'd eased her loneliness, and she hoped they wouldn't be gone for very many days. She knew—because they'd talked about it—the approximate amount of time it would take for them to travel back and forth, but none of them had any idea how much time it would take to conduct the precarious business of getting the children away from the people who had sent Rodney and Biff to kill Dougal.

Sylvia forced all of that out of her head and kissed Dougal once more before she forced herself to step back, saying softly, "Good night and rest well."

"And you," he said as she picked up the candle she'd brought with her and left the parlor. She could feel his eyes on her until she started up the stairs and could no longer be seen. In that moment she seemed to experience some kind of delayed reaction from the way he'd kissed her. The quickened pace of her heartbeat and the quivering in her stomach almost made it impossible to keep moving up the stairs, but she took a deep breath and kept going toward her room, silently praying that Dougal and the others would be able to accomplish their endeavor quickly and safely, and that he would very soon come back to her.

It was still very dark outside when all the occupants of Sylvia's home gathered around the table to enjoy one of Millie's typically hearty breakfasts. Millie had set her alarm clock to wake her at four so she could be certain of sending the men off with full stomachs. If Sylvia had known about her plan, she would have set her own alarm clock early enough to be able to help her. But she had been awakened by a knock at her door and George's voice telling her that breakfast was hot and ready.

Now that they were all seated and eating, very little conversation was taking place. Sylvia knew from previous discussions that they wanted to leave in the dark so they could get well beyond the area where Sylvia's carriage might be recognized before the sun came up. Sylvia was glad for the farewell kisses she and Dougal had exchanged the previous night, but she found herself discreetly watching him and dreading his departure.

Recalling a thought she'd had the previous evening after Rodney and George and Millie had gone to bed, Sylvia said, "Rodney, I'm wondering what you will do after you get your son back. I assume you have a home where you were living before all of this happened. Will you go back there or—"

"Oh, I don't want t' try and settle anywhere those people could find us," Rodney said, clearly afraid. "The place we was livin' was rented and we been gone long enough now that I'm sure someone else is livin' there now. I know how t' do lots o' things so I can get work t' care for me and my boy. I'm thinkin' I'll just pick myself a town or village on the way back and stay."

"That means I'll likely not see you again," Sylvia said, realizing as she did so that she actually felt some sadness. She'd quickly grown fond of the man with his stark humility and tender emotions. Impulsively but instinctively believing it was right and good, she added, "If you don't find a place that feels right to you, Rodney, you come back here with your son and we'll find work enough for you to do. I can give you both a roof over your heads and food to eat. Perhaps you wouldn't want to remain permanently, but maybe you need some time to be more prepared to make a fresh start elsewhere."

Rodney looked only a little more astonished than everyone else sitting at the table, but Rodney was quick to say, "That's awful kind o' ye, Missus. Ye've already done so much for me. I don't want t' impose but it's nice t' know that if we don't find a good place t' stay we won't be without a home. I can manage well enough on my own, but I got t' take care o' my boy."

"Yes, you do," Sylvia said with growing confidence. "And you wouldn't be imposing because we will be putting you to work." She laughed softly. "Both the barn and the house need painting and the inside of the barn needs some repairs and—"

"The animal's stalls all need to be practically built new," George piped in with enthusiasm and Sylvia could have hugged him. "And the loft where we keep the straw needs some work."

Millie interjected, "The shelves in the larder are in bad shape. They could stand to be rebuilt before they fall and something breaks."

"Well, Rodney," Dougal said, "it seems you would be needed here should you decide that's what you want to do."

Rodney just nodded appreciatively with tears glistening in his eyes. Sylvia didn't know if his tendency to cry easily was due to the fact that he'd recently lost his closest friend and he was filled with fear on behalf of his son, or if he was simply that kind of man. Either way, his tenderness warmed her, and she sincerely hoped he would decide to return.

Sylvia was surprised by the thought that if Rodney brought his son here, then Rachel would have a playmate rather than being the only child among a group of secluded adults. She almost gasped aloud as she realized for the first time that the final goal of this escapade was to safely retrieve two children, and they would be coming here—at least one of them would for certain. Given her growing feelings for Dougal and her accompanying hope that he would never leave, she had to fully accept the fact that he had a daughter. They certainly had sufficient bedrooms in the house for everyone—although Rodney and his son would have to share a room, but she doubted he would mind that. Still, the reality of having children here felt deeply thrilling. This house had been far too quiet, and she prayed that all would go well with their journey and the result would indeed be having two children living in her home.

Sylvia found it difficult to say goodbye to the men and was glad for the way that Millie hurried them along and hardly gave anyone time to even think about their departure before they were on their way. Millie and Sylvia stood outside the house in the dark as the carriage rolled away, neither of them saying a word until they could no longer hear the sound of the wheels on the road.

"Well, that's that," Millie finally said and went into the house with Sylvia following her. "It's going to be awfully dull after all the fuss that's been going on."

"It will indeed," Sylvia said, and the two women set to work to put the kitchen in order.

"We can take a nap later," Millie said while they were working. She then chuckled. "In fact, we can do anything we want."

Sylvia laughed with her. "We certainly can," she said, unable to deny that a peaceful day would be welcome, although she already missed Dougal very much, and she suspected that Millie would be sorely longing to see George long before he returned.

Within a few days Sylvia began to lose track of how many days the men had been gone. Given the isolated life she'd lived for years, she'd stopped keeping track of days long ago. She kept track of the seasons by the changes in the weather and nature and the length of time the sun was visible in the sky. But she rarely knew which day of the week it was, except for when Millie would let her know it was Sunday and they always had their own little church meeting in the parlor.

Sylvia and Millie did well at keeping each other company and making certain all the chores were accomplished. The weather remained mostly fair, with only some light rain now and then, and they both hoped the men were also being blessed with fair weather. The farther away they got, the more likely it was that they could be dealing with much different weather.

When the time began to drag without the men there, and it was evident that both Millie and Sylvia were starting to worry more, Sylvia was grateful for Millie's idea to put the spare bedrooms in pristine order in anticipation for the arrival of children. Of course, they didn't know for certain if Rachel would come back with her father, or if Rodney would return here at all, with or without his son. But the women decided that assuming they *would* return was perhaps a form of trusting in God to help make all of this turn out well, and working to get the rooms ready in anticipation of their return was an act of faith.

"I don't know why I didn't think of it before," Millie said as they discussed their plans over breakfast on a cloudy morning. Then they talked about which rooms would be best for their new occupants. With the possibility of Rodney returning and bringing his son, they determined that they should use a room that had two narrow beds, as opposed to the room Rodney had been using previously which only had one bed. The room Rodney had been using would become Rachel's.

"And let's hope we don't find any more strays to take in," Millie laughed, "because we don't got no more rooms."

"We certainly will have a houseful," Sylvia said and sipped her tea, inhaling its soothing fragrance, "but the more I've thought about having children here, the more I've grown to like the idea. It's the way it should be."

"Perhaps," Millie said with compassion, "this might help heal the hole you carry in your heart."

"Perhaps," Sylvia said in reply but didn't want to talk about that, so she began listing aloud all they would need to do in these two bedrooms to get them ready.

Sylvia and Millie spent all that day and the day after putting the two bedrooms in perfect order, and the day after that Millie declared that the men and children surely had to be returning any day now, so she began some special baking projects. "They'll all be needing some good meals when they get here," she said, "but I can't very well be cooking large amounts of food that you and me won't be able to eat. The baked goods will keep better, however, and will give them something tasty." She went on to tell Sylvia about her plans to make two different kinds of sweet biscuits that the children would enjoy, and she also planned to make a cake that she would carefully cover and keep in the larder to keep it moist. She also endeavored to make two flavors of scones and some buns. Sylvia enjoyed helping Millie with her baking projects, and being able to visit with her while they worked. They were both growing more anxious over the absence of the men and their concern for the children—even though they'd known they couldn't possibly estimate how many days they would be gone.

When there was nothing more to bake, the women took on some extra cleaning projects around the house, both of them staying far too busy to think much about the situation, and wearing themselves out enough that they were too exhausted at night to do anything but fall asleep. Sylvia was glad to be able to stay busy, but she was becoming as physically exhausted as she was emotionally strained with all the working and waiting, and she woke up one morning missing Dougal so much that she could have sworn there was literal pain around her heart. Rather than trying to avoid thinking about him, she remained in bed longer than usual and allowed herself to feel the ache. She wept over his absence and the uncertainty of such a strange relationship, and just as she had done hourly since he'd departed with the other men, she prayed that they were all safe and that their goal of retrieving the children would go well.

At breakfast Sylvia told Millie she felt exhausted and it was her opinion that they needed to enjoy a more relaxing day and only do the absolute minimum of chores.

"I think we've earned it," Sylvia said. "Besides, I don't know if there's much more we can clean."

"I dare say you're right," Millie said. They'd even thoroughly cleaned the other bedrooms. "I only hope and pray they return soon. I've never been away from my George for so long and I just . . ." Her voice cracked and she put her hand over her mouth.

"It's all right," Sylvia said. "I know you miss him, and I too hope and pray it won't be much longer. It's all right to cry, Millie." Sylvia told Millie how she'd cried in bed earlier, and they sat at the table long after they'd finished their breakfast, sipping tea and talking and crying and expressing every possible hope that they would see their loved ones again soon.

Sylvia was surprised to hear Millie say, "I do believe you're growing to love Dougal. He's not your Daniel, as you've said many times—but he's a good man, and he's here. What I mean by that is . . . well, he seems very comfortable here—he fits in well. We've just assumed that he would stay here with his daughter—at least that's what I assumed, and I assumed that's what you were assuming as well." Sylvia laughed softly over the silliness of the sentence and Millie chuckled before she became more serious and said, "But it seems to me your feelings toward him are changing. I'm thinking he's become more than a friend. And the way you miss him is only more evidence of that."

"I can't deny it," Sylvia said, "nevertheless I think a great deal of time is needed to know if we *should* be more than friends. There's so much he doesn't know about me—and the other way around, I'm certain. So, for now we'll leave it at that."

"As you wish, Missus," Millie said and stood to begin clearing the table.

Rain began falling later that morning, which was more than a drizzle but much less than a downpour, nevertheless it remained steady throughout the day while Millie read a book and Sylvia spent some time grinding herbs. After a simple lunch they both took a nap then prepared a simple supper and did the necessary chores before going to bed.

Sylvia found it more difficult to fall asleep after a day of not exerting much physical energy, but she finally slept with dreams filling her head with strange images of Dougal turning into Daniel and back again. She came awake with a start in the darkness and her immediate thought was that such a dream was understandable considering their physical resemblance, and the way that Dougal had pretended to be Daniel. In the midst of the thought, Sylvia gasped, distinctly hearing the sounds of a carriage and horses going slowly past her windows.

"Oh, good heavens," she muttered before she lit a lamp and pulled on a dressing gown. She rushed into the hall, heading toward Millie's room, but Millie appeared in the hall before Sylvia got there.

"I think they're here," Sylvia declared.

"They are indeed," Millie said with delighted laughter. "I looked out the window and despite the dark I could see that it's our carriage, sure enough."

The two women hurried down the stairs and Sylvia set down the lamp she was carrying long enough to put on Daniel's old boots and also a cloak over her dressing gown. Standing this close to the door she could hear that it was still raining so she pulled the hood of the cloak up over her head just as Millie said, "I'll light the stove in the kitchen and get the kettles heating on the chance they need some warming up. And I'll warm up some scones too."

"They may want to just get into their beds and rest," Sylvia said, "but some relaxing tea wouldn't go amiss if that's the case."

"Indeed," Millie said, and Sylvia went outside where she could see three lanterns burning inside the barn, with the doors swung open wide.

Her heart thumped painfully at the thought of seeing Dougal. She would certainly be happy to see George; she'd missed him as well. And the possibility of Dougal and Rodney having their children with them created a nervous jittering in her stomach.

But more than anything she longed to see Dougal. His absence had certainly made her realize how much she'd grown to care for him. After all of these unnumbered days of waiting for the men to return, they were finally here, and Sylvia could hardly believe it. The rain helped her realize that she wasn't dreaming as she hurried toward where she could see Dougal and George unharnessing the horses from the carriage. Even as bundled up against the weather as they were, Sylvia had no trouble recognizing either one of them.

Sylvia ran as quickly as she could manage with the oversized boots on her feet, then she paused just inside the barn to watch Dougal lead one of the horses into a stall and secure it there while George walked around to the other side of the horses that were still harnessed. The moment Dougal had latched the stall door, Sylvia ran toward him and all but threw herself into his arms. He'd barely had time to even see her there before they were sharing a tight embrace and he lifted her feet off the ground, laughing in a way that reminded her of Daniel, but she pushed all thoughts of her dead husband away in order to fully enjoy this moment.

"I take it you're happy to see me," he said and laughed again.

"Oh, I am!" she said and kissed him.

"Careful," he murmured with a wide grin as he set her feet back on the ground, "you could stir up a scandal if anyone sees that sort of thing."

"Millie's already figured out there's something between us, and if Millie knows then George does too. I'm afraid it's too late to be concerned about that."

"Well, then," he said and kissed her again, "I missed you too. However . . ." he motioned toward the horses and carriage, "I believe I'd do well to take care of this."

"I'll help you," she said, well accustomed to handling the horses.

"How delightful," he said and walked toward the carriage.

George passed them, leading the third of the four horses into the barn. "Hello, George," Sylvia said brightly and he grinned at her.

"Hello, Missus," he said. "It's mighty good to see your face."

"And yours," she replied and set to work helping Dougal unfasten the buckles on the harness of the remaining horse. "I can't wait another moment," she said. "You must tell me if you were successful." It occurred to her that both Dougal and George both seemed in very good spirits. She hoped that meant they *had* been successful as opposed to simply being glad to be home.

Dougal led the horse into the barn and Sylvia fell into step beside him. "We were very blessed," he said. "It took time and there were some complications, but . . ." he laughed again as if he couldn't suppress his happiness, ". . . yes, we were successful."

"Oh, that's wonderful!" Sylvia said and glanced over her shoulder, realizing that Rachel must be inside the carriage. She was just about to ask if Rodney had decided to come back with them when she saw him on top of the carriage untying the ropes that held a large tarpaulin over the luggage to keep it dry and secure. "And Rodney came back," she added.

"He did, indeed," Dougal said and stopped walking a moment as if he needed to look directly at her when he said this. "He proved himself to be a man of true courage and integrity. I must admit that he surprised me more than once. He's a good man, Sylvia."

"I believed that was true, but I'm glad to hear more evidence in that regard . . . especially if he'll be making himself a part of our household."

"*Our* household?" he asked with a pleasant smirk.

"You know what I mean," she said and looked down.

Dougal began to walk again, leading the horse into the stall and he latched the door before he turned to her and asked, "Do you think you're ready to have two children in your home?"

"It will be an adventure," she said, feeling both thrilled and a little nervous, "but I'm ready. You must be so happy to have Rachel back."

"Yes, I am," he said, smiling at her.

"Are the children in the—"

"They're both asleep so we decided to take care of everything first and take them into the house last of all. If they wake up and feel disoriented, we want to be nearby."

"Of course," Sylvia said, then helped Dougal make certain the horses were cared for while George and Rodney took the luggage into the house. The men had taken very little with them, but Sylvia noticed from a glance out the barn door as they were unloading the bags and trunks that they'd returned with more—but of course that would be the case since they'd brought back two more people.

Sylvia felt deeply curious to see the children, but as their fathers took turns removing them from the carriage, they were wrapped in blankets and the glow of the lamp George held revealed little more than hair on the top of their heads, and Sylvia couldn't even tell what color it was except that the child Rodney carried had darker hair than the child Dougal was carrying.

George led the way into the house with a lantern, and Sylvia followed the two men holding their sleeping children. As she watched them enter the house, she felt a strange sensation that the changes coming into her life were far greater than she could begin to comprehend. She stopped walking for a moment, so overcome with the sensation, then she hurried to catch up.

By the time Sylvia hung up her cloak and got her feet out of Daniel's boots, Rodney and Dougal were at the top of the stairs. George's voice startled Sylvia when he said, "Millie went up to get them to the right rooms."

"Excellent," Sylvia said, trying to suppress her stark curiosity over the children, but it would be silly for her to follow the others upstairs with the hope of getting just a glimpse of them as they were put into their beds. She'd be able to meet them in the morning, and she suspected that it would take no time at all for them to be so at home here that it would be difficult to remember life without them. Perhaps that was the reason she felt so overcome with the changes before them.

Since George was having a cup of tea and a scone, Sylvia sat at the table to join him once she'd checked her dressing gown to make certain it was tied tightly over her nightgown.

"Ahh," George drawled, stretching his arms up over his head, "it's good to be home, Missus. It sure enough is."

"It's very good to *have* you home!" Sylvia replied with enthusiasm. "Millie and I have kept very busy, but I dare say she's surely grown bored of my company."

This made George chuckle, the sound emphasizing to Sylvia how very glad she was to have him home. She'd truly missed George and Dougal, and her relief to have them home—and to know they were safe—left her feeling as if a great weight had been lifted off her shoulders. On top of that, she now knew they had been successful in the mission that had taken them away. She felt anxious to hear what had happened, but assumed they would all talk about it when they were together.

She assumed Dougal and Rodney would come back downstairs for some tea, but she suddenly wondered if maybe they were just going to bed and she'd have to wait until morning to hear the details of their adventure. She then heard multiple sets of footfalls on the stairs and she could tell that both of the men and Millie were on their way down. She managed to suppress any urge to make a fool of herself when Dougal entered the room, but she couldn't keep herself from returning the smile he gave her.

"Oh, it's grand to be home!" Dougal said and sat down next to Sylvia. "I dare say there's no place in the world that has tea and scones the likes of which can be found in this kitchen."

"Hear hear," George said and took a big bite of a buttered scone. "Between our missus making the teas herself, and my Millie's brewing and baking, we are blessed indeed."

"Yes, indeed," Rodney said, taking a seat.

Millie got more hot water for the tea before she sat down herself and Sylvia said, "I'm so glad you decided to come back, Rodney."

"I'da been a fool t' not take ye up on such an offer," he said. "Once I had my little Bob with me again, I wondered how I could ever work enough t' meet our needs and still see him taken care of. He's such a small lad. I'll do whatever work ye want me t' do, Missus," he said. "And ye don't need t' pay me none, or not much at least. I'd only need money when Bob grows out of his clothes. Just havin' a home and friends and plenty t' eat is all I could ever ask for and I thank ye. I'll work hard for ye; I promise that."

"I'm not worried about that," Sylvia said. "And you *will* get a wage for your work to meet your personal needs—along with room and board, just as George and Millie do. It's not much but it's—"

"It's plenty good," George said. "Our needs are met and then some; we don't need more than that."

Sylvia thought of the money she'd found and realized that she could afford to give her employees a raise, but she would consider that after she'd had the opportunity to return the money owed to those from whom it had been taken, and then she would know exactly how much she had. Sylvia felt somewhat impatient to return the money, but she hadn't wanted to tell Millie about the discovery yet, and she doubted she could have accomplished such a task without having Millie find out she was busy at something secretive. And she preferred to have Dougal help her. Now that he was back, they would talk about that at the first opportunity. For now, she just wanted to sit here and soak in the peace and joy she felt to have everyone safely within the walls of her home.

Chapter Ten

A Houseful of Family

"Now," Millie said, pouring herself a cup of tea, "I'm certain that none of us should be staying up too long given that we'll have children to care for once they've had their fill of sleep, but I think I speak for the missus as well as myself when I say that we can't bear the curiosity of knowing what happened."

"Yes," Sylvia said, "I am in complete agreement. Just tell us the brief version, and you can fill in details tomorrow."

The men all exchanged glances as if to silently decide who would begin. Rodney quickly looked down, declaring that *he* would not be telling the story. George then nodded at Dougal who took in a deep breath and began, "Well . . . the brief version . . ." He cleared his throat and the others waited in anticipation, even the other men who already knew everything that had happened. "Firstly, we took your advice and sought out the help of the constable. He serves more than one village—rather a large area in truth—and has a few officers employed to assist him. He knew of my wife's family but was not personally acquainted with them which I think was in our favor. Rodney and I simply told him both of our stories from the beginning and he was in complete agreement, however he told us that we needed the approval of a judge in order to legally get the children. The problem we faced was that the judge responsible for this area, was also responsible for an area much larger, and therefore he had to travel in order to hear our case and issue a warrant."

"A what?" Sylvia asked, not wanting to sound ignorant but more importantly wanting to understand what had happened exactly.

"It's a legal document that . . . well . . . in our case it stated that Rachel's grandparents had no legal rights to have the children in their care and they needed to turn them over to us immediately. There was also the matter of kidnapping and conspiracy to have a murder committed. It was the constable's advice that we focus on getting the children back because the other issues might be more difficult to prove, but a great deal depended on how the judge viewed the situation, since he had the legal authority necessary to help us. The constable sent word to the judge that he was needed but he expected we wouldn't see him for a few days at least, so we got rooms at a pub and just . . . waited."

"Bored out of our minds we were," George muttered.

"And I was wearin' out the floor with my pacin' back and forth, worried about my boy," Rodney spoke up. "In a strange sorta way it was more difficult knowin' he was so close and I couldn't do nothin' about it cuz the constable had warned us to mind our manners and not cause any trouble if we wanted the judge t' be on our side."

"Very wise," Millie said, and all eyes turned again to Dougal, wanting him to finish the story.

"It was five days before the judge arrived," Dougal said, "and I think we were all near to going mad by then. But once we were able to meet with the judge—having the constable with us—and we told our stories to him, the judge had his clerk write up a warrant then and there so we could get the children back. He was in agreement with the constable about the other crimes these people had committed, that they would be difficult if not impossible to prove, and he simply wanted to get the children back to their fathers. He did tell the constable, however, to keep a close eye on these people and if they caused any further trouble for any reason, he wanted to know about it."

Dougal sighed and smiled more to himself before he continued. "The constable and his officers went with us the minute we had that warrant to collect the children. We waited in the carriage while they conducted their legal business, and it seemed to take very long even though we know it was only half an hour or so before Rachel and Bob were brought to the carriage. Rachel was a little hesitant about going with me. She's not had me in her life for a very long time, although she did see me many times when I was trying to get her back. We've talked on the journey back and she's admitted again that she hated living in that house and she was glad to get away. She's quickly warmed up to me and all is well." Dougal nodded toward Rodney. "Of course it's not been nearly so long since Bob had seen his father, and he was missing him very much. They were very glad to see each other."

"That's right enough," Rodney said and wiped the back of his hand over his eyes. Sylvia was touched to see that he hadn't lost his tenderness since she'd last seen him.

"I believe the children didn't like the people in the house, but Rachel quickly became friends with Bob after having been the only child there for so long. They were mostly left on their own to play and not allowed outside, but from everything they've told us they were never hurt—they were yelled at a great deal, it seems, but never physically hurt, for which we can be grateful."

"Amen t' that," Rodney said, mopping his eyes more fervently. He had clearly been traumatized by the entire situation and overcome with gratitude to have his son back, although he was likely still grieving over the loss of his friend Biff, and much had changed in his life. Sylvia felt warm inside to think that she could help Rodney and his son have a better life, and that they would all benefit by having another able-bodied man around to help with all the work that had fallen behind, and if Rachel and Bob had become friends during their imprisonment, it was likely far better for Rachel to not be the only child living in this house—especially considering the isolated way they lived their lives due to Sylvia's distorted reputation.

Dougal took in a deep breath and blew it out slowly. "In truth, I think that's all there is to tell. As an added precaution, both Rodney and I were given legal documents stating that these children belong in our custody in order to prevent any further problems. I don't think there are any other details that really matter, except . . . well, the children left with nothing except for a doll that Rachel was holding to very tightly, so we purchased some things for them—all of the minimally necessary clothing they would need, and a few toys. And we had to buy a trunk to put all of it in."

"I will earn off the money used for my boy," Rodney said strongly. "I would have ye take it from my wages until it's all made right and—"

"Don't you worry about that, Rodney," Sylvia said, then looked at Dougal. "Nor you. I am nothing but happy to be able to contribute to helping these children have a new start in life, and I can't wait to meet them." She sighed, feeling tired even though she wasn't necessarily sleepy. "However, I do believe we should all try to get some rest. If the children slept in the carriage, then they will be up at a normal time in the morning no matter how tired we adults might be."

"No need for you to worry about that," Dougal said. "We will take care of the children and I'll see that the morning chores are done since I'll be awake anyway. You rest as long as you like."

"But—" Sylvia began but Dougal interrupted her.

"If we need to nap in the afternoon, you can help watch out for the children. By then you won't be a complete stranger to them."

"Very well," she said and repeated, "and I can't wait to meet them."

It only took a few minutes to put the kitchen in order before everyone went upstairs to their rooms to get some sleep. Sylvia wished for an opportunity to kiss Dougal goodnight, but with the others nearby it would have been impossible without creating an awkward scene.

Sylvia went into her room and crawled back into her bed, mentally reviewing all that had happened since she'd been startled out of her sleep by the sound of the carriage arriving. She couldn't keep herself from smiling to consider that their mission had been successful, and that having the children in their fathers' care was now legal and couldn't be questioned. And she actually giggled softly to recall the greeting she'd shared with Dougal, and how much she'd missed being in his arms and feeling his kiss upon her lips. Oh, how glad she was to have him back!

When Sylvia awoke, she was surprised at how long and how deeply she'd slept. The clock told her she'd long ago missed breakfast, even if the heavy clouds outside had left the room dim. She'd expected to be awakened by the sound of children being noisy—as children naturally were. But she'd slept deeply and hadn't heard a sound—at least not anything loud enough to wake her. Realizing that rain was hitting the roof and windows, she wondered if that had helped buffer other noises.

Sylvia hurried to get ready for the day and left her room to stand in the hall for a long moment, hearing no evidence of anyone else being upstairs. She went down to the kitchen where Millie was putting something in the oven.

"Oh, there you are," Millie said. "I'm glad you got yourself some sleep, but you must be half starved."

"I *am* hungry," Sylvia said, "but where are . . ."

Millie pointed past Sylvia and said quietly, "In the parlor. Quiet little things. I suspect they weren't allowed to make a peep in that awful house where they was being kept. I dare say with time they'll learn how to be normal children again."

"I do hope so," Sylvia said.

As if Millie had fully grasped Sylvia's curiosity, she said, "You go and meet them, and I'll warm up some breakfast for you."

"Thank you," Sylvia said, "but don't go to too much trouble."

"It's no trouble at all," Millie smiled and motioned with her hand toward the parlor.

Sylvia moved quietly into the doorway to see the children each kneeling opposite each other next to the table between the sofas, concentrating on a picture puzzle they were attempting to assemble. All three men were seated around the children, showing a great interest in the puzzle. Bob had a head of thick dark brown hair that looked as if it didn't know how to remain in place. Rachel's blonde hair hung down her back like a silky waterfall, and it was evident it had been brushed through very well not too long ago. She wondered if Dougal was responsible for that. Until now Sylvia had not once even thought about the actual ages of the children. She could see that Bob was likely a few years younger than Rachel, and he was probably four or five. Sylvia hoped they would like her, and she wondered if she truly had anything in her that might be naturally nurturing toward children. Well, with two of them living among them, they would all certainly find out.

"Hello," she said, and all eyes turned toward her, which gave Sylvia her first view of the children's faces. Rachel's features were soft and gentle, and her skin was as white as a porcelain doll. She was truly a beautiful child, almost like a fine lady in miniature, and there was an obvious resemblance to her father that Sylvia found intriguing. Bob had large eyes and a round, mildly chubby face even though he was not at all a chubby child. Quite simply, he was adorable. His appearance gave Sylvia the urge to just hug him tightly.

"I'm Sylvia," she said. "I—"

"Papa told us all about you," Rachel said very maturely. "He said you are very kind and you are letting us live in your house with you."

"I'm very glad to have you here." Sylvia moved her eyes back and forth between the children and added, "Both of you."

Bob said with the slightest hint of a lisp, "Do you make cakes like Millie? She let us have cake after breakfast."

Sylvia laughed softly. "Millie makes very delicious cakes. In fact, I think everything that Millie makes is delicious. Sometimes I help Millie, but I only do what she tells me. I'm afraid I couldn't make a cake on my own, and if I tried it would probably taste very nasty." She made a face that mimicked having tasted something terrible, which made the children laugh.

Turning her attention to the puzzle, Sylvia asked, "What do we have here?"

"We saw this in a shop during one of our stops on the way home," Dougal said. "Sometimes we had to just take a walk through a village to stretch our legs and get some fresh air. The children were very intrigued with it, so we indulged and brought it home with us. They've been excited to actually have a table where they could put it together."

"It looks as if it's coming together very well," Sylvia said, leaning over the table to get a better look at the painted picture of some farm animals. "You know, we have some of those animals out in the barn." The children looked up at her, showing some excitement. "You met our horses since they were pulling the carriage that brought you here, but we also have a pig and a cow and some chickens. And they all have names."

Bob turned to Rodney and asked, "Can we look at th' animals?"

Rodney spoke to his son with genuine fondness. "It's rainin' right now, little man. We'll all go out t' the barn when it's not so wet." Rodney glanced toward Sylvia and added, "If that's all right with the missus."

"Of course it's all right," Sylvia said with a little laugh. "You needn't consult me on your activities."

Sylvia was about to sit down next to Dougal and join the observation of the puzzle coming together when Millie appeared and told her that her breakfast was ready.

"I'd best get something to eat," Sylvia said. "I'm afraid I slept far too long."

"Not too long if you needed the rest," Dougal said, giving her a smile that made her heart quicken.

She nodded at him then said to the children, "Keep up the good work. I can't wait to see the puzzle when it's finished."

After Sylvia had enjoyed appeasing her hunger and Millie had completed her work in the kitchen, the women joined everyone else in the parlor to watch the evolution of the puzzle coming together. The adults just watched and allowed the children to fit the pieces together, and they did so very well without any guidance. Occasionally it took them a minute or more to find the right piece to fit in a particular place, but they were both clearly very bright. When the puzzle was completed, everyone cheered and applauded as if it were the greatest accomplishment to ever occur in the history of the world. Millie insisted that they needed to celebrate with more cake and the children ran to the dining table to be seated, eager and excited to have more of Millie's delicious cake, and Millie quickly followed after them, chuckling with pleasure.

"They're delightful children," Sylvia said to the men while they were coming to their feet. "I look forward to getting to know them better."

"After having been away from Rachel for so long," Dougal said, "I look forward to getting to know her myself."

Dougal and Sylvia exchanged a smile and then everyone was seated around the table to enjoy a slice of Millie's cake. When Millie declared that the cake was almost gone, the children almost looked as if they might cry. Then Millie declared that she would just have to make another, and she would need the help of Rachel and Bob to mix the batter. This made the children clap their hands with excitement.

While Millie had the children engaged in helping her, Sylvia asked Dougal if she could speak to him privately, saying in front of the others, "I need your advice on some household business matters."

"Of course," Dougal said and agreed to meet her in the workroom in a few minutes. George and Rodney went outside to do some work in the barn since only the bare minimum had been taken care of in their absence, and both men were heard telling each other they'd far rather work in the barn than have to deal with any kind of business matters.

Sylvia sat down in her workroom to wait for Dougal. It was only a moment before she heard his footsteps approaching. Sylvia's heart quickened when Dougal entered the room and closed the door behind him. He sat beside her with their backs to the windows where rain drizzled over the glass in continual streams.

"I do need to discuss some business with you," she said immediately, in order to make him aware of her motives, "but mostly I just wanted to be alone with you for a few minutes."

"I would never argue with that," he said and quickly kissed her. He drew back to look into her eyes, saying in a husky whisper, "Oh, I missed you! Forgive me if this sounds presumptuous, and please know that I'm well aware we are not in a position to be making any decisions for the future, but . . . I just have to say that I don't ever want to leave here again. A moment hardly passed while I was away when I didn't have you in my thoughts."

"It was the same for me," she said. "We kept very busy, but . . . I couldn't stop thinking about you, and . . . perhaps we need to talk about exactly what we might want to have happen in our future . . . even if it would be prudent to take some time to actually make any decisions."

"I've already told you what I want, Sylvia," he said with ardent adoration in his eyes. "But I must admit that I feel . . . well . . . a man is supposed to care for a woman, to provide for her needs, and . . . the way I came here with nothing, and still I have nothing, and . . . Oh! Before I forget . . ." He reached inside of his shirt and pulled out a small stack of banknotes. "Here's the money we didn't need."

Sylvia took it and quickly thumbed through the stack, making a quick estimation of what was there. "You didn't spend as much as I thought you would—not that it would have mattered."

"I hope it's all right that we purchased things for the children, and—"

"Of course it's all right," Sylvia said. "In fact, I think I'd very much like to spend a great deal more on the children. The house could use more toys and games and puzzles, I think. I want them both to feel completely at home here, and to be able to have fun—as children should."

"You're such a generous woman, Sylvia, and so kind. I want to echo what Rodney said. I will do whatever work you need done for as long as you need it in order to earn off all that you have spent to help me get Rachel back . . . and to provide so much for her—and for me. You have been generous on my behalf right from the start. I find it difficult to believe that we would be so blessed."

"I feel blessed as well, Dougal. And I don't feel as if I'm making any great sacrifices. It's nice to have all of you here. It feels more like a home with the place all filled up."

"Well, I'm glad you feel that way," Dougal said with a small laugh. "Once the children become accustomed to being here, they might well test our patience."

"What are children for?" Sylvia said, reflecting his laughter. She then recalled one of her purposes for needing to speak with him. "I've done nothing with trying to return the money to its rightful owners. I couldn't really do anything about it with only me and Millie here because we spent practically every waking minute together. And I also wanted your help . . . or at the very least your advice . . . on how to go about it and—"

"I've given the matter some thought," Dougal said. "If you're not opposed to paying his fees, I believe it might be best to put the matter into the hands of a solicitor and for him to return the money personally, as opposed to trusting the post which can be subject to unpredictability. I assume you want the money returned anonymously . . . as opposed to having these people know who you are and where you live. Putting your location on the envelope would be necessary in order to post them so that they would get returned if they weren't deliverable. If someone delivers the money personally, they will know whether or not it gets into the right hands. And I don't at all think that you should be traveling to complete such an endeavor, and if *I* do it, people who knew Daniel will assume that it's me, and they might be glad to receive the money owed to them, but not necessarily glad to see me. What do you think?"

"I think it's a very good idea," Sylvia said, actually feeling some relief. He'd thought of all the possible problems that she'd been thinking about.

"Have you worked with a solicitor before? Is there someone in the area? Someone you can trust?"

"There is a Mr. Simpleton who worked with Daniel, and a little with Daniel's father prior to his death. Daniel had Mr. Simpleton come here before he left for war to help me understand how to handle financial matters regarding the estate in Daniel's absence. I've consulted him a few times in the years since. I like him very much and I do believe he can be trusted."

"That's good, then," Dougal said. "Perhaps next time George and Millie go into town for supplies they can deliver a message to Mr. Simpleton and he might be willing to come here for a meeting—since I assume you won't be going into town."

"He's always come here before," she said. "He understands the situation and has always been very kind."

"That's especially good," Dougal said. "So, we will deal with that matter when Mr. Simpleton is able to meet with us here. In the meantime, I think we can put the right amount of money into individual envelopes and properly address them. If you like, I could help you whenever the time is right."

"Thank you," Sylvia said. "I do appreciate your help. I know it isn't so terribly complicated, but . . . perhaps because it's somewhat of a sensitive matter. Daniel and I argued so much over this very kind of thing. To be able to return this money feels like a miracle to me. It feels somewhat healing in regard to my memories of him. I'm very glad to not have to face taking care of it alone. With you there I won't be so prone to allowing my mind to wander into difficult memories."

"I'm glad to help in any way I can, and I'm very glad that you trust me to help you with something so . . . sensitive." He came to his feet and urged her to do the same, easing her into his arms where he kissed her ardently before she even had a chance to realize he was going to. But it was easy and natural to return his affection, and she loved the way her spirit felt soothed by the evidence that she was not alone in her feelings. Reluctantly easing away from her, he added, "Now, I think we should go and see how that cake is coming along."

"Excellent idea," Sylvia said, and they both went to the kitchen to see that the children were having a marvelous time under Millie's supervision, and she too was clearly enjoying herself.

The remainder of the day went smoothly while Sylvia felt drawn to the children and enjoyed getting to know them. She liked asking them questions and learning about their preferences and personalities.

That evening after supper was over and the evening chores had been seen to—both in the house and in the barn—Rodney took Bob upstairs to get him ready for bed and Dougal told Rachel to go upstairs and change into her nightgown. Sylvia was pleasantly surprised when Dougal discreetly guided her into her workroom and kissed her, whispering near her ear, "I needed a good-night kiss."

"I'm so glad," she said, and he kissed her again.

"I told Rachel I would check on her shortly, and I'm obligated to tell her a bedtime story. I left a lamp burning in her room, but she's naturally a little uneasy about being in a strange place. I think at least for tonight I should stay close by." He bent over and kissed Sylvia once more. "I will see you in the morning."

"I'll look forward to it," Sylvia said, then a thought occurred to her. "Oh, one more thing. Do you think I should tell George and Millie about the money? About what we're doing?"

"I think that's entirely up to you," Dougal said before he smiled and winked and left the room.

Sylvia remained where she was for a short while, pondering all that had changed in her life since Dougal had frightened her in the barn with his appearance. And just today those changes had become much more dramatic. But she felt far more happy than anxious over the prospect of getting to know the children better. Thankfully, they would be well cared for by their fathers—and George and Millie had already stepped in like doting grandparents—and Sylvia could just learn how to interact with them by observing and just spending time with them, day by day.

Sylvia felt relief over Dougal's suggestion on how to deal with the money, and she looked forward to the day when that would all be taken care of. For now, she just wanted to sleep. It had been a very eventful day and she felt suddenly very tired. After carefully hiding the money in her room, Sylvia got ready for bed and slid beneath the bedcovers, her last thoughts being of the sensation of Dougal's kiss before she drifted into a contented slumber.

Two days later, George and Millie went into town for supplies and they all decided that the children would enjoy going with them. Rodney went as well to help. Now that the drama surrounding Rodney had been settled, they'd all decided that no one in the household really cared about what anyone might think of the fact that Rodney now worked for Sylvia and lived in her home. Sylvia had given George some extra money to purchase something for the children that they might enjoy playing with. It was decided that Dougal should remain away from the public eye—at least for now—given his resemblance to Daniel Hewitt. Of course gossip in the village had surely spread that Daniel was alive and well, but Dougal didn't feel ready to face the way people might react to him and want to talk to him. And Sylvia never went into town, which gave them the perfect opportunity to use envelopes and sealing wax that Sylvia had in ample supply and prepare the money to be put into the hands of the solicitor. They also included a brief note of explanation inside each envelope. It took some time, but they were able to complete the task and safely hide the envelopes before the others returned from town to report that all had gone well.

The men unloaded feed for the animals in the barn and brought food into the house that was put into the pantry and the larder. In the midst of putting everything in its proper order, George whispered to Sylvia, "I gave Mr. Simpleton your message. He will be coming to see you tomorrow afternoon."

"Excellent," Sylvia said, and George smiled before he resumed his work. Neither he nor Millie knew her reasons for needing to meet with her solicitor, but they respected her privacy. She couldn't think of any reason *not* to tell them. Quite simply, they just hadn't had an opportunity to speak without others around. It was not something to be discussed in front of the children, and there was no reason for Rodney to know about the past misdeeds of Daniel Hewitt.

Sylvia had been so busy helping organize the pantry that something strange suddenly occurred to her. "Where are the children?" she asked in a teasing voice. "You didn't leave them in town, did you?"

"No," George chuckled, "we didn't leave them. Rodney's keeping an eye on them while he organizes some things in the barn. They each chose a new hobbyhorse and they're wanting to do a great deal of running."

"It's good for them to get some proper exercise," Millie commented as both women went to the back door, curious to see the children at play. They both laughed to see Rachel and Bob following each other about with a large, smooth stick between their legs and dragging on the ground, and a horse's head fashioned out of wood attached to the other end. The children were laughing and imitating the noises that horses made, and Sylvia couldn't help but feel delighted to see them having so much fun.

"I dare say," Dougal said, appearing behind the women to look over their shoulders, "the little tykes might be sleeping with their new horses."

"As long as the horses are clean," Sylvia said, mesmerized by watching the children, "I don't see anything wrong with that."

"Indeed," Millie said and chuckled before she returned to her work, but Sylvia chose to watch a little longer and loved the way that Dougal remained in the doorway, watching with her.

That night the horses did indeed get put to bed in the children's rooms. Rachel was content to have hers on the floor beside her bed, although she wanted a blanket over the stick so only the head was showing above it. Bob, however, was quite insistent about having the horse in his bed with him. The adults all laughed about it while they shared tea around the table after the children had been put to bed. Doing so had quickly become a habit, and Sylvia enjoyed this time with all of the adults. Rodney was starting to warm up more to the others and seemed more at ease, and Sylvia was pleased to see evidence that he was feeling more relaxed in her home. He had already proven that he was indeed willing to work hard, and he had a fair amount of skill in doing whatever task might be required.

The following day Mr. Simpleton came as promised and Sylvia met privately with him in her workroom, since it was a place where the doors could be closed and they could talk without being overheard. He accepted Sylvia's request very matter-of-factly with the minimal explanation she gave him, and he promised her that he would see the matter taken care of, assuring her that he didn't take her trust lightly and he would do right by her. And the amount he charged her for such an endeavor was not as much as she'd thought it might be. He asked for half his payment at that time, and he would come and collect the other half when the matter was all taken care of. Sylvia knew if she had decided to personally travel to deliver them herself it would have cost far more, and if she sent them by post she would always wonder if they had been safely delivered to the right person.

Sylvia felt an enormous relief to see Mr. Simpleton leave with his promise to help her make things right on Daniel's behalf. She couldn't deny a sense of healing in regard to her relationship with Daniel, and she was glad he'd made it possible for her to do this.

Over the next few weeks, Sylvia's household settled into a new routine that Sylvia liked very much. Everyone had their daily responsibilities, and the children had each been given some simple tasks that were appropriate for their age. Neither of them complained about the little bit of work they needed to do. Millie had suggested that it was good to put these expectations into place before the children became too comfortable in their new surroundings without being expected to do anything, and then it would become an easy habit and nothing for them to whine or complain about. Sylvia appreciated Millie's wisdom, and she knew the two fathers did as well. Dougal had not been in charge of his daughter for years, and Rodney had admitted that he didn't know much about the proper raising of a child. He'd only been doing what he thought was best, but he'd often doubted himself, and was therefore grateful for any help or advice.

As green plants began to appear in the garden, everyone put some time in every few days to remove the weeds and leave the vegetables to be able to thrive on the rain and sunshine. The children even helped pulling weeds—probably for the fact that it allowed them to get their hands very dirty—although they had to be closely supervised by an adult in order to be able to tell the weeds from the plants they wanted to keep. As the vegetables grew bigger it would be easier to tell the difference.

With supplies purchased in town, the men began doing the repairs and painting that was all long overdue. They'd decided to paint the barn first and then do the outside of the house. George kept to his usual routine while Dougal and Rodney took on the extra projects, although both Millie and George enjoyed helping care for the children while their fathers were busy. Sylvia also contributed to watching over the children, and now that she'd had the opportunity to get to know them better, she found she was becoming sincerely attached to them.

Sometimes she would look around at her home and the people there and realize that she never could have imagined such a situation, but she liked it very much and hoped that everyone who lived here now would remain indefinitely.

Of course, when the children became adults they would likely go elsewhere to find their way. It was easy to imagine Rachel growing into a beautiful young lady who could surely find a good husband and be happy with him. And Bob seemed destined to become a hard worker like his father and would surely be able to make a living doing whatever he might choose to do, and also have a family of his own. But their adulthood was many years off, and Sylvia was determined to enjoy every moment of the time they were here.

She also enjoyed the company of every adult now living in her home. She shared a unique relationship with each of them but couldn't imagine her life with any one of them absent. In fact, it was difficult to even recall how her life had been before their home had become so full.

Occasionally the children got into some kind of argument with each other, and there were times when one or both of them were resistant to doing their assigned chores. But the adults were all unified in how to handle such situations, and nothing ever got too much out of hand.

A stretch of many days of rain made it impossible to work in the garden or do any painting on the outside of the barn. So, Dougal and Rodney worked inside the barn, and also did some repairs in the house. Millie kept busy in the kitchen, sometimes having the children help her, although that always made a bigger mess and took longer than if Millie simply did the work herself. But she didn't mind. In fact, she rather seemed to enjoy it. Sylvia helped Millie some in the kitchen as she always had, and she also regularly spent time in her workroom, grinding herbs and making salves and powders and tinctures. The children were curious about what she was doing, and she gladly explained it to them. She told them they were allowed to watch but they couldn't touch anything because her methods and mixtures had to be exactly right, and everything needed to remain very clean. Rachel and Bob followed her rules perfectly, likely so they could have their curiosity eased and because they didn't want to be expelled from the room. And once they'd watched her enough to become bored, they left her to do her work and found other things to do.

The children made good use of the toys, games, puzzles, and books that had been purchased for them, and George began a new tradition of reading to them for a while each afternoon, which George likely enjoyed at least as much as the children.

After five days of rain, Rachel came into the kitchen early one afternoon where Sylvia and Millie were working and asked if she and Bob could have their own tea later on, instead of having tea with the adults. They talked about it and decided that the children would have tea an hour prior to the time when the adults would have tea, and during *that* time the children would do something quiet so the adults could enjoy *their* teatime. Rachel and Bob were both excited and Sylvia wondered over the source of the idea, but she and Millie both found it endearing the way that the children insisted on helping prepare the little sandwiches for their tea, and to properly arrange biscuits and scones on little plates. They set one end of the table with the proper dishes, and shared tea very maturely with little help from the women. Within a few days the new schedule for tea had become a habit and the children seemed to enjoy behaving like grownups while they shared tea, and the adults very much enjoyed having tea without the children creating noise and chaos.

Nearly four weeks after Mr. Simpleton had left to see to his business on Sylvia's behalf, he returned and met with her to report that all of the deliveries had been made successfully. "Only one of these people was not at the same address, but they were tracked down easily enough, still in the same town," the solicitor reported. She was surprised when Mr. Simpleton provided a ledger page for Sylvia on which each of the recipients had signed their names as proof of having been given the envelopes she'd sent for them. She *did* trust Mr. Simpleton, but having this piece of paper in her hands gave the project a stronger sense of finality.

Sylvia was pleased and paid the man the remainder of what she owed him, and he reminded her before he left that he was always available to help her with any financial or legal matter. She was glad to know that was the case but hoped there would never be any need of his services again. Knowing the matter was taken care of gave her added peace, and she was able to more fully put the matter behind her.

As more time passed, Sylvia felt an added security having the significant amount of money Daniel had left her hidden safely away. She'd never felt concerned about having their needs met, finding her inherited property and income sufficient. Nevertheless, there had been very little extra, and she'd always had the hovering worry there wouldn't be enough if they had been met with any challenges. She no longer needed to worry about that.

Along with feeling more secure financially, Sylvia discovered a new contentment in her life as spring stretched into summer, settling into many warm days and much beauty in the nature around them. They had all settled comfortably into a routine that revolved around the needs of the children, and it was rather quaint the way each of the adults had their time every day when they helped the children or shared an activity with them. Sylvia had grown to love them very quickly, and she prayed that neither Dougal nor Rodney would ever leave and take these precious children with them. She'd grown to care for Rodney and admire him in many ways, and she grew to care for Dougal more every day in an entirely different manner.

The two of them managed to sneak a kiss here and there when no one was looking, and sometimes they were actually able to share some private conversation. But it seemed to Sylvia that their relationship had reached some kind of plateau. He was pretending to be her husband on the chance that anyone might come to the farm and encounter him. Also, having a husband added another layer of security for Sylvia—especially when she was so ostracized by the community. His presence made her feel safer, made her life feel more normal. And yet he was *not* her husband. They slept in rooms at opposite ends of the house, and for all their little romantic moments each day, they never talked of the future possibilities of their relationship. Sylvia began to wonder if Dougal would be forever content to keep things between them as they were, or if he might be waiting for her to address the matter. Perhaps the fact that he was living in her home—and in some strange way employed by her—he didn't feel that he could share his feelings on the matter honestly.

Sylvia sincerely didn't know what to do about the problem. She wondered if she should take the lead and initiate a conversation to address exactly where they stood. On one hand she didn't want to frighten him off by expecting more than he felt willing—or capable—of giving. On the other hand, she didn't think she could bear going forward indefinitely with the love they shared remaining in such a place of stagnancy.

Chapter Eleven

The Wrong Man

Rainy days always kept the children indoors, and any outdoor projects the adults might be working on came to a temporary halt. But that was the nature of life in a place where rain was a frequent occurrence. Nevertheless, Sylvia loved the rain. She loved the coziness it created when everyone was secure within the safety and protection of their home, and she loved the way it nourished the garden and all of the surrounding grounds and meadows.

Today she settled into her workroom. Customers came consistently—one or two a week and always late at night. They had gotten past the spring months when colds and the flu were more common, but her supply had been depleted. She'd been waiting for summer to offer many plants she gathered and dried to then either be crushed or boiled to be made into her inventory of powders, creams, poultices, and tinctures. Sylvia had taken the children with her more than once to search for and pick baskets full of leaves from the gingko trees and chamomile flowers, as well as lavender, primrose, and others. The children had enjoyed the excursions and Sylvia had appreciated the help since she'd needed large quantities of the plants and flowers. The baskets weren't heavy but Sylvia could only carry so many at a time.

Now, all of these offerings of nature had been thoroughly dried and were ready for the real work to begin. Occasionally the children came into her workroom to see what she was doing and ask a question or two, but they quickly became bored since Sylvia felt strongly about needing to do the actual work herself. This wasn't like helping in the kitchen—everything had to be handled very carefully at this stage, and no mistakes could be made. A mistake in the kitchen might result in less-than-tasty scones or cake, but a mistake in Sylvia's work could create the wrong remedy and cause problems for the patient. The children had understood Sylvia's explanation of this, but they still seemed to need to check on her every once in a while and just see how she was doing, and to examine the progress of her work.

Sylvia had come to enjoy their interruptions and the little bits of conversation that took place when they came to visit with her, and she wondered how she had ever managed to live in this house without them. As they left the workroom in a hurry, they almost bumped into Dougal as he entered. He laughed and told them to slow down a little and save their running for outside on a sunny day. They ignored him and their footsteps could be heard on the stairs, obviously going to their rooms to see what they might be able to play with to ease the boredom of a rainy day.

"I hope they aren't causing you any trouble," Dougal said, sitting down and casually crossing his ankle over his knee.

"Not at all," she said. "Don't worry. I'm not afraid to get after them if they're misbehaving."

"Good," he said with a small laugh, then added more seriously, "I'm very grateful for the way you help watch out for them, and needless to say, for the way you've opened your home so graciously to all of us. Rachel would be terribly lonely and sad without Bob to play with, therefore having him and his father here is an added blessing. You know Rachel and Bob don't always get along and they have their challenges, but I think they'd be lost without each other."

"I know all of this, Dougal," she said, vigorously mashing the pestle into the mortar in order to create a fine powder that would easily dissolve in liquid. "Why are you saying things you've said many times?"

"I just don't want you to ever think that I'm not grateful. I wish I could do more to help you and—"

"You do plenty to help around here," she said, a little astonished. "I'm not at all overworked or feeling taken advantage of, I can assure you."

"That's good, then," Dougal said as if he'd just needed the reassurance. He then added, "So how are you feeling about having two rather loud and energetic children in your home now that they've had time to completely settle in? Rachel loves it here. From what she tells me, she always hated being with her grandparents, and living here is something akin to heaven for her."

"I'm so glad," Sylvia said and stopped working for a moment to take that in. The very idea made her deeply happy. "And to answer your question," she said, resuming her work, "I enjoy having them here. I like having the house full. I think we all make a comfortable group and as far as I can see, things are going well. Since I can't have children of my own, having them here is . . . well, I think it fills something in me that I had believed would never be filled. Having children in the house is just . . . well . . . quite frankly I love it, and . . ."

Sylvia stopped what she was doing abruptly when she glanced up at Dougal and saw an expression of shock and perhaps some degree of horror on his face. She set down the pestle with a thud and asked, "What's wrong?"

"You can't have children?" he asked in a voice that sounded almost panicked. "How do you know for certain?"

"Now, that's a personal question!" Sylvia countered, not wanting to talk about it. "Are you trying to say that any possibility of a future between us would be negated by this fact?"

Dougal looked a little startled and hurried to say, "No! That's not at all what I'm saying!" She wondered if that meant there *was* the possibility of a future between them. "I'm simply . . . surprised. You've never said anything about it before and—"

"It's not the kind of thing a woman brings up in casual conversation," Sylvia said firmly.

"I thought we shared something more than simply . . . casual conversation."

"Do we?" she asked, hoping to steer the conversation away from her most sensitive personal issue and perhaps be able to get some answers to the questions she'd had simmering in the back of her mind.

"I trust you and I enjoy the relationship we share, but nothing has changed for months. We haven't talked at all about where we stand or what we want to happen between us in the future or—"

"Sylvia," he interrupted and leaned forward a little, "I love you and I want to stay here with you forever, but as I've pointed out many times, I have nothing to offer you and—"

"Are you saying that you have hesitated declaring your intentions because of . . . what? Your pride? Is it not all right for our lives to go on as they are? For you to live in my home, simply because it's *my* home and I'm a woman? Of course you're the wrong man to—"

"What?" he asked, sounding defensive.

"Just let me finish. All of the adults living here know your true identity, but as far as anyone else knows you're my husband. Except that you are *not* my husband. Therefore, if you intend to remain here indefinitely—which I hope you will—that would have to be remedied."

"Yes," he said, "that would certainly have to be remedied, but . . . it's also more complicated than that." She waited for him to explain but he didn't.

"Can we not talk about such complications?" she asked.

"Sylvia," he said gently, "you're right that we need to talk about these things, and . . . just give me a little time to come to terms with some things that have been troubling me, and I promise you that we will talk about everything . . . and we will make plans for our future—our future together."

Sylvia took a long moment to absorb what he'd said before she nodded and looked down. "Very well," she said, thinking she should pick up the pestle again and continue her work, but her thoughts were stuck on his reaction to her admitting that she couldn't have children. She usually worked hard to not think about her condition, but at the moment she didn't feel the strength to push the memories away and she unconsciously moved to a chair.

"Are you all right?" Dougal asked and moved his own chair next to hers so that he could take her hand.

"Just . . . some difficult memories," she admitted, wanting to be honest.

"Does it have anything to do with your not being able to have children?" he asked, and she looked up at him, startled by his perception until she reminded herself that he was not only perceptive, he had come to know her well.

"I'm afraid it does," she said, realizing she needed to tell him the reasons. She could not seriously be considering a future with him and not be completely honest about her past. And she wanted more than anything to be with him forever. Perhaps sharing her darkest, most sensitive experience might be an act of faith toward that future. It had certainly occurred to her that her inability to bear a child would affect Dougal if they were to marry. Before he'd shown up here, she had completely given up on the possibility of ever marrying again. But he *was* here, and they had grown to love each other. He had the right to know.

"You don't have to tell me," he said, "except that . . . I want to share your burdens, Sylvia."

"I *do* have to tell you," she said, "because I don't think we should have any secrets between us. This isn't really a secret; it's just something I don't like to talk about, but . . ." She sighed loudly. "But you should know what happened." She sighed again and just dove in if only so she could get it over with as quickly as possible. "It was only days after Daniel left that I realized I was pregnant." She heard him draw in a sharp breath but tried to ignore his responses in order to just get through this. "With this realization I knew I needed to hire someone to live here and help me. I'd considered the idea. Daniel and I had even talked about it, and I had felt hesitant. But with a baby coming I knew I could never manage everything on my own. So that's when I brought George and Millie into my home. They were in need of work and a place to live right at the moment I needed them. It was a miracle."

"Indeed," Dougal said solemnly and said nothing more, which prompted Sylvia to press forward.

"About six months into the pregnancy, I began having terrible pains and . . . bleeding." It only took Sylvia a moment to realize that he was a grown man and he would know what she meant. "George went for the doctor. At that time, I'd had no reason to dislike him because quite simply I didn't know him. I had been attending church and going into town for errands, but I was shy and I hadn't interacted with people much. Very few people made an effort to speak with *me,* and I believe now in looking back that my shyness had given people the impression that I was standoffish, which contributed to the terrible rumors when they began to spread, but . . . I'm digressing. Forgive me."

"It's fine," Dougal said. "I'm glad to know anything you want to tell me."

His words encouraged her to go on. "By the time the doctor arrived with George, I was in terrible pain. I was having contractions very close together, and it was far too soon for the baby to come and be able to live, so I was naturally very upset. The doctor was . . . forthright. He stated facts without offering any compassion or kindness, but I just kept thinking that I needed his help and it was his expertise that mattered." She took in a deep, sustaining breath before she reached toward the most difficult part of this story. "The labor was difficult and painful, but when the baby—a girl—was born already dead, I wanted to die myself. And then . . . then . . . the doctor said that I was bleeding too much and I would bleed to death if he didn't do something and fast. I had no idea what to expect . . . what he meant by doing *something,* but to put it as briefly as possible, he performed a very hurried surgery on me. I'm not certain what he did exactly, but the result was having my womb permanently damaged, so much so that I would never be able to carry another baby."

He looked horrified and she well understood the feeling. "Did you have anything to ease the pain?" he asked.

"A spoonful of something that in my opinion didn't help in the least," Sylvia stated. "Quite honestly, I never imagined such pain could be possible. I felt . . . everything. Millie was with me, praise heaven. And the doctor did everything very efficiently, but without a single kind word."

Dougal leaned forward and hung his head into his hands, and she heard him sniffling. Was her story so upsetting? *Yes,* she thought. It was horrid. And she knew Dougal loved her. In truth, his reaction helped compensate somehow for the coldness of the doctor at the time and the extreme pain she'd endured. Dougal had been a soldier, and she knew from things he'd told her that he'd witnessed men experiencing unspeakable pain. He likely had some comprehension of what she'd been through from things he'd seen and heard before. Although Sylvia *still* had trouble comprehending it. She'd lost her baby. She'd

194

lost her ability to ever have another baby. And the surgical procedure that had permanently damaged her had been far more painful and traumatic than her labor and the loss of her baby combined. She still couldn't think about it without cringing and wanting to scream.

Sylvia paused now that she'd gotten past the worst of her story, and she noticed Dougal taking a handkerchief out of his pocket and using it to wipe his face. She couldn't *see* his face, given the way he had leaned forward and was looking at the floor, but there was no question that he was crying.

Wanting to get this completely over and done, Sylvia went on to tell him what she considered important facts. "Needless to say, after this ordeal it took me a very long time to recover physically, and I never would have survived without Millie and George to take care of me and everything else around here. But the physical pain was only worsened by my deep grief. Not only had I lost my baby and my ability to give birth, I kept having this instinctive feeling that the surgery had not been necessary. I didn't know if my mind was simply trying to cope with my grief, or if my hunch was right. Millie suggested that I needed more information. There was no other doctor or even a midwife anywhere in this area, so I wrote letters to the doctor and a midwife in the village where I'd grown up. I wrote in detail what had happened and asked them to share their honest opinions based on their training and experiences. Both of them wrote back and they each told me almost exactly the same thing." She took a deep breath, wondering if she could say it aloud without becoming even more emotional than Dougal was at the moment. "Excessive bleeding following a birth is not terribly uncommon. There are methods of stopping it by massaging the womb or . . . well . . . I don't remember exactly but they both said there were a number of things that should have been tried before taking such drastic measures. In essence, what this doctor did to me was the most drastic thing he could have done, and in the medical profession it is considered to be absolutely the last possible option to save a woman's life. He tried nothing else before he just . . . put me through this horrible procedure and . . . took away my ability to be a mother."

Sylvia realized she was crying now and hurriedly wiped her hands over her cheeks. She knew there was one more thing she had to say and she rushed to do so. "I can't be certain, of course, but . . . I know the doctor was aware of my . . . remedies . . . and that he strongly disagreed with such an approach to healing. And I've wondered if he's the kind of man who is callous and harsh in *all* of his medical decisions, or if his dislike of me influenced the way he handled my situation."

Dougal looked toward her abruptly with a rage in his eyes that couldn't disguise the fact that he'd been crying a great deal more than she'd realized. "Are you saying he did this to you out of some kind of . . . jealousy . . . or . . . or vengeance?"

"I don't know, Dougal," Sylvia said. "And it doesn't matter. It's long in the past, and what's done is done. Holding onto anger against him for that or any other reason will only poison myself. I don't like him and I don't trust him, but I forgave him a long time ago. I have no wish to carry such a burden, Dougal. God will judge him for his actions one day. Only God knows his heart and his motives."

"Well, I might need a little time to be able to follow your very noble Christian example," Dougal said and stood so quickly that his chair almost tipped over. "I can't believe he did this to you." He began pacing frantically. "I can't believe . . . you had to go through all of that."

"Dougal," she said gently and stood to face him, taking hold of his arms to stop his pacing. "I'm all right. I know it's tragic, but I'm all right. And if you can be all right with my inability to have a child, then—"

"I'm not upset about that," he said. "I mean . . . I am, but not because I consider you any less valuable as a woman because of it. I'm just . . . upset." He took in a loud, deep breath and blew it out slowly as if he were consciously attempting to calm himself. "Oh, Sylvia," he said with a quivering voice and wrapped her in his arms, "I'm so sorry you had to go through all of that . . . alone."

"I wasn't alone," she said, holding to him as tightly as he held to her. "George and Millie took very good care of me."

"Without your husband here with you," he clarified.

"It couldn't be helped," she said, and he drew back just enough to kiss her brow before he stepped away and looked at her with deep compassion in his expression, but there was still rage in his eyes.

"Thank you for telling me," he said. "I . . . I need to be alone. We'll talk later."

Sylvia nodded and he hurried from the room as if the tears he'd been crying were only the beginning of an explosion of emotion that was threatening to burst out of him and he didn't want to be with her when it happened. She wondered why her story would upset him so deeply, and concluded that he truly did love her.

Feeling a little weak from having repeated the worst experience of her life, Sylvia sank back onto her chair and cried silently for several minutes before she pushed her memories of the event back into the place in her mind she'd created for them where they couldn't be felt. She got back to work in order to distract herself, and loved the sound of the children coming noisily down the stairs. In her mind, God had given her a miracle. She would never be able to give birth, but He had brought two beautiful children into her home and having them here gave her great joy.

The following day the sun was out and they all took advantage of the warmth to work together to pull the weeds out of the moist, soft earth in the garden. The children were each required to work for half an hour and then could clean their hands and play while the adults worked together to make certain the garden was completely free of weeds.

When that was finished, they all went their separate ways to work on other projects in the yard, the barn, and the kitchen. Sylvia noticed that Dougal still seemed unusually somber since the conversation they'd shared the previous day in the workroom. By all accounts he was interacting with everyone normally, and putting on a good front that made it easy to believe he was fine and all was as it should be. But Sylvia had gotten to know him well enough that she could see some kind of sorrow or grief hovering around him, and she wondered again why her story would have affected him so deeply. She wondered if there was someone in his past that had lost a child or had been treated badly by a doctor. His mother? A sister? Rachel's mother? He'd told her that she'd died in childbirth; perhaps the trauma of that experience was weighing on him. Sylvia knew all of these women were now deceased, but she knew very little about them, and she had to consider the possibility that her story had awakened some difficult memories for him, and perhaps that was the reason for his carefully concealed heartache. Sylvia wanted to talk to him about it, but he was putting a great deal of effort into avoiding any opportunity for the two of them to be alone at all. He'd told her he needed time, and she felt the need to respect his request and just allow him some time to come to terms with what she'd told him—whatever the reasons might be.

A few days after Sylvia had shared the most traumatic experience of her life with Dougal, she was working in the kitchen with Millie when Dougal came through the back door, his shirt splattered with an excessive amount of mud.

"This," he said somewhat melodramatically, "is what happens when you attempt to repair the corner of the pig trough and all of the pigs come to investigate. Thankfully I was kneeling outside the trough fence and my trousers were spared."

"Oh, dear," Sylvia said and couldn't keep from chuckling.

"You can't win a fight with a pig," Millie said and chuckled as well. More seriously she said, "I've got some hot water on the stove. I'll have George bring it to your room so you can change and clean up."

"Thank you," Dougal said and removed his boots before he hurried up the stairs.

"Where *is* George?" Millie asked as if his availability hadn't occurred to her when she'd promised he would help Dougal.

"I think he went outside with the children quite a while ago for a walk," Sylvia said. "They could be anywhere. Not to worry. I'll take the water up and leave it outside of his door."

"Very good," Millie said and poured both cold and boiling water into a clean bucket, intermittently checking the temperature to make certain it was perfect. They had a handful of buckets for this very purpose that were always kept clean, and Millie filled two of them with the correct temperature of water for Dougal to get cleaned up.

"Are those too heavy for you?" Millie asked as Sylvia picked them up.

"No, it's fine."

"Just give a knock on the door and tell him the water is there," Millie instructed, "and also tell him to just leave the muddy shirt on the floor by the door and I'll get it laundered." She let out a jolly little laugh. "It's certainly not the first time we've dealt with mud in this house."

"No, it certainly isn't," Sylvia said and headed up the stairs. She was surprised as she approached Dougal's room to find the door open, but since he was only changing his shirt, she didn't feel concerned about seeing anything that might be an embarrassment for either of them. Of course, he'd been expecting George, and he likely hadn't wanted to make it necessary for George to knock or open the door. Sylvia stepped into the doorway just as Dougal was sliding the muddy shirt off his back, which was turned toward her. She froze where she stood just as surely as if a sudden blizzard had burst into the hallway to leave her incapable of moving or speaking.

Dougal's voice startled her back to the moment. "Thank you, George," he said. "Just leave the water there."

Sylvia set the buckets down so abruptly that she felt a slosh of water soak through one of her stockings. She had to check herself carefully, to know that she wasn't imaging what she saw, while every interaction with this man since the day he'd appeared in her barn in such desperation raced and swirled in her mind. But it only took her a few seconds to be absolutely certain that what she was seeing was real. There was a very distinctive scar on his upper back, behind his right shoulder. And she knew it well. This man was not Dougal Heywood, and he never had been.

"Daniel," she muttered, her voice trembling. In fact every part of her was trembling with a combination of fear and confusion and *rage*.

He turned abruptly toward her, and his eyes widened in horror, his countenance was immediately overcome with guilt. "Sylvia," he said and moved toward her, but she backed away. "Oh, Sylvia. There are reasons for this. You must allow me to explain. You must—"

"What is there to say?" she demanded in a voice that was little more than a quavering whisper. "You've been lying to me all this time . . . living here . . . wooing me . . . pretending . . . for what? *What?*"

"I can explain, my love," he said desperately, "but it's complicated and—"

"There's nothing you can say that would ever convince me this *charade* was necessary," she insisted and felt a sudden need to just get away from him. She could feel herself on the verge of completely crumbling, and she hurried to her own room so she could attempt to contend privately with what she had just learned.

Sylvia hadn't meant to slam the door, but the sound of it closing startled her. She hurried to lock it then found herself incapable of even moving another step. She dropped to her knees then sat on the floor, lifting her apron to her face just as heaving sobs erupted from the center of her chest, creating literal pain as she wept. She couldn't believe it! She just couldn't believe it! All this time the man she'd believed to be Dougal—while at the same time believing that Daniel was long dead—had in actuality been Daniel. She'd been entirely convinced that *both* men had changed their scoundrel's ways, but she'd been completely duped and made a fool. And perhaps worst of all was the fact that she had fallen in love with Dougal. She'd embraced hopes and dreams of a future with him with the belief that they would share a good, long life together. And now every conversation she'd had with Dougal came back to her in a painful barrage as she attempted to accept that it had been Daniel—her husband—pretending not to know her, telling her tales of a life that was not his, but that of a dead man. Or perhaps there was no Dougal at all! Perhaps Daniel had simply made up the story of this man who looked so much like him.

She immediately squelched that theory with the existence of Rachel and her undeniable resemblance to Daniel, and yet for all of his crimes, Sylvia absolutely knew that Daniel could not be her father. She knew Rachel's age and birthday now, and Daniel had been living in the village where he'd met Sylvia at the time of Rachel's conception, and he'd lived there for quite some time. There was also the fact that Rachel's grandparents certainly would have known what Rachel's father looked like, and they'd known him from his youth, so there had to have been a Dougal Heywood, but . . . Oh! It was all so confusing! Such a mess! And when she reached beyond the confusion and heartache that fueled her tears, she just felt so *angry!* He'd lied to her, taken advantage of her, made a fool out of her. She wanted to slap him good and hard—over and over—as if that might somehow give him just a little bit of the pain she was experiencing.

Hearing a loud knocking on her door, Sylvia was startled so badly that she let out a gasp on the wake of a little scream. She pressed her apron tightly to her face in order to help keep her tears silent, but she felt certain that whoever was at the door had already heard her very vocal sobbing before they'd knocked. And she felt relatively certain it was Daniel. *Daniel! Daniel?* She couldn't believe it!

When she didn't respond, the knocking repeated more loudly, followed by Daniel saying through the door, "Sylvia, I know you're in there. Please . . . talk to me . . . or just listen. Let me explain."

"Go away!" she shouted in response, giving her anger some degree of escape with the excessive volume of her voice. "Just . . . go away and leave me alone! You're a liar and a swindler—just as you always were. Go away and leave me in peace!"

"I can't," he said. "I can't until you hear what I have to say. There are reasons for this, Sylvia. I was going to tell you everything . . . and soon. I swear to you that I was, but—"

"Not soon enough, obviously."

"And do you think you would have reacted any differently if I'd just told you . . . oh, by the way, my dear, I'm actually Daniel, your husband?"

Sylvia felt no response to his question except a volatile rage that had nowhere to go. She groaned and grabbed a shoe on the floor nearby and threw it at the door, then she threw the other one. "Go away! I don't want to see you!"

"Sylvia, please! I'm begging you! Please, I just—"

"What in the world is going on up here?" Sylvia heard Millie say from the hallway. "It's a right good thing everyone else is outside. This kind of screaming and yelling would have the children terrified."

Sylvia shouted, "Tell him to leave me in peace, Millie! I don't want to talk to him."

Millie's voice came closer to the door. "I can tell him to give you some time to calm down, Missus, but you and I both know that no problem is going to get solved without talking it through. Whatever this is about I think you owe him the chance to speak his piece."

"I don't think I owe him *anything!*" Sylvia shouted in response.

"Come now, Missus," Millie said in a gentle voice, "I can't imagine what's got you so upset. I've not seen you so upset since . . . well . . . that don't matter. Surely you can talk about what's troubling you once you've calmed down."

Sylvia begrudgingly realized that Millie was right. They had to talk. As much as she had no desire to hear anything he had to say, she would be a hypocrite and a terrible example to just kick Daniel out of the house without at least hearing what he had to say—even if she might only be doing so as a courtesy that would not change her mind whatsoever.

If only to make it possible to be left alone, Sylvia finally said, "Fine, I'll talk to him—later. And I want you and George present for this conversation. Rodney can keep the children busy elsewhere because they certainly don't need to be exposed to such drama."

"I can agree with that!" Millie said. "And if you want me and George there, we'll be there. Are you in agreement with that?" Millie asked and Sylvia knew the question was being directed at Daniel—the man Millie believed to be Dougal.

"Yes," he said, "thank you."

"Very well," Sylvia shouted. "Now leave me in peace."

"When might this conversation take place?" Millie asked, clearly wanting some kind of commitment from Sylvia.

"I don't know," she shouted more softly. "Later. Tomorrow. Never."

"I will not accept *never*, Missus," Millie said, speaking to her as if she were a child even while she used the title of respect she'd always used. "I don't think waiting until tomorrow is wise given how upset you are. So *later* it is. After supper is over and cleaned up, we'll have Rodney watch over the children upstairs and put them to bed. He'll understand. Now, that's that."

Sylvia expected more to be said from the other side of the door, or for Millie to demand that Sylvia agree to those terms. But she only heard footsteps moving away, finally honoring her request to be left in peace. She was glad for the time alone; she certainly needed it. But oh how she dreaded the conversation that would take place later. She was glad to know that George and Millie would be there. They needed to know the truth and she didn't want to have to tell them. Daniel was the author of these lies and the creator of this astoundingly horrible situation. *He* should be the one to tell them. And then he could attempt to give them the explanations that he claimed were valid. She already knew there was nothing he could ever say that would make this all right.

He didn't deserve to be here, and she didn't want him here. Then it occurred to her that this was Daniel. He was alive! And that meant that the house and the property all belonged to him, not to her. She didn't have the right to kick him out. If anyone needed to leave, it would have to be her. And where would she go? What would she do? And even if Daniel *did* leave, what about Rachel? His daughter. No! Not *his* daughter! Oh, she felt as if her head might explode! And right now she just wanted nothing more than to simply be left alone so that she could cry and be angry. But her mind continued to spin with the uncertainty ahead of her now that she knew the truth.

If Daniel intended to remain here, then she would have to leave, and she had the money Daniel had left for her hidden here in this room. She needed to find a way to keep it on her person, beneath her clothes, every moment of every day and night until she left so that he could never take it from her. She'd earned it! And if he wasn't willing to leave, she needed a way to support herself when she walked away from here. The very idea of leaving her home and the people she loved provoked a fresh explosion of sobbing, but she managed to make it to the bed where she curled around a pillow and wept so long and so hard that she almost believed a person could die from weeping.

Sylvia eventually stopped crying only to find herself staring at the wall, unable to move, unable to put her thoughts together enough to feel capable of ever getting off of this bed. She was startled by a light knock at the door and realized she had lost all sense of time. It was as if she had mentally been transported to another realm in time and space. She then heard Millie's voice say gently, "I've left a lunch tray outside your door. You need to try and eat, Missus. I know you're upset but you need to keep your strength up." She paused more than long enough for Sylvia to respond but she couldn't think of anything to say. "Is there anything else you need, Missus?"

"No," Sylvia croaked, her throat raspy from so much crying, "thank you."

She heard Millie leave but still didn't move. A few minutes later her stomach rumbled as if it knew there was food on the other side of the door. She didn't feel like eating, but she did feel hungry, and she agreed with Millie's suggestion that she needed to keep up her strength.

Surprised by the weakness and exhaustion she felt as she stood and made her way to the door, Sylvia opened it tentatively and peered into the hallway to make certain it was empty before she slid the tray into her room, then again closed and locked the door.

The food on the tray smelled good and her stomach rumbled again as she moved the tray to her bed and just stared at what was there before she was finally able to make herself put the fork in her hand and begin to eat. With every bite her body felt more strengthened, but her thoughts were still spinning helplessly with the bizarre reality that Daniel was alive and here and he'd been pretending to be someone else all these months. She felt deeply betrayed, and utterly brokenhearted. And she felt like such a fool! But right now she could only pray that by the time she was required to make herself present for the conversation that Millie had insisted upon, she would be able to remain calm and dignified, and that her tears would be all dried up. Daniel already knew she was upset, but she didn't want to humiliate herself further by crying in his presence. She just had to get through this day, even though she couldn't imagine how life might be tomorrow.

At some point in the afternoon, Sylvia actually managed to fall asleep in the midst of staring at the wall. She woke to realize it was almost time for supper, but she couldn't bear the thought of sitting at the same table as Daniel—not with all she'd come to realize about his true identity. It was going to be difficult enough to sit in the same room with him and force herself to be engaged in a civil conversation, but sharing supper was simply not possible. She wondered if Millie would be understanding of this and was grateful when she brought a tray to the door just as she'd done at lunchtime.

Before Millie left, she said through the door, "I'll come for you in a while when we're ready to talk."

"I'll be ready," Sylvia replied, feeling as if she were lying. She couldn't imagine *ever* being ready to have such a conversation.

She wasn't able to eat very much of her supper while thoughts of having to face Daniel churned inside of her. For all of the hours she'd locked herself away, she still couldn't comprehend what she'd discovered, what had been taking place all this time, and what in the world could be done about the situation given the vast number of complications now that there were children living here, and their welfare was surely more important than anything else.

Sylvia stared at the uneaten food on her plate while she listened to sounds coming from downstairs that indicated the others had finished eating and dishes were now being cleaned and put away. Her heart quickened and refused to slow down, making it difficult to take in the deep breath she desperately needed to sustain herself. The problem only grew worse when she heard Rodney escorting the children upstairs and to the room he shared with Bob. She distinctly heard him say from the hallway, "The other grownups that lived here before we came needs t' have a grownup meetin' so we're gonna play some games and read some stories until it's time for bed."

Sylvia startled herself from a daze to the realization that Millie would soon be coming to tell her that it was time for her to show herself downstairs, and she would have no choice but to hear Daniel's explanation of his most recent devious ways. All of the hurt and trouble he'd caused her in the past came rushing forward to join the anger and heartache over this newest discovery, and she doubted her own ability to remain objective. But she told herself over and over that she absolutely needed to remain calm and dignified. She knew that Millie would be compassionate to Sylvia's feelings, but she could be very mother-like when it came to dealing with irrational outbursts, and she quite simply wouldn't tolerate it.

Sylvia forced herself to abandon any further efforts to eat and she hurried to freshen up, deciding it would be best if she showed herself in the parlor before Millie had to come and get her. She kept telling herself to have courage, to be firm in her convictions, and to not allow Daniel to manipulate her in any way. Still, she couldn't even begin to fathom how she was going to get through this without either exploding into some kind of tantrum, or dissolving into a heap of helpless sobbing.

Chapter Twelve

Love and Anger

Sylvia went quietly down the stairs in stockinged feet that would make no noise. At the foot of the stairs, she glanced into the parlor only long enough to see that George and Daniel were sitting there. George was drinking a cup of tea as was his habit after supper, and Daniel looked more somber than she had likely ever seen him.

Unwilling to go in there without Millie, Sylvia slipped quietly into the kitchen and asked, "Is there something I can do to help?" She wished she had brought down her supper tray but decided it could wait.

Millie looked surprised to see her and said, "No, no. I'm almost finished." She focused on wiping off the worktable with a clean rag. "I was thinking I'd have to come up there and drag you down the stairs." She let out a small laugh to indicate she wasn't being entirely serious, although Sylvia wasn't at all surprised that Millie knew how reluctant she felt about this little meeting they were about to have.

"And yet here I am," Sylvia said, "and you should know that despite how badly I don't want to do this, I'm grateful to you for insisting that we talk . . . and for you and George being willing to put yourselves in the middle of this . . . terrible mess."

"It can't be *that* terrible, now can it?" Millie smiled toward her as she hung the wet rag up to dry.

"You haven't yet heard the reasons I feel so . . . furious with him."

"No, but . . . I'm certain it can be worked out," Millie said, walking past Sylvia toward the parlor. She wished she could share Millie's confidence, but at the moment she couldn't imagine *ever* being able to work this out.

Sylvia felt Daniel's eyes on her as she entered the parlor, but she forced herself not to look at him as she sat down as far away from him as possible. The moment Millie was settled into her chair near George, she said, "All right, then. It's evident the two of you have had some kind of serious disagreement, and sometimes people just need help from those who care about them in order to work things out and come to a compromise. We live here with the both of you and we *do* care about you, so we want to help."

George said to Millie, "You're missing the part about how it might be private and they don't *want* to talk to us about it."

Millie cleared her throat and added, "We *do* respect your privacy, and you certainly don't have to tell us anything you don't feel you should, nevertheless, we all live under the same roof and we can't have that kind of shouting going on—especially with children in the house."

"I want you to know everything," Daniel said firmly. "I owe Sylvia an explanation, and it's complicated. She has every right to be angry with me. And I want the two of you to know, as well. You're like family. You have been to Sylvia for years, and you've come to feel that way to me in the time that I've been here. You need to know what's going on; you need to know the truth, because . . . I've been deceiving all of you, and Sylvia figured that out this morning. I've been intending to tell her the truth, but I kept finding reasons to put it off, and then . . . well . . . now she knows and she's . . . well, as I said, she has a right to be angry with me. I simply want her to hear out my reasons for doing what I've done, and—"

"*What* did you find out this morning?" Millie asked, looking at Sylvia. "I don't think this conversation is going to make much sense until we know exactly what the problem is."

Sylvia sighed and looked at the floor, mostly to avoid Daniel's gaze when she felt his eyes turn toward her. She cleared her throat and drew back her shoulders before she just said what needed to be said. "This morning when Dou. . ." she almost said the name of the man Daniel had been pretending to be but she couldn't call him that anymore.

"When he got muddy and went upstairs to change his shirt . . . and you . . ." she glanced at Millie, ". . . had said that George would bring some water for him to wash up, but then George was busy, so I took it up. I assumed the bedroom door would be closed and I would just set the water in the hall and let him know it was there. But the door was open . . . and he was removing his shirt and . . ." Sylvia coughed in an effort to fight back a sudden rise of emotion that was more rooted in sorrow and betrayal than anger, and yet anger felt safer; anger made her feel stronger, and she didn't want to let on to the truth of what she was feeling. She coughed again and continued with a steady voice. "I saw a scar on his back."

When she said nothing more for a long moment, Millie said with impatience, "And?"

"I know the scar very well," Sylvia said now looking at Daniel, surprised to find him looking back at her, but she saw nothing but humility and regret in his eyes. She wanted to see defiance and defensiveness—both of which she'd become very familiar with in years gone by. Seeing such things from him might help her feel more justified in being so angry with him. For now, she ignored what she saw and just finished her explanation. "Daniel got that scar as a child; an accident with a rake when he'd been playing in the barn." Sylvia heard both George and Millie gasp as the problem became obvious, but she had to say it anyway. Motioning toward Daniel while she looked at George and Millie, Sylvia said, "This is not Dougal Heywood. This is my husband . . . Daniel . . . who has been pretending to be Dougal Heywood for months."

George and Millie both turned astonished, accusing eyes toward Daniel. It was George who broke the silence by saying with an anger in his voice that felt validating to Sylvia, "You've been here in this house . . . deceiving your own wife . . . all this time?"

Daniel sighed loudly and answered. "Yes. Yes, I have. But . . . it's complicated." He turned to look at Sylvia. "I know I've deceived you, Sylvia, and your anger in that regard is justified—I expected it. But I had my reasons, and I need you to hear the whole story. I need you to at least try and understand why I did what I did. I don't know if you can ever forgive me, and I wouldn't blame you if you couldn't, but . . . I am *not* the man I used to be. I needed the chance to prove that. You were so angry with me when I left—and for good reason—but I feared coming back to only settle back into that anger between us again. It would seem I went about it all wrong, despite my best intentions, and . . . there were other factors in the situation." He sighed again and looked down, leaning his forearms on his thighs. "I think I just need to start at the beginning . . . if you'll let me."

Millie spoke up vehemently, "I think we all need to hear this story from the beginning. I don't see any hope of working things out in the right way if we don't know *everything*. And since it's not just our missus here that you've deceived, I think that me and George do indeed need to hear what you have to say."

"I agree," Daniel said. "We have some big decisions ahead of us given . . . what I've done, and all of us are affected by my actions. I humbly take accountability for every choice I've made . . . everything I've done. I just . . ." He hung his head and seemed to have completely run out of words to say.

"Why don't you just start at the beginning," George said, "like you said you would."

"Of course," Daniel said but kept his head down. He took a deep breath and began, "When I first met Dougal it was likely the strangest experience of my life." He looked up long enough to meet the eyes of each person in the room. "Everything I told you about the two of us meeting, and our friendship, and the way we both decided that we needed to make right all of the wrongs in our lives—that was all true—all of it." He looked more directly at Sylvia. "When I told you how Daniel died . . . it was all true except that it was Dougal who died. I was wracked with guilt, wishing it had been me. Dougal had literally saved my life—twice. He didn't deserve to die that way. He had a daughter to go home to. He'd made a very specific plan about returning home and making things right with all of the people he'd cheated, and then he would get his daughter back and find a new place to settle down with her."

Daniel looked at the floor again and clasped his hands together as if doing so might give him strength. "The moment I realized he was dead, all I could think about was Rachel, and how desperate he had been to get her away from her despicable grandparents. Knowing I wouldn't even be alive if not for this man, I determined then and there that I needed to honor his memory by taking care of the things he'd felt so strongly about doing—even though that meant allowing you to believe I was dead." He looked up at Sylvia and she saw his chin quivering before he looked down again as if he didn't want her to see him cry. "Our marriage had been so difficult . . . and you had been so angry with me for all the trouble I'd caused . . . and I take responsibility for that. You were always a good wife—such a good woman. I didn't deserve you, and I sincerely believed it was best if I was dead to you, that it would be better if I never came home."

Sylvia wanted to say that it *would* have been better if he'd never come home, but she forced herself to keep quiet and just listen—even if she didn't want to. Some of what he'd said actually made sense, and a part of her didn't *want* him to have valid reasons for doing what he'd done. She was angry and she wanted to remain angry.

Daniel sighed and she could hear a definite air of sadness in it, but she just listened as he went on. "Because Dougal and I had eased our boredom during the long stretches of days and weeks between battles by learning to pretend to be each other—all in good fun—it was surprisingly easy for me to become him once I knew he was dead. The two of us were alone in a hidden spot at the edge of the battlefield, and it only took a couple of minutes to exchange anything that would identify us. I cried like a baby while I was doing this . . . and trying to accept that he was gone . . . and attempting to come to terms with what I was committing to do on his behalf by trading our identities. But he'd saved my life and I had to do it. So . . ." he drawled, ". . . I knew everything I needed to know in order to find my way to the village where he'd grown up. Not far into my journey I was able to get a tattoo on my finger that strongly resembles Dougal's mole. I'd spent enough time with him that I knew exactly where it was and what it looked like, and I knew it needed to be there if I had any hope of convincing people who had known him that *I* was him."

Daniel sighed and shook his head as if he too had trouble believing this was real. "I have a fairly good memory, but I also had his personal belongings in my possession, and he'd written down the names of the people to whom he owed restitution and for what exactly. Therefore, I was able to figure all of that out and take care of it, although it took a great deal of time, and before I knew it I had been living in this village for more than a year and a half. I had visited Rachel when I'd first arrived although her grandparents barely allowed us to spend a minute together. Rachel seemed drawn to me, believing I was her father, but I could tell how unhappy she was, which increased my determination to get her away from these people and allow her to believe I was her father so that I could raise her. I had nothing, but I knew how to make money and I was committed to giving her a better life than she was getting by living with those people. I knew nothing about raising children, but I often had a strange feeling that Dougal was guiding me, helping me, that he was grateful for what I was doing and that somehow everything would work out all right."

Daniel shifted in his chair and leaned back, crossing an ankle over his knee while he looked toward the window, somewhat dazed. "A day came when I realized there was nothing more I could do to try and get Rachel back without getting myself in trouble because these people were so influential and manipulated their neighbors. I felt overcome with the need to return home and make certain you were all right, even though I wasn't certain how I would go about coming back from the grave. As I traveled, I just kept thinking about the arguments we'd had before I left, and I desperately wished we could somehow make a fresh start . . . without having to wade through all of that anger . . . and all of the terrible things I'd done to hurt you. Then it occurred to me that if the people Dougal had grown up with had believed I was him, then perhaps you might believe it too, and it would give me some time to prove to you that I had forever traded away my unsavory methods of making a living by cheating others. I thought it might give us a chance to get to know each other again without the interference of the past. I look back and realize now how awful it was of me, but at the time . . . I was thrilled with the supposed need to learn to speak like . . . Daniel . . . because I could tell you were avoiding me and I longed to be able to spend time with you, and this gave me that opportunity. I wanted to show you that I had changed, that I only wanted to do good . . . and to be a good man and to—"

"Except that you were being deceptive from the first moment I found you in the barn," Sylvia blurted. "How can you possibly think that you could prove you'd changed by being deceptive?"

Daniel sighed and hung his head again, looking overtly ashamed. "I can only say that in my mind it made sense at the time. In my mind I believed that we could get to know each other all over again without all of the muddiness of the past between us. I knew that eventually I would have to tell you the truth, but I convinced myself that a day would come when you would be able to see the changes in me enough that you would forgive me. Clearly I went about it all wrong, and for that I am more sorry than I can say. And I certainly hadn't expected to be followed here and shot at and . . . well, everything that happened. There's no need for me to repeat what you already know. And I certainly didn't know that one of the men coming after me was being manipulated because his son was being held hostage—along with Rachel. I had every intention of going back to get her when I could manage it, but . . . well . . . I never expected it to work out the way it did."

"And the money?" Sylvia asked.

"What money?" Millie demanded, which made it necessary for Sylvia to offer George and Millie a brief explanation of the box of money with its ledger and the extra amount that had made it possible for Sylvia to fund the excursion to retrieve the children.

Sylvia then looked at Daniel and repeated, "What about the money?"

"What about it?" Daniel countered, sounding much more calm and kind than she was managing to be. "I left the box of money just as it was when we found it. I don't know if you'll believe me, but I had honestly forgotten about it when I left, and for a long time afterwards, or I would have told you about it in a letter. I knew you had the income from the rent that came in every month. I truly believed you would be well provided for, and I certainly wouldn't have kept such a detailed account of where the money had come from if I'd not intended to return it. I'd worked hard for that money—even if gambling might be considered a dubious profession, what I did was legal and I earned every bit of the money in that box legitimately. Everything I told you about it was true even if I omitted details. And every bit of the money that's left now after repaying the debts belongs to you."

Daniel shifted in his seat and looked directly—even fiercely—at Sylvia. "Listen to me, Sylvia, and please listen with an open mind and an open heart. I may have handled the situation all wrong, but I swear to you that with the exception of telling you my true identity, everything I've told you since I've returned is true. My feelings for you are real. I needed to honor my friend and make things right for him and try to get his daughter back. Now, with your help, she's in a good home and will be well cared for, and I thank you for your assistance and support in that. I do believe that even if you'd known the truth about my identity before we'd gone to get her, you still would have been supportive of the endeavor because you would not have wanted Dougal's child—or Rodney's—to be in such a terrible situation. You're a good woman with a good heart, and I have wondered a thousand times and more if you would have been far better off to have married someone else. I surely don't deserve you. Nevertheless, I love you, Sylvia. I love you with my whole soul. I love you more than I was ever able to feel back when I was putting so much effort into hiding my misdeeds and trying not to get caught. I am a changed man, Sylvia. I swear to you that I am. And I pray that you will not base my integrity or my character on this stupid mistake I've made by pretending to be Dougal, thinking that it would give us a chance to fall in love again without all of the anger and frustration between us from the past. In my opinion I think it worked—except that I know you're so furious with me now that I doubt you will ever forgive me."

A terrible silence fell over the room following Daniel's impassioned speech. Sylvia knew it was up to her to say something now, but she couldn't think of anything at all that wouldn't sound snippy or rude. She now understood his motives more clearly, and she could appreciate some degree of why he'd done what he'd done. But she *did* still feel furious, and she *didn't* know if she could forgive him. She finally just stated the truth. "I appreciate your explanations. At this moment I'm too overwhelmed to be able to express my feelings without the risk of saying something I will regret. With all the complexities of our relationship, the possibility of forgiveness is complicated, and I can't make any promises."

Following more arduous silence, Daniel said with firm conviction, "Perhaps I should leave here and leave you in peace. If any of the locals even care or show curiosity over my absence, you can tell them I've gone away for work—as I used to do for long stretches of time. And

I just won't come back. I wouldn't blame you at all for not wanting me here. I deceived you and I'm prepared to take accountability for that. The problem is Rachel. She needs stability, a home, consistency, and love. I know you always wanted to be a mother, and I know now that it's not possible for you to have a baby. If you would be willing to take on Rachel's care and consider the money I've given you a fair donation to that care, I would be eternally grateful. And I'll leave if you want me to."

Sylvia considered what he was saying for many long moments before she concluded, "I need to think about it. I know two things for certain: First, Rachel needs to stay here. You're right in that she needs a home and stability, and I *am* willing to take her on as my own and do my best to raise her with love and consistency. Second, I know that I am *not* leaving here. I didn't do anything wrong. I didn't set out to deceive you or anyone else. You've been dead to me for years, and everything I've *inherited* from you, I've earned with all of the grief you've given me. Whether you should leave is something I need to think about, and I'm far too . . . overwhelmed . . . and angry . . . to talk about it anymore tonight." She stood up, needing to put an end to this conversation because she simply didn't have the strength to endure any more of this right now. "We'll talk tomorrow. In the meantime, we will all make certain that Rodney and the children have no reason to suspect there is a problem. There will be peace in this house. I insist upon it. Good night."

Sylvia left the room and hurried upstairs, fearing she might once again burst into a painful bout of sobbing, but at the same time feeling far too exhausted to cry a single tear. She took her time in getting ready for bed and was about to extinguish the lamp when a light knocking sounded at the door.

"Who is it?" she called.

"It's Millie," she replied softly. "Might I have a word before you go to sleep?"

"Of course. Come in," Sylvia said and sat on the edge of the bed. Millie slipped into the room and closed the door behind her, sitting on a nearby chair where she could face Sylvia.

"You might think it's none of my business, and maybe it's not— except that me and George live in this house, and we love you dearly

and would do almost anything for you short of committing murder."
She let out a small laugh. At another time Sylvia might have found
it humorous but right now she just didn't have the strength to laugh.
"Before I say anything else, let me make it clear that I spoke with
George about what I wanted to say to you, and he agrees. And we
want you both to know that we're full aware you're the mistress of this
house and any final decision is up to you and we will respect that decision, but that doesn't mean we don't have the right to offer our opinion on the matter. Would you be in agreement with that, Missus?"

"Yes," Sylvia said. "I do believe that's how it works with us, and I
appreciate knowing that you will stand by whatever decision I make."

"Good enough," Millie said. "Now, given this situation
with . . . Daniel—I almost said Dougal. Oh, it is confusing!"

"It is indeed," Sylvia said with a bitter edge.

"But the thing is . . . me and George ain't no fools, Missus. We
never knew Daniel so of course we never knew what he looked like,
and we only had your stories about him to know what he'd been like,
but . . . we both believe that what Daniel is saying now is true. The
man that has been living in this house since you found him in the
barn is a sincere and honest man. He may well have gone about the situation all wrong—as he admitted himself. But that doesn't mean his
intentions weren't good, and it doesn't mean he hasn't changed in all
the ways that he claims. Now, forgiveness can be a long and complicated thing to work out, and you have the right to take all the time you
need—and if you choose not to forgive him, that's your right, Missus.
Trust is something that has to be earned, and you learning what you
did today has certainly broken that trust. But if trust is measured out
by a person's words and deeds, me and my George believe he's proven
trustworthy many times over since he's come here, and it's important
to keep this particular issue—big as it is—separate from everything
else he's done to try and earn your trust and prove himself—remember that's what he was trying to do, Missus, even if he was misguided
on that count. Still, from the outside looking in on this situation, we
can understand why he would want a fresh start . . . why he would
want to be someone different when he came home to you. For all
that you're angry and you have a right to be, you can't deny that his
motives show evidence of his desire to do right by you."

Sylvia couldn't deny that there was a great deal of sound reason in all that Millie was saying, but she still felt so confused and over-whelmed—less angry, perhaps, which was surely a good thing, since she knew well enough that it was impossible to make sound decisions when in a state of anger.

"You make a fair case," Sylvia said, "although I still have a great deal to think about and I still feel entirely overcome."

"And that's fair enough," Millie said.

"I assume you're attempting to get to a point," Sylvia said.

"I am indeed," Millie declared. "Me and my George believe that you should give yourself some time to consider whether you can trust Daniel, and whether you can forgive him. Still, it don't seem right for you to just send him packing to find a new life on his own when you look at all the good he's done, and the fact that he *is* your husband, and this land and house rightfully belong to him. It gives credit to his humility and remorse that he would be willing to leave and give you all that is his, but can you truly live with such a decision, Missus? Would you not perhaps in the future come to regret allowing him to leave when you're surely still too confused and angry to be making such a decision? And what if you never saw him again? What if one day you realize you *have* forgiven him, but you don't know where to find him? I'm just saying that you don't know what the future will bring, and perhaps you should allow him to stay here until you've had a chance to think things through a great deal more. And the children love the man. Would they not forever be wondering why he left and never came back? I can't see the fairness in that for them."

Sylvia only had to think about that for a moment before she said, "I'm sure you're right. In spite of all my muddled thinking, I believe something inside of me knew that I couldn't in good conscience allow him to just leave. That matter *does* deserve some time, and I dare say we can tolerate each other politely while we *do* give it time."

"There now," Millie said. "I think that's a fair and reasonable deci-sion. And me and George are here for you no matter what. Do you want to speak with Daniel yourself about this, or would you like me and George to be there so you—"

"No, but thank you," Sylvia said. "I do believe I've calmed down enough to be able to speak with him civilly." Recalling just how angry she had been, Sylvia added, "Thank you for your patience with me . . . and for your sound wisdom and insight while I'm not thinking clearly. I'm grateful for you, Millie, and George too. I can't say it enough—I don't know what I ever would have done without you."

"It's the other way around, Missus," Millie said and stood, but she bent over and placed a kiss on Sylvia's cheek before she said, "Everything will be all right. It will. However this turns out, it'll be all right."

"Thank you, Millie."

"You get some rest now," Millie said before she left the room.

Sylvia remained where she was for several minutes, allowing Millie's advice to repeat itself in her mind and to soak in so she could manage separating the issues of trust and forgiveness and love. *Love?* Millie hadn't said anything about love. But Sylvia had to acknowledge that she'd always loved Daniel despite their differences, and she'd grown to love Dougal—or the man she'd believed to be Dougal. She *had* fallen in love with Daniel all over again. And learning of his deception had not changed the way she felt about him. It was the trust and forgiveness she needed to work on. But Millie had been right—that didn't necessarily mean she should kick him out of the house with the desire to never see him again. That *wasn't* what she wanted, even if she appreciated his willingness to leave if that's what she *did* want.

Sylvia was startled from her deep thoughts with a sudden need to tell Daniel tonight that she didn't want him to leave. She doubted she could get any sleep if she didn't tell him now, and she hoped he hadn't already gone to bed. She didn't want to wake him but doubted he would have been able to fall asleep very easily given the likelihood that his mind was as overwhelmed as her own.

Sylvia put on a dressing gown and tied it tightly around herself before she picked up the lamp and hurried down the hall as quietly as she could manage. She knocked very lightly on Daniel's door before she lost her courage, and she hoped that no one else would hear her knocking.

The door came open so abruptly that it startled Sylvia. "What?" Daniel demanded too quickly for him to have even known who had come to his room so late. He looked surprised to see her, but it was also evident that he'd been crying—long and hard—and he was in fact *still* crying. It was impossible to not see in the lamp's glow the tears streaming down his face.

"Yes," he quietly demanded, "I've been crying like a baby, but I am beyond caring what anyone in this house thinks about what I do or why, because I'm done with secrets, I'm done with trying to hide who I am or how I feel, so . . . let me have it, Mrs. Hewitt."

Sylvia felt softened even more with the evidence of his emotion and the convictions behind it. She knew she could work herself back into a storm of anger toward him with very little effort, but she put her effort instead toward handling this situation appropriately.

"Have you come to tell me to have my things packed and be on my way first thing in the morning?" Daniel asked. "Or have you—"

"Actually," Sylvia said in a gentle tone that seemed to calm him down a bit, "I've come to tell you that you need to stay . . . at least for now. I admit that I'm overwhelmed and confused and . . . yes, struggling with some anger, though not so much as earlier. For all of my shortcomings, I am wise enough to know that big decisions should not be made in anger. There's a great deal I need to think about . . . and I need time. Trust and forgiveness are very big issues . . . especially with all that's happened. But . . . that doesn't change how I feel about you, and . . . you need to stay—at least for now. For the sake of the children . . . and for all of us in the household . . . I believe we need to just allow things to go on as they have . . . as long as you understand that I *don't* trust you, and I don't know if I'll ever be able to forgive you. But this is your house . . . your land. For that and a great many more reasons, you need to stay, Daniel." She sighed. "That's all I have to say. I think we both have the ability to be civil and polite and pretend that all is still the same as it was before, especially when Rodney or the children are around—for their sakes."

"Thank you," Daniel said on the wake of a long, deep sigh that seemed to come from the deepest part of him. "I can't say what that means to me. Even if you can never forgive me . . . or never trust me again . . . I will continue to strive to prove myself trustworthy. You may not want to hear it, but . . . I have to say it. I love you, Sylvia. I always have, I always will. I know that love and trust are not the same. We talked about that—argued about that—a great deal before the war. Nevertheless, that's how I feel, and . . . well . . . enough said for now. Thank you . . . for allowing me to stay. If it's all right with you, we can revisit this issue in a few weeks, and if you want me to leave, I will."

"We can do that," she said and nodded, figuring there was nothing more to be said right now, and she was afraid she might start crying herself if she didn't leave, so she did, rushing quietly to her room, feeling as if this day had been some kind of strange, terrible dream—the kind of dream that made no sense after you'd awakened and tried to recall it and put the pieces of it together.

Sylvia went to bed but wasn't surprised when sleep eluded her. After she'd mentally reviewed the drama of the day several times, she finally drifted into a restless sleep, praying inwardly that they would all be able to settle back into a comfortable routine and move forward. She was glad to know she had the option to separate from Daniel, and they could revisit the decision in a few weeks. She was also glad to know that he would be here for the forthcoming stretch of time. Despite all of her anger, she couldn't imagine this household without him. She just had to figure out how to manage her own feelings over the matter, and the deep contradictions that assaulted her when she thought of Daniel with tears on his face declaring his love for her. But then there was the reality of how the same Daniel had been deceiving her in so many ways for months now, and the very thought lured her toward a raging anger she was too exhausted to even look at. Yes, she certainly had a great deal to work out within herself. She was simply glad to have some time to do so.

Sylvia was more relieved than she could have ever expressed when everyone gathered around the table for breakfast and everything felt completely normal. Rodney didn't ask about the important conversation that had taken place in the parlor the previous evening. They all just talked and laughed as they always did, and the children's antics provided a great deal of joy for Sylvia that had been absent in her life prior to their coming here.

Throughout the day Sylvia was pleased to find that she and Daniel could interact normally and not let on that a tumultuous secret had come to light and created a huge discord between them. As days passed and eased into weeks, she felt deeply relieved to assess the strange circumstances in her household and realize that her anger toward Daniel had calmed down a great deal, although she was careful to avoid sharing any personal interaction or conversation with him.

Rather than focusing on all that had gone wrong with the relationship between the two of them, she put her attention toward observing him with the children and the way he so endearingly played with them and teased them and appropriately disciplined them when necessary. She was well aware of the work he did each and every day to help repair her home and the barn, and neatly groom the surrounding grounds. He worked hard alongside the other men and remained cheerful despite the distinct sadness and remorse she could see in his eyes whenever she gathered enough courage to look at him directly. Sometimes he caught her at it and stared back, making her heart pound hard and fast until she could force herself to look away, wondering how she could ever bring herself to send him away, and at the same time wondering how she could ever bear to live under the same roof with him indefinitely and make peace with the fact that she was desperately in love with a man she couldn't trust and couldn't forgive.

She'd told herself a thousand times or more that she could learn to trust him again as long as he continued to remain trustworthy. Surely anyone deserved the opportunity to change and to become worthy of being trusted. She trusted Rodney despite her terrifying initial encounter with him. When it came to the possibility of forgiving Daniel, she couldn't think about it without stirring up a battle inside her mind between the evidence that he had changed and his reasons for doing what he'd done—all of which warred against the very fact that he had been living in her house and declaring his love for her while pretending to be someone else. She felt betrayed and foolish and gullible, and it made her angry if she allowed herself to think about it for more than a moment.

Her anger was so deep that she couldn't imagine *ever* being able to forgive him. Nevertheless, she'd come to see that she also couldn't imagine ever having him leave. The personal relationship between them might well be over and done, but that didn't mean he had to leave here—not when that meant taking Rachel's father away from her. At least as far as Rachel believed, he was her father. And despite how much grief this man had given her, she couldn't find a way to justify having him leave the land and home that legally belonged to him. Nor could she find any good reason for *her* to leave. This was her home. She'd surely earned the right to live here, and she believed the children needed her. She'd gained relationships with both of them, and each day she took part in caring for them.

There was a great deal about this bizarre situation that she felt confused over, but she absolutely knew that both she and Daniel needed to stay, even if that meant forever sleeping in separate rooms and maintaining a relationship that avoided any kind of personal interaction or conversation—despite the fact that they were legally husband and wife.

Sylvia knew that she needed to tell Daniel the conclusions she'd come to so he wouldn't be left to just wait and wonder, but she kept finding ways to avoid such a conversation. Instead, she often found herself just watching him while he wasn't aware, and inevitably her heart would quicken, her stomach would flutter, sweat would rise in her palms. And sometimes tears even came to her eyes. The issues of trust and forgiveness left her increasingly frustrated as she came to accept more and more with each passing day that she was as deeply in love with him as she had ever been. She was lonely and she missed him. He was physically here and yet they shared nothing.

Sylvia spoke with Millie about her feelings, knowing she could trust her completely and she needed another woman with whom to share such personal and complicated emotions. Millie was kind and wise and insightful, but in the end, she had no advice to offer that Sylvia didn't already know. She had to choose to allow Daniel to prove that she *could* trust him. She needed to sincerely strive to come to terms with the misdeeds he had owned up to and apologized for and seek to forgive him. The fact that he *had* willfully deceived her about his identity was impossible to overlook, and yet there was a great deal of evidence she could not ignore that proved he *had* changed, and he *was* a better man. And she absolutely had to acknowledge to herself— and to him—that she loved him deeply and irrevocably.

It took Sylvia what seemed a great deal of time to ponder the intricacy of such a tangled web of emotions and the situation she'd found herself in regarding her husband. She finally came to the conclusion that she just needed to have a private conversation with Daniel. Until she told him honestly how she was feeling, and took the time to hear what *he* was feeling, she would never be able to move forward. The very idea terrified Sylvia, but she awoke on a warm sunny morning with the realization that she needed to talk to him or she would drive herself to madness.

Near the end of breakfast, Sylvia tried to quell the pounding of her heart and force a steady voice as she said, "Daniel, I wonder if we might discuss some things. Perhaps we could go for a walk?"

Daniel looked so astonished that for a moment she thought he might say or do something that would draw undue attention from the others. But he cleared his throat carefully and said, "Of course. I just need to—"

"I'll take care o' that," Rodney said. "Ye go ahead and see t' yer business with the missus."

"Thank you," Daniel said.

"I'll see to the kitchen," Millie said, beginning to clear the table. "If you're going for a walk, you should do so before it gets too warm."

"Thank you," Sylvia said to Millie and hurried outside, aware of Daniel following her.

The two of them walked in silence for minutes, until the house and barn were no longer in sight due to the way the meadow rolled downward.

Daniel finally said, "I don't believe anyone will be able to hear us now. If you feel the need to scold me for any reason, you should do so."

"I have no need to scold you," she said, trying not to sound offended. She had to remind herself that he had no idea where her mind might be. He might even be believing that she was about to tell him he needed to leave. In that moment she felt a strange burst of empathy for how grueling these weeks must have been for him while he'd left his fate completely in her hands and had had no choice but to wait and see what she would decide. Actually, he'd had a choice; he could have just left. But he hadn't. He'd stayed. And Sylvia had to accept that his doing so was an indication of his character.

Acting on her deepest instincts and praying they would serve her well, Sylvia stopped walking and he did the same. She stood to face him and decided she just needed to quickly summarize how she felt and be done with it.

"Daniel," she said, looking into his eyes, hearing more affection in her voice than any kind of anger or bitterness. "I mostly just wanted to say that . . . I don't want you to leave. You shouldn't leave. Not ever." The surprise in his expression made her believe even more that he'd been expecting her to send him away and she was nearly moved to tears. "You belong here. This is your home and your land more than it is mine. And the children need you." She paused to take a deep breath. "*I* need you." His eyes widened as his astonishment became more evident, but Sylvia tried to ignore what she saw in his expression and just get this over with. "I still feel confused and overwhelmed, Daniel. You were . . . dead . . . and now you're here, and . . . you *are* different, I know you are, but . . . I still feel weighed down by all of the difficulties of the past . . . and . . ." She shook her head and closed her eyes briefly. "And . . . I can't say I'm not still upset over your making me believe you were a different man, nevertheless . . . I see evidence of your sincere efforts to prove that you are trustworthy, and . . . I want to forgive you. I'm trying to forgive you but it's proving difficult and . . . I need time."

"I understand," he said gently. "And I would understand if you were never able to forgive me. I've done so much that hurt you . . . and brought grief into your life. I understand. But, oh! I cannot deny how relieved and grateful I am that you would allow me to stay. I want to stay, Sylvia. I don't ever want to leave this place again. We have a good life here that we're sharing with good people. We're a family; a strange and wonderful family. And I desperately want to be a part of that. So . . . thank you . . . for letting me stay. I swear to you that I will never betray your trust again, because I never want to risk losing all that I have here."

Sylvia could only nod, grateful for all he was saying, and for the sincerity she could feel as much as she could see in his expression. For the first time since she had discovered the truth about Daniel's identity, Sylvia actually felt a deeply undeniable hope that the future might actually bring her the true happiness she had always longed for.

Chapter Thirteen

A Matter of Judgment

Daniel turned away to walk back toward the house, but Sylvia stopped him. She knew she needed to say something more and her heart was pounding so hard that she feared it might completely give out on her if she didn't just say it. "There's something else I must tell you," she said and attempted to fill her lungs with air.

"I'm listening," he said when she didn't go on.

"I . . . don't know what it means . . . or what can be done about it . . . given the complications of our relationship, but . . . I still have to say it. You need to know, and I can't hold it inside any longer."

"Then just say it," he said, his brow furrowed with concern while his eyes showed deep curiosity.

Looking into his eyes now she wondered how she ever could have believed that these were not Daniel's eyes. She'd been convinced that this was Dougal and she believed that she had accepted this belief as truth and she'd quickly stopped looking for evidence to the contrary. But now she could see Daniel so clearly.

"First of all," she said, "you should know that once I'd gotten past the worst of my anger, I realized that I'd been blessed with a miracle."

"A miracle?" he echoed dubiously.

"Yes, Daniel, a miracle. You were dead and then you came back to me."

"But . . ." he sounded perplexed, ". . . I would have thought that—with as bad as things had become between us—you would have preferred I *not* come back."

"I can't deny how difficult certain aspects were in our relationship—and still are in some respects—but Daniel . . . oh, Daniel . . . the most important thing I need to tell you is . . . I love you. I love you. I loved Dougal because he was the best of you. I know there are issues between us that . . . need time, but . . . I love you, Daniel, and . . ." her voice quivered and tears stung her eyes, ". . . you mustn't ever leave here again because . . . I need you. I love you. I ask that you be patient with me regarding the difficult feelings I'm still struggling with, but . . . you need to know that those difficulties do not change the fact that I love you with all my heart and soul." She laughed on the wake of a sob. "I'm so grateful that you came back to me."

Sylvia impulsively put her hands on the sides of his face, something she'd been wanting to do for many days now. And she breathed in a refreshing sigh of relief when he held her face the same way. Before she could even think about how long she'd been longing for him to kiss her, he did. She knew she'd been struggling with confusion over the love she'd come to feel for Dougal, and then realizing that he had been Daniel all along. But all she felt now was relief just to feel his lips against hers. Oh, how she'd missed him!

"I love you too, my precious Sylvia," he murmured, his lips so close to hers she could feel them moving as he spoke. "I love you more than life. I would do anything for you, Sylvia. Anything! And I swear to you that I will never do anything to hurt you again." He resumed kissing her and then he was holding her in his arms and Sylvia's arms went quite naturally around him and she held him as close as humanly possible. For a long moment they looked into each other's eyes and she saw moisture glimmering in his just before the moisture in her own eyes made her view of him blurry, but she closed her eyes and he kissed her again, over and over, the kind of kiss she'd experienced often before he'd gone off to war, the way a man should kiss his wife. Kisses that expressed the love they'd always shared and the way it had always been when difficulties were set aside and neither of them were aware of anything but the love they felt for each other.

Daniel finally stepped back but took both of her hands into his. With the hint of a smile, he said, "I suppose we must continue to sleep in separate rooms."

It was difficult for Sylvia to reply, "For now. Besides the fact that Rodney and the children still believe you are Dougal . . . I need . . . some time."

"I understand, Sylvia," he said. "I really do. I just . . . miss you. And I hope that eventually we will be able to get beyond all that's between us."

"I hope for that too," she said. "In the meantime, I think we should more frequently make the time for long walks together."

"I would like that," he said. "Perhaps we would do well to talk more about our experiences while we were apart."

"That would probably be good," Sylvia agreed.

"Speaking of which . . . I don't want to upset you . . . but I just have to say that . . ." He squeezed her hands more tightly but looked down as if to hide his expression and she suspected what he was trying to say. She didn't want to talk about it, but she could understand why he might feel the need to say something—now that she knew this man was her husband. He cleared his throat, but his voice quivered when he spoke. "I felt as if the world had fallen out from under me when you told me about the baby . . . and everything you went through when you lost her." He looked up at her with deep sorrow etched into his countenance. "Why didn't you write and tell me?"

"You were at war," Sylvia said. "I didn't want to add to your grief. I just . . . believed we would talk about it when you came home, and then . . ."

"I died," he said with shame as he squeezed his eyes closed and shook his head in disbelief. "I just have to say," his eyes still closed, "I've had difficulty coming to terms with . . . the fact that we had a baby . . . and she's gone." He opened his eyes and looked firmly at Sylvia. "She was my daughter too, and she's dead. And when I think of what that doctor did to you . . ."

"It's in the past," Sylvia said, "but I can understand your need to grieve. And you should—as much as it's necessary for you to come to terms with it. Of course when I told you, I didn't know that . . ."

"That I was the father of that baby," Daniel said with self-recrimination. "And that's my fault."

"Now I can understand why you were so upset and trying so hard to keep me from knowing just how upset you were."

"It wasn't easy," Daniel said, "and that night I cried myself to sleep, if you must know." He sighed deeply. "Now, I just want to say that . . . I'm more sorry than I can say for what you went through . . . alone. I know you had George and Millie, but I should have been here."

"You couldn't have known, and you couldn't have done anything about it even if you *had* known. Come," she began to walk back the direction they'd come, holding his hand, "I want to show you something."

They walked together in comfortable silence while Sylvia took in how deeply relieved she felt for all that they'd just shared both in conversation and affection. There were indeed issues between them that still needed time, but now she knew he was never leaving, and she felt hope that eventually they might be able to share a good and complete life together, devoid of all the difficulties that had once torn them apart.

Rather than going toward the house, Sylvia veered to the right toward a wooded area that wasn't terribly far from the house. In fact, it was the same wooded area where Biff had been buried after his tragic death. But Sylvia led Daniel to a different grave, the grave of their infant daughter. She'd been born too soon and had been very tiny, but her features and form had been perfect. Millie had made a little white gown for the baby to be buried in while George had built a tiny casket. They'd said in both cases that it was nothing fancy, but it met the needs for this child to be given a proper and dignified burial—and Sylvia had been infinitely grateful for their insights as well as their efforts. George had also found a large, flat stone with rounded edges on which he'd used a chisel to carve the essential memorial for this child. Sylvia explained all of this to Daniel as they held hands and looked down at the simple marker which simply read: *Baby Girl Hewitt* followed by the date she had been born dead.

"I'm glad to know this is here," Daniel said. "And . . . there's something strangely poetic about Rachel ending up in our care."

"Yes, I've thought the same many times," Sylvia said. "I'm so glad she's here." She turned to face Daniel. "And I'm so glad you were willing to work so hard to take on her care even though she wasn't your daughter."

"It was the right thing to do," Daniel said, "although I know very little about caring for children, therefore I'm very grateful for everyone in our household who adds their wisdom and assistance to doing so."

"I'd say it's working out nicely," Sylvia said.

Daniel laughed softly and embraced her. "Much more nicely than it was before we took this walk, I'm glad to say."

"Yes, I'm glad for that, too," Sylvia said and just held tightly to her husband.

They returned together to the house then went their separate ways so that Daniel could pull weeds in the garden, and Sylvia could help Millie with whatever work in the house needed to be seen to. She found Millie busy at laundering clothes, and after exchanging a quick greeting, she set to work helping.

A minute later Millie said, "I take it your walk with Mr. Hewitt went well."

"Why do you say that?" Sylvia said, trying to sound innocent while she kept her focus on rinsing the soap out of a man's shirt that Millie had just washed in a separate tub of warm water.

Millie chuckled and said, "If you could see your face now you wouldn't ask such a silly question. I've not seen you looking so happy since before you found out that it was your Daniel here pretending to be Dougal."

Sylvia felt herself blush and she was overcome with a sudden weakness. She plopped onto a chair after dropping the wet shirt back into the tub of water. "Oh, Millie. I love him! And I can't deny my gratitude that he's here and alive."

"Did you tell him so?"

"I did," Sylvia said, so very glad that she had. "And I told him that he needs to stay."

"I'm very glad to hear it."

"But . . ."

When she didn't finish, Millie guessed, "But you're not sure about trusting him . . . and forgiving him."

"That's exactly right," Sylvia said.

"Which is how you always felt before the war with your Daniel," Millie said, which offered Sylvia some enlightenment. "And you were weary of always having to weigh your love against such difficulties in your heart. But if I may say so, by all accounts as far as I can see he is not the man you described to me and George as such a scoundrel. I would say in all fairness that his reasons for not telling you the truth about his identity make sense. I believe his intentions were good even if he might not have thought it through as carefully as he should have. And I believe as a general rule that people should be trusted until they give you a reason not to be—with caution, of course. Only a fool would lay their wealth out for a stranger to steal if he chose to."

"And would it be only a fool who would open her heart to a man who has brought so much grief into her life?" Sylvia asked the question with severity and a quivering voice.

Millie stopped her own work and sat beside Sylvia, putting a hand over hers. "I believe he's proven himself enough to at least earn your heart. Of course neither of us can say for certain that he will forever remain committed to the good changes in himself. But I think deep in your heart you trust him, and the only way to know if trust is warranted is simply to trust. I don't know everything, Missus, but it's my opinion that you should give him a fair chance. We can both pray that the change in him is sincere, but I think we all have good cause to believe that it is—and I think everyone deserves a second chance."

Sylvia thought about that and nodded in agreement, but she had to say, "And what of forgiveness, Millie? For all that I love him and want him to be a part of my life . . . and I do believe I can trust him . . . when I think of certain things he's done—not the least of which is pretending to be Dougal all this time—I still feel . . . angry . . . and betrayed. How do I forgive him? How do I find peace over that and not have it interfering with all the good we might share?"

"I would say forgiveness is something that for the most part happens a little at a time. I think it requires a good deal of prayer . . . and looking into your heart . . . and just . . . well, making an effort to not hold onto those bad feelings. Just . . . give it time, Missus. And for now, it's my opinion that you have no good reason not to open your heart to him. He's your husband, Missus, and he's come back from the dead. It's a miracle."

"It is, isn't it," she stated conclusively and smiled. She *did* need to work toward forgiveness, but that didn't mean she couldn't also be working on mending her relationship with Daniel. He *was* her husband, and she loved him with all her heart. And no one was perfect, certainly. Surely, she could give herself time in her efforts to forgive him and still learn to share her life with him again. The very idea made her almost burst with happiness as she went back to work, chatting comfortably with Millie about how she and Daniel had talked about the loss of the baby, and how she'd taken him to the grave.

"I'd say that's a big step toward mending your hearts together," Millie said.

"Yes, I do believe it is," Sylvia agreed.

They weren't yet finished washing and rinsing the laundry when it was time for lunch, but they washed up and set out the makings for sandwiches with bread Millie had made the day before, and slices of cold lamb. Sylvia found herself avoiding even a glance toward Daniel, fearing she would blush visibly and everyone would become suspicious of the reasons. The moment they'd finished eating, everyone scattered in different directions, the children to play and the adults to work on their chores.

Sylvia and Millie finished washing and rinsing everything that was dirty, and the two women took all of the clean laundry outside to hang it on the clotheslines in the sun. While Sylvia was doing so, she couldn't help glancing frequently to where Daniel was working in the garden, which provoked a fluttering inside of her each and every time. She felt disappointed to have to go back into the house, but she had supper to look forward to while she continued helping Millie with the work that needed their attention. Together they cleaned the laundry tubs and prepared a fine meal for their "strange and wonderful family," as Daniel had put it.

When everyone was cleaned up and gathered around the table, Sylvia looked around while they shared conversation and laughter and wondered if she had ever felt so happy. She was glad to feel Daniel looking at her discreetly as often as he might get away with it, and occasionally they shared a knowing glance and a wink. Their time together earlier today consumed Sylvia's thoughts, and when she recalled the way he had held her close and kissed her, she found it difficult to keep the thrill inside of her from showing.

Sylvia took notice of the way Daniel was so attentive to Rachel, giving her help whenever she needed it. When she had believed this beautiful little girl was Dougal's daughter, such things had seemed completely natural. In the weeks since she'd discovered Daniel's true identity, she had been so consumed with her own emotions that she'd not bothered to notice what was very clear before her now. Daniel had taken on the care of his friend's daughter, and he took that role very seriously. His tenderness with Rachel made Sylvia love him all the more, and she felt so overcome with gratitude that she had to fight back the threat of joyful tears.

Later when the children were asleep and the adults were all preparing for bed, Sylvia and Daniel managed to steal a secretive kiss in the hallway before going their separate ways to sleep. Three nights later after another quickly stolen kiss, Sylvia lay in her bed and stared into the darkness above her, realizing this situation had become ridiculous. Daniel was her husband, and they'd come far in healing their relationship. She felt so deeply lonely that it ached inside of her, and she suspected he felt the same.

Before Sylvia had any time to talk herself out of it, she lit a candle and moved quietly to the other end of the long hallway in her bare feet. She didn't even bother knocking at Daniel's door, fearing someone else might hear the sound and become suspicious. Until they spoke frankly with everyone in the household about the fact that Daniel was in actuality Sylvia's husband, they wouldn't want anyone to know that Sylvia might be doing something so audacious as sneaking into his room in the middle of the night. She closed the door carefully behind her, wondering if Daniel was asleep, but he turned over and lifted his head, then sat up.

"What are you doing?" he whispered, sounding more delighted than astonished.

"I'm sick to death of being alone," she spoke in a soft voice. "And I'm your wife." She set the candle on his bedside table and sat on the edge of his bed.

"Well, isn't that a lovely coincidence," he said, taking her face into his hands. "Because I am your husband, and I too am sick to death of being alone." He kissed her. "It's been so long, Sylvia." He kissed her again. "I thought I would die without ever seeing you again. And then all of this ludicrous pretending that I've been doing. I often thought that if I just had the courage to tell you the truth, we could be together again, but I had lied to you and I was a coward and—"

"Hush," Sylvia said and put her fingers over his lips. "I love you, Daniel. We're together now."

"Indeed we are," he said and wrapped her in his arms as he kissed her over and over. And Sylvia could only think once again that it *was* a miracle. He'd been dead, and then he'd come home to her. She was truly blessed.

Sylvia settled her head on Daniel's shoulder as he put his arm around her, using his other hand to thread his fingers between hers.

"We need to tell Rodney and the children the truth," Sylvia said. "That you and I are married and have been for a long time. I doubt it will make much of an impact on Rodney or Bob, but . . . telling Rachel means telling her that her father is dead, but . . . I believe it would be far worse to allow her to believe otherwise."

"I think you're right," Daniel said, "but that's a lot for a child to take in. We need to handle it carefully."

"Of course," Sylvia said, "and we need to allow her to grieve, which might mean some difficult behavior . . . depending on how she reacts. But we must remember that we're giving her love and security and a stable home, and with time she will feel the benefits of that."

"I think she already has," Daniel said. "I simply hope that—"

A loud knocking on the front door startled both of them and Sylvia hurried to put on her nightgown, not wanting to get caught in Daniel's room in the middle of the night—although she remembered that George and Millie knew the truth, so hopefully Rodney just stayed in his room with little Bob and ignored the intrusion on their sleep.

"A customer?" Daniel asked, pulling on his trousers then grabbing his shirt. "This late? Truly?"

"It's rare but it happens," Sylvia said. Daniel had become accustomed to the late-night visits of those who wished to purchase Sylvia's remedies, but no one had ever come this late.

"I'll get the door," he said, picking up the candle. "You'd do well to at least get a dressing gown from your room."

"Of course," she said and peered out into the hall, glad to see it empty. She hoped no one would open their door before she had a chance to get back to her room. George and Millie generally remained in their room while Sylvia dealt with her customers, and she hoped that would be the case tonight. She dashed down the hallway in the darkness while Daniel headed down the stairs just as the knock at the door was repeated, more loudly.

Sylvia put on her dressing gown before she lit a candle and hurried down the stairs. Daniel was standing at the open door and turned toward her when she approached.

"They told me they would only speak with you," Daniel said and stepped back, but she sensed his desire to remain close by. Perhaps he was curious, perhaps he felt protective. Either way, she was glad to have him there.

Sylvia managed to keep from gasping as she faced the two people standing in her doorway.

"I'm certain you know who I am," the vicar said.

"I know who you are," Sylvia replied. "I just can't imagine what you're doing *here*, especially at this time of night."

"This is Bertha Belder—the doctor's wife," he said, motioning to the woman standing beside him. "I've accompanied her here at her request." He then turned to Bertha as if he expected her to offer an explanation.

"It's my husband. He's very ill." She was clearly upset. "He accidentally cut himself rather badly . . . with a kitchen knife. I helped him stitch it . . . and we thought we had disinfected it sufficiently . . . but the wound looks worse every day . . . and he has a fever, and . . . ."

"Does he know you're here?" Sylvia asked.

"He's become delirious, Mrs. Hewitt," she said in a respectful tone. "He's aware of very little. I know your reputation, and I personally have never cared about the ridiculous suspicions that others talk about. I am in need of your expertise. I'm asking you to come with me . . . and to do all you can to try and save my husband."

"And if I can't?" Sylvia asked. "It's possible the infection is too far along and—"

"Then we will know that we did everything we can," Bertha said. "Please. I'm begging you."

Sylvia felt drawn to go but still hesitant. She turned to Daniel as if he might have the answers and he was quick to say, "I'm coming with you." That was all Sylvia needed to hear to believe that she would be safe going out on such a strange endeavor. "You get dressed and gather all you need. I'll write a note for the others so they know where we've gone. I'm certain all will be well here."

Sylvia nodded gratefully toward Daniel then turned and said to their visitors, "If you'll just give us a few minutes to—"

"We'll be in the carriage," the vicar said, "whenever you're ready."

"Thank you," Bertha said. "Thank you."

Sylvia nodded and closed the door as the two of them turned and walked toward a waiting carriage.

"Good heavens!" Sylvia exclaimed softly. "I certainly never expected *this* to come up in my life."

"Life is full of surprises," Daniel said and kissed her quickly before they both went to get ready to go.

Once Sylvia was adequately dressed for such an outing, she went to her workroom and filled a basket with every possible remedy that she thought might help. Fearing she might have forgotten something, or might not have enough of something else, it occurred to her that Daniel could borrow one of the Belder's horses and return to get more if necessary.

It felt strange to Sylvia to climb into the carriage with the vicar and the doctor's wife, but once Daniel was seated beside her, she felt safe and calm. Through the drive into the village, Sylvia considered all that the doctor and the vicar had done to make her life difficult, and she wondered if she should really be doing this. But she only had to wonder for a moment. Their behavior did not impact her own beliefs about helping those in need, and Bertha's plea had certainly touched her heart. Discreetly observing the vicar made her believe that he was only doing this for the sake of Mrs. Belder, and that his opinions of Sylvia hadn't changed. But Sylvia really didn't care.

The strangeness of this situation deepened as they went into the doctor's home with Bertha hurriedly leading Sylvia up the stairs to the patient's bedroom. Sylvia was most keenly aware of two things: Daniel following directly behind her as if he might protect her from any possible danger, and the opulence of the house which made it evident to Sylvia that this man made far too much money providing medical care to the locals who were mostly only making a moderate income and could not afford such exorbitant prices for their medical care. But Sylvia focused on her purpose for being here rather than placing any judgment on her patient. Right now he was ill and suffering, and a person could certainly die from the kind of infection Bertha had described. Sylvia couldn't leave here without knowing she had done everything in her power to save him; otherwise, she would be haunted by regret for the rest of her life.

Once in the well-lit bedroom, Sylvia was glad for the doctor's delirium, since she doubted he would let her anywhere near him otherwise. She asked for clean water and soap to wash her hands before she examined the wound which was on the inside of his forearm. It was red and puffy and pus oozed from between the stitches. Sylvia said quietly to Bertha who was right beside her, "I'm going to remove the stitches which is more likely to help it heal, even though there might be more of a scar. The stitches themselves are now full of infection.

Bertha nodded and Sylvia added, "Do you think—in his current state—that you would be able to get him to drink a small amount of water or tea?"

Bertha glanced at her husband. "I think so; I can try."

"I have a tincture we can put into it that will help him rest and help ease his pain, and another that is capable of killing the infection from inside the body."

Bertha nodded and left to get something for the patient to drink.

Sylvia then found Daniel right beside her, saying softly, "Tell me what you need. Let me help you."

With Daniel handing her things from her basket as she asked for them, Sylvia removed the stitches, then cleaned the wound, which brought on a painful response from the doctor, but he still seemed unaware of what was going on around him. Sylvia stopped working while Bertha got him to drink a small amount of water with the two tinctures in it, and they were both glad that he'd gotten that inside of him.

Sylvia then applied a poultice on the wound that would help draw the infection out, and she wrapped clean bandaging around it to hold it in place. She then said to Bertha who was now standing on the opposite side of the bed, watching her closely with both concern and curiosity showing in her face, "While the infection is so severe, I need to change the poultice every hour, so I think it's best if we stay for now."

"Of course," Bertha said. "I'd be grateful to you for doing so. We'll make certain you have all that you need. And of course, I'll pay you well for your time and efforts."

"We can talk about that when he's doing better," Sylvia said, distinctly uncomfortable over the thought of taking money that had been earned by charging too much for medical care.

Once Sylvia had done all she could for now, she took in her surroundings with more careful observation. The bedroom was large, decorated finely, and designed for comfort. She was glad for the availability of high-backed comfortable chairs and she decided to move one close to the doctor's bedside so that she could keep a close eye on him. Before she could move the chair, Daniel stepped in and moved it for her, as if he'd read her mind. She thanked him and was surprised when he moved another chair right beside hers so they could sit close together.

Bertha told them quietly, "I'm going to try and rest here beside him." She kicked off her slippers and laid down on the bed. "I confess I've not been able to sleep much since he became so ill. You will wake me if anything changes . . . or if I'm needed?"

"We will," Sylvia promised. "Try and get some rest while you can. This certainly won't be over quickly."

Bertha pulled a blanket up over herself and rested her head on the pillow while she put a loving hand on her husband's arm. Sylvia watched them and felt a new perspective settling into her. Since the day she'd lost her baby and her ability to have another due to his callous and impulsive decisions on how to solve a problem that had other viable solutions, she had only seen this man as a villain. His perpetuation of the terrible rumors about her that had ostracized her from the community had only added fuel to her belief that he was simply a horrible man. Seeing him so vulnerable now, quite literally on the brink of death, she saw him only as another human being, as vulnerable and subjective to suffering as any other. His wife clearly cared about him, which for some reason surprised Sylvia. In her mind she had come to believe that no one could love such a beastly man.

Then it occurred to her that she had always loved Daniel, even when he had been taking unfair advantage of other people, people who had probably hated and despised him. Daniel had changed his ways and had worked hard to make restitution for his crimes. The doctor who had impulsively subjected her to an excruciating surgical procedure that had made it impossible for her to ever be a mother had no way of making restitution. It could never be undone or reversed. And yet it was in the past; the deed was done.

Sylvia often had moments of wishing she could have had a baby, but she had long ago stopped feeling any anger or resentment toward this man. It was not her desire to carry such a burden; she only wanted peace in her own life, and with time she had found it. And now she'd been blessed with the miracle of Rachel coming into her home and her family. And Bob too added joy to their household. Looking at the doctor as he slept more comfortably, Sylvia felt no animosity toward him, but that didn't mean she necessarily liked him. Right now, however, he was simply a man who needed the help of her expertise, and as soon as he had improved enough to be aware of his surroundings, she planned on being long gone from here. Sylvia would leave Bertha with the necessary items to care for him, and all of the instructions she would need to use them properly.

"You should rest as well," Daniel said quietly to Sylvia. "I can keep an eye on him."

"Thank you, but . . . I feel too restless to relax right now. Perhaps *you* should rest so you can take over when I *do* feel tired."

"I'm fine," he said and put his arm around her, urging her head to his shoulder.

Sylvia listened to the silence surrounding her for a long while until her eyelids began to feel heavy. Her next awareness was Daniel nudging her as he whispered, "It's been more than an hour. Should we not change the poultice?"

"Yes, thank you." She rubbed her hands over her face as if that might bring her more fully into consciousness. "Oh, my. It seems I wasn't as restless as I thought."

"It's fine," Daniel said with a small laugh. "I like holding you while you sleep."

She passed him a warm smile and set to work gathering all she needed to change the poultice on the doctor's arm. Daniel was once again by her side, handing her what she needed and making the process much more quick and efficient. The patient winced when the wound was flooded with disinfectant, but he remained asleep which was good for all of them. Bertha sat up in bed when she realized what Sylvia and Daniel were doing. She offered her assistance, but Sylvia assured her that they had everything taken care of and she should rest.

After Sylvia and Daniel changed the poultice two more times—dozing a little in between—the patient emerged from his calm slumber into an agitated, somewhat delirious state. Sylvia helped Bertha give him more of the tinctures, which had to be put into a small amount of water since he wasn't capable of drinking very much in this condition. But he relaxed again rather quickly, and those caring for him took advantage of this time to rest themselves.

When daylight had fully arrived, a woman brought a large tray of breakfast to the room for Bertha, Daniel, and Sylvia, which she set on top of a large bureau. Bertha only introduced her as our loyal cook and housekeeper, before the woman left and came back a couple of minutes later with a tray of cups and saucers, a teapot, milk, and sugar. There wasn't a table in the room where they could sit down, but there were places to set their teacups, and they each managed to hold their plates and eat. Sylvia was reminded of the times that she and George and Millie had gathered in Daniel's room—who was known to be Dougal at the time—to share meals or cake.

The food and tea tasted especially good to Sylvia and she was grateful for the sustenance they offered. Once they had all eaten, Bertha told Sylvia and Daniel there was a guest room not far down the hall that they were welcome to use for as long as Sylvia felt the need to remain close by. Since it was a room with one large bed, Sylvia wondered what they would have done if she and Daniel were still just *pretending* that Daniel was her husband—or Dougal as she had believed. And it had only been last night that they'd shared a bed for the first time since before he'd left for the war. Thankfully, the timing was good in that regard, and they simply thanked Bertha for the room after which Bertha suggested they get some rest and either she or the housekeeper would wake them when the poultice needed changing.

Despite the interruptions of caring for their patient, both Sylvia and Daniel were able to get a fair amount of rest, which was much easier in a bed as opposed to the chairs available in the patient's room. They were given a fine lunch, tea, and supper which they were able to eat in the dining room with Bertha, who didn't say much but was cordial. She seemed to be entirely consumed with worry for her husband.

After supper, when they changed the poultice, Sylvia could see a visible improvement in the wound, and urged Bertha to see for herself.

"Oh, that's remarkable!" she declared. "A miracle."

Sylvia took the opportunity to state what she firmly believed, "It's simply the use of plants and herbs that God has given us for the purpose of healing. But we don't know how much infection has spread through his body from the wound. I think we can cut back to changing the poultice every two hours, and we'll continue to give him the tinctures when he wakes up enough to do so. Beyond that, all we can do is wait and see how he responds."

"I understand," Bertha said, gazing at her husband with adoration. Looking back at Sylvia she added, "I could never thank you enough for what you're doing. Do you have what you need?"

"Yes, thank you," Sylvia said.

She and Daniel got more sleep that night with not needing to change the poultice as frequently, and the following morning after breakfast Daniel borrowed one of their host's horses to go home and make certain all was well, and also to get some fresh clothing for both himself and Sylvia, and a list of medical supplies that were beginning to run low. Sylvia knew that Millie could help him find what she'd written down, and it was more practical for Daniel to take care of the errand—especially since she knew the doctor would never want her to be seen in daylight leaving his home. But knowing that Daniel was going home, even for just a short while, made her miss her family greatly, especially the children. She would be glad when this ordeal was over, but she was certainly committed to seeing it through.

For three more days Sylvia and Daniel remained in the doctor's home, caring for him meticulously, and doing their best to offer reassurance and comfort to Bertha. Each day the wound looked better until there were no visible signs of infection at all, which felt very satisfying to Sylvia, but Bertha was beside herself with joy, even though they still weren't certain if the infection in the patient's body would yet be conquered.

Along with Sylvia's satisfaction in seeing evidence of the doctor's improvement, she'd begun to feel a strange shift in her feelings toward this man throughout the time and effort she had put into watching over him and genuinely hoping and praying for his recovery. She found herself examining her knowledge of Christianity which was at the heart of who she was and all that she believed. And a thought occurred to her that she'd never considered before. She truly believed that she had forgiven this doctor for what he'd done to her and how he'd negatively impacted her life, and she could sincerely say before God that she felt no ill will toward him, nor was she angry or holding onto any grudges over their differences. Not trusting the man, and preferring to avoid him, were not the same issue as forgiveness—at least that's the way she saw it. But what occurred to Sylvia now was the matter of judgment. She didn't feel as if she'd been judgmental toward him, but now she found herself considering the fact that she did not know this man's heart, or his mind, or his intentions. In fact, she hardly knew him at all. She didn't know if he had regret over what he'd done—although that was entirely between him and God. The overall message that seemed to be forming in her mind was the fact that she couldn't *fully* forgive him until she acknowledged that she had judged him as being a terrible person, a true villain. He had indeed done much that had affected her life adversely, but she was all right; God had blessed her greatly despite such challenges. And it simply wasn't her place to judge this man in any way; the Bible made that very clear.

As Sylvia spent hours at his bedside and continued the routine of caring for the wound and giving him the medicine he needed to rest and heal, she gradually came to see him entirely as a man in need, a man suffering and clinging to life, a man like any other man. She felt a warmth come over her as if to tell her that in letting go of her judgment of him and his actions, her forgiveness toward him was complete, and she felt as if a burden were truly lifted from off her shoulders—a burden that she hadn't even realized she'd still been carrying.

Sylvia cried silent tears as a new peace over the matter settled into her every fiber, and she was glad to be alone in the room, knowing that Daniel was resting in the guest room and Bertha was visiting with the housekeeper over household matters.

Only a moment after Sylvia had wiped away her tears and took in a deep breath of this fresh new perspective, Daniel came into the room. He bent over to kiss the top of her head before he went to the window to look out and she found herself just watching him with the sunlight outside illuminating his features. The love she felt for him surged through her, accompanied by a deep gratitude for the miracles that had brought him back to her—however strangely they had come to pass. And then it occurred to her that if she could forgive the man she hardly knew who had taken away her ability to have children and then had maligned her publicly to the point that she'd been completely ostracized from the community, why could she not forgive Daniel for his past offenses? He'd expressed his regret over and over. He'd apologized profusely and with sincerity. He'd proven himself trustworthy and a changed man. And for all that his deception in pretending to be Dougal had been very hurtful and his motives questionable, he had boldly declared that he had likely made a mistake in how he'd handled the situation, but he'd been afraid and confused. If Sylvia could acknowledge that she had no idea what the doctor's intentions might be, that she didn't know his heart or his mind, that she had no right to judge him in any way, how could she possibly judge Daniel's thoughts or feelings or intentions? Was she holding onto her own old hurts as a reason to hold back her forgiveness? She believed that God allowed people time to work through their struggles as a prerequisite to forgiveness. But had she not been allowed more than sufficient time for such a process? If she was truly the Christian woman she claimed to be and *wanted* to be, then she certainly needed to examine her behavior in that light. And it was clear to her now that she needed to let go of any degree of being judgmental toward others, and to allow forgiveness to fill her heart and cleanse it of the need to hold onto any of the wounds from her past.

Suddenly Sylvia couldn't get to her husband's side fast enough, and she immediately wrapped her arms around him, holding him tightly against her.

"Well, hello," he chuckled. "What is this?"

Sylvia looked up at him, not surprised by the cleansing tears that slid down her face without warning. "I just need to tell you that . . . well . . . forgive me, Daniel."

"Forgive *you?* For what? You've done absolutely nothing that would require me to—"

"Forgive me for holding onto my anger and judgment toward you. I was holding onto my old hurts, and I was assuming things about your possible motives and intentions that I had no right to assume. I love you. I trust you. And I forgive you . . . for everything. And I hope and pray you can forgive *me,* and we can truly begin again and start a new life together."

Sylvia saw tears gather in Daniel's eyes as if to add one final declaration of his sincerity. "Oh, my love," he said and pressed a hand over her face and into her hair. "I don't blame you at all for needing time to adjust to all that I've done . . . and the way everything happened. There's nothing to forgive. I'm only grateful that you can forgive *me.* And I don't think I've ever been happier than in this moment."

"I do believe I feel the same," she said, and he kissed her. They both laughed softly and he kissed her again.

Chapter Fourteen

Forgiven

The following morning Sylvia and Daniel went to the doctor's room right after they'd finished breakfast where they settled in for their usual vigil. Sylvia had checked on him just before breakfast and he'd been sleeping soundly. And he still was. But it was only a short while later that she heard a noise from the bed, indicating that their patient was waking up.

Sylvia moved to his bedside in an effort to assess how he was doing. Each time he became somewhat conscious she watched him for signs of how ill he felt. He'd not had a fever now for more than a day, but he'd still barely shown any awareness of his surroundings when he'd awakened, and he'd still seemed miserable. But now Sylvia saw his eyes focusing on her and his brow furrowed in confusion.

"What are you doing here?" he asked, his voice raspy.

Before Sylvia could explain she heard Daniel say, "I'll get Bertha."

"Your wife and the vicar came to get me," Sylvia said, her heart pounding as she feared what his response might be. "The wound on your arm had become severely infected and you were very ill. I'm glad to say that it appears all is well and you're going to recover."

Thankfully before he could respond Bertha hurried into the room and sat on the edge of the bed, turning his attention to her. "Oh, my dearest!" she said, weeping. "You're all right. You're going to be all right. She saved your life."

Bertha looked at Sylvia and her husband did the same, but Sylvia didn't feel the need to remain any longer and wonder how he might respond to her being in his home. Whatever he might feel about the situation was between him and his Maker. Sylvia felt at peace and had no need for him to thank her or acknowledge her assistance. And she certainly didn't need to risk having him say something to her that might be hurtful. She knew now not to judge him for his behavior—whatever it might be. And she'd forgiven him completely. But that didn't mean she needed to expose herself to his possible negative attitudes toward her. So she hurried from the room and Daniel followed her.

"He's fine now," she said to him. "We need to go."

"I can't say I won't be glad to leave here and go home," he said as they went into the guest room to gather their things.

"Amen to that," she said.

While Daniel went downstairs to make arrangements for them to be taken home, Sylvia set out on the bureau all that Bertha would need to care for her husband until he was completely healed—provided he would allow her to use Sylvia's concoctions now that he was conscious and aware.

Bertha entered through the open door and said with some disappointment, "You're leaving?"

"He's going to be fine now," Sylvia said with a smile. She motioned toward the items she'd just been putting in order. "I'm leaving everything you need to care for him. You know what to do. If you need more of anything, or another problem arises, you know where to find me, and I'm glad to help."

"You've been so incredibly kind," Bertha said. "And I cannot thank you enough. You have indeed saved his life."

"I'm sincerely glad that I could help," Sylvia said.

"I need to pay you. Just give me a moment to go and get—"

"That's not necessary," Sylvia insisted. She'd had plenty of time to think about this a great deal, and she knew this was important for a number of reasons. "I'm glad you came to get me, and I'm glad we were able to help. Consider this a neighborly gift. I only ask that you give your husband this." Sylvia picked up a letter off the bedside table which she had written the previous day. "Or perhaps you can read it to him. It's nothing of concern," Sylvia assured Bertha. "I just want him to know that all is forgiven."

Bertha got tears in her eyes and offered no warning before she was hugging Sylvia tightly. Sylvia returned the embrace and Bertha stepped back. "You are a good woman."

"As are you," Sylvia said and Bertha hurried away, obviously anxious to be at her husband's side, especially since he was now awake.

Thankfully it didn't take long for the carriage to be harnessed and Daniel and Sylvia were soon on their way home. It felt like months to Sylvia since she'd seen her strange and wonderful family, and her heart quickened with anticipation to think that it was only a matter of minutes before they would be able to put this bizarre adventure behind them. She was truly ready to begin a new life with her beloved husband who had proven himself to be a new man. She'd never imagined the possibility of feeling so thoroughly happy.

Sylvia was so glad to see her home come into view that she laughed aloud and Daniel laughed with her, squeezing her hand before he kissed it and then kissed her lips. Before the carriage had halted, the children were running out of the door with all three adults coming behind them, and Sylvia had barely set her feet upon the ground before both Rachel and Bob overwhelmed her with hugs and laughter. Once they'd sufficiently greeted her, they did the same to Daniel. Sylvia also shared hugs with Millie and George. Rodney didn't seem to be a hugging kind of man, but he was all smiles and didn't hesitate to say how glad he was to see them.

"It just don't seem right at all around here without the two o' ye," he said.

"Well, it didn't seem at all right not to be here," Sylvia said, and they all went into the house as the doctor's carriage rolled away.

Once inside, Millie insisted they all sit around the table while she put the kettle on so it could heat up for some tea while they visited. The children showed no interest in the details of Sylvia and Daniel's experiences; they were only glad to have them back. But the adults were *very* interested, especially given all they knew about the past animosity between the doctor and Sylvia and all the related problems it had caused.

Sylvia and Daniel took turns repeating exactly what had happened, and the others seemed disappointed that the story hadn't been much longer. They'd been gone for days, but the majority of their time away had been spent watching over a mostly unconscious patient and administering the same remedies over and over, so there was very little to tell in that regard. But Sylvia felt inclined to share with them her personal epiphany regarding her feelings toward the doctor, and how she had been able to forgive him more deeply. She noticed Millie dabbing at her eyes with her apron, but Rodney discreetly wiped away a few tears as well. He only knew that this doctor had disliked Sylvia and had spread vicious rumors about her, but apparently that was enough for him to appreciate Sylvia's change of heart.

"So, I wrote him a letter to tell him how I felt, and I charged them nothing for our time and efforts—not to mention the large amount of supplies we used. I believe that offering my services as a gift is the charitable thing to do. It helps me feel better about putting away all of the unkind thoughts and feelings I've had toward him. And now it's over and done. I don't expect anything in response, but I have been able to completely put the matter to rest, so in essence this little unexpected adventure was somewhat of a divine gift of healing for me."

"That's lovely, Missus," Millie said with a sniffle. "Just lovely."

When there was no more to say, Sylvia declared the desire to be able to get things back to normal. Within a short while she was helping Millie make a cake and Daniel had gone outside to pull weeds in the garden. Given the long, especially warm days of summer, the vegetable plants were all getting larger, but so were the weeds and it was an almost daily task to keep up with removing them. As the children ran in and out of the house, often very loudly, Sylvia felt a deep joy and contentment over their presence here. In fact, all things combined, she felt a new sense of peace—a kind of peace she'd never felt before. Her household felt complete. Daniel had come back to her a new man, the kind of man she'd always longed for him to be. And her new level of forgiveness toward the doctor and others who had hurt her left her feeling as if she were literally beginning a new life. There was only one more matter that needed to be taken care of, and just after lunch she whispered to Daniel that they needed to tell Rodney and the children the truth about his identity so they could stop dreading it. He agreed and they decided to take care of it after supper and before bedtime.

When supper was over and done, everyone gathered in the parlor, and only George and Millie showed a lack of curiosity. Sylvia had told Millie earlier of their intentions, and of course George and Millie knew everything about the situation already. Rodney believed this man was Dougal, and given his own part in how all of this had evolved, he certainly deserved to hear the entire story. And most importantly, Rachel needed to know that her father was dead and Daniel had come for her at her father's request. Both Sylvia and Daniel were determined to make certain that there were no lies or secrets in their home, and this was the final piece of putting the truth out into the open.

Once everyone was settled, Daniel began by telling everyone straight out that he was in truth Daniel Hewitt and not Dougal Heywood, and he asked for their patience while he explained everything. Rachel was surprisingly without expression, and Rodney just muttered, "Just when I think I got it straight . . ."

Daniel went on to tell everyone about how he'd met Dougal and their mutual astonishment over how much alike they'd looked. He went on to tell the entire story, including how he had purposely deceived Sylvia and how upset she'd been when she found out. Sylvia interjected a brief recounting of how she had forgiven him and that she knew he was a good man who could be trusted. Daniel then went on to tell any other pertinent details before he looked directly at Rachel and said, "Sweetheart, do you know what this means? It means that I'm not *really* your father, although I'm going to take care of you like a father for the rest of my life, and Sylvia is going to be a mother to you. But . . . sweetheart . . . this means that your father died in the war, and—"

"I know," Rachel said, showing no shock or surprise whatsoever.

"You know?" Daniel countered, astonished. "How?"

"My father wrote letters to me. Grandmama told the servants they were supposed to burn my letters, but I knew from spying that they were kept in a special drawer and I would read them before *I* burned them so no one else would know what they said. I learned to read before Papa left for the war. And Papa wrote to me and told me that he prayed every day I would be safe, and that I would be able to read his letters and our secrets wouldn't be discovered by anyone else. I couldn't write back to him but I prayed too and I think our prayers were answered.

"Papa told me about his friend who looked like him, and that if anything happened to him, it was possible that his friend would come for me, and I needed to let everyone believe he was my father, and I needed to let him be my father, and he wanted me to know that he loved me and everything would be all right."

A strange silence followed Rachel's confession until Daniel scooped her into his arms and held her tightly. They cried a little and laughed a great deal as the acknowledgment of their sorrow over Dougal's death was swallowed up by their joy of being together as a family, and they'd had many weeks of seeing the evidence that Rachel was happy here.

While no one seemed to have anything to say, Rodney declared with confused astonishment, "Well, if that isn't the strangest tale I've ever heard of."

"It is, indeed," Daniel said.

"And even though I lost my man Biff," Rodney said, "I know God surely must have smiled down on me t' bring me here. Seems to me that lots o' prayers have been heard for all o' us. Me and my boy Bob ain't never been so happy. I'm mighty grateful t' all o' ye here."

"And we're so glad to have you here," Sylvia said. "I can't even imagine what our household would be like without you or Bob."

"Rachel would be awfully lonely without sweet Bob," Millie said.

"And you've done a lot of fine work around here," George added.

"Indeed," Daniel agreed. "In fact, I dare say we needed you perhaps more than you needed us."

Rodney gave a scoffing laugh. "I'll argue that t' the grave."

"You go ahead and do that, my friend," Daniel said. "As long as you stay here with us, you can argue as much as you like."

"If that turns out t' be the way things go," Rodney said more severely, "promise me you'll put my grave in the woods next t' my man Biff."

"There's no need to be concerned about such things for many, many years to come," Daniel said, "but we promise."

The children were getting restless with the conversation. It had held little interest for Bob, and once Rachel had stated what she knew, she became distracted by Bob's antics.

"I think it's time to get these little ones to bed," Daniel said and scooped Rachel into his arms in a way that made her giggle.

Rodney did the same with Bob and the men went up the stairs to help the children get ready for bed and to read them a story. Sylvia had gradually become more and more involved with the care of the children—especially Rachel since her husband had taken on the role of the child's father—but when Sylvia had believed Daniel was Dougal and he was actually Rachel's father, it had been natural for him to oversee this bedtime routine. And since Daniel's true identity had come to light, he'd still insisted on being in charge of bedtime and spending this hour of the evening with Rachel. He truly had become a father to Rachel, and it was evident that Rachel had grown to love Daniel as much as he had grown to love her. And Sylvia loved them both.

Once the entire household knew that it was in truth Daniel Hewitt living in the house, his things were moved into Sylvia's room. This left an empty room which Sylvia declared made it possible for Rodney and Bob to not have to share a room, but they both insisted that they liked sharing a room and wanted to continue doing so.

"The house we lived in before wasn't so large," Rodney explained. "We always shared a room. I don't know if little Bob would feel safe or comfortable if we didn't."

"That makes sense," Sylvia said. "But perhaps when he's older he'll feel differently. For now, an empty room certainly isn't any cause for concern."

Summer moved toward autumn while everyone settled more deeply into their new way of life. Sylvia loved having the house and barn painted before winter, and also to have a great many repairs completed that had been long overdue. Having two more men around who were both hard workers had been a blessing in many ways.

The final harvest of the garden took place as the weather turned cold and the remaining root vegetables were pulled up and put into the cellar, along with some winter squash and pumpkins. Sylvia also enlisted the help of Daniel and the children to help gather every possible plant that could be dried and used to create her remedies before the frost of winter killed them all.

Fires were kept burning in every room on the ground floor all through the day so that everyone could stay warm while they were indoors, and the children were only allowed to play outside for a short time each day—and only if the sun was out; no one wanted them getting sick. Sylvia had come to enjoy a new habit of sitting in the parlor with Daniel late in the evenings after the children were asleep and the other adults had gone up to bed. They would extinguish all of the lamps and just sit in front of the fire and talk. They never ran out of things to talk about—their hopes for the future, their coming to terms with the past, and their gratitude for all that was good in the present. Excluding facts that simply couldn't be changed, Sylvia couldn't think of a single thing she would want to change about her life. She felt deeply contented and happy, and she never let a day pass without telling Daniel so. She didn't ever want him to think that she took for granted the miracle of his being alive, nor the miracle of the way he had changed so much for the better. And Daniel was equally appreciative of Sylvia. They both believed that remaining mindful of their gratitude for each other would help keep their marriage strong and therefore they would both be happier throughout the remainder of their lives.

A knock at the door startled both of them but Sylvia was quick to say, "A customer, no doubt."

"Or perhaps," Daniel said facetiously as they both stood up, "the doctor has wounded himself again." He hurried to light a lamp and carried it as he followed her to the front door.

"Unlikely," Sylvia said and opened the door only to catch her breath as she saw the doctor, the vicar, and Bertha standing before her. Sylvia put her focus on Bertha since they'd developed an amiable relationship, and she had no idea what to expect from these men.

"May we come in?" Bertha asked. "We know it's late, but we have an urgent matter to discuss with you and . . . it is rather chilly, and . . ."

"Of course," Sylvia said as she and Daniel stepped aside, and the three visitors entered. She closed the door and motioned toward the parlor, not wanting all of them standing near the door while they discussed whatever this urgent matter might be.

"Thank you," Bertha said and led the way while the men remained mute. Perhaps they feared Sylvia would cast an evil spell upon them if they spoke.

Daniel set down the lamp and turned up the wick before he lit another lamp so the room wasn't quite so dark. He also stoked up the fire and added some wood, creating more light as well as warmth, but Bertha still kept her cloak pulled tightly around her as she sat down carefully on one of the sofas, with her husband on one side of her and the vicar on the other. Daniel and Sylvia sat down across from them and Daniel took Sylvia's hand as if to offer silent support.

"What is it that we can do for you?" Sylvia asked, noting that they all bore grave expressions. "Is someone ill?"

"Mrs. Hewitt," Bertha said, "a strange and terrible thing has happened, and—"

"I believe I should say something first," the doctor said with a nod toward his wife. He then looked directly at Sylvia. "I owe you a profound apology. I don't know that it's possible to recount all the ways I have wronged you, Mrs. Hewitt, nevertheless I would like to express my remorse and also my gratitude for all that you did to save my life."

"Thank you," Sylvia said, feeling a temptation to cry but fighting it back. "I humbly accept your apology. It means a great deal."

The doctor nodded and offered a wan smile just before the vicar said, "I do hope and pray that you will also accept *my* apology, Mrs. Hewitt. Perhaps at some future date we might discuss how to go forward with more acceptance and respect."

"I would like that," Sylvia said, then silence blanketed the room until she looked at Bertha and said, "You were going to tell me about something strange and terrible that's happened. Whatever it was, I can't imagine what it might have to do with us. But I assume you didn't just come here at this hour to offer your apologies."

"The apologies are long overdue," Bertha said in a way that hinted at a subtle scolding toward her husband and his friend the vicar. "What we need to discuss with you tonight is rather urgent. You see . . . a young woman died not an hour ago—nineteen years old, bless her." Bertha's voice trembled. "She was a seamstress, working for the tailor in the village since her husband was killed in an accident only a few months ago. Perhaps peace can be found in thinking that they might be together."

"That is truly tragic," Sylvia said with compassion. "Still . . . I'm not certain what it might have to do with me . . . or us."

"Neither her nor her husband had any family," Bertha went on, "which left us with a terrible dilemma, and yet the three of us—who were all with her when she passed—all seemed to know at the same moment that you were the answer to this dilemma."

"Which is?" Sylvia asked and was surprised when the doctor answered.

"There are some mistakes for which restitution is never possible," he said, his voice trembling as well. "And therefore they are the mistakes for which we feel the most remorse, I believe. But sometimes prayers are truly heard, Mrs. Hewitt, and miracles happen. I am not at all saying that this young woman's death was a miracle; it is a tragedy to be sure. But perhaps God sometimes brings something wonderful out of tragedy, and allows some tiny measure of restitution to be possible."

"That is a lovely sentiment," Sylvia said, "but—"

Bertha interrupted, "She died giving birth, Sylvia." Bertha then opened her cloak to reveal that she was holding a sleeping infant and Sylvia could hardly breathe as the implication began to settle in and she felt Daniel's grip on her hand tighten. "He has no family, no home. And every person we could think of that would be good enough to bring an orphan into their home and treat him well already has their hands full with their own very young children. But you . . . you are a good woman with a good husband . . . and a fine home, and . . ." Bertha sniffled as she stood and moved directly in front of Sylvia, leaning over to place the infant in her arms. "He belongs with you, my dear. We all know it to be true. We hope that you will be in agreement, because we know you will give him a good life."

Sylvia fought to catch her breath while she took in the feel of a living, breathing infant in her arms. Her mind swirled with everything that had been said by her visitors leading up to this baby being placed in her arms. Daniel put his arm around her shoulders, and she could hear evidence that he was crying before she realized that tears were streaming down her own face and every cell in her body felt immediately connected to this child. She had worked very hard to accept the fact that she would never have a baby of her own, a child to raise from infancy as her own. And now there was a miracle in her arms, and she couldn't begin to comprehend the possibility that it might be real.

"But . . . how can this be?" she asked, looking through tear-filled eyes at the three visitors sitting across from her who had brought this baby into her life.

"God does indeed work in mysterious ways," the vicar said humbly but with a slight smile.

"This child is meant to be yours," the doctor said. "He's meant to be raised in this home, with this family."

"But . . ." Sylvia still had trouble accepting the reality of what she was being told, "it feels too good to be true. I feel as if . . . it will end and . . ." The urge to sob got stuck in her throat, making it impossible to speak until she let it out. Realizing it was fruitless to attempt hiding the depth of her emotion from these people, she let out a sharp sob, and then another. "I fear this won't last . . . and our hearts will be broken all over again. Please tell me that—"

"This child is yours," the vicar said. "We will see that the legalities are properly taken care of. There is no need to fear losing him, Mrs. Hewitt. And . . . in my own effort to make restitution for my sins against you, I would humbly ask that you and your household might consider attending church this coming Sunday. There is something I would like to say over the pulpit to the entire community, and it would mean a great deal to me if you were present when I did so."

Sylvia became unable to speak due to a huge onslaught of confusion and fear, even though she instinctively believed the vicar was being sincere and the very idea of being able to attend church again filled her heart with an added layer of joy. She'd come to accept her isolated way of life, but in that moment she was fully able to acknowledge to herself that she didn't necessarily like it. She'd simply become accustomed to not complaining about something she hadn't had the power to change. But how could she not at least accept the vicar's offer and make the effort to try? The worst possible outcome was that things would remain the same. But she looked down at the sleeping infant in her arms and realized that nothing would *ever* be the same. With or without the support of the community, she had the very thing she'd always longed for and had come to believe she would never have. The depth and breadth of such a miracle was impossible to comprehend.

When Sylvia didn't speak and the expectancy in the room became thick, Daniel said, "My wife and I will be at church on Sunday. Thank you for the invitation. We will also be bringing the child we've taken in to raise as our own, a little girl named Rachel who is the daughter of one of the men I fought with in the war who has lost both of her parents." He looked at the baby in Sylvia's arms. "And now she has a little brother. She will likely be almost as happy about that as we are."

"Tell me about his parents," Sylvia said to the people who had brought her this baby. "I need to know who he came from . . . so that we can tell him about them when he's old enough; it's only right."

Sylvia saw tears in Bertha's eyes as she smiled and leaned forward a little. Sylvia guessed that Bertha had known these people and was pleased with Sylvia's interest in them. She told Sylvia and Daniel that the baby's father had been a farmer who had worked very hard but had also known how to relax and have fun when the work was done. He'd been known for initiating social gatherings with other people in the village, and he'd been well-liked by everyone. He'd died after he'd fallen from a ladder while attempting to make repairs on the roof of his home, and his wife had been devastated. She too had been a very social person until the loss of her husband, when she had become hesitant to receive visitors and had seemed to lose the desire to live except for the sake of her unborn child. It was the unanimous opinion of all three of the people sitting across from Daniel and Sylvia that the baby's mother had only wanted to be with her husband once she'd been able to bring her child safely into the world.

"Such an idea might sound strange," the vicar said, "unless it is viewed through a spiritual lens, nevertheless, we were all with her when she died, and that is what we have all felt."

Sylvia could only nod, fearing that she would start to sob again. Instead, she just held the baby more tightly against herself while the entire life of this boy appeared in her mind, and she could feel the joy he would bring to their family.

When the baby began to squirm and make funny noises, the sounds prompted all three visitors to stand up and Daniel did the same, but Sylvia felt too weak to do so and just held her baby close, still overcome with such an enormous miracle.

"Rose—the baby's mother," Bertha said, "had everything gathered for the anticipation of the baby. Many women in the village had made gifts; blankets and clothes and the like. She had a lovely bassinet so he has a safe place to sleep while he's still tiny. You'll be needing to get a proper crib as he grows bigger and moves around more on his own. But for now there is plenty of everything you'll need, including bottles to feed him in case she wasn't able to breast feed him adequately, as is the case with some women. Rose had even acquired a goat for its milk, which you will be needing. And we have everything in the carriage."

"You have a goat in the carriage?" Daniel asked.

"We do indeed," Bertha said with a little laugh. More seriously she said as she looked directly at Sylvia, "I must ask . . . *we* must ask—just to be certain—if you are entirely in agreement with taking on this child. We just assumed, but we need to know."

"Yes!" Sylvia said. "Oh, yes!" She looked up at Daniel, realizing it wasn't only up to her.

"Absolutely yes!" Daniel said with stark enthusiasm. "It's a miracle! I think I can speak for my wife when I say that we are terribly sorry for the untimely deaths of this child's natural parents, but we are more than glad to be able to bring this precious boy into our family."

"Excellent," the doctor said. "We'll go and get everything out of the carriage then, and—"

"I'll help you," Daniel said and followed the others outside, leaving Sylvia alone with her new son. Before she'd lost her baby, she'd basked often in the dream of her baby being born alive and well, and she'd hoped for Daniel to return from the war and they would have more children. Her dreams had been shattered and she'd struggled a great deal to come to terms with the losses in her life. And now she had been blessed with a series of miracles that she never could have imagined. How could she have ever even thought to pray that Daniel would come back to her a changed man when she had believed him to be dead? And how could she have prayed for the miracle of having this precious baby put into her hands? All she could do now was bask in the joy consuming her and thank God for His unfathomable generosity and mercy.

Still alone with her new son, she looked down at him as he wriggled and grunted comically. "Hello, little one," she said, "I'm your new mother. The woman who gave you life will always watch over you—and your father too who has passed on; they will be your angels. And Daniel and I will care for you and love you all the days of our lives. I love you already, my little one. We will have a good life together—I swear it."

Sylvia kissed the baby's head and inhaled his sweet fragrance, freshly bathed and perhaps carrying a subtle aroma of heaven that might still be clinging to him. To Sylvia, he seemed the very personification of heaven, and she couldn't imagine feeling any more blessed than she felt in that moment.

The next little while felt entirely dreamlike as Sylvia just held the baby, feeling somewhat dazed and unable to do anything more while Bertha made herself at home in the kitchen to prepare a bottle for the baby with some fresh goat's milk while the men were apparently all out in the barn making certain the goat—who was also a new addition to the family—was comfortable and cared for.

"Now," Bertha said, "he won't eat very much at first, so don't be alarmed if he doesn't. The best advice I can give is to follow your instincts as a mother. A woman doesn't need to give birth to a child to have the instincts of a mother." Sylvia nodded, tempted to cry again. "And if you have any problems . . . or questions . . . just send for me and I'll come and help. My children are long grown and have moved away. I don't get to see my grandchildren very often. If it's all right with you, I'll check in regularly and see what I can do to help, which would be a great blessing for me."

"I would like that very much," Sylvia said, "and I'm certain I can use all the help and expertise I can get. I have Millie to help me; she works for me. But she never had children of her own. Still, she has *very* good instincts. Nevertheless, your expertise will be very much appreciated."

"I'll check back tomorrow, then," Bertha said. "Right now, let's change his nappy and see if he'll drink just a little, and that should help you get started."

Sylvia nodded with appreciation and watched as Bertha did what needed to be done, glad for the opportunity to watch a woman who had experience with babies take care of his basic needs enough for Sylvia to know what to do.

"Tomorrow I will show you how to bathe him," Bertha said. "That's something that can feel a bit frightening with such a tiny one, but I know some tricks that will make it easy."

"Thank you," Sylvia said. "I can't thank you enough."

"No, it is you who should be thanked, my dear," Bertha said. "Taking on a child that is not your own is no small thing. You are a good woman, and I pray you will be happy in this endeavor."

After the baby had been prompted to let out a tiny burp after being fed, the visitors left and Sylvia and Daniel were left alone with their new son. Sylvia encouraged Daniel to hold the baby who was sleeping again, and she eased him into the crook of his arm.

"I can't believe it," Daniel said, looking down at the baby. "Could it be my imagination that he looks a little like you?"

"Probably," Sylvia said with a tiny laugh.

"He's so very little," Daniel observed. "And so very beautiful."

"He is indeed!"

"What will we call him?" Daniel asked, looking up at Sylvia.

"Actually," Sylvia said, "I gave that matter a great deal of thought when I was pregnant with the baby I lost. If you don't want this name, there are many other options, I'm sure, and we don't have to rush, but . . . if the baby had been a boy, I wanted to call him Daniel Harrison—the middle name after my father, and of course the first name after *his* father—and I wanted to call him Danny. What do you think, my love? Shall we call him Danny?"

Daniel's voice quavered as he said, "It would be such a great honor to have this miracle child named after me, and of course using your father's name as well is perfect. I know he was a good man and you loved him dearly. I think Danny is perfect, and I think that his name will always remind me that I need to forever be the kind of man who is worthy of such miracles in my life."

Sylvia smiled tearfully at her husband and he reached over the baby he was holding to kiss her. And Sylvia realized she felt complete and whole in a way she never had before. She hadn't realized that anything was missing from her life, or perhaps she hadn't allowed herself to even wonder what it would be like to have a baby of her own, because she'd known it simply wasn't possible. But it had happened. With Daniel by her side and little Danny in their lives—along with every other blessing they'd already had—how could she ever ask for anything more?

After Daniel quietly carried the bassinet up the stairs and into their bedroom, Sylvia laid little Danny in it and just watched him for several minutes before she gave into Daniel's insistence that she try to get some rest.

"We have an infant to care for, my love," he said. "We're going to need all the sleep we can get."

Sylvia finally forced herself to go to bed, glad to feel Daniel close beside her, but neither of them could sleep. Instead, they talked about the miracle that had happened in the last couple of hours, and the indescribable joy they both felt.

"Sylvia," Daniel said, "I want you to know that your inability to have a child never made me love you any less, or feel any less desire to spend my life with you—even though I would have preferred to have a baby together, just as I knew you would have. I was content with the life we were settling into together. I don't want you to ever question that. Still, I cannot deny the joy of this miracle."

"I couldn't have said it better myself," she murmured and shifted her head on his shoulder. "Still, thank you for saying it." She sighed contentedly and added, "I love you, Daniel Hewitt. Thank you for coming back to me."

"Thank you for letting me stay," he said with a chuckle that seemed an indication of how they had put all of the trauma of the past behind them. Now, they only had a bright and wonderful future before them.

The following day was full of more joy than Sylvia believed she could ever hold as everyone in the household was overcome with the surprise of waking up to find that a brand new baby boy had joined their family. The adults were as fascinated with little Danny as were the children. They all took turns holding him—the children getting assistance from the adults. Even Rodney was convinced that he should get used to holding little Danny since they all needed to be a part of raising this precious boy and giving him all the love he deserved. Everyone was so thoroughly happy that Sylvia felt as if the roof of the house might explode into the sky simply because the house couldn't contain all the mutual joy they felt.

By the time Sunday came, Sylvia and Danny had become mostly accustomed to caring for Danny, and Millie had been extremely helpful. George and Rodney liked to hold Danny now and then when he was sleeping, but otherwise preferred leaving his care to others. The children found Danny boring when he was sleeping, and they were completely intrigued with him when he was awake.

They all decided that they would accept the vicar's invitation to attend church, and they would all go together if only to be seen in public as the family unit they had become. Earlier in the week after Sylvia had shared what the vicar had said, the men had all gone into town to purchase new clothes that would be suitable for attending church, and the children had gone with them since they were both in need of new clothes as well. Sylvia and Millie already owned dresses that would be appropriate, and the baby had many lovely things to wear that had been given to him prior to his birth.

When Sunday arrived, they all huddled in the carriage except for Rodney and George who sat on the box seat, George handling the four horses pulling them toward the village. Thankfully it was a lovely day, and the weather didn't cause any grief for them.

Sylvia felt decidedly nervous by the time they'd arrived, despite how much she'd kept reminding herself that the vicar's invitation had been sincere and humble, and this was surely a good thing. As every member of their household stayed close together entering the chapel, Sylvia could feel people looking their way with curiosity and sometimes disdain, but no one said anything to them, and they just found a place to sit near the back where Sylvia could slip out easily with Danny if he got fussy.

After some hymns and prayer, the vicar stood at the pulpit and began his sermon, which increased Sylvia's nervousness as she began to wonder if she'd misread his apparent sincerity. Perhaps they'd been lured here only for her to be further ridiculed as a supposed witch, which would condemn every member of her household by association. But Sylvia's fears melted into astonishment and then warmed her with gratitude as the vicar began to speak about the need for people to have sufficient humility to be able to admit that they had been wrong, or they'd made a mistake. And a deep irony settled into Sylvia considering her own recent discoveries about herself as the vicar talked about the need to not judge others when it was impossible to know their hearts or their intentions—and that only God knew such things. And then, much to Sylvia's astonishment, he came right out and asked the forgiveness of the congregation and especially to Mrs. Hewitt for his own unrighteous judgment toward her. He declared boldly that he now knew that she was a good woman and he welcomed her and her family back into their community. He also explained how Mr. and Mrs. Hewitt had taken on the care of the orphaned infant of people that were obviously well known in the community, and he expressed gratitude for their willingness to love this child as their own.

Sylvia was glad to have Danny sound asleep in one of her arms and not needing attention while she used her free hand to wipe away tears with her handkerchief. She saw the vicar smile and nod toward her at the conclusion of his sermon and she returned the same. After the meeting was over, it was as if every member of the community had been magically altered in their attitudes toward Sylvia and her family. They gathered around to offer greetings and to fuss over the baby with kindness, and some even offered apologies. Sylvia recognized some of these people as her secretive customers, and she suspected they would be as glad as she was that they no longer had to sneak to her home under cover of darkness to purchase her remedies.

Sylvia was most surprised of all to have the doctor and Bertha approach her, and to hear the doctor say in a voice that many could hear, "How nice to have you here with us. I hope we will see you often."

"As do I," Bertha said.

On the way home from church the adults in the carriage were mostly silent as they attempted to take in the dramatic event they'd just experienced. Sylvia was glad for the children's chatter and their obliviousness to what had just happened and what it meant to Sylvia's life.

After they were home and settled, the children went upstairs to play and the adults gathered in the parlor to talk. Rodney asked a few questions about details he'd been unaware of, and Millie took it upon herself to answer them. She then went on to express her awe and gratitude for the miraculous events that had unfolded at church, and each person in the room expressed wonder over such a series of miracles. Sylvia mostly listened, overcome with inexplicable gratitude as she considered how her efforts to help the doctor in his illness had begun a series of events that had led to the blessing of little Danny now being a part of their lives, and a complete change of attitude from the people who had previously ostracized her from the community.

Late that evening after everyone else had gone to bed, Sylvia and Daniel sat in the parlor in front of the fire, with Danny sleeping soundly in the crook of his father's arm. Sylvia rested her head on Daniel's shoulder and sighed contentedly as he pressed a kiss into her hair. There were no words needed for either of them to express that they both considered the life they shared to be nothing less than perfect.

About the Author

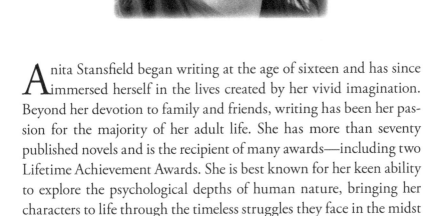

A nita Stansfield began writing at the age of sixteen and has since immersed herself in the lives created by her vivid imagination. Beyond her devotion to family and friends, writing has been her passion for the majority of her adult life. She has more than seventy published novels and is the recipient of many awards—including two Lifetime Achievement Awards. She is best known for her keen ability to explore the psychological depths of human nature, bringing her characters to life through the timeless struggles they face in the midst of exquisite dramas.

For more information on the author and her books, follow her on Instagram or go to anitastansfield.com.

Scan to visit

www.anitastansfield.com

AUTHORS WANTED

You've dreamed of accomplishing your publishing goal for ages—holding *that* book in your hands. We want to partner with you in bringing this dream to light.

Whether you're an aspiring author looking to publish your first book or a seasoned author who's been published before, we want to hear from you. Please submit your manuscript to:

CEDARFORT.SUBMITTABLE.COM/SUBMIT

CEDAR FORT
Publishing & Media

**CEDAR FORT IS CURRENTLY PUBLISHING
BOOKS IN THE FOLLOWING GENRES:**

- LDS Nonfiction
- Cookbooks
- Biographies
- Comic & Activity books
- Children's books with customizable characters

- General Nonfiction
- Children's
- Self-Help